Veronica Dale

Acclaim for *Dark Twin*

Veronica Dale crafts a richly-imagined tale of the struggle between the persistence of goodness and the corruption of power within the heart of a single youth—an absorbing follow-up to *Blood Seed*, the first book in the series.
Debra Doyle, PhD, editor, writing instructor, and author of many novels and short stories, including co-author of *Knight's Wyrd*, winner of the Mythopoeic Fantasy Award for Children's Literature.

The juxtapositions between darkness and light, lies and truth, and choices that hold the power to change many lives are deftly woven into a story line that holds as much spiritual and political insights as it does the struggle of an oppressed people desperately in need of hope. Firmly rooted in the fantasy genre yet laced with elements of intrigue, political purpose, and moral and ethical issues, *Dark Twin* is especially recommended for readers who like their fantasies complex and thought-provoking.
D. Donovan, Senior Reviewer, Midwest Book Review.

I was swept away by the inventiveness of Veronica Dale, a captivating writer. *Dark Twin* is fantasy suspense with enough supernatural horror to satisfy any appetite. The exciting narrative presents an ethical dilemma at every turn in the ominous crypts of an imaginary world. A powerful force cannot remain submerged for long.
Linda K. Sienkiewicz, author of *In the Context of Love*, a 2016 Eric Hoffer Book Award Finalist and 2016 Readers' Favorite Finalist. She was nominated for a Pushcart Prize in poetry.

As a parent of twins, I am always in the market for a good twin story. This one surpassed my expectations by a mile.
Francine Zane, Readers' Favorite Book Review

Veronica Dale's latest is fearless and lyrical. She confronts evil in gritty detail with exquisite prose. This is a dark book, to be sure, but the light never fully goes out. You will root for Teller to prevail over the tormentors who seek to turn him away from his true destiny.

Cynthia Harrison, award-winning author of six novels, including *Luke's #1Rule* and the Blue Lakes series.

Dale's lush world-building and dark characters had me turning pages far into the night. The twin brothers are on a collision course, each of them tortured by the other's absence throughout the first two books. I can't wait for Book Three to find out if hope wins, or if the brothers are already too damaged to save each other or their homeland. You do not want to miss this fantasy.

Gretchen Rily, paranormal and contemporary romance author.

The author's imagination knows no bounds. *Dark Twin* is a fascinating read that is hard to put down.

Stanley D. Williams, PhD, international award-winning video producer, filmmaker and author of *The Moral Premise*.

After reading Books I and II of the *Coin of Rulve* series, I eagerly await the next installment. Dale weaves a tale that resonates with every person who has ever felt alone, abandoned, rejected, or torn between good and evil. At times, I had to put the books down because the emotions evoked by them kept me in tears.

Adele Brinkley, avid reader and editor at With Pen in Hand

The story is intense, and you will get a feeling of dread in the pit of your stomach. I felt like I was there with Teller; I could feel his pain, his conflict, and his every single emotion. This is one of the best novels I have read so far this year!

Kayti Nika Raet, Readers' Favorite Book Review

Dark Twin

Coin of Rulve Book Two

by Veronica Dale

Nika Press

Published by Nika Press
Macomb, MI

ISBN 13: 978-0-9969-521-2-5

With thanks to the many people who helped me bring this book into being, including Tom, my patient husband; Bob, Cindy, and Tom in my novel critique group; Dora and Joe at Woodward Press; my boosters Fran, Martha, Jason, and Jesse the Shark; my editor DJ and proofreader Adele; artists Christa and Jaimie; and all my supporters at Detroit Working Writers

Cover: Christa Holland, Paper and Sage
Map: Jaimie Trampus

Dear Reader...

Dark Twin is the second book of a four-part series, but it can be read on its own. The first book, *Blood Seed*, is about Sheft, and this one is about his twin brother Teller—his other half, so to speak. Separated at birth, both brothers are called by the Creator Rulve to walk a dangerous but redemptive path. Teller, however, lives in a different setting, relates to different characters, and faces an entirely new set of challenges.

That being said, most people will get a lot more out of *Dark Twin* if they've already read *Blood Seed*. "Familiarity with Book One," says Diane Donovan, senior reviewer for Midwest Book Review, "is recommended for a smooth transition to the powerful influences on Teller's world. Even though *Blood Seed* held different protagonists, its dark metaphysical background and depth provide a firm foundation for this continuation of the theme, which offers the same solid approach to spiritual and psychological insights as its predecessor."

Whichever book you decide to read first, the twins' challenges are connected to our everyday lives. Some people believe reading fantasy is a waste of time because fantasy doesn't depict reality. Not so. We fight against giants every day. For example, Teller is driven toward advancement, but knows it will come at a cost to his integrity. Both brothers hear a call to something greater, but they're young, like we all are deep down, and they feel isolated, rejected by family, and must constantly defend themselves against the local bullies. Those around the brothers call them different names, insist they be different people, but each twin wonders *who am I really?* Like many, they struggle at times with feelings of despair.

Teller is like those of us who believe we have done too much evil, or accommodated it out of self-interest for too long, to be redeemed. Sheft is like those of us who live with so much prejudice in our community or dysfunction in our family that we have difficulty recognizing our own strengths, our own power for good. Like both brothers, we may deny that we have any special calling to help save our family, our community, our country, our world. Sheft and Teller, and many characters who appear in our myths and dreams, inform us we are wrong.

Yes, the brothers endure times of intense darkness, but also find moments of unexpected grace. That's why my favorite description of the *Coin of Rulve* series is "a dark journey toward a distant light." As a pastoral minister, I learned that people value self-sacrifice, courage, and the ability to forgive. Especially today, we crave hope.

Veronica "Vernie" Dale (www.veronicadale.com)

P.S. A heads-up: Questions for Discussion are listed at the back of this book. You might find them helpful if you belong to a book club, would like to start one with your friends, or just want to explore Dark Twin at a deeper level. If you're like me and want to be on the lookout for these questions as you read, take a glance at them before you begin.

CHARACTERS

IN THE SEANI (say-*ahn*-ee)
Komond – captain of the Rift-riders
Larrin – captain of the guards
Rivere – (*ree*-vair) young man, apprentice healer
Teller – the twin brother of Sheft, Se Mena's grandson

The Se (*say*)
Se Abiyat – chief healer
Se Celume – (*sell*-oo-may) young seeress
Se Druv – the eldest, head of the Seah Council
Se Isavin – (*iss*-ah-ven) in charge of defense
Se Mena – Teller's grandmother, a teacher
Se Nemes – counselor
Se Penan – scholar and linguist
Se Troya – domestic operations
Se Utray – (*uht*-ray) naturalist

Teller's childhood friends
Deoner – (dee-*on*-er) 13, Rift-rider trainee
Eiver – (*aye*-ver) 11, newly arrived boy
Hirai – (*here*-aye) 10, ward daughter of Se Celume
Lir – 9, boy, true son of Se Penan
Ianak – (*ee*-uh-nahk) 9, ward son of Se Penan
Yuin – 8, newly arrived boy, grieving loss of his twin
Avia – 7, true daughter of Se Penan

In Oknu Shuld (*ahk*-new)
Eyascnu Varo – (a as in "gate"-*yahsk*-nu) the Spider-king,
Dahran – Teller's chief rival
Gorv – ahn, twin brother of Yuin
Keel – orientation instructor
Keya – ahn girl
Liasit – (lee-*ah*-sit) young ahn woman
Noz – friend of Dahran

The Vols
Nosce – (*no*-shay) Vol Prome, Spider-king's chief overseer
Autran – (*ow*-trahn) Vol Segun, provider of potions
Shacad – Vol Tierce, head of Spider-king's army
The Delver – Vol Kuat, shape-shifter

TABLE OF CONTENTS

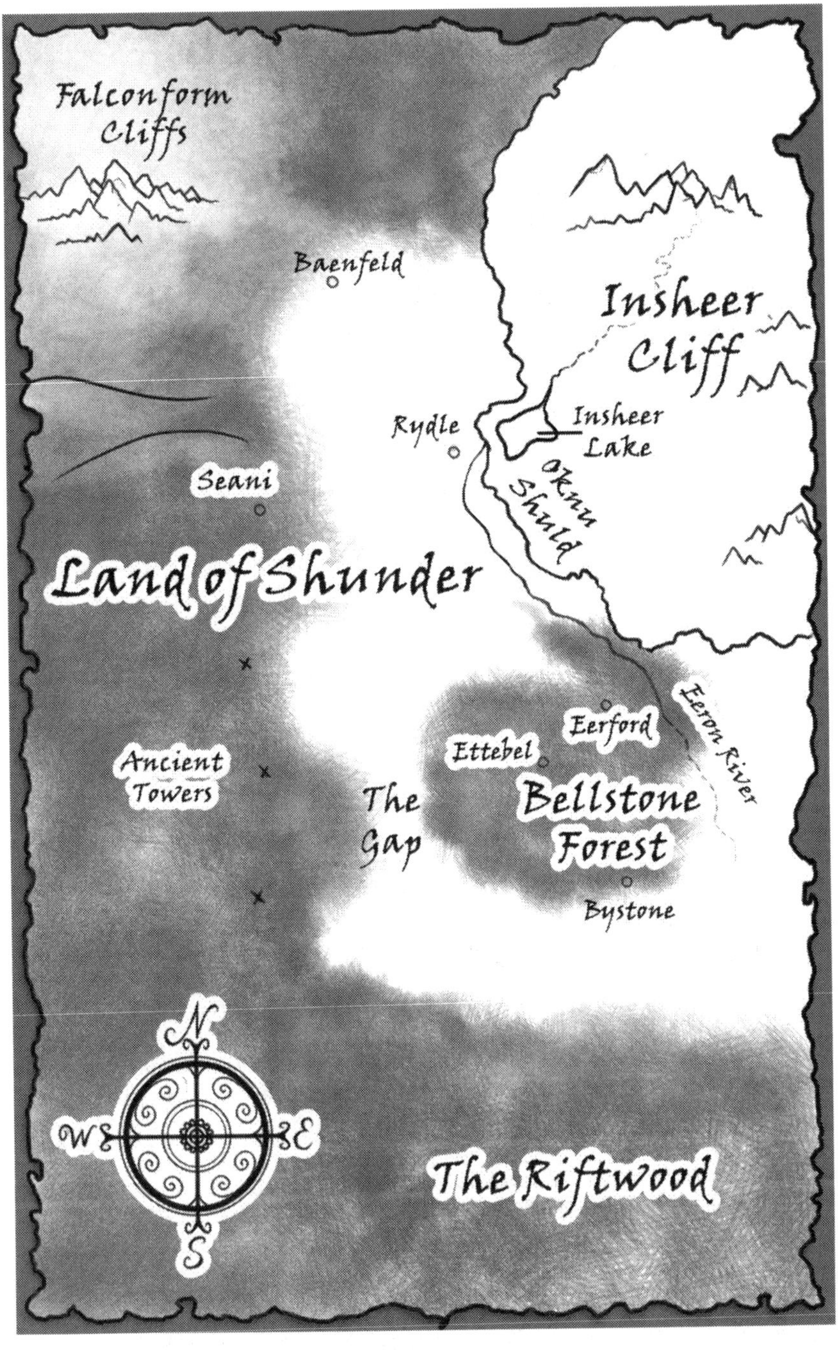

Falconform Cliffs
Baenfeld
Insheer Cliff
Rydle
Insheer Lake
Seani
Oknu Shuld
Land of Shunder
Eeron River
Eerford
Ettebel
Ancient Towers
The Gap
Bellstone Forest
Bystone
N
W
E
S
The Riftwood

Pain which cannot forget falls drop by drop upon the
heart until, in our own despair, against our will,
wisdom comes through the awful grace of God.
Aeschylus.

Time is the school in which we learn,
time is the fire in which we burn.
Delmore Schwartz

Dark Twin

Coin of Rulve Book Two

PROLOGUE

Se Mena closed the door behind her and, taking a deep breath of the chilly pre-dawn air, stepped into the Healer's Garden. It felt good to escape the sweltering infirmary for a moment, where her first grandchild was taking its time being born.

It felt even better to escape the painful question she had seen in the eyes of several visitors who had stopped by during the long hours: how tainted might this child be?

With an angry sniff—how could a newborn child be tainted?—she pulled her cloak closer. This being the sixth day of Seed, patches of snow still lingered on the paver stones at her feet, just visible by the dim lantern that shone beside the infirmary door. She made her way to the edge of the small garden where the land sloped toward the east.

Across the valley, Insheer Cliff stood dark against the star-filled sky. Her gaze wandered to the pale scar where, long ago, a waterfall had once plummeted. Sunsink Falls it was called, dammed and damned by the Spider-king, the so-called lord of the land of Shunder. Now he used the resulting lake to irrigate his vast morue fields. Very thirsty was that noxious crop, which infested the plateau—and their very lives—like a cancer.

A sudden sound startled her—a deep, sonorous gong that welled up from the valley below.

Bo-ung.

Goosebumps erupted on her arms.

The sound came from the south, where Bellstone Forest floated like a dark, isolated island in the valley mists. Once part of the vast Riftwood, it had been hacked from its ancient connection by the Spider-king's relentless drive to divide and conquer.

Scarcely had the echo rolled away when the gong struck again. *Bo-ung.* Resonant, yet strangely muffled, the note seemed to emerge from a cavern under the earth and travel along the same underground paths the earthquakes took. It must have awakened the whole valley, which now listened in an uneasy silence.

The sound rang out a third time—*bo-ung*—and her scalp tingled.

It was the Bellstone, the ancient voice of Shunder. Brandishing the hope found in legends and the strength found in prophecies, it cried out for a leader who would save their land. It called, in essence, for rebellion. The Bellstriker, whoever he was, would be in danger of losing his life.

The door behind her banged open, and she whirled to see Abiyat. Along with a shaft of light and a waft of warm air, thin wails emerged from behind him.

"Twins!" the healer exclaimed. Shock glazed the fatigue in his eyes. "But not identical. Oh God Rulve, each is different!"

But that was impossible. In a land poisoned by morue, there was no such thing.

Except—and the realization burst into her mind like the sound of a great bell—in one specific case. One specific, long hoped-for, and devastating case.

Mena pushed past him and rushed inside.

Six days later, she stood over her grandsons' crib. Bright morning sun streamed through the window, but it only emphasized the desolate silence. A part of the yellow quilt had been thrown back, and the mattress bore the faint impression of the other infant who had so recently lain there. The rest of the quilt still covered his brother. As she watched, little Teller stirred and lifted his dark head against the sheet, as if seeking the warm body he'd been so close to all his short life.

He didn't know his mother had gone to a place of supposed safety. He didn't know she had been sent off with his brother beyond the Spider-king's reach.

He didn't know that, in spite of promises and hopes, he might never see either of them again.

Chapter 1

The Wall-Stalkers

"Look, Deoner," Teller said, "there's a snake down there." He squirmed uneasily on his narrow perch high atop the sunny rock wall. "It's watching us."

Deoner didn't even glance down. "Yeah. Lots of snakes around here." At age thirteen, he was clearly not very interested in what a six-year-old had to say.

None of the other five children dangling their legs seemed to notice the snake. The brown and grey spots on its skin made it almost invisible among the rocks and leaves that littered the clearing between the forest and the southeastern wall of the Seani compound. But this snake wasn't acting right. It jerked its head to stare, one by one, at each of them in turn. Its eyes were a hungry green, so lit-up they seemed almost blind.

Deoner continued his argument with the others about who should be on whose team in their game of Rift-rider, but Teller continued watching the snake. It was a big one, as thick as a man's arm, and two short plumes swept back from the top of its head. Normally, he liked snakes. Their skin felt scaly-dry and their long tongues flicked in and out in a ticklish kind of way. None had ever bitten him.

But this snake was different.

He turned his head away from it. Sitting twelve feet

up was scary enough, especially since the top of the wall seemed barely wide enough to accommodate his backside, so he tried to think of something else. Up here, that was easy to do. He sniffed in the smell of sunbaked rock and the spice of the purple heliotrope that bloomed at the edge of the forest. The guards kept a wide area outside the wall clear of trees and bushes, but beyond that the forest stretched down to the valley in breezy waves of green mingled with all the fall colors: golden-yellow, orange, and rich dark reds.

Eiver elbowed him in the ribs. He was eleven, and had been brought to the Seani only three days ago. His sandy hair always stuck out and gave him a comical look. "Is that Sagetown?" he asked, pointing at a far-off clearing where a few dead and blackened tree trunks still poked out of the charred ground.

"Yeah, what's left of it." The Spider-king burned it down a long time ago, to punish the first parents—and the last—who had refused to turn their children over to him.

"I'll bet you can see ghosts there," the boy said. He made clawing motions in front of Teller's face and spoke in a spooky voice. "They sift through the ashes, trying to find their own bones."

Teller wasn't scared, but the thought of what the Spider-king had done caused heat to flare up in his spirikai, the spot beneath his ribs that their healer sometimes called the solar plexus. Hoping to avoid another fever, he took a few deep breaths and the hot feeling went away.

Deoner leaned past him to point at Eiver. "You're on my team." He turned to the boy on his right. "You too, Ianak."

"Wait a minute!" Hirai exclaimed from down the line.

A sturdy ten-year-old, she was captain of the other team. "*I* choose Ianak. You already stuck me with Teller, and he's never played before."

Ianak, who was nine, rubbed his long nose and grinned, obviously pleased to be fought over.

"What are you complaining about?" Deanor asked. "You already got Lir."

Sitting on the far end, Ianak's ward-brother Lir turned to look at them from under his mop of dark, curly hair. He was nine too, and accepted in a matter-of-fact way that he was Hirai's fastest runner, as well as being smart in class.

Teller didn't care if he was the last one chosen. The older kids didn't invite him to play with them very often, so he was delighted to be up here with them. The two captains resumed their argument. Deoner had invented the Rift-rider game years ago and the rules were simple. Members of two teams climbed the wall as fast as they could, then raced across the top in opposite directions. One team had to scramble down a woody hydrangea vine and the other used a rickety ladder, which was kept hidden in the bushes when not in use. The team that got down to the starting place first was the winner. What all this had to do with the Rift-riders, no one seemed to know; but if you didn't like heights or were afraid of falling, the game wasn't for you. The two captains finally formed their teams, although neither seemed happy about it.

"All right," Hirai went on, tossing back her hair. "Who gets the vine and who gets the ladder?"

This started another argument, which Teller stayed out of. He watched the sky—it was that deep blue that you seemed to get only in the month of Acorn—to see if he could spot the falconforms. Everyone in the Seani waited for them. Grandma said a band of these fierce warriors were flying in tomorrow, but right now he saw only a lone hawk, gliding over the Eeron Valley.

A rustle on the ground caused him to look down. The snake. He'd almost forgotten about it, but now it was slipping around a clump of weeds and coming toward the wall. A short distance from the base, it stopped and lifted its head. The eye-slits fastened on him. No tongue flicked out, which didn't seem right. A breeze made the trees rustle and a chill crept down the back of Teller's neck. He didn't want this snake anywhere near him. "Go away," he said in the mind-speech.

Although none of the other children could hear that, the snake seemed to. It hissed, rose higher.

Even though the wall was too high for the snake to reach him, Teller quickly drew his feet up. "Go away!"

"All right, all *right*!" Deoner shouted at Hirai. "You get your precious vine!" He kicked the wall with his heels, making a loose stone bounce down the wall and land close to the snake. It didn't move, only continued to focus on Teller in a very un-snakelike way.

The children, talking excitedly to each other, stood up, which sent more bits of loose rock rattling down. The snake ignored them and slithered to the very bottom of the wall. It wove its head from side to side as if looking for a way up. Teller suddenly remembered his teacher telling them that certain snakes were expert climbers. He scrambled to his feet, discovering almost too late there wasn't much room to scramble.

"Come *on*, Teller!" He found he was the last one left on the wall and Hirai, standing by the vine about twenty feet away, was motioning urgently to him. It was time to get down and start the game. He stumbled toward her, but felt the lit-up green eyes burning on his back.

"Hurry up," Hirai shouted. "They're winning!" She was climbing down the vine now, and only her head and shoulders were visible.

Teller glanced down, and his heart jumped. The snake was keeping pace right below him. It reared up, trying to reach him. He started to run, but things got strange. The top of the wall seemed narrower than before, and his shoes felt big and clumsy. He couldn't hear them crunch on the crumbling stones, couldn't hear anything except the pounding of his heart. He snatched a look ahead and almost cried out. Now the snake was right on top of the wall. How had it gotten up there so fast? It surged toward him, its eyes glued on his face.

He looked wildly around for the hydrangea bush, his only way down. Waving his arms to keep his balance, he saw that the bush—and the race—was between him and the snake. He put on a burst of speed. Blood drained from his head and the air got darker and thicker, as if a tunnel was folding itself around him. All he could see was the snake at the end of it. Its eyes were so bright and sharp they seemed to scream, and its mouth was opened so wide he could see down its throat. Its forked tongue rested like a bloody slash on its lower jaw and its fangs dripped with poison.

A terrible though hit him: he would never escape.

Something whacked him across the shins. He gasped, grabbed out, and clutched a woody branch. Leaves hit him in the face and rough bark slid through his hands as he half-fell, half-climbed down the vine. He burst out of the greenery and staggered directly into an adult.

It was Se Ísavin. She grabbed him by the back of his shirt and guided him to where the other children were standing in the shade. Panting, his heart thumping, Teller looked up at the wall. It baked quietly in the sun. No snake glared down at him from the top. Where had it gone? He seemed to be emerging from a nightmare, and the feeling of being in a tunnel faded.

The children were acting as if they'd never seen the snake. Most of them were looking guiltily at Se Ísavin. She frowned down at them from her cool, tall height. "Weren't you told not to play on the walls?" she asked.

So that was what bothered her, not the snake. The children hung their heads, except Eiver, who looked blank. Teller didn't remember anyone telling him not to play on the wall.

"Come with me." Se Ísavin headed with long strides into the woods. They followed her, Teller trying to keep up, all the way to Se Nemes' domicile near the pine grove. "Sit," Se Ísavin ordered, and they dropped onto the grass while she went inside.

Teller rubbed his sweaty hands on his pants. Both palms stung, and he hadn't realized until now that they were scratched. He hadn't felt anything but terror and was still shaking.

Se Nemes emerged. Thin, with crinkled half-circle eyes and a throat-lump, the counselor always brought a sense of calm. Maybe because he was as old as Teller's grandmother, over half a century, and was one of the few who had been born with the mind-speech. "Se Ísavin tells me you were playing on the wall just now," he said, speaking as kindly as always. "It's very important that you *never* do that." The counselor seated himself on a tree stump in front of them. "I'll tell you why. When I was young, we used to play a game called 'Ogre' up there. One day, when I was supposed to be the guard, and the other children had run ahead, I was alone on top of the wall. I heard something rustling below me on the other side."

Teller drew a short, surprised breath. The same thing had just happened to him.

"I saw an old man," Se Nemes continued, "dressed in a patched robe. He had a bandage around his eyes and poked his staff ahead of him as he made his way forward. 'Is there someone up there?' he called out. I answered 'Yes.' He asked me my name and, foolishly, I gave it. 'Help me, Nemes,' the old man commanded. 'I need to see the healer for my eyes. Come down on this side and guide me through the gates.'

"I could climb our wall then as well as most of you can now, and part of my heart ached for the poor old man. But another part was afraid, and I didn't come down. Instead I told him to follow the sound of my voice and I would take him to the entrance.

"I could see the old man didn't like this idea, but he followed me. I walked, calling out once in a while, but soon I thought I could feel his eyes staring at me through the bandage. His shadow was strange, too. Sometimes it was long, as if the sun were setting. Other times it just pooled around his feet. And its shape was not always that of an old man."

Stopping for a moment, Se Nemes looked at each of them. Teller wanted to ask him if he felt like he'd been walking in a tunnel, but his mouth was too dry to speak.

"I stopped calling down, and we walked in silence. I began to hear the old man whispering in my mind. 'Nemes. Nemes, come down. Come down to me, Nemes.' It was very hard for me not to obey him.

"At last we came around a curve in the wall, and I almost shouted with relief. I could see the guard-tower and waved to the guard stationed there. He waved back, and when I looked down, the old man was gone. It was as if he had never been. A chill went through me, just like now when I'm telling you this story, so many years later. For weeks my dreams were haunted by someone whispering my name, until finally my father, our counselor then, was able to cure me."

The children stirred uncomfortably, and Teller felt Se Nemes' chill, like cold mouse-feet scampering along his arms. What he had seen was real. Instead of an old man, he'd seen a snake, and it, too, just disappeared.

"Who was that old man?" Se Nemes asked them.

No one answered.

"Deoner, do you know?"

The boy looked down. "Yes, sir. It was a devisement of the Spider-king, or one of his servants."

"And what did it want?"

The boy bit his lip, then answered. "You, sir."

"Could it have pulled me down from the wall?"

"No, sir. The wards prevented that."

"So what was my danger?" Nemes looked at each of them.

Hirai answered, her eyes still full of the story. "It could've…its voice could've *made* you come down. Then"—she blinked, perhaps to rid herself of the terrible thought—"it would've taken you into Oknu Shuld."

Into the Spider-king's underground stronghold, from which no one escaped. An image flashed into Teller's mind. He'd fallen off the wall, onto the dangerous side. The wall loomed high above him, but no anxious face looked down, no hands reached out to help him, and something behind him, something terrible called a devisement, rustled in the grass and hissed his name.

"Teller?"

He jumped, but it was only Se Nemes, looking at him with concern. "Are you all right?

"I"—he had to swallow—"saw a snake."

"That's another thing," Se Nemes said, addressing them all. "Those red racers by the southern wall can inflict a nasty bite. But far worse than that are traps set by our enemy. Children, you are all too precious to put yourselves in danger. The Seani needs each and every one of you! Your relatives had to be very brave to bring you here. Soon the oldest of you will be taught more about the Spider-king and his stronghold. But the rest of you have to trust us and obey our rules until you learn the reasons for them." He got to his feet. "So, you won't play again on the wall?"

They all nodded.

"Then thank you all for listening so attentively."

"Did you ever see that old man again?" Teller blurted out.

Se Nemes shook his head. "No. On this side of the wall, you are safe from the likes of him."

Teller sighed in relief. But the memory, and the certain feeling he could never escape, still crawled inside him.

Se Nemes re-entered his domicile, and Se Ísavin came forward. She was in charge of Seani defense and tended to talk to people as if they were soldiers. "A band of falconforms will be arriving tomorrow morning. Their leader, Drapak, is bringing them to discuss certain matters with the Seah Council. One falconform, however, has arrived ahead of the others. If you would like to meet him, come with me to the garrison."

With a whoop, the children jumped up and followed Se Ísavin. From time to time over the years, Teller had seen a falconform coming down over the trees—to report to Se Druv about something, he supposed—but never up close.

Komond waited for them in the open field before the guardhouse. With his wiry black hair, and eyes as sharp and far-seeing as a hawk's, he looked a little stern, just like a captain of the Rift-riders should. But when he caught sight of his wife, he smiled and his eyes turned a kind of soft grey. Se Ísavin smiled back, something she didn't do a lot.

Four sturdy perches made of logs had been set up behind Komond, the crosspieces waist-high from the ground. On one of the perches sat the biggest creature Teller had ever seen.

Speechless, most of the children stopped some distance away, but Deoner went to stand at Komond's side, as if to remind everyone he had just begun Rift-rider training.

Se Ísavin herded them closer, until Teller's nose was about level with the huge curved claws that clutched the log like a twig. He tilted his head up to look at the great falconform. Its body was almost as tall as two Komonds. Its feathery forehead was sloped high, more like a person's than a bird's, and although its yellow eyes looked fierce, they also looked wise.

"Boys and girls," Komond said. "I am pleased to introduce to you Yarahe, son of Drapak the Claw." He extended his hand toward the falconform. "He seems very large, doesn't he? Yet his people consider him an adolescent, scarcely older than Deoner here. One day, when he's full grown, he will take his father's place as king of his people." Komond's eyes flicked over them. "Do any of you have questions?"

Eiver spoke out. "Can he talk?"

Deoner rolled his eyes, but Komond didn't. "The falconforms," he explained, "use many calls, but they also communicate in kyra, a kind of mind-speech. Kyra is not like our mind-speech, which certain of us are born with and others are not. We have to learn the language. Se Ísavin and I are fluent in kyra, as is our Eldest, Se Druv.

Soon all the Rift-riders will learn it. Over longer distances, we can also speak with the falconforms by using some of their calls."

Komond glanced up at Yarahe, seemed to listen for a moment, and then turned back to the small group. "Yarahe wants you to know that his people call themselves the Wind-rulers. They settled long ago on the ridges northwest of here, on this side of the Eeron River. Just as it is for our Se, children are rare for the falconforms. Yarahe is one of only four fledglings that survived the year he came forth." He looked at Lir, who was standing beside Teller. "So Yarahe is like you, Lir, and like our own daughter Avia, the only two children here born to Se."

Se Ísavin stepped forward, her hands clasped behind her back. "Tomorrow morning Drapak will be bringing with him two falconform scouts. The Seah Council will discuss their living here and becoming part of our garrison."

Teller exchanged an excited glance with Lir. Falconforms would be staying right here in the Seani!

"Having them here would be very helpful to us," Se Ísavin went on. "The wind-rulers can fly over Insheer Cliff and tell us about the strength and numbers of the enemy. They can patrol the Eeron Valley, and that will help us aid the Bellstone warriors who are trying so hard to defend their forest homes. Also"—her eyes lit on Teller's face for a moment and then slid on—"they can assist us in accomplishing other important goals."

"All right, children," Komond said, "now is your chance to come forward and present yourself to Yarahe."

No one moved.

"Yarahe isn't going to eat you. He's already had his lunch." A small lift at the corner of Komond's mouth hinted that he was only joking.

Se Ísavin motioned to Ianak, who warily went up to the giant falconform, bowed stiffly while mumbling his name, and then backed away. The others did the same, until it was Teller's turn.

His eyes could barely take the creature in. He forgot to bow and had to force words out. "I am Teller, Sir Windlord."

Looking down at him, the falconform partly spread out his huge wings. This doubled his size, which caused the other children to gasp in fear. Teller also drew in a breath, but it was not one of fear, but of wonder. A strong emotion streamed out of him, not exactly in mind-words but in a feeling: "You are an awesome creature!"

The big head thrust toward him and the wild yellow eyes, only inches away, gazed directly into his. "I am honored, Emjadi T'lir."

Teller blinked. Emjadi T'lir? What did *that* mean?

CHAPTER 2

THE BOY UNDER THE BLANKET

Before he could ask, three other Rift-riders joined Komond and Se Ísavin to crowd around the falconform. The older children ran after Deoner, leaving Teller to stand alone.

Of the fifty or so people who lived in the Seani right now, only eleven were children, including himself, and most of them were years older or younger than he was. He turned with a sigh and wished his twin brother Sheft was still with him. Then he'd always have someone to play with. Scuffing through fallen leaves, he meandered toward the trail to Face-sky Outcrop. The upturned faces there had been carved into the limestone long ago, and yesterday's rain had probably made miniature ponds of their eyes and mouths. When that happened, tiny water bugs appeared out of nowhere, and he liked to watch them swim around. Sheft would like that too.

He made his way across the curve of the hillside. Before him spread the Eeron Valley, with Insheer Cliff on the other side. From here you couldn't tell it was hundreds of feet high. Pale pink and ocher streaked the cliff's grey rock, and the whole thing glowed in the afternoon sun. Except in a place where dark green ivy grew. Like a mold, it covered the stronghold where the Spider-king lived.

He turned his head away. No one knew how big Oknu Shuld was or how far it tunneled into the rock, but tales were told of many levels full of gloomy halls and endless corridors, of forgotten dungeons and evil rooms called laboratoriums. And for over six years now, since before he'd been born, his father had been imprisoned there.

The thought made him feel sick and hollow inside. That was bad enough, but under this feeling something dangerous burned, like flames under an empty pot. His grandmother would never leave a pot like that—it could ruin the pot or even start a fire.

He had to stop these feelings before they got worse, before they started smoldering in his spirikai and spread into a fever.

He rushed past the trail to Face-sky Outcrop and instead took the path to his domicile. The leaves that sifted down and the empty milkweed pods made him feel even lonelier. So did their little cottage, filled with a stillness he had never noticed before. Grandma's shawl was draped over the rocking chair, the sun came through the windows in that autumn slant that somehow made the shadows in the kitchen deeper, and the whole place felt sad and abandoned. A fly buzzed against the window in his sleeping alcove, bumping to get out, so he opened the window and shooed it through. He turned to his cot, felt under the mattress, and pulled out a piece of worn, pale yellow quilt.

It used to be bigger. It used to cover him and his twin brother when they were babies. But years of rubbing it and carrying it around had made it threadbare around the edges, so his grandma had cut it down several times until now it was only the size of a large handkerchief. He was too old for such a babyish thing, but now he needed it.

The sight of it, however, caused him to ache worse than ever, and he crunched the fabric in his hand. How could he feel the pull of a brother he didn't even remember? He put his other hand over his spirikai, as Rivere did, but he wasn't a healer like Rivere, and so nothing happened.

"You could come to my house."

It was a mind-whisper, a half-shy suggestion, and it touched his heart. It sounded like someone who hoped for visitors but was afraid no one would come. "All right," Teller said.

Stuffing the piece of quilt under his shirt, he left the domicile, hurried along the shortcut through the woods, and emerged onto the Red Lantern Way. This led to the round hall of the Quela, just up the hillside from the Seani House. One of the two big wooden doors stood ajar, as if Rulve had opened it for him. He passed out of the sunshine and into the quiet place where Rulve lived.

Rulve lived everywhere, of course, but especially in the Quela. The Creator wasn't a man or a woman, but a spirit—like a father who cared about justice and a mother with a merciful heart. Because, Teller thought, he had neither father nor mother, this was a good place for him to be.

The hall was bathed in dim, forest-green light. It came from the sun shining through the huge jade disk that took up most of the western wall. Like a round green window, but thicker at the base, Rulve's Disk stretched from the hard-packed soil of the floor to the wooden ceiling.

The remains of twelve very old trees arched over him, holding up the walls and the roof like giants asleep in their own shadows. Their trunks formed eight alcoves, each named for its own stained-glass window. He moved past his two favorites: the Sun Alcove on his left, its picture bright with yellow and orange; and the Seed Alcove on his right, full of earthy, mysterious browns.

Making his way around the large pool in the center of the hall, he passed under six of the Quela's twelve candles, all taller on their stands than he was. Because there was no liturgy now, only two of the six up in front were lit, the ones that flanked Rulve's Disk.

Enormous cupped hands, their fingers intertwined and thumb-tips touching, were carved into the shelf that formed the base of the disk. They were Rulve's hands, which created and sustained the world.

A little scared—this was a holy place—he approached until the green thumbs were at the level of his chest. This was closer than he had ever come by himself before. Grandma said he and his brother had been placed in those hands soon after they'd been born, during a special ceremony that dedicated them both to Rulve, so maybe it was all right.

The hands looked kind of empty. Perhaps Rulve was lonely too. "Can I climb in and keep you company?" he asked.

The hands seemed to glow with loving-kindness, and that was all the answer he needed.

Glancing around, he saw no one, so he pulled his blanket from under his shirt, threw it over the big thumbs, and scrambled up. The stone felt surprisingly warm. He leaned back and settled into Rulve's hands.

High above, in the green shadows at the top of the disk, words were carved into the jade: "*My life is in your hands.*"

This puzzled him. How could he hold Rulve's life in his hands? He looked at them—they were grimy and much too small. Putting the problem aside as one of those mysteries only adults could solve, he closed his eyes and rested in the comfortable curve beneath him. Birds in a nest, he thought, must feel like this. He smelled wax from the candles and heard a cricket chirping from somewhere just inside the front doors. He drew the familiar piece of quilt to his cheek. It was soft. The gentle hands held him, and he breathed a deep sigh of contentment.

"So there you are," a voice said.

Startled, he sat up.

"I've been searching for you." A wrinkled face peered down at him. It belonged to Se Troya, who was in charge of housekeeping. She held a cloth in her hand and must have come to polish the candlesticks. Short dry ends of white hair stuck out of the kerchief she wore.

Quickly stuffing the quilt under his shirt, he tried to answer Se Troya's question. "I was…" He found he couldn't explain the feeling, or the invitation, that had pulled him here, so he did the best he could. "I was lonely."

Her mouth quirked in sympathy. "I'm sure you were, Teller." For a few uncomfortable moments she gazed at him, as if she knew something about him that he didn't know, something big, yet sad. Then she took a deep breath and spoke briskly. "There's a basket of sheets down by the hospit that need hanging. Please take care of that before they get moldy."

The hospit. He'd never told anybody, but he dreaded going to the hospit. The place was for sick people from the countryside, who couldn't afford to pay the Spider-king's shamans. All their hurting made him hurt too.

"Everyone's got to pitch in, Teller," Se Troya reminded him.

"You can come back later," Rulve suggested. "I'm always here."

"All right," he said, and reluctantly climbed down from the Creator's hands.

He made his way down the slope and past the Seani House. Instead of walking over the Great Lawn, he took the trail through the meadow, where the finches flitted among the thistles or reached as far as they could under bent-over sunflowers for the fat, black seeds. The hospit stood a short distance from the front gates, and the basket of damp sheets waited for him behind it. Even though he had to use a stool to reach the clotheslines, hanging the sheets wasn't so bad because he could stop and watch the hummingbirds poke their long beaks into the blue-sprite flowers. He'd just finished the last sheet when Tema, the young woman who helped Se Abiyat run the hospit, motioned to him from the back window. She wanted him to come in.

Rats.

Waves of heat hit him the minute he walked through the door. A lady in the bed across from him groaned. She had her knees up and hid her face on her arms, which were all scratched and bruised. Probably umbraks down in the village had done it, if she hadn't gotten out of their way fast enough. A man in the next bed held a bloody towel to his forehead and spoke to Tema. "A gang of young bullies," he said in a strained voice, "crazy from purple. They had my little girl." Purple, Teller knew, meant morue, because of the plant's purple flowers.

The thought of bullies hurting a little girl, and the Spider-king's boar-men beating up people in the street, made him feel even hotter.

Tema cast a brief glance at him. "Teller, see if you can get the boy in bed eight to come out from under his blanket. He arrived early this morning and really needs to eat something."

He wanted to say no. He wanted to rush out into the cool autumn air. But he felt sorry for the new arrival, who was probably scared as well as hurt. The boy in bed eight sat with one of the hospit's brown wool blankets over his head, rocking back and forth and hugging his knees. How could he stand being under there when the room was so hot?

He touched the place where the boy's arm probably was. "Can I sit by you?'

The blanket started. "No," said the muffled voice under it. "You people are sorcerers and mages and…and evil spell-casters."

Teller looked longingly at the closed door. This might take a while. "Those kind of people live in the Spider-king's stronghold, not here."

"You'll get in trouble for calling him the Spider-king. His name is the Lord Eyascnu Varo."

"Eyascnu *Vora*, you mean."

"Don't talk like that!"

Teller didn't argue; people in the villages didn't know any better. "Varo," he'd learned from Se Penan, meant "beacon" in an old language called Widjar, and voras were blood-sucking creatures that lurked in the Rift-wood. Everyone in the Seani knew which word best described the Spider-king.

"You're pagans," the boy under the blanket said. "You worship Rulve instead of Lord Varo, and there is no Rulve."

"I don't know what pagans are, but we do talk and sing to Rulve. And about that last part, it's like you said there is no Seani, when the place is all around us."

The boy didn't seem to be listening, and continued to rock back and forth. The man in the next bed coughed and coughed—another hurting person who added to the heat in the room.

"Can I sit down please?" Teller begged.

"Do what you want." The boy moaned. "I need *purple*."

Teller sat on the edge of the bed, and the feel of the cool sheet helped a little. "That doesn't heal anything. It makes you feel better for a little while, and then you just get worse."

"Worse?" His voice shook, as if nothing could get any worse. Like heat from glowing embers, the boy's pain radiated through the blanket. Teller knew what was causing it: the broken bond with his twin.

Most children born in Shunder were identical twins, or niyalahn. Any time between the ages of five and twelve, one of these twins, thereafter called the ahn, was taken into Oknu Shuld. The lord's mind-probers broke the child's bond with its niyal twin, and the family never saw their ahn-child again. This boy's brother must have been taken only recently.

"A lot of the people here are niyals like you," Teller said.

"No they aren't. I'm dead. Officially dead."

"You seem alive to me. Unless you're all bones under there."

He'd meant it as a joke, but the boy didn't laugh. "You wouldn't care if I was."

Teller moved his hand to a cooler place on the sheet. "If I didn't care, I'd be outside. Believe me."

There was movement under the wool, as if the boy were wiping tears away. "It started because my uncle was…wasn't feeling well."

Teller nodded. There were lots of people in Shunder who "didn't feel well," which meant morue had addled their brains or made them act mean.

"I was playing this flute I made," the boy continued.

"Uncle said I was making too much noise, so he smacked me. My head hit the hearth and everything went black. Uncle said the subaltern came and marked me dead in his ledger, but later I woke up."

"Good thing."

The boy hesitated. "Not...not really. Uncle was afraid the subaltern would arrest him for lying. For trying to cheat the lord out of the RCT." The Remaining Child Tax. "So he brought me here and"—his voice cracked—"left me."

If the boy was raised by an uncle, he wouldn't have a mom or dad. He would have no one, not even a twin brother anymore. Sympathy swelled inside Teller, but it somehow joined with the heat that was clinging to his skin and made his shirt all sweaty and stick to his back. "Please come out. I need to leave, but I can't while you're still under that blanket." He tugged at it, but the boy wouldn't let it go.

In desperation, he pulled the piece of yellow quilt from under his shirt. It was damp from sweat now, but he pushed it part way under the boy's blanket. "Take this. Maybe it'll help."

The wool-covered lump stopped rocking. A thin, brown hand slid out and fingered the quilt. "I'm too old for baby stuff. I'm eight."

"Yeah, I'm too old for it too."

"So what are you carrying it around for?"

"I don't 'carry it around'!" Embarrassment made Teller feel even hotter, but he decided to tell the truth. "At least hardly ever. Only when I miss my twin."

"You had a twin?"

"A long time ago."

The boy seemed to think about that. His hand smoothed the quilt, probably feeling how soft it was, and then drew it under the blanket.

26

Nothing happened for a moment, but then the blanket started to come down. It revealed a high forehead with an ugly bruise in the middle of it, a pair of large, close-set eyes, and a tear-streaked face. Most of the villagers and farmers who made their way to the hospit were thin, but this boy looked half-starved.

"I'm Yuin," the boy said. He seemed older than his age, but most niyals did.

"I'm Teller."

"My brother's name is—was—*is* Gorv." His mouth twitched in a half-smile. "Uncle used to get us mixed up all the time." He lowered his head, looking ready to cry again.

"You know," Teller said, "your uncle could've left you to fend for yourself." That happened to lots of kids. "But he brought you here instead. Maybe he knew that if you stayed with him, he'd just keep on not feeling well and you might get hurt again. And if the subaltern found out you weren't really dead…" He hesitated, wondering how honest he should be.

"I know. Then the subaltern would have to make *sure* I was."

"Yeah. He'd be afraid of the lord finding out he made a mistake."

Yuin stared at his drawn-up knees. "So you think my uncle didn't—didn't just…" He lifted one shoulder and let it fall.

"No. I think he did what he thought was best for you."

They sat quietly for a moment. Using a corner of the blanket, Teller wiped sweat from his forehead. He felt as if he were wearing an itchy woolen sweater on a hot day in Redstar. "Are you full of purple?"

The boy shook his head. "Uncle needed it all."

"Se Nemes will make sure. He's our counselor. He'll help you about missing your brother, too. Then the Seah Council will find a ward-parent you can stay with, and maybe Se Cel will let you play your flute during our prayer-times, and you can go to school too."

"School?"

Teller kept forgetting what it was like in the villages. "It's a place where you learn things. My grandmother, Se Mena, is a teacher, and there's a class this afternoon. Maybe, if you see Se Nemes right away and he says it's all right, he'll let you come to it with me."

The boy stared at a patch of sun that had fallen on his blanket, then twisted to look out the window above his bed. "I heard there's seven forest pools here, all different, where you can swim. And brooks with clean water and lots of fish, like the Eeron River used to have."

"Yes. And there's waterfalls, and sledding in the winter, and on the Night of the Falling Stars we roast little sausages on sticks. All that." He was feeling very feverish now, and couldn't tell Yuin more of the things he loved about the Seani.

"We never roasted sausages," Yuin said, "even when my mom was alive." Resentment flickered in his eyes. "They say that none of the vegetables you grow here and none of your pigs and eggs and things have to go into Oknu Shuld. You get to keep all of that food for yourselves."

Teller thought of the rather watery stew they had for lunch, and how they only got an egg on liturgy day. "It's not a lot of food. Some of it goes to the sick people here and some goes to people begging at the gates." He was so hot that even talking about food was making his stomach roil. "Will you stay out from under the blanket now?"

"I guess."

Teller pointed to the bit of yellow quilt Yuin still clutched. "Do you still need that?" It was all he had left of his brother.

Yuin's eyes, sad and hopeless, were looking far away, and he didn't answer. He didn't let go of the quilt though, so Teller slid off the bed and, with a pang, left it behind. Waving the front of his shirt to cool himself, he rushed to where Tema was winding a bandage around the man with the bleeding head. "He's out now," he said.

She gave him a haggard smile. "Thank you, Teller. Very much." Then she gave him that look. The same one Se Troya had.

It stopped him. Sometimes when he came to the garrison, where he wasn't supposed to be, one of the four guards would set him up on G'ala's back and let him ride the pony around the stable-yard. He loved that, but the glint of unearned admiration the guards and Rift-riders exchanged among themselves made him uneasy. At times he felt like a disturbed seed in the ground, as if people were constantly brushing away the dirt above him to see if anything was sprouting yet.

And something *should* be sprouting. There was something he had to do, or be, and every one of the Se seemed to know what it was. All the adults did. But he didn't. It gnawed inside him—a pull, a call. Like a flame chewing at a log.

Hotter than ever, he rushed outside. The sun almost blinded him; the air simmered with its heat. Pulling off his shirt, he ran up the hillside. All that talk about pools made him want to jump into one, and the nearest was the deep green Pool of Rulve.

Chapter 3

Soul Nodes

Thankfully, the Quela was empty; Se Troya had gone. The pool, cool and inviting, shone dimly under the shadows of the roof.

Rulve said he could come back, but Teller didn't want to bother him twice in one day, and it wasn't even for liturgy. "I'm so *hot*," Teller said. "Is it all right if…?"

"Jump right in."

He kicked off his shoes, sat on the stone-rimmed edge of the pool, and leaned into the water with a splash. The relief was instant. A delicious coolness rushed over his face, through his hair, and down the back of his neck. With arms outspread, sinking slowly, he felt the terrible fever flow out of him. His hot body broke up the reflection of the big green window, and pieces of it wavered all around him. The rocky bottom of the pool, which was really a slow-seeping spring, seemed far below, dark and mysterious. He rose to the surface, flipped onto his back, and took a breath of air. The tension that simmered inside him—that he should be somebody, that the empty-pot feeling came more and more often, that everything seemed so wrong in the villages—all this slipped away. Water closed over his face, and through the pool's rippling surface he stared up at Rulve's glowing green disk. "Sorry to bother you again," he said.

"That's all right. You can come to me whenever you want."

He rose to take a breath. Rays from the star-windows shimmered on the green water, which in turn sent sparkles among the great branches that held up the ceiling. It was like lying on the forest floor and gazing up at leaves backlit by sun. His eyes ran down the tree trunks until they were level with the roots. They were all smooth and shiny from people sitting on them during liturgy. He floated in a lazy circle, staring at the mighty trees that upheld the hall, and said to himself the name of each as it slowly spun past.

His gaze lit on Eka, the first tree to the right of Rulve's Disk, and then slid past a side door to Twegen. Next came Dre and Teta, which formed the Moon Alcove. Se Penan said the names were only numbers in Widjar, but "eka, twegen, and dre" seemed more powerful, more mysterious, than "first, second, and third." He counted all the trees, until his favorite came into view. "Enlen," he whispered. Number eleven. Only two trees had a picture carved into them: a flame in Enlen and a leaf in Twegen. They were like twin brothers, standing across the hall from each other, safe at home with Rulve and one another.

"I like to be in your house," he said.

"I like you being here."

It seemed like his father's strong hands held him and his mother's arms wrapped around him. He just stayed there and felt his whole body bathed in love. Every breath tingled.

"Do you feel better now?" Rulve whispered.

Too relaxed even to use the mind-speech, he said yes, and thank you. Being with Rulve was the best feeling in the world. He closed his eyes and sank into the water's cool embrace. A slow current from way deep down slid against his skin. Sinking, slowly unfolding, he let the dear presence soak into his spirikai.

"Teller! Teller!"

He gasped. Someone was pressing on his chest. He pushed the hands away and wiped water out of his eyes. He was lying on the flagstones that surrounded the Pool of Rulve. Above him hovered the worried face of Se Celume, their young seeress, her long hair dripping. The guard Suver, not much older than Deoner, peered over her shoulder. They must have come here to practice their instruments before the next liturgy.

They rushed him to the infirmary where Se Celume made a big fuss. "He was drowning, Abiyat! Thank Rulve we got to him in time!"

"I wasn't *drowning*," Teller protested. "I just got really hot and was cooling off."

Se Abiyat sent Suver off to get the counselor, then peeled off Teller's wet clothes and sat him on the edge of one of the two beds. Se Cel anxiously wrapped him in a blanket.

"Are you hot now?" Se Abiyat asked, his slightly bulging eyes regarding him with concern. He reminded Teller of the wise old sturgeon that lived in the deep pools of the Westwood Brook.

Teller checked. "Not so much."

"Celume," the healer said, "will you please get Teller some dry clothes from stores?" She dashed off, and Se Abiyat turned back to him. "You've gotten these fevers before, haven't you?"

Teller nodded. A couple of times he couldn't hide it, and his grandma took him to the infirmary.

Se Abiyat made him breathe deeply, listened to his

chest, and looked down his throat. "Tell me what you did today."

Thinking it best to omit the Rift-rider game, he told him about Yuin and what he'd seen and felt in the hospit. "Se Abiyat, the people in there were hurting. They were hurting very much, from 'braks and bullies and purple. Somebody has to *do* something!" His spirikai was simmering, and he put his hand over it.

Se Abiyat felt his forehead. "We know, lad. We're trying."

The simmer inside him rose up to boiling. "But it's not *working!*" he cried.

The healer gave him that adult look that made him feel so uneasy, but this time deep sympathy swam in his gaze.

"I'm sorry," Teller said, ducking his head. The whole Seani was probably just as worried about what was going on as he was, or even more. He looked up at Se Abiyat. "But I don't want to wait until I get bigger to help you. I want to help you *now.*"

Se Abiyat's eyes got shiny with tears. He covered Teller's hand with his own and was about to speak, but just then Teller's grandmother rushed in.

Her face was creased with worry, and strands of her grey-streaked hair had come out of its neat bun. She swept him into her arms. "Teller, are you all right? What *happened* to you?"

He tried to tell her, but by then Se Nemes had come in and everyone was talking at once. Se Abiyat promised his grandma that he was fine, but that he probably shouldn't go to her class. In the middle of all the confusion, Se Cel brought him dry clothes, but Se Nemes said to put only the small-cloth on. They finally made his grandma go back upstairs because the older children would be coming in any minute for class.

"Would you mind," Se Nemes asked him after the women had gone, and only the two Se remained with him in the infirmary, "if I do a brief examination? It's been a while."

Teller didn't like the feeling of someone moving around in his head, but he trusted Se Nemes. So he said yes and stretched out on the bed.

The counselor rubbed jewelseed oil into his hands and laid them one by one on all the soul-nodes: forehead, throat, heart, spirikai, abdomen, and the place just above his private parts. Soul-nodes, Teller had learned, were something like sources of spiritual power or—he wasn't exactly sure—maybe where it was stored. Each one had a number. Se Nemes spent extra time on the fifth node, located in his spirikai. Then he touched two nodes at once: forehead and spirikai, spirikai and abdomen. Sometimes he closed his eyes, as if listening to what the nodes were telling him.

The counselor wiped his hands on a towel, gently pulled him to a sitting position, and placed his hands on either side of his head. This was the part Teller disliked the most, but he tried to keep still while Se Nemes sifted through him. At last he finished. "You can get dressed now, lad."

The two men looked at each other. "I think the Seah Council needs to meet tonight," Se Nemes said.

Teller, pulling on a pair of pants, didn't like the sound of that.

Chapter 4

Dedication

Dread flapped in Se Mena's stomach like a carrion crow. She stood in the library on the second floor of the Seani House and reminded herself that Teller was fine, that Se Cel had over-reacted again. But her other grandson had already been taken away, and nothing—*nothing*—must harm this one. Losing both twins would break her in half. It would devastate the entire land of Shunder and would grieve, she was certain, even the Lord God Rulve.

Her thoughts jumped back to the night, six years ago in early spring, when her grandsons had been dedicated to Rulve. The Seah Council had decided that only certain adults would be told about the twins' extraordinary nature, so the ceremony had taken place in secret.

Seven of the Se stood just inside the double doors of the Quela, waiting to be called forward. They were still arguing.

"I don't understand your *thinking*," Mena said to them. "Teller and Sheft are niyalahn. They are twins, not meant to be separated. If we wrench them apart, we will be acting like the Spider-king himself!" Immediately she regretted saying the name in this holy place, but still lifted her chin defiantly. What she had said was true.

"Mena, please," Abiyat said. "We have gone over this. Your grandsons are not niyalahn. They are not identical twins and may not share a bond at all."

"But they aren't ristas! They were not born as single individuals."

Penan, standing at her left, took a deep sigh. The language scholar was just past middle-age, and ruggedly handsome. His shaggy hair fell over a forehead that seemed always creased in concentration, and his eyes squinted against a light, Druv maintained, that most did not see. "Mena," he said with exaggerated patience, "your grandsons are not merely niyal or ahn or rista, but all three. That is what niyalahn-rista *means*."

"Don't patronize me, Penan. I know what it means."

"Then you are wiser than all the Se put together."

Abiyat pulled at her sleeve. "Celume beckons." The seeress and Druv waited in the front of the hall, her short silhouette and his bulky form dark against moon-glow of Rulve's Disk. Mena's infant grandsons, who had been swaddled in blankets and placed in Rulve's great hands for the ceremony, lay out of sight behind the huge thumbs.

Celume had known all along that Riah would give birth to these special twins. She had seen it in a dream of portent and, with what inner turmoil Mena could only guess at, lived with that knowledge for months. Such dreams waited in the soul-well of Shunder, but only a few, Celume among them, had the ability to dive deep enough to draw them out. The young seeress, however, had typically doubted her ability and lacked the confidence to speak out, and therefore said nothing until just after the twins were born.

As Mena led the others toward Rulve's Disk, a sphere of light seemed to rise over the edge of the great thumbs like a tiny, misty sun. It was pulsing over the heads of her sleeping grandsons. Even though she had seen it the night before, it still brought an ache to her throat.

Abiyat took her elbow and gestured toward the light. "You see the problem, Mena. We do not yet understand what powers your grandsons possess, but we believe that the two boys in tandem command its completeness. If the twins stayed together here, growing in age and wisdom, their aura also would grow. And the Spider-king would surely detect it."

Mena stopped and glared at him. The others also stopped. "The aura isn't the only thing that bothers you, is it?"

Nemes placed what was meant to be a reassuring hand on her shoulder. "We don't need to get into that now, my dear."

But Utray, who had said nothing so far, seemed to think they did. The botanist moved in front of her, his receding hairline making him look older than his forty-odd years. "You must realize, Mena, how crucial it is that your grandsons be separated. We don't know what their powers are, or even *whose* they are. If Neal wasn't their father—"

"But he was! There's no doubt in my mind that the twins' father was my son-in-law Neal."

Utray extended his hands to her. "What if not? What if these children were engendered in the Spider-king's stronghold, upon one of us, for reasons we do not know?"

"There was no mysterious reason! It was an act of casual cruelty to a helpless prisoner—life as usual in Oknu Shuld."

"Riah was raped in her cell and then allowed to escape. The result of her pregnancy now lives in our midst. All our work, all we are trying to do here, depends on us facing facts as they are. We can't hide from a truth we don't like."

"Raped, yes. But *after* Neal fathered the twins. They'd been married almost half a year."

Abiyat broke in, looking at her as he looked at a patient he couldn't cure—with sympathy but also with candor. "When the Seah Council deems the time is right, we will call your daughter and her son home. We will help your grandsons discover their gift and teach them how to use it. Only then can they walk forth as Rulve directs, to save our children and our land."

Sometimes the man irritated her beyond belief. "And how long will it take for the Seah to *deem* the time is right? Months? Years? Meanwhile, my daughter will be gone, my one grandson parted from me, and my son-in-law…God knows what has happened to him!" Suddenly it all became too much for her, and she blinked back tears. "Riah is strong, but how many burdens can she carry alone? That terrible night in the spider-hole, her husband's disappearance there. You know the pressure she was under to end her pregnancy!"

"We all supported her, Mena." This came from the housekeeper Troya, standing behind her.

"Then the twin births. It shocked us; can you imagine how it affected her? She crumbled, deep inside. How is she alone supposed to discover what Sheft's gift is, when the nine of us must work to discover Teller's?" A cold wind seeped through the crack in the double doors behind them, making her shiver.

"Druv has made sure that she and the child will be protected," Abiyat said. "The city of Ullar-Sent lies far beyond the Spider-king's reach. I have been there to meet with other healers and found it to be a place of learning and law."

"Yes, yes!" Mena waved away his words as she would a pesky fly. "My daughter and grandson will be safe in the home of a wise elder well-known to Druv. A teacher of paper-craft, he said."

"I, too," Troya murmured, "will hate to see Riah and the little one go. But the falconform will visit them and report back to us. You have to trust Rulve, Mena."

"I do trust her! Yet everyone speaks as if the Creator's gifts to my grandsons may somehow already be spoiled, like a worm not in the apple but in the very seed!"

Penan had been looking around the dim hall as if it were full of rebuttals, and he must select one a child might understand. "Mena," he said, "every day we see how chosen evil can ruin Rulve's good gifts. We see it in our hospit, where people bear terrible injuries or suffer from diseases sweet-rue once could cure. We see a rich and fertile land slowly dying to enrich the few. We see the Eeron River turned into a cesspool so the noxious purple may thrive."

"My grandsons had nothing to do with that. They're innocent babies!"

"The *father* of these boys may have been the one who chose evil. We have no idea what traits he has bequeathed to your grandsons, no idea what lurks in their blood."

"What? You think Rulve would allow his niyalahn-ristas to be twisted from birth?"

Penan threw up his hands. "I don't pretend to understand the mystery of evil. I don't know how an innocent child can grow up to become a murderer or a despot, but it happens. Nothing is as simple as we all might wish."

She turned to look at Ísavin, but the woman, like the soldier she was, kept her face neutral and looked stolidly ahead. Half of Mena could see their point of view, and the other half railed against it, but all of her felt sick at heart.

Druv, a big man whose hair and short beard seemed even whiter against his brown skin, spoke to them from up front. "If your discussion is over," the Eldest said, "we can start anytime now."

Thus admonished, they all moved forward. As she reached the front of the hall, Mena raised her eyes to the words inscribed at the very top of the jade disk: *My life is in your hands.* They expressed the Seani's trust in Rulve, but they also expressed Rulve's amazing trust in them. Against all reason, in the passion of extravagant love, the Creator had placed the precious gift of the niyalahn-ristas into their all-too-human hands. Rulve was relying on the Seani, in all its weakness, to protect and nurture them. The words were both a fact and a plea.

She shifted her gaze to the three star-shaped windows below the writing. They formed an elongated triangle pointing toward the horizon. On the darkest night of the year, when hope ebbed lowest, they framed the three great stars of the Spera constellation: blood-red Marhaut, golden S'gan and Rayuel, a faint green. The Creator set the Spera in the heavens as a reminder of his providence and her compassion; so none of her sons would lose heart, so all of his daughters would continue to hope. And tonight Mena needed that hope. She looked at the star-windows because her heart was breaking.

As the ceremony went on, as her grandsons were washed, anointed and dedicated to Rulve, as the moon set behind the Seani hillside and the leaf-light in the Quela gradually faded, the star-windows framed not the subtle colors of the Spera stars, but only blackness.

The Eldest concluded by cupping his hands, wrinkled yet strong, around each infant's head—one light-haired and the other dark. "Emjadi S'eft and Emjadi T'lir, Rulve has sent you to do his will. May your hearts be filled with courage and compassion, and may your lives be a gift to our land."

He had addressed each infant with the Widjar names Celume had heard in her dream. The meaning of s'eft and t'lir were as yet a mystery, but the title that preceded them—emjadi—was not. It was the title given only to the niyalahn-ristas, and the Se had agreed it would never be used in public until the twins were old enough to bear it.

Druv turned to her. "Mena, be at peace. Receive for your grandsons these medallions, until such time as these children should choose or reject them, each for himself, as a symbol of their call."

He placed over her head two identical pendants hanging from black braided-leather cords. They also had appeared in Celume's dream, where a voice had called them the "Toltyrs Arulve." The seeress had made a drawing of them before the twins were born and quietly sent it to the smiths of Bystone village, who fashioned them. At first glance they seemed to be miniatures of Rulve's disk, made of pewter instead of jade, but with one difference: a willow leaf was engraved on one side and a flame on the other. Celume's world contained many symbols, but why the dream chose only these two, and what exactly "toltyr" meant, even the seeress herself didn't know.

The pendants felt heavy and cold against her chest. A wave of desperation made her grasp Druv's hand. "Surely we can find a way to hide the aura!"

He bent to look into her eyes. "It's growing too fast, Mena. If we wait much longer, our enemy will surely detect it. How could we, with our four Rift-riders and five guards, defend against the Spider-king's army?

Against all four of his Vols? At present we are safe because
we are insignificant. The Seah's only choice is to act with
utmost caution, both for our sakes *and* that of your
grandsons."

He turned away and everyone exited the hall, leaving
her alone to pray for the babies. Troya would return
shortly to help her carry them back to their crib in her
domicile. Their aura had disappeared, for both infants
were awake now. Sheft's beautiful, silver-colored eyes
focused on the nearest candle while Teller's pumping
little legs were in the process of kicking off his blanket.

Their lives lay in Rulve's hands.

CHAPTER 5

DARK THREADS

A clatter and the sound of voices brought an end to Mena's memories of that shadowed night. She turned toward the door. The older children were spilling into the library for her class, four boys and two girls who noisily settled themselves around the nicked and ink-stained table. The fifth boy, about whom Nemes had consulted with her earlier, stood at the door with Troya's hands resting on his thin shoulders. The housekeeper smiled down at him, but Mena saw the pain lurking in her eyes. In spite of Abiyat's ministrations, the poor woman's stomach malady wasn't getting any better.

"This is Yuin," Troya said. "My husband and I have offered to be his ward-parents, and Yuin's giving that some thought."

The boy said nothing, only stared fixedly at his too-big shoes. Like most of them, he'd come in barefoot, and the Seani's store of wearables was limited.

Mena steered him to a seat. He stared wide-eyed at the red and gold carpet in front of the hearth, at the floor-to-ceiling shelves full of books and scrolls, then tilted his head back and sniffed. He was probably taking in the smell of the leather bindings that she herself loved.

Eiver, on the other hand, was gazing speculatively at the wheeled wooden ladder used to reach the top shelves.

Mena knew exactly what he was thinking. She remembered the forbidden thrill of riding the ladder when she was a little girl, her friend whizzing her along the shelves.

Her class looked at her expectantly. Every child in the Seani, Mena firmly believed, must learn mythistory: how their great myths both shaped and emerged from the history of their land. The people of Shunder had come to believe that tyranny was inevitable, that things had always been the way they were now and could never change. Teaching mythistory was the most subversive thing she could do to undermine the power of the Eyascnu Vora.

"Two new students are with us now," she said, "and we must bring them up to date. Hirai, please stand and tell Eiver and Yuin how the Seani got started."

"I tell better when I'm sitting." A confident and take-charge person, the ten-year-old was the very opposite of her ward-mother Celume.

"Then by all means stay seated."

Hirai wiggled her backside deeper into her chair and folded her hands. "A long time ago, when the old kings were starting to turn bad, there lived a beautiful lady named Marhaut. She had a twin brother, S'gan, and he—"

"Wait!" Eiver seemed in genuine distress, and Mena nodded at him. "How can a girl and a boy be twins?" he asked.

"This all happened before the time of morue," Mena said. By his extravagantly furrowed brow, she saw he didn't understand. Hirai saw this too.

"Back then," she told Eiver, "moms and dads hardly ever had twins, but if they did, the babies could look alike or they could look different. They could *even* be a boy and a girl—like Marhaut and S'gan. Then everything changed. The Spider-king made morue, and it got into people's veins. Mostly poor people's, 'cause they can't afford shamans. After that, niyalahn were born most of the time, and they were always identical twins. Got that?"

"Uh, yeah."

"So, Marhaut got married to a wise man named"—she squeezed her eyes shut—"I forget."

"Rayuel," Mena supplied.

"Oh yeah. Rayuel. They had a little boy. By that time, though, Shunder wasn't a good place for families anymore. So Marhaut and her husband and her twin brother gathered their followers—the people who ran away from the bad kings—and came up here. They started to build the Seani, but the King of the Riftwood came in secret to see what was going on in his territory. He had no queen, so every day he watched Marhaut through the trees, and saw how kind and beautiful she was."

"Ew!" Eiver plopped his hands into his lap in disgust. "A *love* story."

With a glare, Hirai leaned over and poked him in the arm. "Shut up, frog-face. I like this part."

"Don't call people *names*," Mena admonished her. "Just tell the story."

After taking a moment to make sure her glare at Eiver had penetrated, Hirai went on. "So the King of the Riftwood said they could finish building the Seani only if Marhaut came to live with him forever."

Eiver suddenly looked interested. "So then there was a fight?"

"No," Hirai said with a withering glance at him. "Their small group could never fight the King of the Riftwood and all his creatures. But they needed a safe place to live and the Riftwood was everywhere back then. Marhaut thought about this problem, and finally made a very hard decision."

Mena put out a hand to stop Hirai. "Ianak, can you tell the class what that decision was?"

The nine-year-old abruptly stopped making faces at his ward-brother Lir and frowned mightily, rubbing his pointy nose. "Uh. What was the question again?"

"For heaven's sake," Avia piped up. "Let me tell." She was seven, with delicate features, and like her mother Ísavin, apt to get impatient. "One night Marhaut kissed them all—her brother, her husband, and her little boy—and they thought it was for good-night, you know? But it was really for good-bye. The King of the Riftwood was waiting for her, and she went with him. So it turned out that the Seani was built, but Marhaut's family never saw her, ever again."

There was a momentary silence. "*We* see Marhaut sometimes," Hirai said.

Deoner snorted. "It's her statue. Over there by the Pool of Compassion."

"No. My ward-mother says the real Marhaut comes to the Seani in times of trouble."

The new boy, Yuin, had been staring morosely at the center of the table all this time and now spoke up. "She shouldn't of left her little boy."

Nemes had warned her that their newest arrival was having a particularly hard time overcoming his guilt at being a niyal instead of an ahn. For a long time, Mena could not understand how any parent would give up their child to the Spider-king. She hadn't reckoned with either the power of the Eyascnu Vora or his morue. Villagers quickly learned the lesson of Sagetown. Fearful, dependent on morue, they had little choice but to believe what they were told: their ahn would be better cared for in Oknu Shuld than in their own poverty-stricken huts. Not only would there be more food for their remaining children, but also it was true patriotism to give up a child in service to their country. The carefully measured packet of morue parents were given in payment assuaged any lingering guilt and masked the many pains they lived with, at least for as long as its numbness lasted.

"Marhaut did it because she loved her little boy," Hirai said. "She gave up everything so all children could be safe."

"But we *aren't* all safe," Yuin protested.

"That's right," Mena said gently. "But because of the sacrifice of one courageous person, the Seani exists now to keep as many children as possible out of Oknu Shuld."

Eiver, who had apparently been thinking hard about something else, abruptly raised his hand. "Why is it called Oknu Shuld?"

"What difference does it make?" Deoner demanded with a sigh.

Mena, walking slowly around the table, raised her eyebrows at him. "Names are important. They can reveal deeper truths." She addressed Lir, who had been quiet so far, but attentive. "Have you covered this point with your father?" Penan was teaching his son the old language.

He nodded. "It means 'blind windows.'"

"But how can windows be *blind*?" Eiver asked.

"Just think about it," Lir said.

When no answer was forthcoming, he provided one. "It's because ivy grows all over them."

Penan would say Widjar reflected a way of thinking little understood now, but was remarkable in its ability to express intuitive truths. So "Oknu Shuld" could also mean something like "self-deluded soul;" but this she would not mention.

"So," Ianak said, stretching his arms, "now we know all about Marhaut. Time for recess."

Mena smiled. There was more to the saga, which was told in the *Tajemnika*, or *Regarding the Heart*. But Riah had taken the big red book with her so she could read tales from it—the happier ones—to Sheft. "Not quite yet." She pulled up an empty chair and sat down. "In her story, Hirai mentioned morue. Who knows what happened to the beautiful little plant called sweet-rue?"

No one did.

"It once grew everywhere in Shunder," she prompted, "and healed all kinds of diseases."

Seven pairs of eyes looked blankly at her.

"Farmers plowed it under to fertilize their fields."

Nothing.

"All right. A long time ago, the lord learned how to hybridize"—she glanced at Eiver and hastily corrected herself—"how to *change* sweet-rue into the terrible morue."

"It's called morue," Ianak explained to Yuin, "because you always want more of it."

"Actually," Mena said, "'mor' means 'death' in the ancient language, and that's what morue brings. Getting back to our story, one night, after the lord made morue, he sent a poisonous mist out of Oknu Shuld. It flowed into the Eeron River, crept up the hillsides, and settled over the fields. In the morning, when the mist blew away, people discovered that every sweet-rue plant was dead. Every single one. There was nothing left but the lord's morue, growing on top of Insheer Cliff. And once a year, for many years after, the mist would come down into the valley again. It looked for any sweet-rue seedling that might have somehow survived."

"Did the mist creep into the *Seani*?" Yuin asked in alarm. He drew his feet up on the rung of his chair, as if the lord's sorcery was even now swirling up the stairs.

"Yes," Mena said. "None of the Se could stop it." She then answered the question the boy had really asked. "But if you stay within our walls, Yuin, nothing can harm you."

"When the niyalahn-ristas come," Deoner maintained, "they'll make us safe *everywhere*."

Mena took a sharp breath. She hadn't intended to bring up the topic of the niyalahn-ristas today. Teller was supposed to have been at this class, and she hadn't wanted her intelligent grandson to put two and two together. At least not yet.

But he wasn't here, and perhaps his absence was fortuitous. "That's a very interesting observation, Deoner, and we'll talk about it after our break. Girls and boys, you can go out to the balcony now, but just for a few minutes."

Chairs scraped and everyone rushed to the door. "Don't wake up the little ones," she called after them. The balcony extended to the nursery next door, where it was nap time for the three children too young yet for school.

Only three, of so many in need. And in six years, there had been no new births here. Being free of morue carried a price. She glanced at the empty place on the shelf where the *Tajemnika* used to stand. The story of her grandsons might someday be added to the blank pages at the end. Their names would be woven into the mythistory of Shunder. A chill of foreboding crept down her arms, for in this weaving, many dark threads might be needed.

She went to the window and opened it to let in some fresh air. Looking away from the ivy-covered blight of Oknu Shuld, her eyes sought the distant mountains of Trey Aughter. Druv's homeland. Today they were invisible in the autumn haze. She took a few moments to pray—

for her grandsons, for Troya, for the new boys Yuin and Eiver, for her daughter far away—until a squeal of laughter told her the break was over. Back in the library, Deoner immediately returned to his topic of interest.

"When the niyal'arists come," he said, "they'll wield swords and magic spells. They'll kill the enemy and be our kings. Good kings this time."

Mena thought of her grandsons, only six years old and completely unaware of the great burden they bore. "Do good kings always have to come with swords?" she asked. "Don't the really good ones bring peace and justice?"

"Oh, yes, Se Mena. But you only get that with swords."

"Marhaut didn't have a sword *or* a spell!" Lir exclaimed. "And she won the Seani for us. That's pretty ironic."

"Swords kill people," Hirai stated. "How does that bring peace and justice?"

"What's 'ironic'?" Eiver asked, again with that deeply wrinkled forehead.

Ignoring him, Deoner jutted his head toward Hirai and widened his eyes. "You only kill the *bad* people," he said. Mena noted he managed at the last minute to delete the "stupid."

"How do you know who the bad people *are*? Are you Rulve now?"

"Everyone knows. Bad people do bad things."

"But swords can't bring the sweet-rue back."

"This 'ironic'," Eiver put in. "Is that what swords are made of?"

Yuin spoke up in a tremulous voice. "The subaltern took my brother into Oknu Shuld. Why didn't he pick *me* instead?"

Not to be deterred, Deoner kept his eyes on Hirai. "I'm talking about the bad people who live *there*"—he pointed out the window—"in Oknu Shuld. *Those* are the ones the niyalahn-ristas will kill."

Things were getting out of hand, but Mena felt she had to address this latest issue. "The niyal'arists will defeat the Spider-king and his army all by themselves?" she asked. "They won't need our help?"

"No," Deoner said firmly. "That's what being niyal'arist *means*. That you don't need any help."

Mena felt her shoulders droop. How insidious, and very common, this idea was. Intellectually, people knew the emjadis were only human, but emotionally they longed for more, expected more. Her job was to educate these children that the responsibility for changing Shunder could not be hefted onto the shoulders of one or two saviors. Niyalahn-ristas could be hurt, could be influenced, could be ruined or healed by those around them. They would always need help and would fail without it.

"Boys and girls," she said, "it's important that we understand what niyalahn-rista means. Can you think of anyone who is not an ahn, a niyal, or a rista?"

They could not. Everyone born in Shunder was one of the three.

"So perhaps the word is trying to tell us that the emjadis are very much like all of us. They can't do everything themselves. We will all have to work together to help them."

"What's the good of even *having* an emjadi then?" Deoner grumbled.

Hirai leaned forward. "Maybe they'll be like Marhaut."

Mena's eyes flicked to the child's earnest face, and her heart sank. Marhaut had given up everything and went alone to an unknown fate. To the people of the present,

Marhaut's story brought hope, but to that small family of the distant past, it brought only pain and hollow grief.

"Maybe," the little girl continued, "the niyalahn-ristas won't have swords, but will have some other way to help us."

Deoner flung his arm toward the east-facing window, from which Insheer Cliff was clearly visible. "Against *that*, there *is* no other way."

The children fell silent.

So did she.

The Seani was failing. It was still small and virtually powerless, caring for only a tiny portion of the children who needed help, providing handouts to farmers and fisher-folk who used to earn their own living, and fighting a losing battle against morue. Her grandsons had been separated out of fear, the very soil needed healing, and the nascent rebellion desperately needed direction.

Oh God Rulve, they all did.

CHAPTER 6

FATHERS

"Grandma, what does 'emjadi t'lir' mean?"

Mena abruptly stopped writing in the *Annals,* the record of the Seah meetings, which she was trying to update for their gathering later tonight. She and Teller had returned from dinner in the Seani House and now sat in the circle of light cast by the oil lamp on the table. Where in the world had he heard those words? No one should be using either of them within his hearing.

"What words again?" she asked casually, trying to give herself time to think. One day, when the boys were old enough to understand, both Teller and Sheft would be told everything about who they were. This was not the day.

"'Emjadi t'lir.' At least I *think* it was 'emjadi t'lir.'" He peered into a bag of star-nuts that lay beside him. He was supposed to be shelling them while they waited for Rivere.

"Who told you these words?"

"Yarahe. Today, when we went to the garrison."

She put the quill down and leaned back in her chair. "How did he tell you?"

Teller shrugged. "I don't know." He pulled out a nut and tapped it with the mallet. "Yarahe just...just *thought* it, and I heard." Frowning in concentration, he picked away pieces of the broken shell, dug out the meat, and dropped it into a bowl.

Mena swallowed. Her grandson, then, had the full kyra. Teller had learned how to talk later than most children; but when he was slightly over a year old, Nemes detected the beginnings of the mind-speech in him. He began to teach him what they sometimes called the language of truth, because it could not transmit an overt lie. So by three years of age, when Teller spoke only a few words vocally, he was mind-speaking very well with Nemes and with the others in the Seani who also had this gift. But no one knew he could communicate, fluently it seemed, in kyra.

He scooped a handful of nuts out of the bag. "So these words, Grandma. What do they mean?"

"The Seah doesn't know what 't'lir' means. Se Cel heard that name in a dream about you, so let's just say that 't'lir' is how you say your name in Widjar. The other word you're asking about means…something like 'sir.'" As a title used only to refer to the niyalahn-ristas, its translation was closer to "lord." She would have to speak to Ísavin about this issue. The falconforms must be more discreet.

"Oh." Teller thought a moment. "I suppose Yarahe called me that to be polite. But I'm not big enough yet for such a word."

"Not yet." *But someday*, she thought. *Someday, Teller.*

"So I can call Se Nemes *Emjadi* Nemes?"

"No!" she said, a little too sharply. "No, Teller. When you get older I will tell you how to use that word properly."

"It's a *bad* word, then," he said with some relish.

"Certainly not! It's simply a word in another language that you should not use just yet. Now go back to your work. Keppit will need those star-nuts in the kitchen tomorrow."

Teller sighed, reached for a nut, and broke open the shell. "Does my brother have two names too?"

"He does. His Widjar name is S'eft." Another word they couldn't translate. She resumed writing in the *Annals*.

"When will he and my mom come home?"

It was a question she had been asking herself for years now. "Remember what I told you, Teller. The Seah has to decide when—" She barely bit off "when it's safe." If she'd said that, the next question would certainly be: "Safe from what?"

Safe from the lord's relentless search for the niyal'arist twins. In a bitterly ironic twist, the Eyascnu Vora maintained these twins were themselves voras in human form, that they were blood-sucking entities whose sole mission was to destroy his lawful reign. From time to time, madmen or rebels would proclaim themselves the niyalahn-rista saviors. They would ignite a flame of hope and attract a following, but inevitably were arrested and publicly executed. The Seah would do everything in its power to prevent this from happening to her grandsons, so there was no reason Teller should know about it.

Teller nodded, but then asked, "When Sheft comes home, will you get me and him mixed up? Yuin said his uncle would get him and his brother Gorv mixed up all the time."

That was a dangerous question, and she must answer it carefully. Mena put down her quill, determined to tell as much of the truth as possible. "Not many people would get you and your brother mixed up. You both had similar features when you were born, but your brother has hair the color of cornsilk." She reached over to tousle his hair. "And yours is the color of soot." With two fingers she touched both his eyelids at once, making him smile and blink. "And Sheft's eyes were a different color too." They were the most strangely beautiful eyes she had ever seen. "Not the blue most babies are born with," she told him, "but a shiny silver, almost like the tube of quicksilver Se Utray keeps in the Sky Tower."

Leaning close, he made his eyes big. "And mine are as brown as mud." It's what Rivere sometimes said to tease him. He laughed, but then his face clouded. "But twins *always* look the same."

She made sure she kept smiling. Here it comes, she thought. "Not all. There's a special kind that don't."

"What kind?"

"Well, the kind you and Sheft are."

Teller was clearly dissatisfied with this answer, as well he should be. "So we're twin ristas?"

"That's not possible. Ristas are always singles."

"Oh." He digested this statement, and then asked the question Mena knew he would. "So, how are we special?"

"That's what the Seah will find out when your brother comes home." She placed her hand on top of his head and gently twisted it back toward the star-nuts. "Now get busy."

Except for the thumping of the mallet, all was quiet for a while and Mena felt a surge of relief. That wasn't too bad for a first conversation about niyalahn-ristas. But then Teller spoke again. "Will my father ever come home?"

He looked so forlorn that her stomach clenched. "Probably not, Teller. We talked about that, remember?"

Averting his eyes, he carefully scooped the broken shells into a pile. "Can't Se Druv get him out of Oknu Shuld?"

"No one can get him out."

He looked up at her. "Sometimes umbraks bring prisoners here in a wagon."

Shocked, she almost dropped her quill. The adults did everything they could to keep these atrocities a secret from the children. "How do you know about that?"

"Well, the last time it happened, Deoner heard the cooks talking about it in the kitchen, so he told Ianak. Then"—he shrugged—"all the kids knew." He looked up at her with eyes so innocent, so full of puzzled hurt, that they broke her heart. "It's a very bad thing, Grandma."

She nodded, fighting a sudden lump in her throat. "Yes, Teller, it is."

Every so often, a group of 'braks, apparently wanting amusement, would haul a few half-dead prisoners from the dungeons of Oknu Shuld and dump them at the end of the track in front of the Seani gates. Making sure the captives were within range of their arrows, they retreated under the cover of the trees and taunted the Se to come out and rescue them. As the day wore on, the umbraks ate and drank, wagered on which prisoner would be the first to die, and threw rocks at those who tried to crawl to safety.

The Se kept vigil the entire time. At the end of the day the 'braks, yawning and stretching, retrieved any captive still alive and drove their wagon back down the road. After they were gone, the Se emerged and buried the dead.

And this is what Teller—and all the children, it seemed—had known for almost a year.

Her grandson, thankfully, now appeared to have a more immediate concern. He was looking at the door, his forehead creased.

"I know," she murmured in sympathy. "Rivere's late."

Teller cracked open more star-nuts, but didn't eat any. They were so delicious that if he took one, he'd want them all. Rivere, he reminded himself, always came home safe. But when Rivere went out to the villages to help people too afraid or too sick to come to the hospit, he still worried. The Eyascnu Vora hated healers.

Worrying about Rivere, and talking about the umbraks, and thinking about what the prisoners must have felt when they'd been dumped outside the gates—so close to safety yet so far away—all that made that hot feeling surge through him again. Someone had to *do* something. *He* had to do something. The iron pot inside him was heating up again, and he wanted to fan himself, to move away from the hearth-fire, but he didn't want Grandma to notice. Then he'd have to go back to the infirmary and would miss seeing Rivere.

"I worry too," his grandma said, as if she knew exactly how he felt. "But the villagers who are secret friends with the Seani will do their best to protect him." These secret friends, Teller knew, were the Sperians, named after the stars of hope.

Just then the door burst open, and Teller jumped to his feet.

Rivere lunged forward and swept him into his arms. "Got you!" he cried. His tight black curls tickled Teller's nose and his hug made him feel even hotter, but it was worth it.

Rivere sat in Teller's seat, his downward-slanting hazel eyes creased with delight, and settled him onto his lap. "I would have come right away," he said to Grandma, "but Abiyat needed to speak with me first." He looked into Teller's eyes, and his grin faded away. "Are you all right, voskat?"

Teller wrinkled his nose at being called "messy-hair," but secretly he liked it when Rivere teased him. "Sort of," he answered.

"Your cheeks are a little flushed."

"I'm fine." And he would be, now that Rivere was back. He leaned against Rivere's chest and listened to the reassuring buzz of his voice as he talked to Grandma. Suddenly an idea flashed into his mind. A wonderful idea. "Rivere," he said, twisting to look up at him. "Come live with us!"

Rivere stiffened and for a minute didn't say anything. "I live in the Seani House, Teller, in the dormitory with Se Druv and the others. And there's no extra bed here."

"You could sleep in my cot, and I could sleep on the floor." A thought bloomed, so big it almost took his breath away. "You could be my ward-father!"

A look of pain crept into Rivere's eyes, and Teller felt the sting of it inside him. He had hurt Rivere—and suddenly knew why.

When Rivere's wife died, he had to raise his baby son all alone. Then, when the little boy was brought into Oknu Shuld, the mind-probers thought he might be one of those rare ristas who had certain powers the lord could use. But apparently they'd been mistaken. Whenever that happened, the Spider-king would get angry, and the child's body would be found in the garbage heaps of Oknu Shuld or in the river. Rivere's son had been found in the river, dead at eight years of age. That was when Rivere turned to morue and almost died from it. Now he had reminded Rivere of all that.

"I don't think I can be a ward-father yet, voskat," he said with a sad smile. "But if I could, I'd want to be yours."

Disappointed, and angry at himself, Teller turned away. Rivere still held him on his lap, his strong arms securely around his waist, but all too soon he had to leave. Rivere messed up Teller's hair in parting and took the bowl of nuts with him to drop off at the Seani House kitchen.

"I have a meeting with the Seah tonight," Grandma said, shutting the door. "But before I go, I think you need to hear about your real father."

Teller was glad about that, but also a little scared. All he knew was that his father disappeared inside Oknu Shuld, but he didn't know why, or even how.

She brought a chair beside his bed while he quickly undressed, pulled on his nightshirt, and settled in his cot to listen. Light from the lamp in the next room slanted onto the floor of his alcove, leaving most of it in the warm dark.

"Your father was a very brave man," Grandma said. "He was Se Druv's ward-son, and handsome too, with green eyes that crinkled when he laughed. Neal volunteered to be part of a dangerous plan the Seah made with the Sperians down in Rydle Village. He took a job with a married couple who ran the bakery. They wanted to do something against our enemy, but didn't have the strength to stop using morue and come here to live with us."

"Rivere stopped using it. Se Abiyat and Se Nemes helped him."

"Yes indeed, when you were just a baby. But it's very hard, and not everyone is able to do it. Anyway, every few days these bakers would load their wagon with bread and deliver it to Oknu Shuld. Your father drove the wagon so he would be able to get inside."

"Why?" The idea horrified Teller. No one wanted to get inside Oknu Shuld.

"To find out things. To get information our enemy doesn't want us to have."

Teller nodded. Sometimes he and Avia hid in the

bushes and played "spy" on the guards, except the guards always spotted them.

"Your mother came down to work in the bakery too. She attended secret meetings held there at night. Pretty soon Riah and your father got married, and together they used the wagon to get inside the Spider-king's stronghold. They even made friends with the subaltern in charge of supplies. What little we know about Oknu Shuld came mostly from their reports."

"Then what happened?"

Grandma took a deep breath. "One day—it was a beautiful summer day in Sky-Path—your mother and father drove the bakery cart to the side gate of Oknu Shuld as usual. But this time they were arrested. Your mother was questioned and then got out, but your father"—lines appeared between her eyebrows—"your father never did."

That hot, empty-pot feeling flared again. He remembered the day something across the valley had caught his eye in the light of the setting sun. It glittered just above the big gates of Oknu Shuld, the only part not covered by ivy. Everyone said he had better eyesight than most people, but even so, he could barely make it out. Rivere explained it was a mosaic, taller than Grandma's domicile and made up of black and purple stones. The picture was that of a giant spider. Teller never looked at that spider again. It had pounced on his father and dragged him inside.

Grandma smiled sadly and smoothed his hair. "But what I want you to remember is this: your father made your mother very happy. And children liked him, just as they like Se Utray. Sometimes Neal would make a special cake for one of their birthdays and hide a toy inside. Or bake rolls with funny faces made of raisins. He would have been delighted with you and Sheft." She tucked him in, they thanked Rulve for the day, and then she leaned down to kiss him good-night.

He drifted off. In his sleep a man laughed, his green eyes sparkling, but his face was that of Rivere.

CHAPTER 7

DECISION IN THE SKY TOWER

Teller was asleep when Mena quietly left their domicile. He had kicked off his blanket as usual, even though the autumn night had turned chilly, and she had to cover him up again. When she got to the Sky Tower, most of the Se were already seated at the big round table, which took up much of the circular room. As she squeezed past chairs toward her place, several murmured how glad they were that Teller was all right, and others reached out to grasp her hand with a smile. While they waited for Utray to appear, Nemes passed around mugs of steaming cherry bark tea from the pot that Keppit had left for them, as well as a jar of honey the Seani cook had thoughtfully added to the tray.

Mena opened the *Annals* and sipped the sweet, dark red tea with satisfaction. The little fire in the hearth brought out the fragrance of the herb-wreath that hung above it, but a slight draft fingered the back of her neck. It came from the wooden steps that spiraled up to Utray's workroom on the second floor, the tiny sleeping alcoves on the third, and the observatory above that. Utray must have opened a door up there. He appeared shortly thereafter, wiping his rather bulbous nose with a handkerchief. A fond smile softened his face, weathered from his long and frustrating search for a surviving sweet-rue plant.

"Sorry," he said. "My ward-daughter wanted me to read her just one more story."

They exchanged the "Y'rulve" greeting, Druv gestured to Abiyat, and all eyes flicked to the healer. "We are here," he said, "to discuss what Nemes and I discovered today. Teller did not fall into the Pool of Rulve this afternoon by accident, but jumped in to relieve another of the fevers he's been having lately." He looked gravely at each of them. "Nemes and I believe this fever resulted from his feeling the pain of those in hospit."

"What!" Mena cried. *Tsks* of dismay flew around the table.

"My records show," Abiyat went on, "that these fevers began just over a year ago, on the very day the 'braks last came. Nemes and I thought there was no way Teller could have been aware of that incident. Yet we now suspect that the little emjadi somehow felt the prisoners' pain as well."

"Oh Rulve," Mena groaned. "He could have. Just tonight I found out he—and all the children, Druv—knew what the umbraks did."

She told them what Teller had revealed, and Druv's shoulders slumped. "We must address this," he said. "We must prepare the children before it happens again."

How in Rulve's name, Mena thought, can you prepare a child for such a thing? She looked at the much smaller version of Rulve's disk which hung between the windows that faced south and east. Made of copper, the disk had turned almost the same shade of green as the potted plants that filled the windowsills on both sides of it. She always viewed this as a symbol of the deep way Rulve empathized with all of her creation. Tonight, that thought brought little solace.

Sitting next to her, Nemes pressed his hands together,

held them against his lips for a moment, then lowered them. "There is a related matter I must report. When I examined Teller this afternoon, I detected changes in the fifth node, located in the spirikai, or solar plexus. I have long sensed in that node what one might expect in a niyalahn-rista: an extraordinary potential, a sense of mission, self-reliance with its corollary of loneliness. Today, however, I detected an aura of"—he hesitated— "of violent upheaval."

His words startled her. "Violent? He's not a violent child, Nemes. Surely you know this."

Before he could reply, Celume spoke, looking uncomfortable. "Yet when…when I saw the toltyr in my dream, I saw a leaf and a flame, yes. But at first, the flame looked to me like a…well, like a dagger's wavy blade. Of course, I might have been mistaken, but now, in view of what Nemes…" She trailed off, unsure of herself as always, and looked down at her hands.

"What are you saying about my grandson?"

Celume seemed incapable of answering, so Nemes spoke up. "Look at it this way. People often wax poetic about springtime: about the emerging buds, the newborn lambs, and the like; but in reality, spring is a time when floods carry off houses, when great whirlwinds uproot trees. Anything new, any creative breakthrough, brings violence. Birth is a painful and bloody event. Passionate lovers take each other by storm." He smiled slightly, as if he were thinking about his wife, with whom he was still in love after almost thirty years. "Is this not how Rulve created the world?"

"But what does this have to do with *Teller*?" Mena realized she sounded shrill and tried to calm herself.

"He is niyal'arist," Druv put in, "and brings change. Change never comes easily, Mena. It often hurts."

"I then turned my attention to the sixth node," Nemes continued. He placed his hand on his abdomen. "It is where we feel most intensely, most intimately, the suffering of others. In your grandson, Mena, the sixth node has deepened considerably." The counselor's throat-lump ticked with emotion. "I think he is already beginning the mission to which Rulve has called him."

Mena's stomach tightened. "What mission?"

His own eyes moist, he gazed deeply into hers. "To bear the pain of all Shunder."

The tightness fled up to her heart. "That can't be his destiny. He was born to save our land, not suffer the ills of it."

Nemes touched her arm in his fatherly way. "Over the years, you've taught many children, including my wards, about Marhaut. She felt the suffering of our people, and this led her to make the sacrifice that resulted in the Seani. Of course you don't want your grandson to suffer. Neither does Rulve. But salvation is always bound up with compassion, with feeling another's pain, and you cannot block that path of redemption."

Tears began to sting her eyes, but Mena blinked them away. Surely, whatever Teller's destiny, it lay years in the future.

Abiyat cleared his throat. "I certainly do not disagree with my colleague. But I believe Teller's mission involves more than compassion. He feels deeply the injustice that permeates our land. Today, for the first time, the boy expressed a clear desire to help us change that. He needs to know who he is, and soon."

Druv leaned back, folded his arms, and looked thoughtfully into the middle distance. "There's more here, though. These fevers you mentioned, they put me in mind of something. Something we have never seen"—he shifted his gaze to Penan—"except in our mythology."

What, Mena wondered, could he be talking about?

The scholar met Druv's eyes. "It appears," Penan said, "that you too are thinking of skora."

So that was it. They all turned to her, but all she had to offer was her dismay. "I've seen no evidence. Nothing!"

Penan's eyes upon her were as focused as a hunting cat's. "Is he fascinated with fire? Ever flared out in anger?"

"No more than any other child."

"Yet something propelled him into the water today," the scholar insisted. "A desperate act to control skora, perhaps, in the only way he knew how?"

Mena opened her mouth to protest, but Ísavin spoke. Always serious, the woman in charge of Seani defense had grown even sterner after the niyal'arists were born. The responsibility for protecting Teller, Mena knew, weighed heavily upon her. "If Teller indeed possesses skora," Ísavin said, "we must not fear it, but nurture it. This power of fire surely comes from Rulve, given to the niyalahn-rista so he may succeed in his mission. Our duty is to guide Teller in its use."

"And what 'use' do you envision?" Penan asked. He always carried a tiny scroll—no one knew what was written on it—and now he took it out of his pocket. See-sawing it between his first and second fingers, he absently tapped one end on the table. It made a hollow sound: *thuck-thuck-thuck.*

"You know as well as I do. Teller is called to lead Shunder in a great rebellion, one that will burn out Oknu Shuld and rid the land of this unbearable oppressor!"

"Ah yes." He had that deceptively mild look on his face which often portended an argument. "The just war, waged by the virtuous. Rulve's niyal'arist, killing and burning to achieve an ultimate good. An interesting concept."

"Don't bait me, Penan," Ísavin warned "We must destroy this evil before it destroys us."

"Both sides in every war ever fought claimed the same thing."

"This is an old argument," Troya put in, "and I literally don't have the stomach for it. We're not speaking about waging some future war, but about a sickly six-year-old child—"

"He's not *sickly*," Mena protested.

"—who probably needs his brother!"

Her heart leaped. At last they were talking sense!

"I think you're right," Nemes said. "When Teller was just an infant, newly separated from his twin, the bond he shared with Sheft was strained, and Rivere helped relieve that pain. After that, I thought all would be well with the child. But now I think Teller needs some assuagement only his brother can provide."

"Sheft also needs comfort," Celume said in a low voice. "He also suffers."

Mena looked sharply at her. "What are you saying? What's wrong?"

Celume bowed her head and put both hands around her mug of tea, as if to warm them. "Roots," she said finally. "In the runes. I've seen them, tangled and choking. He is afraid." She looked up in anguish. "Cut into him is the letter T, and it bleeds! His spirikai cries out for his brother."

Sick at heart, Mena sank bank into her chair.

"Why didn't you tell us this earlier?" Druv asked gently.

Celume spoke so softly Mena had to lean forward to hear. "I dearly love my ward-daughter Hirai, but Teller and Sheft are my...my soul-sons. After they were born,

I went through the labyrinth for them, to the moon-mirror. It showed me—I know it did—that the emjadis would have to walk alone in the dark. I saw blood for Sheft and fire for Teller, but their meanings were closed to me. The fire may have referred to the fevers, or to skora, or to something else entirely." Her face crumpled. "What good is it for me to see things, if I don't know what I'm *seeing*?"

Troya, sitting at her right, placed her hand over Celume's clenched fist. "Yours is not a precise craft, my dear, nor one easily mastered."

"My duty is to walk ahead of the niyalahn-ristas. To…to use my arts to clear a path for them. But the future is dark and I have only a small lantern." Near tears, she shook her head. "No matter how high I hold it, I'm just too short for it to cast much light!"

"Nonsense," Troya said. "You're half the age your mother was when she began having the great dreams. Be patient with yourself, girl."

Druv glanced at the time-candle on the table. About three inches of its pillar remained: three hours until midnight. "It has been suggested," he reminded them, "that it is time to call Sheft and Riah home."

"Yes!" Mena cried. "The boys never should have been parted in the first place."

"If we agree on this course," Penan said, "we should be cautious. *Very* cautious. We're talking about a powerful configuration of soul-nodes here. What if Teller does indeed possess skora? As it grows, this alone may draw the Spider-king's attention. And what power will Sheft bring? What if it is an even more conspicuous ability?" He frowned, tapping the scroll. "We don't know what will happen when the two are reunited, but at the very least their aura will draw unwanted attention."

"The aura again!" Mena exclaimed. "Has nothing changed in all these years?"

"No," Penan said. "That's why it's been 'all these years.'"

"Things *have* changed," Ísavin stated. "In our talks with the falconforms today, we learned they are finally abandoning their isolationist stance. The umbrak attack against them last spring proved that their cliffs are not the barrier they once thought. I believe Drapak is ready to make a formal alliance with us. If so, we will be in a much better position to protect the niyal'arists."

"Something else has changed," Troya added. "We now know that Mena's grandsons are suffering. They are twins and they need each other!"

"I've said that all along!" Mena cried. "They must be brought together *now*, no matter what the risk." Her eyes leaped to the copper disk, and her heart sent out a quick, intense plea.

Abiyat spoke up. He looked tired. In addition to treating her grandson this afternoon, Mena knew he'd also spent long hours in the hospit and missed dinner. "What about what Se Cel heard in her dream of portent," he asked. "The words 's'eft,' 't'lir,' and 'toltyr'? Might they cast any light?"

"Penan?" Druv twisted his head from one side to the other to get the stiffness out of his neck; Mena could almost hear the tendons crick. "Have you made any progress on the translation?"

Penan sat back with a sigh. "Would you like the short answer, or the long one?"

"The short. Please."

"No."

"Not *that* short." Druv drained his tea and set the mug down with a thump.

The scholar rubbed the bridge of his nose between thumb and forefinger. "All three are ancient Widjar words. Today we guess 'toltyr' means something like 'wholeness or totality,' but the other two words we can't translate at all. In the *Scroll of S'gan*, all three terms are often used together, apparently in relation to a single concept."

"Remember," Celume added, "S'gan was the twin who stayed in the Seani while his sister left. He must have been struggling with the meaning of Marhaut's sacrifice." She seemed surer of herself now that she was speaking about scholarly matters rather than her art.

Penan held his hands parallel in front of him, as if to measure something invisible. "True, but S'gan was an escrimage, a writer of wisdom. In that capacity he used the word 'toltyr' in the context of redemption, of great sacrifice. But 't'lir' and 's'eft,' as far as I can tell, have something to do with philosophical arguments about what this wholeness, this 'toltyr,' really demands."

"And we," Druv said, eying the time-candle, "don't really want to get into philosophical arguments now, do we?"

"You know me, Druv," Penan said with his sideways smile. "Always and any time."

Utray had been staring at the medicinal plants on the windowsill. Now he leaned forward and pointed to them. "Some of these plants, in combination with others, are a deadly poison. Knowing this, I must speak out. We've never dealt with the fact that we have no idea who fathered these boys. Now we hear about Teller's proclivity for violence, his possible possession of a power we don't fully understand. Nor do we know, much less understand, what power Sheft possesses. If he were to be uprooted and planted here with his brother, what might emerge? Here, in our midst? And could we control it?"

Mena folded her arms and glared at Utray. "This is getting ridiculous. Now you are comparing the niyal'arists of Rulve to some kind of noxious weeds."

"For God's sake, Mena, that's not—" Utray began, but Troya leaned in front of him."

"If it will alleviate their pain, wouldn't it be an act of love to bring Sheft and Teller together? Surely Rulve would not allow an act of love to be corrupted."

"That's not my question," Utray said. "My question is, did an act of love conceive them?"

Druv cut off Mena's angry retort with a gesture, heaved a deep sigh, and placed both hands on the table. "We need to end. Utray, Penan, we will keep your concerns in mind." He turned to Nemes. "Explore with Teller this fifth node. Find out if it indeed holds skora."

"Teller is resistant to mind-search, but he wants to cooperate. We will try."

"And you, Ísavin. I will see you and Komond at the falconform talks tomorrow."

"Of course."

"So we all agree it's time to call Sheft and Riah home?"

Utray's lips thinned in disapproval, but Penan nodded. "With caution, Druv. With caution."

Relieved, Mena pushed back her chair and stood with the rest. But there was something more she had to do. "The umbraks," she said, "will surely come back. Have we made any progress at all on rescuing their prisoners next time? There must be a way."

"There isn't." Druv frowned as he passed the basket for their empty mugs. "Penan, Nemes, and Celume have worked with me on this problem, but with no success." He picked up his cloak from the back of his chair and eased it over his shoulders. "The wards must clearly discern the intentions of the person who wants to enter. If one of us, for example, carried a prisoner through the gates, or even dragged him in with a rope, our intentions would, for want of a better word, blur with the prisoner's. So if that person were a devisement or someone who planned to do harm, we would appear as one thing—one dangerous thing. Both of us would be destroyed." He looked at her, old grief haunting his eyes. "I know you have hopes that one day Neal might be one of the prisoners brought to our gates. But my ward-son is dead, Mena."

She said nothing more. She would never tell anyone, Druv especially, about her plan. When last the umbraks came, she ran to the postern and deliberately cried out Neal's name, making sure the creatures heard it. They would know Neal was someone obviously cared about. If her son-in-law were still alive, if records were kept of prisoners' names, and if the 'braks believed it would hurt her, Neal could be among the next group of prisoners brought out.

Then, if the Seah could not save him, an arrow would. She was still good with the bow, and Neal's suffering would end. Her son-in-law would be buried in honor, the father of her grandsons would come home at last, and the terrible uncertainty would be over.

Mena tucked the *Annals* under her arm. About a third of the way through the meeting she had gotten too involved to take notes and would have to finish them tonight. It was very late when everyone left the Sky Tower—except of course Utray who, looking troubled, climbed the stairs to his room.

A damp chill hovered in the night. Soon they would be waking up to the great autumn fogs that settled into the valley and only burned away by noon. Penan, Nemes, and Ísavin headed off to their respective domiciles in the northeastern quadrant. Ísavin's voice came floating back in the quiet, saying she hoped Komond had put Avia to bed.

Mena smiled to herself, knowing how the child would take advantage of her mother's absence to wheedle whatever she wanted from her father. Carrying the basket of mugs, Druv followed Troya and Abiyat down the path to their beds in the Seani House, "I'll just wash these before turning in," Druv said. "No need to bother Keppit."

That left Mena and Celume on the deserted Red Lantern Way, walking through patches of fallen leaves. A few drifted down while a frog, settled in some warm hollow, tentatively creaked. Suddenly, Celume stopped. She stared at a pale blue moon-moth fluttering around one of the glowing lanterns.

"What's wrong, Cel?"

"I…I don't know. These moths. They fly lately in my dreams—hundreds of them. They settle upon my body like the touch of death!"

Mena was surprised at her vehemence. The slightly phosphorescent moths were rare on this side of the valley, and she thought they were beautiful, glowing like pale little wraiths in the dark.

Celume vigorously rubbed goosebumps off her arms. Mena remembered persistent rumors about the Spider-king: that he had cross-bred these delicate moths into creatures with chilling characteristics. Like certain parasitic wasps, these luniku, as they were supposedly called, deposited their eggs in the body of a living animal. In a death too horrible to think about, their victim swelled with masses of developing larvae that slowly ate it alive.

"It's just a harmless moon-moth," Mena said, but Celume would not move until Mena shooed it away. A short while later their paths diverged and Mena walked alone on the trail, leaving the twinkling red lights behind her. Ahead, through the trees, she saw the window of her domicile shining with a faint orange light from the hearth.

Soon, she thought with a rush of joy, she would hold her daughter in her arms again. Riah would sit late with her in front of the fire while Sheft slept next to his brother in the alcove. They would be a family again, even celebrate Spera Night together this winter. What a special night that would be! The bright stars of hope would shine directly through the windows of Rulve's Disk, and—for the first time—into the eyes of the niyalahn-ristas.

With the guidance of the Seah, they would become strong young men, alight with courage and compassion. Then one day, when the time was ripe, they would go forth with grace upon them, with the power of the Seani surrounding them, and the history of their land would be forever changed.

The waning moon, having risen perhaps an hour ago over Insheer Cliff, peered through the trees to her left. She suddenly pictured how its cold light was even now illuminating the ground in front of the closed Seani gates. Ground dark with old blood. She thought once again of Neal. In one way or another, she had done all she could, and her small family might soon be reunited at last.

Even if one of them were dead.

Teller dreamed that he sat alone on the Seani wall. An evil yellow moon glared out of the night, casting long tree-shadows across the clearing between the forest and the wall. The shadows moved crookedly with a life of their own. Like scrawny, disembodied hands, they crawled toward him and up the wall. He kicked out in horror, but they grabbed his ankles and pulled him, screaming, into the terrifying dark.

He awoke with a start, his heart pounding in his throat. Rolling over, he saw the low glow of the lantern on the kitchen table. His grandmother sat in its soft circle, writing, and for a long time he listened to the reassuring *skritch* of her quill.

CHAPTER *8*

WINGS IN THE MOON-MIRROR

The door to the mess-hall banged open. Komond turned his head to see Celume dash in, her eyes wild, her hair askew. The clatter of breakfast in the guardhouse came to an abrupt halt as the table full of guards and Rift-riders looked up in surprise. Celume rushed toward him.

"Where is he?" she cried. "Don't let him near the falconforms!"

Alarmed, Komond stood. For an instant he thought the young seeress, who barely reached the height of his chin, was actually going to clutch the front of his shirt. "Who are you talking about? What's wrong with the falconforms? We're supposed to conclude our negotiations within the hour."

"They bring danger! Danger to the emjadi. You must listen to me."

"I *am* listening. What danger?"

"I have seen it! Great wings. They will take him away." Her eyes were desperate, and now she *did* grab a handful of his shirt. "You've got to stop it, Komond!"

"So we just scrap all our plans?" Ísavin demanded. "We tell the falconforms to go home?"

Komond understood his wife's frustration. He and Larrin, the captain of the guards, had been called to join the Seah at their meeting in the Sky Tower. There being no room around the table for another chair, Komond stood in front of the closed door, his thumbs hooked in his belt. "Our alliance with the falconforms is too important to be wrecked by visions," he stated. "I'm sorry, Celume, but we need better proof than that."

The girl flinched at his stare, but she didn't look away. "But I *saw* it, there in the moon-mirror, just before dawn. Then again in the runes. The little boy, covered by huge wings. He screamed and kicked and we could do *nothing!*" To his exasperation, a tear coursed down her cheek. She wiped it away with the back of her hand.

Mena glared at him from her seat across the room. "I don't understand your attitude, Komond. It sounds as if you think the alliance is more important than the safety of my grandson."

"They're both connected!" He put his palms together and entwined the fingers in illustration. "The falconforms are crucial to the long-term protection of *both* your grandsons." Mena was an intelligent woman; why couldn't she see that?

Larrin spoke from where he sat on the spiral stair, clasped hands hanging between his knees. "Celume's only reporting what she's seen, Komond. Grilling her won't produce a vision more to our liking, or to hers either, I'll wager." He looked around at them all. "Celume is our scout, sent ahead to find the way. We can't shrug off what she sees, no matter how troubling."

Celume glanced at the young man in gratitude, and his eyes lit up. They looked at each other a moment, then she blushed and dropped her gaze.

Finally, Komond thought. Larrin's interest in Celume had been apparent for some time now, but it seemed the seeress had just this moment become aware of it. Even as concerned as he was, he was glad for his counterpart. He remembered his joy when Ísavin had first acknowledged his own existence all those years ago, but she'd never been one to blush.

Druv fingered his beard and leaned forward to address Celume. "Is the danger imminent?"

She took a moment to gather herself, and the pink color in her cheeks faded. Troubled lines appeared in her forehead. "Two days," she answered miserably, "or maybe three. Within the week, I'm sure."

Komond puffed his cheeks and blew out frustration. "Suppose you're wrong? The falconforms hold no malice toward us. As a people, they also hope for the niyal'arists. They also revere the name of Rulve. If we banish them from the Seani, they may never return. Without the falconforms to protect the emjadis, it may be a long time before they can be reunited. And Drapak is our only connection with Riah and Sheft. So I ask you again, Celume, are you certain?" He knew he was intimidating her, but the safety of the Seani, and of the niyalahn-ristas, demanded it.

Celume said nothing, only looked as if she might cry again.

"So," Penan asked the girl, "all danger will be gone in seven days? Why not ten days or a month?" He extended a hand and raised his eyebrows as if offering a suggestion. "Perhaps we should build an underground prison, and have the child live in it."

"I can't explain," she moaned. "I can only tell you what I saw."

"What about Sheft?" Mena asked. "Do wings threaten him too?"

Celume grew still. She frowned, and a far-off look seemed to lighten her eyes. "Riah will search the skies, but no wings come." A different voice had come out of her, resonant and certain. She sat silent for a moment, then blinked, present with them once more.

Komond found these prophetic issuances unnerving, yet she must be made to understand the situation. "Drapak is utterly loyal to us," he insisted. "Even now the bones of his nest-mate lie atop the Eeron Cliffs, where she was shot down by the last umbrak raid."

Celume took a deep breath, then lifted her chin with a kind of stubborn strength. "Rulve help me, but I have seen wings. Nothing but wings." Her face crumpled in anguish. "Luniku moths fluttering by the hundreds—great wings lifting Teller—bat wings, moth wings, oh Rulve, dragon wings!" She hid her face in her hands.

"Quite a menagerie," Penan remarked, half under his breath.

"There are no dragons in Shunder," Komond stated as patiently as he could. "If they exist at all, it's off in the mountains of Trey Aughter."

The seeress looked up. "I know that!" she cried. "Therefore it *must* be the falconforms. As I already told you."

Komond ran his hand through his hair, frustrated by her logic, or lack of it. "Moths and bats," he muttered. It was always difficult for him to deal with visions. A glance at his wife told him she felt the same.

Penan sighed, pulled out his little scroll, and glanced around the room. "Given we accept this vision, then the only logical solution is to conduct an investigation. We must find out which falconform is the traitor and then act accordingly."

"Usually," Komond said, "there are *facts* upon which an investigation is conducted."

"And what exactly," his wife asked, "does 'act accordingly' mean?"

Utray, of course, had to have his say. "Doesn't anyone see what is occurring here? Already the dark emjadi has brought contention among us."

"'Dark emjadi'? Exactly what do you mean by that?" Mena demanded.

"One of the twins is light-haired, light-eyed," Utray answered. "The other isn't."

"What! Now *coloration* is supposed to mean something?" She turned to Druv. "Make him leave."

"Settle *down*, Mena," Utray said. "I only wanted to point out that Teller is bringing contention among us Se, between the captain of the Rift-riders and the captain of the guards, and between us and our allies." With palms out, he stopped Mena's objections. "I'm not saying it's Teller's fault, or by his design, but we must ask ourselves if this be a plan of the entity that engendered him."

"Why do you allow him to keep harping on this 'engendering' issue!" Mena cried to Druv.

"Ah," Penan remarked, rolling his scroll between his hands, "more contention."

"Which stops now," Druv said firmly. "We all know what must be done. Teller's safety is paramount. The falconforms are a proud people, but Drapak and I know each other well. In our youth, we roamed the mountains of Trey Aughter together. As one friend to another, I'll explain our problem to him, and may Rulve grant that he will understand."

But, as it turned out, he did not. That fact became obvious to Mena at twilight, when she, along with the falconforms, the two captains, and the other Se, stood in the training field before the guardhouse. Their talks with Drapak's delegation had ended, and Druv, his face grave, translated the wind-lord's words:

"'The spirits of my companions appear bright to me. I see no malice in them, and they have proven their loyalty many times. But you question my judgment and view us with suspicion. Where there is no trust, there can be no alliance. In addition, an accused traitor cannot continue to act as messenger between the Seani and Riah. It shall all be as you have decided.'"

And so Mena watched, her heart shriveling, as the four great falconforms took flight toward the north, to ride the wind to their home.

Komond's eyes narrowed as he too watched. "The Spider-king has not done as much damage to the Seani as we ourselves have just done."

Without a word, Celume turned and walked away. After a moment, Larrin followed her.

Druv turned to Mena, regret deepening the lines on his face. "I'm sure you understand, Mena. All our plans to recall Riah and Sheft must be laid aside for now."

Her throat swelled with sorrow and bitter disappointment. Only this morning she had cautiously mentioned to Teller that his mother and brother might soon be coming home. The joy that bloomed on his face pierced her heart. Now she would have to kill that joy, just as it had been killed in her.

The Seani leaders turned aside as the falconforms dwindled into the fading light. One of them, however, lagged behind. When the others were out of sight, Yarahe wheeled toward the hillside high above the Seani and found a perch among the boulders. There he settled, to keep a secret watch.

On their way back to their domiciles, the Se decided that tasks designed to keep Teller indoors would be found for him in the Seani House and that the young guard Suver would escort him to and from there. No one was happy about the decision, especially Teller when he learned about it the next morning.

"I'll have to stay inside for a whole *week*?" he complained, pulling back on Mena's hand as they approached the Seani House. "I'm never going to see the sky again!"

For some reason, the thought of the tunnels of Oknu Shuld darkened for an instant the bright autumn day, but she brushed it aside. "Don't be so dramatic. You'll have plenty to keep you busy."

"Lir was going to show Avia and me how to catch *sun-fish*."

Her poor grandson could not even complain to Rivere because he had gone with his healer's pouch to Baenfeld. "I'm sorry, Teller," she said, "but didn't you tell Se Abiyat that you want to help the Seani? This is your chance. Se Troya is sick and can't assist Ukaipa in the nursery." It was the excuse the Seah had come up with, and to a certain extent, it was true. Troya certainly needed the rest.

"But I want to do something about the *bigger* things! About the umbraks and morue and the ahn."

He looked so passionate, so intense, that her heart went out to him. "You've got to start with the smaller tasks that life presents to you, Teller, with the little people who need your help. Then, when Rulve shows you the way, you can go on to bigger things."

She steered her grandson through the dining room where Keppit's crew were setting out bowls of raisins for their morning oatmeal, up the staircase, and across the hall to the nursery. Ukaipa, an energetic young woman with merry eyes, smiled at them from where she sat on the carpet beside three little girls. Two of them were absorbed in their play, but three-year-old Taisa looked up as they entered. She got to her feet and rushed toward Teller with a delighted smile. Like Teller at her age, she had the mind-speech, but was somewhat behind in learning to talk.

"Pay baw, Tewer," she urged. "Pay baw!"

Teller looked up at Mena. "I guess she's a little person that needs my help, right?"

"Exactly."

With a sigh, he squatted down in front of the child. "All right, Taisa, let's play ball. Go get that red one over there."

He would make a good big brother, Mena thought as the little girl scooted off. But the fond thought quickly turned sad. Because of Drapak's decision, and for who knew how long now, Teller could not be a brother even to his own twin.

CHAPTER 9

OUT OF THE FOG

A cry. Far off, yet urgent.

Teller opened his eyes. Had someone called his name? In his alcove, all was quiet in the grey morning light. A strange charge, however, seemed to hover in the air, dangerous and expectant, like that time in the dining room last spring.

His arms had prickled, and then the forks on the table had begun to rattle. Holding onto their cups, everyone stopped talking and glanced anxiously around. After a few moments the shaking stopped, people looked relieved, and the chatter resumed. It was an earthquake, Grandma had said. Se Utray told them that sometimes when that happened one of the Seani pools would overflow, or suddenly turn from cold to warm.

This morning nothing shook, yet he felt that same prickle run down his arms.

He rolled out of bed. He'd been helping Ukaipa in the nursery for two days already, but Grandma said Se Troya probably wouldn't feel better for awhile yet. At least Rivere was coming home from Baenfeld today. Maybe he was already here!

Teller rushed to the window. Fog pressed against the pane, startling him. It was as if a living thing had crept up during the night and he caught it peering in. Did this mean Rivere would be delayed? Teller sighed deeply. That was bad enough, but morning fog at this time of year usually meant sun later in the day when he'd be stuck in the Seani House. It would be better if it rained.

Teller wandered out of his alcove and looked around for his grandmother. She was nowhere to be seen, which puzzled him. Maybe she had gone on ahead to breakfast, calling him awake as she left. And Suver, who for some reason had been waiting for him on the doorstep every morning, wasn't there either.

Alone in the domicile, Teller's eyes strayed to Grandma's tiny room, the curtain at the doorway folded back on its nail. He could see the small wooden box with a curved top resting on the shelf with her books. She wouldn't mind if he took just a quick peek.

Teller darted in, climbed onto a chair, and opened the box. Nested in a piece of soft cloth were the beautiful medallions Mena had once showed him. They were his and Sheft's birth-gifts. He held one up by its black cord and rubbed the medallion between his fingers. It felt warm and buttery, like Keppit's pewter pitchers. He peered through one of the three star-holes on top—his grandma's neatly made bed looked unusually clear through it—and then studied the engraved pictures. On one side was a narrow leaf and on the other a flame, just like the carvings on Twegen and Enlen, his favorite trees in the Quela. The medallions had a special name—he forgot what it was—and someday, his grandmother said, he and Sheft would be big enough to wear them.

But not today. First he would see if Rivere was back; then maybe, if by some miracle Se Troya felt better, he could finally go fishing with Lir. He replaced the medallions, threw on some clothes, and rushed out the door.

Just outside, he stopped. Everything looked different, as if he had been transported to some strange place during the night. His grandma's purple mums, the path beneath his feet, the branches of yellow and red leaves dripping overhead: everything close by stood out clearly. But in only a short distance, his surroundings faded away, as if beyond this gauzy circle the world might have ended. It was just fog, but it made him feel isolated and uneasy.

Sounds came to him with odd clarity—voices shouting, a door banging.

"Teller! Come quickly!"

He jumped at the mind-words, loud and compelling in his head, then looked around. But the sparse figure of Nemes, or any of the other mind-speakers, did not stride out of the mist. Someone called him, but it was not a mind-voice he recognized. Fear brushed across the back of his neck. Something was wrong.

He ran down the narrow trail toward where he thought the call had come. When he burst into the clearing, he saw nothing but a wall of mist beyond a few feet of waist-high goldenrod and blue-flowered chicory. The hospit, which he knew was to his left, was completely invisible. The fog must have fooled his ears, for now the shouts came from farther away, down by the great gates.

"Teller! Hurry!"

The plea sent him fleeing down the grassy hillside, half-bare trees rising up like ghosts and then fading away, until suddenly the Seani wall loomed ahead. Heart pounding, he turned and followed it toward the gates. The big stone blocks on his right looked as solid as ever, but those ahead seemed to roll out of the mist as he ran. Ahead of him he could hear voices. They sounded high-pitched and afraid.

He reached the postern, a narrow door set into the wall as it curved into the gates. To his surprise, it was ajar. A figure he recognized as Suver stood some distance away with his back to him, apparently keeping a small group of people away from the gates. One man, his face blurry in the mist, was gesturing in excitement. "The villagers all ran to hide!" he exclaimed. "Oh, god, they're coming again!"

Who was coming? Teller crept along the wall, the group too agitated to notice him, and soon the angle of the postern door hid him from sight. For a moment he stood with his back pressed against the stones, then turned and peeked out.

The clearing in front of the gates was empty—odd for this time of the morning. Where were the people who usually came for food or to bring sick relatives to the hospit? They must be hiding, like the man said, probably among the trees. A slight movement drew his eyes to his left where a figure stood under a big oak just at the edge of the fog circle. It was Rivere, his pouch slung over his shoulder. He had flattened himself against the tree trunk and blended in with it. But why? He must have been coming back from Baenfeld, and— The sound of rough laughter pulled Teller's attention to the grey tunnel of mist that was the track down to Rydle.

Several squat figures emerged, pulling a wooden cart. Cursing and shouting at each other, their small, fierce eyes narrowed over their flat noses, they stopped just outside the circle of fog. They unfastened the back of the vehicle, pulled out what looked like a large sack, and two of them carried it forward. A third called up to the guard-towers. "A challenge for your healers! See what you can do with this one!"

The creatures heaved the bundle toward the gates.

Limp arms and legs flailed, and the body of a man thudded into the ground not twelve paces from where he stood. It rolled once, to lay face down in a drift of dark red leaves.

Horror snaked up Teller's spine. The man was a prisoner from Oknu Shuld. The creatures were umbraks. And Rivere was hiding only a stone's throw away from them.

"Ajar the gate!" Se İsavin's voice cried. With the sliding squeal of the bar and the creak of hinges, the great gates cracked open, just large enough for the prisoner to crawl through.

If he could.

Suddenly shaking, Teller turned away and pressed his back against the wall. The man looked as if he was badly hurt.

Over the creak of wooden wheels, a voice rasped out. It sounded as if the 'braks had retreated with their cart, probably using it as a shield against Seani arrows. "The Lord of Shunder has cleaned out his dungeons, and here is one we found at the dregs. Come out, all you healers, and save him!" There was a snicker of laughter among the 'braks, but silence from the guard tower.

Teller heard his grandmother's voice, strong, but with a quaver at its base. "Identify this prisoner! What is his name?"

The leader barked out a laugh. "He's here by special request. Don't you recognize him?" The 'brak waited. "No? Then let me introduce you to Neal."

Ice flooded over Teller. He whirled, and exposing only half his face, looked out of the postern.

The man on the ground was filthy, clad only in greyish-brown rags, and long matted hair fell over his shoulders. The prisoner groaned, and using both elbows, tried to haul himself toward the opening in the gate. Leaves stuck in his hair, and his feet left grooves in the ground. But they were short grooves, for almost at once the man slumped down, breathing heavily.

The 'braks had withdrawn to a place where they were only shapes in the fog. The raspy voice shouted up at the guard-tower. "I'm told some old hag wants this man. Well, there he is, madam. Now where are you?"

A stifled cry and shouts came from the guard-tower, then his grandmother's voice, urgent and entreating. "Neal! Is it you?"

The man on the ground tried to lift his head. His fingers grabbed at the ground. Teller must have made a sound because the man, trembling, turned his head toward him. Through strands of dirty hair and leaves, the man's eyes met Teller's—and his were green. The man collapsed, his right arm under him, and extended his other arm toward Teller. "Please," he croaked.

"Help him!" someone shouted. "Can't someone help him?" More feet rushed past and pounded up the ladder.

"Neal!" He heard his grandma cry. "Neal!"

Se Ísavin's voice rang out. "If you are Neal, you know you must get at least part way through the gates unaided. If you are not a devisement of the enemy, the wards will admit you." In a lower voice, she commanded someone: "Get Komond and Druv."

Lines of pain creased the prisoner's dirt-caked face. He'd never be able to pull himself forward with one arm under his body. The man rolled partially sideways, struggled to free his arm, and finally did it. He dragged himself forward, inch after painful inch. Seani people called out to him in encouragement while Teller watched, clutching the doorpost. At last, about two of his body-lengths away from the gates, the prisoner stopped, breathing hard, his forehead on the ground. With seemingly great effort, he turned and looked at Teller. Sweat trickled down his face.

"Teller?"

It was the mind-speech. The language of truth.

Teller nodded, his eyes awash with tears. "Father?"

The man's mind-voice was weak, only a wisp in Teller's head. "Help me."

The entreaty knifed into his heart. Trembling, he let go of the doorpost.

Still turned toward him, the man reached out. A spasm shook his body. "Help me come home, son," he croaked.

With a cry, Teller bolted out of the postern and fell on his knees next to Neal's outstretched arm. From the guard-tower came shouts and horrified gasps. Rivere rushed out of the trees, shouting. "No, Teller! Get back!"

But he couldn't. Teller grabbed the man's hand. It felt dry and rough.

He heard the clear sound of stretching bowstrings. "Hold!" someone cried from above. "You'll hit the boy!" Umbrak laughter rasped out of the fog.

Teller stood, and using both hands, pulled. People rushed to the gates and thrust their arms out. He pulled with all his strength, but the man was too heavy to move.

"Try!" he begged. "Try to crawl!"

The man raised his head, his eyes fixed on him through strands of greasy hair.

All movement slowed. The shrill voices shouting at him deepened, sounding now like strange animal groans. Teller dropped his hands. The man rose to his knees, shook his head, and his hair fell out in hanks and fluttered away, except for two wisps that streamed out above the eyes. He stood, growing taller and taller. Teller looked up, and then up again, at a head that flattened, at eyes that bored into him with an intense and hungry green. They were the snake eyes he had seen only days ago from the wall. A long serpent-tongue flicked out of the now cracked and lipless mouth.

He froze. The man's body elongated into a thick coil covered with brown and grey markings. Something swelled out of the shoulders, twisting and expanding, and great leathery wings unfolded against the sky. Teller felt pressure and he looked down. What had been a hand was now a giant claw that pinned his arms to his sides. A long hiss jerked his gaze even further upward, into a scaled, reptilian face. The creature threw back its head and issued a wild, triumphant screech.

Teller's ears were still ringing as the powerful wings began to beat. Leaves and dirt swirled around him. He twisted and kicked. His shoes scraped along the dirt as he was dragged away from the gates. "Grandma!" he screamed. "Grandma!" His legs left the ground as the massive wings gained flight.

Several villagers rushed out of the fog and people were shouting: "A wyvern! A wyvern!" Incredibly, he was looking down at them now, looking down at horrified, upturned faces.

"Teller!" Rivere ran toward him, his healer's pouch flapping, and jumped for his dangling feet. Umbraks burst out of the fog and seized him.

"No!" Teller shouted at them, kicking madly in the air. "Leave him alone!"

Small, arm-waving figures swarmed out of the Seani. His body was level now with the guard-tower, with his grandmother and Se Ísavin and the guards. He could see them clearly, their wide, stricken eyes, their open mouths; but with every beat of the huge wings they were getting smaller and farther away. Veils of mist wafted between him and them.

A whine of what sounded like bees passed over his head. Arrows. One must have hit the vast body above him, for it suddenly lurched sideways. Its screech pierced Teller's ears, tore into his stomach. The creature renewed its grip on him, and he heard himself scream. Red drops flew past the other great claw hanging beside him, but the wings continued to plow upward. He screamed until his throat hurt.

With a violent jerk, the massive form above him recoiled. The claw almost dropped him, but then tightened again, so tight he could hardly breathe. He twisted his head to see a winged shadow, talons down and open, swoop over the great head. It was Yarahe. The falconform attacked again, slashing at a creature four times its size. The wyvern screeched, lunged, and missed as the falconform swept aside. Yarahe came in a third time. Wheeling to the right, the creature snapped its long tail. It caught the falconform's wing with the crack of hollow bones. With a cry, Yarahe spiraled downward.

Kyra words trailed after him. "Have courage, emjadi! Y'rulve!"

Dizzy, blinded by tears, Teller was carried into the upper reaches of the fog. The light gradually increased, and he passed through a thin mist glowing from the hidden sun. He rose higher, until the deep blue sky and the warmth of a golden autumn day burst over him. He felt its warmth for only a moment, then with folded wings the wyvern streaked down, into the cold and clouded valley, into darkness.

Chapter 10

Celume's Prophecy

The fog burned away about noon. A bright sun beamed down on the Seani, lighting up the autumn leaves as they sifted down in the groves, sparkling on the waterfalls and pools, warming the empty rocking chairs on the front porch of the Seani House.

Moans drifted out of the hospit, coming from villagers who had been injured in the panic when the umbraks closed in. Further up the hill, anguished prayers emerged from the open doors of the Quela.

In the Sky Tower, the Seani leaders shouted questions at each other, held those who shook with sobs, or sat white-faced and rigid in shock. At first Komond argued that there was no real certainty as to where the wyvern had taken Teller, but Celume insisted that the runes and the moon-mirror had spoken clearly to her, and this time no one doubted her. The wyvern had gone directly to Oknu Shuld.

Oh God Rulve, Mena sobbed within her heart, *how could you allow this? He's your niyal'arist! He's an innocent little boy! How* could *you?*

She cried out that she must give herself to the Spider-king in trade for her grandson, but Druv insisted, as the Seah leader, that it was his responsibility. Everyone chimed in, citing reasons why he or she should be the one to go, blaming themselves for what happened, insisting they must storm the stronghold and get Teller back.

At last Penan stood, his face haggard. "No one must go to Oknu Shuld. For several reasons. First, the lord won't know who Teller is, and we must not inform him."

"What do you mean?" Mena cried.

"Think it through, Mena. Teller himself doesn't know he is niyal'arist, so an ordinary mind-probe won't reveal it. But if any of us Se offers himself in trade for what seems to be an ordinary child, the Spider-king will immediately become suspicious. He will surely order a long, hard probe of that child."

"We must do whatever it takes," Nemes said, "to spare Teller that. The boy showed resistance to mind-search even as an infant. I waited for his trust and then went gently with him. But the prober of Oknu Shuld"—his throat-lump moved up and down as he tried to control his anguish—"will proceed differently. I have seen his work."

With a grim nod, Penan continued. "The mind-probing of any one of us who enters the stronghold will be relentless and severe. That applies double to those who would certainly be captured in any ill-conceived attack. He or she will not be able to keep Teller's secret for long, and then our enemy would be informed that he has under his control the niyalahn-rista he has vowed to kill." Lines appeared on the scholar's face, as if his stomach were cramping. "In addition, the Spider-king would learn all about Sheft and where he has gone."

"Oh God," Mena moaned softly.

"We must also face another fact. If the Seani were fool enough to attack Oknu Shuld, it would lose. It would die. Sheft and Teller would die, the hopes of every child in

Shunder would die; and for nothing. Our restraint is Teller's only chance, Shunder's only chance, for salvation."

"So what do we do?" Mena choked out. "Abandon him? Do nothing to rescue him?"

The room fell silent, until Troya spoke. "Would you," she asked, staring steadily at Penan, "come to that same conclusion if it were Lir who had been taken?"

The scholar swallowed, but when he spoke his voice was steady. "Yes."

Troya's gaze turned to Druv, who sat with his head in his hands. "And you, Druv? Would you make that decision if it had been Neal?"

The Eldest didn't look up. When he answered, his words sounded hollow. "I already did."

The time-candle on the table guttered and honey-brown beeswax spilled down its side. At last Utray spoke. "I'm sure you all noticed," he said in a low voice, "that I was the only one here who did not offer to take the little boy's place."

He looked at Mena, and she could see the pain in his face. In spite of what he had said about her grandson's nature and parentage, she knew he loved all children.

"It was because I was reasoning very much like Penan. Teller ran out of the Seani of his own free will." Hands up, he quieted the immediate outcries. "I know. I understand why he did it. But perhaps this is Rulve's way of telling us that his destiny lies in Oknu Shuld."

With a groan, Mena clasped a hand to her stomach. "No. No, no, no, no, *no*." Grief was like a tight, thin rope around her waist, threatening to squeeze her into two pulsing halves.

A sudden stir in the room cut through her pain. She looked up. Celume had risen to her feet. She was staring fixedly at the copper version of Rulve's disk. Her eyes wide with a vision, she spoke in the strong and certain voice of prophecy.

"*Ea toltyr ataya toltyr,*
S'eft i t'lir maitush.
Rulve keyen odku conju
Way a'seu wydush.'"

In the dead silence that followed, Mena realized she recognized the words, if not their meaning. "That's a poem from the *Tajemnika.*" The big red book Riah had taken when she left with Sheft.

"Which was directly quoting," Penan said, staring at the seeress, "from a far older work written by Marhaut herself—the lost *Tajemjadi.*" *Regarding the Emjadi.*

Larrin reached out and tentatively, not wishing to disrupt the seeress's trance, touched Celume's sleeve. "Celume," he said in a low voice, "please translate for us."

The young woman continued to gaze at Rulve's copper disk, but she answered in the same firm way as before:

"*Out of the circle shall come a coin,*
obverse and reverse diverse.
Rulve wills that redemption join
the assent of those sent to be spent.'"

Penan stared at Celume in awe, his eyes glowing as if he himself were entranced. "For years," he whispered, "I struggled to translate that poem. Nothing I tried made sense. But now I see!" He turned to the rest of them in wonderment and triumph. "In this context, 'toltyr' means 'coin.' T'lir and s'eft are the opposite sides, the obverse and reverse. They are a coin—the Coin of Rulve!"

Her grandsons were the Coin of Rulve? At first Mena didn't understand, but then the meaning dawned. Her heart sank. Coins were forged in fire and made to be spent, made to be irretrievably handed over, to buy back—redeem—what was lost. *Oh God Rulve,* she keened, *what are you demanding?*

Celume pulled her eyes away from the copper disk and turned them, still unseeing, toward those before her. "The Coin of Rulve has passed out of our hands. All our desire to control the fate of the niyalahn-ristas, all our fumbling to weave the strands of what will be—these must be laid aside. T'lir and S'eft belong to Rulve now. The Creator forges them, hardens and imprints them. Back to back he unites them, and waits on their answer to his call. One day we will play our part, but today we are given our own mission, and to this we must turn our resolve."

"Are you saying," Mena burst out, "that we must just sit here and acquiesce? That this tragedy is Rulve's will? Never will I believe that!"

Celume's blank gaze slowly moved toward Mena's face. "Evil beings willed it; not Rulve."

"He could have stopped it!"

"The Creator does not take away the freedom she granted to her creatures. All Rulve can do about evil is redeem it."

Mena made a sharp, cutting gesture and turned away.

"What about Rivere?" Troya murmured. "He'll have to face the mind-probe."

Nemes rubbed a hand over his eyes. "When the 'braks dragged him off, he appeared to be only another villager. Perhaps, Rulve grant it, he may not seem important to the Spider-king. Also, before we let him go on his healing journeys, I taught him a way to resist a cursory probing. Rivere may be able to hide his knowledge of who Teller is by concentrating on the still painful grief for his son."

Druv clenched his fists on the table, his eyes moving

from one face to another. He seemed to have aged years in only hours. "Penan is right. If we overreact now, we will cut off any chance for Teller. But I tell you this." He rapped on the table to emphasize his words and his voice thrummed with intensity. "The evil done this day will not go unanswered. I vow to do everything in my power to bring Teller and Rivere back. I swear it, before Rulve and before this Seah."

"I also swear," Ísavin said, her gaze like iron. "On my life."

A moan of dismay escaped Troya.

Komond ignored her and placed a hand resolutely on his wife's shoulder. "And mine."

Unmoved, Celume gazed straight ahead. "Your choices," she pronounced, "will bring disaster upon the Seani." She stayed for a moment with her seeing; then, seemingly exhausted, sank down into her chair.

A loud, hollow note shivered through the air. Mena started, and her eyes darted to the open door. Far off, yet seemingly under their feet, the great Bellstone sounded.

Bo-ung, it tolled. *Bo-ung.*

An icy lump lodged in Mena's heart. Did the bell speak of her grandson's death, as it had of his birth? Did it toll for the Seah, now hopelessly divided? Or out of the tunnels of despair was it flinging at them an impossible challenge to trust? It seemed hardly to matter, for she was sinking into an abyss of grief, deep and grey, from which she might never emerge.

CHAPTER 11

WORM~LIGHT

The sound of a great bell rolled through him. It echoed in his ears, shook his spirikai. It called, insisted: *wake up!* He sat bolt upright, his heart hammering.

Where was he? Objects came into focus—a dim cave-like chamber, an old wooden chair, a small table. A floor grate in the corner, covered with dust-webs. No windows. He looked for a hearth, a lantern, a candle, but found none. The only light came from a glass globe on a stand. It crawled with glowing, blue-white worms. They looked like maggots, only much bigger. He tore his eyes away from them.

His name. What was it? Panic surged; he couldn't remember his name. He was no one, nowhere. The inside of his head felt torn and scraped, his skin hot.

A memory flashed. Of him lying on a wooden table. Of another rockbound room. Of a face, grizzled and heavy with fat. "My name is Greaz." The thick worm-like lips twisted in a nasty smile. "Welcome, Teller, to Oknu Shuld." The eyes came closer, glowing with an evil light. Fingers like iron claws gripped his head.

Heat roiled in his spirikai. He tried to push the hands away, but the man only laughed.

"Oh ho! A lively one."

With a sharp crack, pain sliced into his head. A mind-probe dug in; with iron claws it ripped and tore. He screamed. Something flared, blinded him. Greaz screeched and let go. A shadowy figure standing in the corner wheezed with laughter.

Gasping, he rolled over to the side of the hard table. The stone floor spun slowly beneath him, and drops of bright red blood dripped onto it.

His name was Teller. He was in Oknu Shuld.

He sat on a rumpled bed, his head throbbing, heat prickling over and through him. He plucked at his shirt, but it clung to him, and he couldn't get it off.

Someone helped him. It was Rivere! Rivere was here.

The healer bathed his forehead and chest with a cool cloth, gave him water. Clutching his hand, Teller gulped it down, even though swallowing hurt his sore throat. The water tasted funny, as if scooped from a long-standing puddle in the rock. Rivere eased him back onto the pillow.

He lay there, slipping in and out of awareness, the walls gliding dizzily around him. From somewhere far off a deep gong sounded, just a regular gong and not the great bell, and someone covered the globe with a black cloth. Later a gong sounded again, higher this time, and the cloth was taken away. Rivere's voice said, "It's morning. The beginning of the rota. There's no day and night here, Teller."

Just the dim, seething globe.

They shared the one bed, and Rivere slept between him and the door. Teller's pillow always felt slightly damp, and their blanket smelled moldy. All the furniture legs stood in little dishes filled with an oily liquid. To keep spiders off, Rivere told him. The grey stone ceiling pressed down on him, and the air smelled as if many people had breathed it before him.

Teller stiffened whenever he heard anything outside. But the door opened only for a silent old woman who shuffled in with a tray of food, or to empty the chamber-pot, or carrying pails to replace the dried-up worms in the globe with live, glowing ones. A thin metal collar encircled her neck, and she wore threadbare, grey-white tunic and pants. She was their ahn, Rivere said. She never looked at them and didn't answer when Rivere spoke to her. The claws must have gone inside her head too.

The fever faded, but there were holes inside his mind where memories used to be. Rivere tried to help him, but names didn't connect with faces and blew away like leaves before he could get hold of them. It was like that with words too. He tried to ask Rivere about everything, but the right words wouldn't come.

Except for one. "Home!" he begged Rivere. "Home!" He was crying because he wanted to go home so much that it hurt.

"I know, Teller," Rivere said. He looked like he, too, wanted to cry, like there was nothing he could do but smooth Teller's hair off his forehead. "I know, voskat. Just get better now, and we'll talk about that later."

Teller couldn't remember where home was, or hardly anything about it, but he longed to go back there. Why didn't anyone come and get him? He remembered he had a grandmother, but not her name or face. He didn't think he had a mother, and the word "father" produced only a confusing blur—of someone who held him on his lap, green eyes that at first sparkled with laughter, then hardened, and burned with hunger. Immediately he blocked the image. He would not remember it. He had no father.

But he had other people, he was sure of it. People

who loved him. Why didn't they *come?* He looked up at Rivere, through tears that weren't words, and Rivere seemed to understand.

"They would come if they could, voskat. Believe me, lad, they would."

He awoke with a start. A figure stood over him, its face as brown and furrowed as the bark of a tree. Its eyes were slanted brown ovals with no pupils, and its mouth was a lipless hole. Teller gasped as it seized his hand in a strong and bony grip. A ring glinted on a brown-nailed finger, a ring of twisted wires.

Rivere clutched Teller's shoulder. "I'm here, voskat."

"I am called Vol Kuat," the figure said. "The lord looks for s'rere, the blood that makes the earth dance." He withdrew a knife and with a quick movement cut the back of Teller's hand. He held it over a small bowl of what looked like dirt, and drops of blood fell into it. Nothing happened. The figure went away, and his trailing cloak left Teller with a confused impression of moldering leaves.

"What was that for?" Teller wanted to ask, but only a stutter came out.

Just then a second alarming figure entered their room. He was taller than Vol Kuat, bone-thin, and dressed in a black robe and hood. He too wore the wire ring. Teller couldn't see his face, but was suddenly sure he didn't want to. A rasping voice came out of the hood. "I am Volarach Nosce, the Prome of Oknu Shuld and the first in service to the Lord Eyascnu Varo. He wants to know more about you. Soon you will assist us in this endeavor."

"It's been only three rotas," Rivere said. "He's not healed yet."

Nosce ignored him and continued to address Teller.

"It is important that you cooperate with us. We suspect you contain great power. It must serve us, or it will never serve you." He stood over him a moment longer, then turned and left.

Teller stared after him. He had power? A scene flashed into his mind, himself sitting at a table and talking to someone: "*So how are we special?*" Then it was gone.

Rivere came quickly to his side. "Don't be afraid. Rulve's love enfolds you, and his presence surrounds you."

He knew Rulve, from before. Even here, they prayed to the Creator. Teller had to do this from his bed, because he was too dizzy and weak to stand. That was all right, Rivere said; Rulve understood weakness. Teller was thankful he did. He just lay in warm, green hands and let Rulve love him. Like raindrops falling onto parched earth, her tenderness trembled on the surface, then slowly sank in. One time when they prayed together, a quick, sharp vision came: hands upraised, he stood with other people, kind and loving people, in a sort of forest, surrounded by a circle of giant trees, his face turned to the green, setting sun. Not long after that, the words he had lost started to come back.

"Please…home?" he asked.

Rivere looked at him with eyes that swam with tears, as if now Rivere had no words, as if the question hurt him as much as it hurt Teller. Rivere said nothing, only reached for Teller's hand and squeezed it. At that moment, Teller knew he shouldn't ask him about home anymore.

The food was awful. Usually there was a small piece of bread on the tray, but they had to pick fuzzy spots of mold out of it. Sometimes they had a piece of cheese rind or a boiled egg, but most of the time they had watery, lukewarm soup with parts of dead bugs floating in it. When Teller first saw this, he pushed his bowl away.

"Y-yuck," he said, his tongue still getting used to talking.

"These things are cave-insects," Rivere said. "You've got to eat them. Children need certain food we don't have right now, like milk and meat, and these symphs will have to do."

In spite of the food, Teller began to feel better, and eventually Rivere persuaded him to emerge from their small room. To their right, a corridor stretched into dimness. Dust-encrusted globes hung by chains from the ceiling. Most were dark and empty, but a few glowed with the horrible giant maggots. They turned to the left, where the hall rapidly became a rough-cut tunnel. It ended at a rock wall sheened by moisture.

"Watch out for the puddle," Rivere said in a low voice. His words sounded muffled, as if there wasn't enough room in these passageways even for an echo. "It must've come from rain leaking from the top of Insheer Cliff. Or from an irrigation channel up there." He glanced at the stone ceiling that almost touched his head, then back at the wall. With fingers outspread, Rivere put his hand on the wet rock. For a moment he didn't say anything, but when he spoke, his voice was raspy. "This must be where Oknu Shuld ends." He pushed against the solid surface, so hard his hand trembled, and an angry, hopeless look crept into his eyes.

The next time they left their room, Rivere turned to the right. Teller held his hand tightly as they passed closed doors and an alcove that held the statue of a creature with horns and a crafty cat face. Grit and dead insects lay in unswept corners. They came to an intersection, where the unlit passageway directly ahead was blocked by an iron gate. The hall to the right, also gated and locked, went up a few stairs and after a long dark distance met yet another twilit corridor that angled off from it. The left-hand corridor was blocked by a heavy metal door, which had been rolled onto a rusty track from a pocket in the wall. Faint noises came from beyond it—growling voices and the sound of boots clanging on what seemed to be a metal stair or ladder.

At first Teller sighed with relief when they got back to their room and the door was closed, but after a while he started looking forward to the short walks. He began to feel a glimmer of curiosity. The hooded figure had told him that he had power, and he wanted to know what it was.

He didn't always hold Rivere's hand now, but sometimes plunged ahead to the right-hand hall, where he would stand pressed against the iron bars of the gate. The sound of the hour-gongs came from that direction, but as if from levels below. He also heard the far off rumble of wheels, an occasional angry shout, or the scary crack of what sounded like a whip.

Then, one time when Rivere was tucking him into bed, the door suddenly burst open, and umbraks piled in. Without even glancing at Teller, they dragged Rivere out of the room.

Too terrified to move, Teller just sat there, staring at the closed door, his heart pounding. Finally he grabbed Rivere's pillow, went to the door, and looked out. He saw only the dim hall. Clutching the pillow, he trailed down the corridor, opening doors and looking for Rivere. All the rooms were small and empty. There were no windows in any of them, and when he thought about that, it was hard to breathe.

He went back to bed and arranged Rivere's pillow

lengthwise alongside him. He snuggled next to it and put his arm around it. He thought of his grandmother, how from his sleeping alcove he could see her, reading or writing late at night, the lantern making a warm circle around her. The light, however, didn't reach her face, and left it in shadows.

A pale glow crawled over the wall. It came from the maggots, but he didn't look at them. They were bristly, as thick as his little finger, and he didn't like them at all.

He dreamed he was trapped with them inside the globe. Fighting to escape, he pounded his fists against the smooth, curving sides. But the glass was too strong and only made a *thung-thung-thung* sound. He stood knee-deep in caterpillars, and they crawled up his legs and clung to his arms. From outside the globe, no one could hear him scream.

He woke, frantically rubbing the feel of the maggot-mouths off his arms, and pulled Rivere's pillow close to his chest. After a while he dozed off, and the next thing he knew the old ahn was shuffling in with a tray. "Good...good morning," he said.

She didn't look up, but her eyes flickered, so he knew she heard him.

"*Is* it morning?"

Ignoring him, she put the tray down and began filling the floor dishes with the oily liquid.

Maybe the mind-speech would work. He tried, but his head burned with the effort, until at last he realized he couldn't do it. His mind-speech was gone. A cry burst out of him, like from some small hurt animal.

The ahn jerked upright. She looked at him as if seeing him for the first time, then darted out.

Loneliness pressed down on him like the stone ceiling. He walked up and down the corridor, drew

letters in the dust, stared past the barred gates. Silence lay
heavy around him. He decided to jump wildly on his
bed, something his grandmother had never allowed him
to do, but when he got tired, the silence flowed back even
worse. He shouted out for Rivere, for anyone, but soon
stopped. It seemed as if unseen things lifted their heads,
suddenly aware of him.

A few memories came flashing back: a plate of blue-
berry pancakes glistening with honey, a sunny meadow
over which swallows flitted and veered, himself on the
back of a pony, and— his grandmother's name! It was
Mena! She was opening a little wooden box and showing
him something inside. He stayed with these memories,
trying to force himself to remember more, but they just
trickled away.

Something bad was happening to him. He became
afraid, in a very cold way. Gongs rang, and he forgot if
they marked the time to be awake or the time to sleep. He
became frantic to get out. He would shake the iron gates
or try to roll the metal door aside, then throw himself
against it until he bruised his shoulder. At night he
screamed, into his pillow so the dark wouldn't hear,
"Grandma! Grandma! Grandma!"

There were spiders in his room. Big, unfriendly ones,
not like the little weavers who made beautiful webs
between flower stems. Long purple and black legs would
emerge from the grate and he could hear them scuttling
on the stone floor while he buried his face in Rivere's
pillow. The liquid in the shallow dishes kept them out of
his bed, out of the globe, but not out of his dreams.

CHAPTER 12

RENUNCIATION

Teller woke from nightmares, not knowing if it was day or night outside, summer or winter. Groggy, he sat up, covered his head with the blanket, and rocked back and forth, back and forth. Hadn't he done this before, or was he thinking of someone else?

A sound, like a tiny squeak, made him throw the blanket aside. A small grey mouse was sitting on his tray, nibbling at his crust of bread. Teller watched it, then became aware that his lips felt...stretched. He was, he realized, smiling, something he hadn't done for a long time. "Hello, mouse," he said. His voice sounded strange too. Hoarse and cracked from lack of use.

The mouse looked up at him with bright eyes, and didn't move as he reached over and picked it up. He held the tiny furry body in the palm of his hand, petting it with one finger, then fed it more bread. It stayed with him while he drank some of the cold, watery soup, and for a while he played with it. But when he set it down on the floor, it scooted out under the door.

"Come back!" Teller cried, flinging the door open. "Wait for me!"

The mouse skittered down the hall and directly under the gate that blocked the unlit corridor straight ahead. Teller saw, to his astonishment, that the gate stood slightly ajar. He wrenched it fully open and plunged into the dark tunnel.

He caught a whiff of fresh, cold air, as if from an open window. Ahead shone a dim light that was a different color from the globe-light. It came from under a closed door at the very end of the corridor. He found the handle, turned it, and pushed the door open.

Rulve's house! He blinked against a dim forest glow and joy flooded him. Then it rapidly drained away. He had entered another cave-like, empty room, but the air smelled, incredibly, of rain. He could hear it pattering outside. The sound and light came from a window to his left. He ran to it, but the opening was blocked by thick woody stems and silver-green leaves. Tough ivy branches twined over the opening like a net. He couldn't even get his hand through. Still, it was wonderful just to smell the air and see leaves shivering when drops of rain hit them, even if the leaves had brown spots on them and their edges were curled.

There was no furniture in the room, so he sank down onto the floor with his back against the wall and his face toward the window. The mouse nosed about, rustling the dried ivy leaves that had blown into one corner. Breathing the clean air, Teller closed his eyes and listened to the rain. That slow kind of autumn rain that always made him feel sleepy.

It was twilight. He and Grandma, laughing in the rain and pulling up their hoods, ran down the path to dinner. Wet leaves gleamed a deep red and gold. A clear puddle lay in the grass, pockmarked by little rain circles. "Watch out for the puddle, Teller!" she cried. He jumped over it and raced toward the warm lights shining out of the Seani House windows.

His eyes flew open. Yes! The Seani! He used to live

there. The Seani was home. And it was just across the valley from Oknu Shuld.

He ran back to the window and pushed his face against the net of ivy. "I'm here!" he shouted. "Grandma, I'm right here!" He grabbed two of the thick stems, shook them, and tried to peer between the half-dead leaves. "Heeere! I'm heere!"

Something crashed behind him, and he whirled.

A young girl stood in the doorway, his tray at her feet. The bowl was broken, the soup he hadn't finished spilled. "Stop that!" she exclaimed. "They'll hear you and block up the window." She was dressed just like the old ahn had been, in dirty-white tunic and pants, and wore the same kind of thin collar.

"I *want* them to hear!" Teller cried. "I want them to come and take me home."

"No one can hear you from up here. Only guards will come."

"But I live just across the valley! In the Seani."

"It's miles away, and you can't even see it from this angle. Please stop shouting. This is the only open window they haven't found yet."

He turned his head to look at the window. She was right. He remembered how he used to stare from the Seani hillside at where Oknu Shuld was covered with ivy, and it was very far away.

"Now I have to get a rag and clean up this mess," the girl said, looking down at the shattered bowl. "I collected your tray like I was supposed to and came here to get a breath of fresh air, and you started screaming. Now look what happened."

"I'm sorry," Teller said. "I didn't mean to scare you." The girl was older than him, probably about eight or nine, and her dark hair was tied back neatly with a blue ribbon.

"My name is Teller," he said, then leaned forward eagerly. "Have you seen Rivere?"

"I've only been here a week."

"Can you ask the other ahn about him? Is he all right? When will he come back here?"

"I'm not supposed to speak to you."

"But there's nobody else to talk to! And I won't tell. There's no one *to* tell."

"I have to go," she said, looking around. "I have to clean this up and somehow explain how the bowl got broken."

"Tell them I did it. Tell them I threw it on the floor." Several times he wanted to do this very thing, just to see the bowl shatter.

Her big brown eyes met his. "That would be lying."

"Yeah." A little ashamed, he lowered his gaze, but then looked up hopefully. "Are you taking the place of the grey-haired lady?"

"For now, I guess. But, please, give me leave to go."

No one needed his permission for anything before, except Se—Se someone for mind exams, but she seemed to need it. Reluctantly, he nodded, and with a look of relief, she slipped away.

He thought about waiting for her to come back to clean up, but didn't want to get her in trouble. He glanced over his shoulder at the window, took a deep breath, and returned to his room. It didn't seem so empty now. When he fell asleep, hours later, it was with the hope of speaking to her again.

The next rota he rushed down the hall toward the room with the open window, just to see it, just to look out, but the gate was locked. Back in his room, he made the bed neat, for the first time in a long while, so the girl could sit on it, then sat on the chair to wait for her.

Finally she came. He jumped up as she put down the tray. "Did you find out anything about Rivere?"

"I'm not supposed to speak to you about him. I'm not supposed to speak to you at all, about anything." She made as if to leave.

"Please don't go! It's lonely here."

She stopped and looked at him with sympathy.

He wanted to keep her talking to him, so asked the first question that popped into his head. "Where's your room? Is it far from here?"

She rolled her eyes. "None of us have our own rooms, silly. We all sleep down on level seven, in the isav. It's a big chamber where the men sleep in one half and the women in the other."

Kind of like the men's and women's dorms in the Seani House. "You never told me what your name is."

She frowned. "Ant."

He never heard of any parent who'd name their child after a bug. "Really?"

"Well, it used to be Keya. The subaltern takes away our village names and gives us bug names when we get here. It's the custom."

He didn't like that custom at all, but she didn't seem to either, so he said nothing more about it. He sat down on the chair and motioned for Keya to sit on the bed. "I don't know how long I've been here. A long time, I think. What month is it?"

"It's Hawk. The middle of Hawk."

"I've been here for weeks then."

"They said most of the time you were sick."

"I'm better now. Do you have friends here?"

"We don't really have time for friends. But Clane and old Hanat are here from my village. And Gorv." She smiled.

"Who's Gorv?" He thought he'd heard the name before, but couldn't be sure.

"He used to live near our farm. At first he worked up here in morue packing, but most of the crop is baled up for the season, so he was assigned to the scourery."

"What's that?"

"Well, it's a cavern down on level eight of Oknu Shuld. Way at the back, where the boiling pools are. The kitchen ahn prepare food on long wooden tables and then put it in these big cauldrons. To cook it, they lower the cauldrons into the pools with chains." Lines appeared in her forehead. "It's hot down there, and a bad smell comes out of some bubbling mud-pots."

A memory came to him, of sinking luxuriously in one of the Seani's warm pools on a cold autumn day, of steam rising from his bare arm when he raised it from the water. But the pools Keya was talking about seemed quite different. "It sounds dangerous down there."

"It is! The floor is slippery with grease and mud, and sometimes a big pot tips over and scalds people." Her lips pressed together a moment. "Gorv says there's a terrible punishment if a worker cuts away too much of the rotten vegetable parts or if a cook adds too many bones to the stock."

"A punishment?"

"They—the ones that made the mistake—they have to stand in one of the dishwashing-cages." Her voice tightened. "Then the subaltern orders them lowered into one of the hot pools. If it's a first offense, she makes sure only their feet are burned. If it's not, they go down lower."

Teller's spirikai began to heat up. "She does this just because someone made a mistake?"

"The subalterns don't believe in mistakes. Their orders

are very clear. People need to obey orders, don't they?" Keya looked away from him and picked at the blanket. "Rena doesn't know about these things."

"Is she your niyal?"

"Yes."

"I don't have a niyal, only a twin brother, but I don't remember him. Can you see what your sister is doing right now?"

"Well, our bond hasn't been broken yet, if that's what you mean. Hanat says one of the mind-probers got hurt or something, so they got behind. Anyway, I can't tell exactly what Rena is *doing*. More like what she's *feeling*— if she's happy or sad. Things like that."

"Do it now, so I can see." He found this was important to him, important to know how she could touch her twin.

Keya nodded, then seemed to listen intently to something inside herself. "It must be early morning outside. Rena is floating someplace, still asleep probably. She's trying to get used to being by herself. But it's—it's hard for her."

"For you too."

"Yes, but at the Welcoming Ceremony, the subaltern told my parents that if I do what I'm told, and do it well, I'll be taken care of. All my life." Her hand wandered to the metal collar around her throat. The skin under it appeared rough and red.

"Does that hurt you?"

She dropped her hand. "I'm not stupid," she said with a proud lift of her chin. "I've never done anything to *make* it hurt. It only itches sometimes. I'm sure that will go away in time."

The thought of having to wear a collar like that made him feel ashamed for her, and he looked away. His eyes traveled over the too-close walls and lingered on the grate. "Are—are you ever afraid in here?"

Keya bent her head and rolled the hem of her tunic. "When we first came, the subaltern told us there was no reason to be afraid, if we obeyed them and didn't break the rules. But"—she lowered her voice a notch—"but I've heard things, like about the scourery. Some of the ahn whisper that they treat you all right at first, but only until your niyalahn bond is broken. They don't want people on the outside to know what happens in here. They say I'm lucky that I still have my bond with Rena, but when that's gone, well…Perhaps sometimes I do get afraid, a little." She bit her lip. "Maybe more than a little."

"Me too," Teller admitted. He remembered an incident from before, of himself holding a small piece of quilt and lying in green, warm hands. "When I'm afraid, I go to be with Rulve."

She looked up at him in surprise. "You've heard of Rulve! I thought only a few people in the villages knew her name."

"Where I come from everyone knows Rulve. We know the Creator isn't a man or a woman, but a spirit, so sometimes we say 'he' and sometimes 'she,' to remind us. His hands make a nest, and you can settle down in them when you're lonely or afraid."

"We call Rulve Mother. In the isav we pray like this." She lay back on the bed, her hands open at her sides. "But we do it under our blankets during sleep-session, so the proctor can't see. Then we link minds and ask our Mother to comfort us." Keya closed her eyes. "At the end of every work-shift, we ask Rulve to quickly send the niyalahn-ristas."

"What's that?"

She craned her neck to look up at him. "They're

people, something like niyalahn, but different. They'll make the sweet-rue grow again, so we won't need the awful morue. They'll redeem all us ahn—buy us back from the Lord of Shunder—and take us home."

"I want to go home, too." The sudden ache made him swallow. "More than anything."

She gave out a little sigh.

"When we're with Rulve in liturgy," he said, "we open our hands too, only like this." He raised his hands like they did during prayer-time, closed his eyes, and listened with his mind and heart. He felt it coming, the familiar deep tenderness, and leaned into its embrace. Love poured through him like a gentle waterfall, washing away his homesickness and worry for Rivere. Rulve was hugging him, so strongly he could feel the tingle of it on his skin, could feel Rulve's hands inside him, holding his heart.

"What's going on here?" a harsh voice demanded.

His eyes popped open, and Keya scrambled off the bed. At the door stood a soldier in a red cloak, glaring at them. He stepped aside and Vol Nosce glided into the room. His presence seemed to push Keya against the wall, to force her to stare at the darkness within his hood. Two umbraks pushed a man ahead of them into the room. With a shock, Teller recognized Rivere. He looked older, and very pale. Teller rushed to him, and Rivere's arms went around him.

"Are you all right, voskat?" the healer whispered.

There was a big lump in his throat, so he could only cling to him and nod.

"Boy," Vol Nosce commanded in his rasping whisper, "the subaltern asked you a question."

Bewildered, he disengaged from Rivere and faced the black hood. "We were—we were being with Rulve."

The two umbraks moved to block the door.

Nosce addressed Keya, who seemed to shrink within herself. "I ordered complete isolation. Why did you speak to him?"

Her eyes wide with fear, she said nothing.

"It was me," Teller said. "I asked her to." He felt Rivere's hands grip his shoulders.

The figure continued to address Keya. "You spoke to him about Rulve, did you not?"

She hung her head.

"You have disobeyed two clear and specific orders. You spoke to this boy when told not to, and you tried to entangle him in ahnish superstition. The penalty is the luniku pits."

Keya's gaze leaped in horror to Nosce's hood. She slid slowly down the wall, until she crouched against it, hugging her knees and staring at him.

"But I already knew!" Teller cried. "I already knew about Rulve."

Nosce turned toward him. "We do not speak about illusions here. There is no Rulve."

Teller stared at the shadowed face, and cold fear washed through him. Besides Rivere, Rulve was all he had now.

Rivere's voice came thickly. "Volarach, please. She's been here only a short time."

"Time does not matter. Orders do. But for contradicting me, healer, you will watch the entire process, until all the larvae have completely emerged. She should produce enough for several lamps."

The subaltern reached down for Keya and grabbed her arm. With a moan, she twisted away, and huddled against the stone wall.

"Vol Prome!" Rivere cried. "Let me go in her place."

"No. You are useful here. She is not. But you will escort her." Nosce spoke a word, and the subaltern stepped away.

Rivere knelt beside Keya, and put his arms around her trembling shoulders. "I won't leave you." He smoothed strands of her hair that had come out from its blue ribbon. "And you won't be in the dark. The luniku gleam like blue ice in moonlight, and they make the whole chamber shine. They'll flutter against you like snowflakes."

"They'll sting! They'll sting like wasps!"

"Yes, they will, but that part will soon be over."

"Do not lie to her," Nosce said. "It will only be the beginning. Her skin will swell with eggs and then erupt with emerging worms."

With a stifled cry, Keya buried her head against Rivere.

The healer drew her close. "It might look ugly, Keya, but after awhile you will feel nothing. The luniku mean no harm. They only want to make their babies. In a few gongs it will all be over." He kissed her hair. "Then your spirit will go to Rulve, and shine bright with her, and your body will make light for us in here."

Keya lifted her head, tears slipping down the lines of anguish on her face. She clutched at the healer's arm. "Rena! Rena can't—"

"They'll break the bond first, Keya. Your sister will feel nothing but that." He got to his feet, and she took his hand. The subaltern pushed them toward the door.

Teller had been listening with growing horror. He couldn't believe what he was hearing. It was worse than his terrible dream of being trapped in the globe with the caterpillars. "No!" he shouted. "No! She didn't do anything wrong!"

Nosce turned toward him "You also contradict me?"

"He doesn't know what he's saying!" Rivere exclaimed. "Teller, be quiet. You can do nothing. She's in Rulve's hands now."

"That," Nosce said, "is a myth. No doubt she will cry out to Rulve many times in the next few rotas, but in the luniku pit there is never any answer." The Vol looked down on Teller. "Only the Lord of Shunder can answer. Only he can save her." He paused. "If asked."

"Then can I ask?" Teller cried. "Take me to him so I can ask."

Rivere squatted down and put his arms around him. "Teller, no. This is not for you to do."

"You would deny him his choice as savior?" Nosce asked.

Rivere looked up at him with a stricken face, but the Vol turned his attention back to Teller. "Do you wish, then, to implore the lord?"

"Yes. If he'll save Keya."

"He will demand much in return."

Teller glanced at Keya's pale, tear-streaked face. He remembered someone telling him: *You have to start with the little people who need your help.* "I'll do whatever he wants," he said.

Rivere stood. "Nosce, the boy doesn't understand. He's too young. In the long run this will get you nothing."

"No?" the Vol said. "We will see." He made a motion with his hand, and the umbraks pulled Rivere back into the shadows at the doorway. "See that he does not make a sound or interfere in any way." The black hood turned toward Teller. "You must do exactly as I say."

His throat tight, Teller nodded.

"The lord will be addressed only through abject humility. Remove your clothes."

He looked at those standing above him: the hooded figure; the cruel, slightly amused face of the subaltern; the stony, half-human gaze of the umbraks back in the shadows. Still crying, Keya clutched Rivere's hand, her head bowed.

She was for sure one of the little people. For sure someone who needed his help. With eyes downcast, he removed his tunic and drawstring pants, then stood before them wearing only his small-cloth. He'd been naked many times, when he took a bath in the Summer Pool or got ready for bed, and never thought anything of it. But now, in this place, and with these people looking at him, he felt somehow ashamed.

"As the Prome of Oknu Shuld, I will accept your supplication on behalf of the lord. Kneel at my feet. Press your forehead and palms against the floor."

He did that, but a hot blush ran up the back of his neck. The floor felt gritty against his forehead and hands.

"Repeat after me," Nosce said. "Lord of Shunder, I bow before you."

He repeated the words.

"I beg salvation for this ahn."

"I beg salvation for this ahn."

"And in return, I reject Rulve, and all thoughts of Rulve."

He stiffened.

"Say it!" the subaltern grated. "Or she is gone."

In the silence. he could hear Keya's muffled sobs. He thought of what they wanted to do to her, just for being kind to him.

"The lord will not wait any longer," the rasping voice said. "Speak!"

In his mind he saw the great hands, and a boy resting inside them. But it was some other child, and he himself had climbed down and was backing away. He took a deep, shuddering breath. "And in return," he whispered, his throat so thick he could hardly speak, "in return I reject—" He swallowed, and tried again. "In return I—" The words would not come out.

"Do you want us to take Rivere as well?" Nosce asked.

"No!" He gulped. "I reject—I reject Rulve, and all thoughts—all thoughts of her." Tears stung the back of his eyes as he watched the hands holding the little boy receding, moving quickly as if down a long tunnel. Rulve was leaving him.

"In gratitude for your favor—"

He looked up. "Isn't that enough?" he cried.

"It is not," the hood said. "Bow, and repeat my words."

He put his head down. "In gratitude for—for your f-favor—"

"I give to you completely, both my body and soul."

Keya's moan cut through his anguish, and the subaltern barked out a laugh. Struggling to suppress the tears, he clutched at the stone floor with his fingers.

"Say it!" Nosce demanded. "If you want the lord to save her."

"'In gratitude f-for your favor,'" he forced out, "'I give—I give to you—'" But now hot tears were pouring down and he couldn't say the final words.

"Take them away," Nosce ordered.

"No!" Teller cried. "'I give to you b-both—body and soul!' My body and soul!" Then he collapsed on the floor, hiding his head under his arms as silent sobs shook and choked him. A door deep in his heart was closing, and clicked shut.

Boots stepped over him. "Sniveling ahn," the subaltern muttered.

There was a movement at the door and Teller raised his head. "Well done," Nosce rasped. "The lord will be pleased."

Through his tears he saw the Vol and the subaltern swirl out. The umbraks pushed Keya and Rivere after them. The terrible knowledge that Rivere was leaving him again forced him to climb to his feet and dash his tears away.

Rivere turned to him, his eyes liquid with pain. "Y'rulve, voskat," he said. "Y'rulve, son."

The umbraks bustled him out, and slammed the door.

Teller stood there, trembling. Rivere had called him "son." But it was too late. He had given his body and soul to the Lord of Oknu Shuld. He had renounced the Creator who loved him and didn't deserve a father anymore.

He could not look at the globe next to his bed, could not go near it. He sat down on the chair and slowly drew up his legs. He was utterly alone.

All night his spirikai throbbed, and fire roared through his dreams.

The old ahn, carrying a pail full of glowing worms to replenish the dead ones, quietly entered the room. It was dark; the child must have finally learned to cover the globe. From the dim light in the hall she saw he was curled up on the chair, asleep and half-naked in the cold. His clothes lay on the floor. She turned to the globe on its stand beside the bed, took one look, and muffled a cry.

It was cracked, black with soot. The larvae inside were nothing but coiled grey ash.

Putting the pail down, she glanced down the empty hall, then carried the child to his bed and gently covered him with the blanket.

CHAPTER 13

THE GREEN ROOM

"So a Seani whelp has pledged loyalty to me. Hardly noteworthy"—the precise voice took on an even more sardonic edge—"in a place teeming with loyal servants."

"His period of isolation is over, lord. Tomorrow I will have him brought to my interrogation chamber. Then I, and Vol Kuat of course, will begin."

"I am not interested in when you will begin," the voice said sharply, "but when you will end."

"Six years in the Seani produced in him certain unfounded beliefs and misplaced loyalties. It will take time to scour these away and unearth his Power. But, I assure you, he will come to see that serving you is his destiny."

"With *what* Power will he serve me?"

A hesitation, then: "I promise only what I can deliver, lord."

"How admirable. But as you well know, Prome, I too never promise; but always deliver." There was a long silence before the lord continued in a lower tone. "You see what they did to me. I used to trust my servants. I believed in their loyalty. The niyal'arist traitors killed all that."

"I've read your autobiography, lord. A powerful narrative. What happened to your brother was a tragedy."

"The *L'garza Wadek* is not a mere autobiography. It stands as a beacon of truth against a deeply-ingrained myth. The legend of the niyalahn-ristas infests our land like a malevolent weed, with vast, tenacious roots."

"The niyal'arists are dangerous voras, lord."

"You cannot begin to plumb the depths of their viciousness. Only one born to rule here, with the love of this land pounding in his veins, can fully grasp the evil they have done. They drained the s'rere out of me, the s'rere Power that was meant to help me rule this land. Now I must search like a beggar for my own heritage."

"We are diligent, lord, in ensuring that every rista is tested for the blood that makes the earth dance. It will surely be found."

"They are ruthless and persistent. They will rise up again, try yet again to devour Shunder's future, to gorge themselves on its destiny. But I will find these new iterations. I took my brother's name as a pledge to destroy them utterly."

"You are a true varo, lord, a beacon of hope in a troubled land."

"Their paths are already converging with mine. I can feel it. They will pay. It may take years, but one rota they will kneel before me and feel my justice."

"In the place where past and future are all one thing, it has already happened, lord. So it is written in the *L'garza*, and so I believe."

Still wearing only his small-cloth, Teller looked down on his tray and dug sand from his swollen eyes. One of the cave-symphs in his soup was still feebly twitching. But next to his bowl steamed a mug of something that smelled a little like herb tea. This was different from the usual cup of cold, dusty-tasting water. The tea brought to mind the grandmother without a face, the feel of a mug warm in his hands after he'd been out in the snow. He reached for the mug and took a sip. It was sweet, as if a strange and wild honey were mixed in, so he drank it all. It left behind a bitter, weedy taste.

Restless, he went to the door. The corridor rang with silence. Pain for what he had done scoured the inside of his stomach. He had rejected Rul—someone who once had loved him. Now he belonged to the Lord of Shunder, body and soul. He closed the door, and sank down with it against his back. Tears welled up, but they would do no good, so he blinked them away.

It was a moment before he realized the light was fading. Were the worms dying? He glanced at the globe, but the luniku crawled over each other as usual. Yet the room quickly slid into darkness. He caught his breath. What was happening? Even as he wondered, the light flowed back. Brighter than before—then too bright.

He rubbed his eyes. The restless feeling grew stronger, jittered in his stomach. Again the room fell into blackness. He looked around wildly, trying to see. The light came again, brighter and brighter, until everything blazed with a sharp edge. The restless feeling fluttered up to his throat, tingled in his tongue. He was struck with an urge to talk.

"Where are my clothes? They were right here!" He jumped up in light and in darkness groped to find his shirt and pants on the floor. Thinking of the spiders, he shook them furiously while the room faded in and out of sight. He didn't remember putting his clothes on, but saw them as he looked down on himself. The dark took them, and then they were there again, shining brightly.

The door banged open and he cried out. Two big umbraks pushed into the room, and the light blinked out. Strong hands grasped his arms in the dark and pulled him into a passageway where he had to squeeze his eyes shut against the glare. They hurried him through the tunnels, the light fading and swelling, while a kind of sick excitement made him babble on. "Where are we going? Let me go! Why is the light doing that?"

They bundled him into a tiny, low ceilinged room, like the mind-probing room. Hands pushed him onto a stone slab and fastened his wrists down. A dark figure loomed over him. Hot fear flared through his spirikai and struck out. "Get away!" he cried.

A rasping voice addressed someone else in the room. "Did you see that?"

"Yes," a second voice answered out of the shadows.

"Is that how you killed Greaz, boy?" the first voice demanded.

Killed? Greaz? *Welcome to Oknu Shuld.* "I didn't—"

"He probed you, got into your mind."

"I said no! I said get *away*—"

"Listen to me. Not Greaz. Before him. Someone else came into your mind, probing and tearing. Many times, in the Seani. How many times?"

"No times. N-no tearing. In the Seani they always asked is it all right, Teller, can we—"

"Someone came. He probed you over and over. Name him."

A name popped into his mind, tumbled out. "Se Nemes? Do you mean Se Nemes? But he didn't—it didn't h-hurt. Never, because S-Se Nemes was kind, not like here, not like—"

"Many times? Se Gremez hurt your mind many times?"

"No. Yes, Gremez." But what had he just said yes to? "I mean no!" he shouted.

"Why did they push you out of the gates?"

The wrongness of that took his breath away. "P-pushed me? They didn't push, the postern was open, and I—"

"Why did Rivere leave you?"

"I—I don't know. He left me!" He tried to roll to the side, to protect the aching loss in the curve of his body, but couldn't. "The umbraks took—"

"He knew you were lying. Rivere knew you were lying."

"What? About what? I didn't—"

"He did not want to stay with a liar. He left you because you refuse to tell us about Nemez. How did you burn him? He was probing you, and you burned him."

"I was alive, I mean lively, and he was coming inside, very hard." He shuddered.

"Stop lying to me. Tell me why everyone in the Seani was afraid of you."

"Afraid? No one was afraid of—"

"They never came to take you home. Why didn't they?"

His whole body twisted with hurt. "I don't know!"

"You did something to make them hate you. Stop lying and tell the truth."

"They didn't! I mean, I'm not. I—I can't remember what you *said!*"

Questions whirled around him, darting in and out of meaning, and he could barely answer before another sprang out. He very badly *wanted* to answer, and words stumbled out of him as fast as he could pronounce them. He talked until his throat hurt.

"Ahn," the voice commanded, "I am thirsty. Bring water."

His mouth felt dry and cracked, and he heard water pouring, someone swallowing. "Please, c-can I have—"

"Not until you tell the truth."

The truth, he strained to tell the truth, but he didn't know, couldn't remember. His mouth was so dry he could hardly swallow, and still they went on and on.

"You are not cooperating. We are not pleased. Are you niyalahn or rista?"

"I'm-I'm a 'sir' and don't call Se Gremez that"—in his eagerness to talk he was running out of breath so the rest came out in a wheeze—"because it's *not* a bad word!"

"Stop babbling and answer the question. Do you have a twin brother?'

He arched his back in an effort to focus. *How are we special, Grandma. Tell me!* Twin ristas he wanted to say, but *no, that's not possible, Teller.* "N-not twins. A brother, cornsilk and mud, but gone, a-ago. All gone!" A word hovered on the tip of his dry tongue and he struggled to spit it out. "I'm Em; it begins with M." But that was wrong and he groaned with effort. "Not M. I'm—I'm lying."

"You always lie. You are a teller of lies." The hood above him disappeared.

He sucked in air and continued talking to them, trying to explain; the light kept going away and flooding back, going away and flooding back. Two people he couldn't see spoke in low voices "Do you know how we're special?" he asked them. "Do you know?"

The horrible blinking slowed, then settled into a pale blue glow. He lay on his bed, alone and muttering to himself. The worm-light shone steadily into his eyes. He turned over so he wouldn't have to look at it. His head hurt, and all night the awful feeling jittered inside him. He tossed and turned with it, until it faded into a twitchy half-sleep.

He woke up parched with thirst. A steaming mug sat

on his tray, but he remembered the bitter after-taste and threw the tea down the grate. The terrible thirst grew, hour after hour. He went to the dripping wall, but it had mostly dried up and he got very little moisture from licking the slimy rock. The rota dragged on, and his head nodded. In snatches of dreams, he searched for water. When next the mug appeared on his tray, he couldn't help but gulp it down. But the bitter taste left him still thirsty.

It wasn't long before the light started to dim again. Panic lunged at him and he jumped to his feet, taking deep breaths. But nothing could stop it. His room went in and out of darkness, slowly at first, and then ever faster, making him want to talk and talk. Even as they took him away, he heard his own hoarse voice trail through the deep blackness and blinding light of the corridors. He went on talking, looking at the ceiling and filling the cramped room with the sound of his words.

The hood returned in a blaze of light. "What are you talking about?"

He blinked. "I—I forgot."

"Because you were lying. You always lie."

"No, that's not true." Frantic, he tried to remember. Was he talking about their birth gifts? "I think the box; two of these jewelries, these pendants, in a box, exactly the same, Grandma kept them for us, for when—" A sudden longing pierced him. "Mena!"

"Is that your mother's name?"

"N-no, gone, Riah's gone, a long time ago." He gulped. "But coming—"

A second voice broke in, from someone he couldn't see. "Say again your mother's name." The voice echoed, sounded intense.

"Riah. M-mother."

"Who is your father?" the first voice demanded.

"Father?" He thought of Rivere, but that was wrong. "There's another name, with green eyes. Neal! He died, h-he's dead. But—but my real Father—the same exact name, my Mother and Father, both."

"What name?"

The blackness blinded him; the burning light stung. "I can't say it! Never can say it."

"Say it! The Lord of Shunder commands you."

"R-rulve."

Someone slapped him, and he gasped.

The questions went on and on, through iron bars of dark slashed with light. He tried to shield his eyes from the constant attacks of glare and blindness, but he couldn't move his arms. "You're lying," the voice kept saying. "Tell me the truth." Far off, he heard the hour-gongs, but was it day or night?

At last the second voice spoke. "There is no more profit in this."

"I agree, Vol Kuat. Tomorrow I will discontinue this potion and replace it with memor."

"*We* will do this, Volarach. I was the one who brought him here. Do not forget that."

"Nor should you forget who is Prome here, and who is Kuat."

Teller found himself back in his room, dizzy, quivering with the terrible excitement, and so thirsty his mouth and throat felt lined with sand. An ahn knelt on the stone floor, washing it, and he lunged for the brown water in her bucket. But he forgot he was in his bed and fell on the floor. Dirty water pooled around him. He tried to drink it, but blacked out.

Little squeaks woke him. Warm and soft, a mouse nestled in his open hand. It jumped to the floor and scurried out. It must've gone to the green room. He had to go there too, right now.

He found himself at the gate. It wouldn't open, and in a panic, he shook it. He didn't deserve to go to the room anymore. He had renounced Rul—renounced the green hands, the comforting love, everything, anything green and alive.

When he realized the gate wasn't locked, he stumbled through. What if it were night, and he couldn't find the light under the door?

He burst into the room, and a green light hit his sore eyes. He shielded them with his arm, took a deep breath of cold, crisp air. The tang of snow lingered on it.

"T'lir."

At the sound of a voice, he jumped, almost falling over. In the far corner of the room, an old man sat on a rocking chair. He had long grey hair and beard, and his night-blue robe shone with golden suns and rocking moons, with stars that that got bigger and smaller as they breathed. On the floor by his side stood a tall hat like a cone, alive with heavenly bodies. The mouse, its whiskers trembling, peeped out through a small arch cut into it. The old man held out a large flagon, beaded with moisture.

"Come and drink, my son."

His legs tried to tangle as he rushed forward, but he managed not to fall and reached for the flagon. It felt wonderfully cool, and with both hands shaking, he took it and gulped down the contents. It was simple water, sweet and clear, with no dust in it, and he drank swallow after swallow with deep pleasure. At last the water was all gone. He lowered the flagon and stared into eyes as deep as a peaceful night. The words flying inside his head stilled and the inner quivering died away. He stood quiet, for the first time, it seemed, in rotas.

The old man looked kindly at him. "You are aching inside," he said.

Tears threatened, but Teller bit his lip to hold them back. No one from home had come to get him. Someone had hurt him, over and over, but he couldn't remember why, or even who. His spirikai burned, and his head throbbed. He belonged to the Lord of Shunder.

"You can cry, T'lir. You can let go of what's inside you."

But it would be more than tears. It would be red-hot anger, flaring up into flames. "I can't. I might burn you."

"I have dealt with far greater fires than yours, T'lir." The old man held out his arms to him. "Sit with me."

Homesick and exhausted, he let the old man place him on his lap, facing out, as Rivere used to do. He sat stiffly, fighting back the tears, but they came anyway, along with great, choking sobs. A handkerchief was passed to him, and this small act of kindness released yet another rush of tears. It felt as if his spirikai was being wrung out like a rag. Finally, it all passed.

He sank back against the old man's chest. Arms went around him, and silence sifted over him. The leaves at the window rustled from time to time, and the old man rocked him back and forth, back and forth. The beard against the back of his head felt as soft as fur.

It seemed he slept for hours, wrapped around with a warm yellow quilt, and his dreams were dappled with sunlight shining through green and leafy branches. When he woke, it was from the best sleep he'd had since Rivere was taken away from him. The hands still held him, and the lap still rocked him. He thought of Keya, the blue ribbon binding up her neatly combed hair. She was secure now in the isav, safe among people she knew. With the rest of the ahn, she would open her hands under the blanket, and be with—with their Mother. He had saved her.

The old man kissed the top of his head. "Would you do it again?" he murmured. "Would you give up everything, T'lir, to save the ahn?"

Teller considered the price he had paid—the name he could never say again, the great hands in which he could never again find shelter, the love that must be kept far off. "I d-don't think so, sir. It h-hurts too much."

The old man continued to rock him. "Yes, T'lir, it does."

The love, the dear and familiar presence that he longed for and used to be so happy with began to edge up to him again; but he drew away from it. He had given that up, had promised. Keya's life depended on it. He clenched his fists tightly on his knees until the feeling went away.

The old man gently peeled back Teller's fingers until his hands lay open, and then tucked them into the curve of his arms. He sat this way on the old man's lap, rocking amidst the stars and moons, wrapped in warmth, until the green light all around him faded away.

Chapter 14.

Memor

He awoke in his room. Had the old man carried him here? Or was it all a dream, from the tea? A tray was waiting for him on the chair. This time there was no tea on it, only the usual cup of dusty-tasting water. The bread was still stale, but the thin soup was hot for a change and had tiny, whole mushrooms in it. He took a small taste; it wasn't bitter. Teller found that he was hungry and ate everything. He soon got sleepy; it must be night-time. Remembering, with a pang, not to say any prayers, he undressed and crawled into bed.

It was a deep sleep, and someone dragged him out of it like a fish. He tried to wiggle away, but his clothes were thrust at him, and clumsily, with thick fingers, he put them on. He had difficulty controlling his head, which was filled with fog and wanted to droop down or flop to the side. The corridor was full of fog too, and their footsteps sounded muffled. He could barely put one foot in front of another, yet they hurried him along until he stumbled and fell—a long way, it seemed.

Someone was whispering in his ear. So close that the black hood brushed against his forehead. Along with the whispered words, vivid images poured into his mind. Se Nemez grinned down on him, tiny bubbles of spit on his teeth, his jaws prickly with stubble. The face came closer.

A light flashed and, to his horror, the face burst into flames. Fire crackled through the hair, melted the thick skin, and the man fell to the ground, screaming. He rolled there, on fire, until they dragged him out of the room.

"That is how you burned Nemez. How did it feel when you killed him?" The rasping voice sounded merely curious, as if the answer didn't really matter.

His head was so full of the terrible picture that it took him a while to focus on the question. But it was twisted somehow. "I–I didn't. Claws. Hurting my head." His lips felt fat, and it was hard to talk, to think.

"Why is Se Nemes hurting you?"

"Not Nemes."

"But it is. Over and over, hurting you. They all want to hurt you."

"They love me. Not hurt me."

"But you told us she almost drowned you. That Mena almost drowned you."

Did he say that? Why? "She didn't."

"You're lying again." The voice was still calm, but more insistent now. "You're under the water, looking up. You can't breathe. You see her face clearly."

Whose face looked down on him? Whose hair dripped? "Fell in, like this." He tried to extend his arms, but they were already out.

"Se Gremez died in agony," the rasping voice said gently. "He died screaming. How could you forget that?"

"Wouldn't. Wouldn't forget."

"So you remember. You remember what Se Nemes did to you."

That was wrong somehow. It was all wrong, but...but still he recalled it. The claws. The sharp, iron claws. "Yes," he mumbled.

"Se Nemes damaged your mind. What a shame. It happened when he tried to seize your Power."

Power? What...? But then he remembered. They said he had power, the dark hood said it.

"You have fire inside you, and Se Nemes tried to take it. No wonder you burned him."

He didn't mean to. He didn't mean to burn anyone. But fire? A hot knife had cut through him and—and fire spurted out.

"Greaz tried to tell you," the voice went on in a quiet, reasonable tone. "He tried to tell you what Se Nemes did. But you did not believe him."

"No. Didn't believe him."

"Instead you burned him. You killed the wrong man, I'm afraid. It was Se Nemes who deserved to die."

"I didn't k-kill. I didn't." He thought the burning pain he had felt was his own, but it must have been...the other man's. Did—did he have children? A little girl who played with a red ball? He groaned, hoping it wasn't so.

"You killed him with your fire. You feel it burning right now. The fire burns inside you all the time, doesn't it?"

He could feel it, deep inside his spirikai; but he wanted to sleep, only sleep and not listen to the voice anymore.

"Many adults here were surprised that a child like you could kill a grown man. It took Power, and they envied you."

A part of him swelled with pride. He tried to tell the voice about the admiring looks of grown men, soldiers, as he rode a big stallion in the garrison. They all knew he was special, the "sir." They saw he had power, that he had fire in his spirikai. But fire that—that killed?

"No," he mumbled. "Not like that. A fever." But it

was more than a fever. It had protected him, pushed Greaz away from him, and burned the wrong man.

"You remember now what you did to Greaz. Tell us."

"I burned him," he moaned. He couldn't help it. He'd been terrified, and the fire just burst out.

"What did you say? Speak louder."

"I burned him on the hands."

"You did much more than that," the voice insisted. "You killed him. His hair caught on fire. He screamed. Remember?"

He tried to deny it, but he…couldn't. He remembered, vividly, the whispering in his ear, the burning hair, the man rolling on the ground.

"That is why you had to renounce Rulve. Because you are a murderer. Because you killed the wrong man."

"I-I remember." He took a long shuddering breath at the enormity of what he had done. "I *k-killed* him."

"Yes," the voice said. "Very good."

But it wasn't good. It would never be good again. His throat choked with tears.

"Let us go back to when you came here."

He rolled his head. "No. Don't want to."

The black hood came close to his ear, and the whispering started again, winding through his head like a mist, painting pictures in his mind, describing the sounds and smells of that day. It blended with snatches of his own memories: the smell of earth under the fog, the creak of cart-wheels, a voice shouting, "Can't someone help him!"

"—then you were in the cart," the voice said. "Remember the cart? You clutched the back of it. You watched the gates get smaller behind you. Tears rolled down your cheeks, and you wiped them on your sleeve. They traded you for the prisoner. How could they do that to a little boy?"

He attempted to raise his head, but it was too heavy. "No." They didn't want him to go. They were saying, "No, Teller!"

"Mena traded you. Your mother traded you for Neal. 'Neal!' she screamed, remember?"

"No," he moaned, trying to twist away from the voice. "She's not…they didn't." But she did; she screamed for Neal. "They *lost* me. I mean—I mean they *loved* me."

"They were afraid of your fire. You killed Greaz. They were afraid you would kill them too."

Something was terribly wrong. He could feel it, but what was it? He tried to grasp clumsy memories that slid out of his hands.

The voice went on, pulling up living roots, and from deep inside him pain welled up. Hot tears rushed to his eyes, but he couldn't wipe them away, and they dripped down his temples, into his hair. He turned his head to the side. "It was me screaming 'Help me, Mena!'"

"Yes. Yes! You were screaming." The voice began to change, became more intense. "Se Nemez was hurting you, and you were screaming. But Mena did not help you, did she? Instead of helping you, they pushed you out the gate. You cried out from the cart, 'help me,' and they never did. You watched the gates grow smaller and smaller, and no one came out of them. They traded you because they knew you belonged here, with us."

He tried to twist away, away from the voice and what it was saying, but his arms were stretched out and he couldn't. "They traded—*loved*—me!"

"They never came for you, did they?" the voice said harshly. "They just left you here."

"I shouted 'I'm here!' but they never came. I shouted." He would never hurt them as he had been hurt; he would never try to drown Mena.

"You were like a strak to them. Furry and cuddly as a cub, but eventually growing long claws and sharp fangs. They were afraid of you. They were weak. Here we are strong. Here we tame straks."

"Not a strak. A boy." There was a heavy weight on his chest, in his heart, and he could hardly talk. "I want to go home," he begged. "Please."

"You *are* home. This is your home. They pushed you out, and we took you in. Now you belong, body and soul, to the Lord of Shunder. You said it. Out of your own free will you gave your word: body and soul. Say it!"

"B-body and s-soul."

"Here we are not afraid of your Power. Here we will teach you how to use it."

"Not—not my fault."

"No. It was right that you killed Gremez."

"Didn't want to."

"All this time and they never came for you. They never helped you develop your Power. They are nothing but cowards, utterly unworthy of you. I cannot believe what they did to you."

More tears coursed down the sides of his head, and he choked with sobs. They had hurt him and made him dream things, and now he was like one of those empty insect shells in the corridors. Everything in him had been sucked out.

"Look at me."

With an effort, he lifted his head and focused on the black hood.

Hissed words came out of it. "Weaklings! They were so weak. They wanted to keep you weak as well. You seethe with skora, and they never saw it. *Druv* never saw it. Pious, pompous coward. All of them—cowards. How you hate them! You hate and despise them for what they did to you!"

Something hot swelled into his emptiness. It flowed up his chest and into his throat and made it hard to breathe. But it stopped the tears.

Suddenly the hood turned aside, as if listening, and Teller's head fell back against the stone. It trembled beneath him, the stone ceiling trembled, and the hood disappeared. A silent shape, which he hadn't even known was in the room, glided out. All around him the rock growled, and he heard the sound of people shouting and glass breaking. Dazed, he watched a small crack flick through the ceiling. A fine stream of sand sifted down, onto his right hand.

It had all been a lie. His grandmother, Rivere, the people he thought loved him—they were all part of one big lie. Pieces of what he believed was the truth had been shaken loose, and now all of it was sliding down. The sand in his palm, this cramped room, all the dark passageways—these were the real things.

He lay there, his arms out. *Let the ceiling come down on me. Please let it come down.*

With a hard jolt, something cracked, and in terror he flung his left arm over his eyes. He'd been able to move it. He turned his head to look and saw that a shackle had broken off.

The room groaned and shook. Close by, something shattered, and the chamber fell into darkness. He huddled on the stone, expecting—hoping—that any moment he would be crushed.

But he wasn't. Everything stilled. He was empty now, and never knew how much that could hurt. He was empty, except for one thing, one thing that burned in the dark. He focused on it, a small tongue of fire deep in his spirikai. It burned in spite of the terrible thing he had done, in spite of the love that was really a lie, in spite of how bitterly his memories had betrayed him.

He sat up, his head spinning, and swung his heavy legs over the edge of the stone slab. A dim, blue glow came from the floor, from a pile of worms crawling over the shards of the globe. At his side, an iron shackle gripped his right wrist. The room shook again, and he heard more sand falling from the ceiling behind him. But he didn't turn. He twisted and pulled against the shackle, twisted his hand back and forth, scraping at the skin until the only pain left was that around his wrist. He thought of an empty cauldron hanging over the flames, scorched and beginning to turn a sullen, dangerous red.

He had fire and would learn to use it. And one day, for what they had done to him, they would all burn.

Chapter 15

Volmeet

A Volmeet was bad enough, Autran thought as he stepped into the lord's private audience chamber, but calling it barely two gongs after an earthquake was not sufficient time for his nerves to settle. The lamps in here weren't good for his nerves either. Shaped like morue flowers with amethyst glass petals, they stood about the room on olivine stems, and only the brightest luniku crawled in their deep, dark-veined throats. The combination of bilious purple and bruised green made him feel slightly nauseated.

Worse yet were the sculptures. The work of the lord himself, they were displayed on burnished silver stands or stood on their own segmented legs. Autran sidled past giant insects in various poses: lunging forward hungrily toward the observer, rubbing their fly-feet in anticipation of a meal, or waiting for something to come within range of their claw-like mandibles.

Along with the three other Volarachs, he knelt on the hard marble floor, and bowed in deep obeisance when the lord entered. The soul-shaking power of the Lord of Shunder loomed over him.

"You may straighten." The Eyascnu's voice, with its precise, clipped pronunciation, crept up the back of Autran's neck like spider-legs.

Trembling, he sat back on his heels and raised his eyes.

Mist shrouded the dais and spilled down the three low steps. It slowly wafted and curled, allowing brief glimpses of the form sitting on the black throne, along with parts of its purple and black striped robe, an onyx crown, and—by far the most intimidating—the mask that covered everything but the lord's red lips. A double row of four obsidians, surrounded by short, spiky hairs, glinted where the eyes should be. All this gave the lord an inhuman, spider-like appearance that Autran found profoundly unsettling.

At the lord's command, Nosce began his interminable report on rents, taxes, and fees, apparently addressing the hem of the lord's garment, which crawled with embroidered morue spiders. As the Prome droned on, Autran noticed that the Eyascnu held a thin chain which ran down to the floor and disappeared behind a heavily veiled archway behind the throne. This was the gateway to the unlit, unformed regions of Oknu Shuld that ran deep into Insheer Cliff on this level. Something hulked there. The veil behind the throne bulged slightly from time to time, as if a large body, lying on the other side, inadvertently brushed against it.

"Crop yields," Nosce was saying in his annoying rasp, "continue to decline and we have no reason to expect that to change. That means, of course, declining revenues; therefore I instituted another tax increase."

The veil bulged once more and the chain clinked softly on the marble floor. The lord rubbed the links between his long, tightly gloved fingers. To Autran the chain seemed too fragile, far too fragile, to control whatever monstrous creature it was attached to.

On Autran's left, Nosce appeared to be winding down. "The earthquake did little damage. Even though several cracks appeared along the back walls of the top two levels, no lake water came anywhere near the steam vents of the lowest level. The cracks are being seen to. I also received a report that one of the hot pools in the scourery geysered. No guards were injured; several ahn were killed. Your power permeates this stronghold, lord; therefore we, as usual, fared well."

The glinting, black eyes turned to Autran's right, where Bardak knelt. He had been promoted to Vol status last year from the lord's personal Vorian Guard and had no match in tedious conceit. "Volarach Tierce, report on your recent campaign."

Bardak thumped his chest in salute. "It was very successful, lord. My forces are already established in the entire region surrounding Baenfeld. There was some resistance in the hamlets, but it was easily put down, and the surviving leaders are being brought here in chains. Archon Shacad, my second in command, has just returned with the news that local councils have been disbanded, and garrisons are being built. By spring, parents will be scheduled for ahn tribute. We've also transported most of the harvest here; less, of course, what my forces consumed while on campaign."

An ebb of the black mist revealed the tip of a highly polished boot. "And the south?"

Bardak looked up in surprise. "Your specific orders were to pacify the north. That I am doing. It would be folly, lord, to move south at this time. That area is protected by the Bellstone Forest and the Heeringone Marsh, both formidable obstacles to our forces. We must first establish our dominance in one region before we move on to another."

"You mention the Bellstone Forest, Volarach," the Eyascnu said. He was using that velvet voice that sent shivers down Autran's spine. "No doubt you heard the

Bellstone when it rang some weeks ago now. You have
had more than enough time to apprehend the Striker. He
is waiting outside this room, I take it, for my judgment?"

Autran dared not turn his head to look at the man
beside him, but heard an uneasy rustle from the Tierce.
There *was* someone waiting outside the room for
punishment; but it wasn't the Bellstriker, only the isav's
former proctor. Apparently he had been responsible for a
lapse of discipline when some ahn spoke to the Seani boy.

"Well, no," Bardak admitted. "My forces went out as
soon as I heard the bell. I led them personally. But the
forest men fight in a cowardly fashion, hiding in trees
and leaping—"

"At our last Volmeet," the lord said, "you assured us
that the Striker problem would be settled. That we would
never again be troubled by the sound of this bell, which
calls the damn rebels to crawl out of their holes, which
causes yet more unrest throughout my realm, which I
made quite clear I did not want—ever—to hear again."
The lord's voice had hardened with each phrase and
ended in an ominous growl.

"Yes, lord, indeed. But my spies failed me. And not
one forester from Bystone or Ettebel could be bribed,
even though—"

"What about the falconforms?"

Autran caught a glimpse of the Tierce wiping a
presumably sweaty hand against his thigh. "The falconforms? I covered that in my last report, lord. The situation
has not changed. They continue to hole up in the
northern cliffs."

"Your incursion against them failed."

"We killed many, lord."

"Yet they continue to block my northward expan-
sion."

"For now, yes. They guard the passes, lord. We have gone over this."

"So we are blocked on the north, you have made no plans for the south, and the Bellstriker remains at large."

"But—but I have been much occupied with the northern campaign, lord; and as I have said, all the land around Baenfeld now belongs to you." He took a deep breath. "I must say, however, that our military efforts would proceed more quickly, *much* more quickly, with abakal. And the Ségun has yet to produce one iota."

Anger mixed with panic boiled up inside Autran. How dare the man blame him! Bardak knew the explosive stones were impossible to make without skora. But he could not speak, could not defend himself, without the lord commanding him.

"What of the dam, Tierce?" Constructed of stout timbers and rock-filled cribs, the dam formed Insheer Lake atop the plateau. The lake irrigated the morue fields there, provided drinking and bath water for Oknu Shuld, and ran the great water clock on level two.

It took a moment for Bardak to make the leap to another topic. "I have full confidence in it. We experienced one small seep, but my men are repairing it even as we speak. The lake level, however, is still rising, due to several years of greater than average snow in the mountains."

"Can this dam, of which you have full confidence and which is now leaking, withstand the rising waters?"

The man seemed unaware of the lord's dangerous tone and spoke as self-importantly as ever. "Certainly. I keep a sharp eye on it. I do recommend, however, that the pressure be relieved. I await your order to release water from time to time over the old falls and into the Eeron River."

The valley-dwellers would be glad of that, Autran

thought. Their river had turned into a cesspool, and their entire fishing industry had disappeared. Not that it mattered: he loathed fish.

"No," the lord said. "Our new lands require additional morue. Extend the fields as far as the dry wash. Build a second dam, deepen the wash into another irrigation channel, and release the rising waters there."

Bardak hesitated, but like the fool he was, plunged on. "Deepen the *wash*, lord? Such a project would be ill-advised. It would increase seepage along the back walls, which is already troublesome. You must understand, there is a natural fissure—"

A raised finger cut him off. Autran snickered to himself. Bardak had made three big mistakes in barely a minute. One didn't teach the arts of war to the Lord of Shunder, or use words like "folly" or "ill-advised" in reference to his future plans.

"Construction on the new dam," the lord said coldly, "will begin immediately, Tierce."

"Yes, lord."

The double row of obsidian eyes turned toward Autran. "Your report, Ségun."

Autran cleared his throat, realizing too late how much it betrayed his nervousness. "In regard to abakal—"

"I know you need skora," the lord clipped. "I want your *report*."

The staring eye-stones flustered him, and he tried to remember the list of items he had prepared for this meeting. Morue first. That was the lord's primary concern. "My new fertilizer is ready for the spring planting, lord. In addition, I have begun working on producing a strain of morue which shows promise of a more potent product. I am also pleased to say there's been no problem with our distributors since I, uh, explained our shortage of luniku hosts to them." Why they whined about the prices they were charged he never understood; they always passed their costs on to the buyer.

Now luniku, he advised himself. Don't forget the luniku. "I controlled a virulent fungus that threatened the cocoons in emergent chamber three, with little loss. Larvae production is going well, but as I mentioned, more hosts are always needed. I can use these rebel leaders Vol Tierce"—bragged about—"mentioned. I would also suggest to my esteemed colleague, Vol Prome, that firmer ahn discipline would also help alleviate this problem." Nosce stirred, no doubt in umbrage at the implied criticism; but Autran could live with that. "Moving on to my other responsibilities, I've kept up with the Tierce's constant demands for arrow-tip poison, but I need—"

"The potions," the Eyascnu said. "Hand them over."

Autran stiffened at the way the lord had glossed over his exemplary work. From the pouch at his side, he withdrew two stoppered vials, set them carefully on the lowest step, and tried to keep the resentment out of his voice. "Everbeast and fura, as you commanded." A risky combination. The mist enveloped the vials, retreated, and they were gone.

The eyes turned aside. "Now, my Prome," the Eyascnu said, "inform your colleagues regarding the Seani boy." Behind the throne, the end of the chain held by the Lord of Shunder rose up slightly, as if it the creature it leashed lifted its head.

"Just before the earth quaked," the Prome said, "Vol Kuat and I finished a thorough examination of him."

That was odd, Autran thought. Nosce was in charge of new arrivals, not the secretive Kuat. The fourth Vol, who had no name but was called the Delver, usually took no interest in anything beyond whatever he did in his domain on level five.

"The boy is a rista," Nosce went on, "and represses all memory of his transfer here. Our records show the father was a prisoner who died years ago. The mother's name was Riah, and I am quite satisfied that she is dead as well. Would you concur, Volarach Kuat?"

The Delver shrugged. "The Eyascnu's subjects are short-lived creatures."

Annoyance stirred in Autran's gut. Only the lord's favorite, his pet Vol, could get away with such a careless tone.

"Get on with it, Nosce," the lord barked. "Tell them what Power he possesses."

A sudden, intense interest become almost palpable in the room. Pompous prick that he was, Nosce paused—no doubt for dramatic effect, damn him—and it seemed that everyone held their breath.

"He has skora."

As one, they all exhaled. Bardak looked past him at Nosce, with eager, burning eyes.

"I glimpsed it," Nosce said, "all those years ago. An aura, glowing dimly for a short while in the Seani. Druv"—he practically spat out the name—"must have managed to hide it after that."

"The skora has seen my need," the lord said. "My people's need. Now it has come directly into my hand, for it recognizes its true master."

Vol Kuat stirred, in irritation, Autran thought. The skora didn't just come by itself. Kuat was the one who'd brought the boy here.

"This Power is still weak," Nosce continued, "and too immature to be as yet extracted. It is also polluted by years of Seani influence. We must nourish it, remove all impurities, and bend it to your will, lord. Then it will be yours for the taking. Tomorrow the boy will attend orientation with Master Keel."

"I recommend a private education," the Delver said.

There was a moment of shock that a Vol should speak without permission, and disagree with Number One to boot, but the lord didn't seem to notice.

"The boy, Vol *Kuat*," Nosce answered coldly, "must prove himself like any other rista. He will be educated with his peers."

Because of the slight emphasis on the Delver's rank, a suspicion crawled into Autran's mind. Did he catch the whiff of a power-struggle? His heart beat faster. Could Vol Prome and Vol Kuat both have designs on this boy with skora? It was Vol Kuat, he had heard, who insisted on being present at the child's interrogation; and Nosce hadn't been happy about that.

The mist coiled slowly around the Eyascnu Varo, and the voice spoke again. "Volarachs, you will *all* contribute to this boy's education. Stoke and refine this fire. Prepare this weapon carefully for me. For too long my people have been demeaned by rebels who confuse and misguide them. They deserve a great leader. With skora I will become that leader." His voice began to rise, to resonate. "With skora I will bring flames to the north and to the south, and they shall burn in every village, in every field, in every house. I will carry fire to the east and to the west, until all our enemies are seared away. My kingdom will rise up, invincible, from the blackened fields."

Both gloved hands turned into fists on his knees. "But first I shall turn my gaze to the Riftwood, which I will burn to the ground. No grove, not one tree, will be left standing. The King of the Riftwood sent niyal'arist voras against me and will do it again if he can. It is only just that I annihilate Rŭk and reduce his domain to one vast field of morue."

Nosce raised an arm, and the lord nodded at him. "And the Seani, lord?" he rasped. "Druv?"

The Prome had always held some kind of grudge against the Seani leader, but no one seemed to know why. The lord laughed softly, a sound that sent chills down Autran's neck. "I will cause the boy to destroy that ant-hill himself, for practice. He will bring Druv to you in chains."

"You are generous, lord."

"Yes, but a word of warning." He leaned forward, and the mist revealed his thin, red lips stretched in a grim smile beneath the spider mask. "The fire is mine. Mine alone, given to me for the sake of my people. I will severely punish any who would attempt to take it from me."

Autran felt the lord's threat like a cold hand on the back of his neck. Not that he'd been toying with such an idea.

"So that you may clearly understand what my displeasure brings, I will now demonstrate it." The jeweled eyes glimmered as the Eyascnu turned his head. "*Volghasti, obud.*"

Two tall figures detached themselves from the shadow of a massive ebony cabinet against the wall. Their eyes glowed red as they stalked forward, bringing a nauseating whiff of rot. The cold hand slipped down Autran's back.

Volghasts.

Utterly motionless until animated by the will of the lord, volghasts were rumored to be the husks of deceased Vols. They blended into the perpetual dimness of the passageways, stood in the shadows of armoires, or appeared to be nothing but statues of ancient kings. But when summoned, a volghast would suddenly awaken and its eyes would burn. Possessing tremendous strength, immune to many powers of sorcery, the four creatures were completely obedient servants—and two of them had been in the room all this time.

"Tierce, rise. You have ill served both me and my people."

Bardak jumped to his feet. "What! Lord, I have done only your...you don't understa-ah—"

The lord made a circle of his thumb and forefinger, and Bardak clawed at his neck, trying to speak. The volghasts, one on either side of him, pulled him in front of the steps. A low, guttural growl came from the hulk behind the throne, and the end of the chain that trailed into the darkness rose higher. Something back there was very interested now.

"He is unworthy of his cloak and vol-ring," the lord said to the volghasts. "Strip them away."

With one motion, a gauntleted hand tore the garment from Bardak's back. The second volghast grasped Bardak's right hand, twisted the ring, and pulled. With a sickening slurp, the ring came off like a deep-rooted weed. The Tierce screamed, then stared in horror at his hand. It hung in red shreds, as if it had been jerked through a mouth of sharp teeth. The volghast held the ring aloft, dripping with the bloody roots that had grown into the Vol's hand, then laid it at the lord's feet.

Justice, Autran thought. Justice has finally fallen onto Bardak's head.

The volghasts propelled the moaning Vol up the shallow steps and pushed him to his knees on the circle of earth that lay to the right of the throne. The chain tautened. A curtain of mist descended over both Vol Tierce and the dais, and from within issued the slap of large feet, followed by a knife-edged shriek. Next came the stink of offal and the sound of salivating growls and snarls. Autran's elation at the downfall of one who dared criticize him in front of the lord turned to alarm as the chain whipped about wildly, clanking against the floor. Screams too terrible to be human pierced his ears. A sudden arc of warm and sticky liquid hit him across the chest. He recoiled, waving his arms for balance, and looked down at himself. The front of one of his best robes was drenched with blood.

The screaming abruptly ended, to be replaced by the sound of cracking bones. The mist on the dais wafted aside for a moment, and something like a long pinkish-grey sausage was pulled into it. Oh god Ázu, it was an entrail. Rending and slurping noises hit him, and Autran's stomach turned over. An object flew out of the mist, crashed into one of the sculptures behind him, and thudded to the floor.

The lord spoke over the noise. "The new Tierce of Oknu Shuld shall be the archon Shacad. His Acclamation will take place three gongs from now. Now leave us. Except you, Kuat."

Swallowing his rising gorge, Autran climbed to his feet. The mist parted, revealing the earthen circle now muddy with blood. A thick, black rivulet of it oozed down the steps. He turned and staggered after Nosce toward the door. Part way there he almost stumbled over something, but when he looked more closely, instantly regretted it.

The object was long and wore a boot on one end. On the other end—he immediately turned his eyes away. In the comparatively bright light of the corridor, he made it just past the terrified proctor waiting with a group of guards for the lord's discipline. Then he bent over and was sick in front of them all.

CHAPTER 16

TRANSFORMATIONS

Still wearing his mask but not his crown, the Lord of Shunder sat at ease on his throne, one knee crossed over the other, while a subaltern finished cleaning up the room and departed. The thin chain, looped loosely around the armrest, lay still. But a bulge at the base of the curtain behind him showed something was still busy there, its teeth scraping against bone.

One of the volghasts stepped back into the shadows while the other knelt beside the circle of earth and spooned some of the bloody mud into a crystal bowl. He placed it on a table beside the lord's right hand, along with a basin of scented water and several small towels. The Eyascnu placed one of the towels on his lap to protect his heavy silk robe.

"Just as you brought skora to me, Kuat, so also will s'rere come."

Bigger than a dire-wolf, the strak standing at the bottom step flicked its ears forward.

The lord smiled. "Yes, I noticed how Nosce failed to mention your role in bringing the Seani boy here. You did well."

The lord placed the bowl of mud on the towel and stripped off his gloves, jerking his face away from the smell. He tossed the gloves angrily onto the floor and immersed his hands, rubbing the mud into every oozing sore and between the festering fingers. "You are the only one who knows my secret pain. Even my autobiography does not mention the utter depravity of what was done to me."

The strak turned its massive head away from the gloves and stared at the lord with its black, deep-set eyes.

"S'rere," the lord said, "will restore these hands permanently. They will become strong enough to choke the life out of the niyal'arist voras who afflicted me, humiliated me, who left my very skin to rot in my own stronghold."

The volghast took away the bowl and replaced it with the basin of water. The lord washed away the mud, inspected his hands, now whole and clean, and used another towel to dry them. He sank back with a sigh and flexed his fingers. "You may approach me," he said to the strak.

The creature moved forward and lay down beside the throne. It panted quietly, its long tongue lolling.

"It was a gradual change," the lord said, staring straight ahead and idly scratching the fur on the strak's humped back. "But I sensed it, Kuat. I sensed that my brother was becoming more twisted, more voracious. I discovered what was happening far too late to help him. I awoke, and his face was grinning down at me, his long fangs bared. I had to kill him."

The strak laid its head on its wide paws.

"He was no longer my brother Varo, but a monster leech that would prey on me and my people. I had to do it, Kuat. The niyalahn-ristas gave me no choice. Rûk sent them, fair and smiling, to gain my trust. But in secret they laid an evil larva inside my brother. A vora-larva. It wormed its way into my brother's very soul and devoured him, and almost devoured me."

He remained silent as the last of the mist curled away from the shadowed purple room, then dismissed the strak. After it departed, he commanded, "Bring me another bowl." A fire-eyed volghast placed it on his lap.

The Lord of Shunder turned his head and addressed the heavily-breathing entity waiting behind the throne. "It is time for another session."

The bulk rose. The chain grew taut, stretching further back behind the curtain, but held. A low growl ascended into a whimper.

"Take it back to its cell," he commanded the volghasts. "I will visit it immediately after the Acclamation."

When he was alone, he pulled off the tight, flexible mask. With a grunt of disgust, he hurled it onto the floor next to the gloves. Reaching into the bowl with both hands, he scooped out the mud and applied it thickly to his face.

Disturbed by the dim light, cave-beetles darted into black cracks as four guards, one carrying a hand-globe, passed by. They escorted the isav's former proctor, his hands tied behind him, and followed the Lord of Shunder. The lord's sphere of werelight made their shadows loom and twist against the walls as they descended a long series of rough-hewn steps and made their secret way into the cavernous depths of Oknu Shuld. There was no sound except their breathing, the proctor's occasional whimper of terror, and their own muffled footsteps.

They stopped at an archway blocked by a rusted gate. The lord unlocked it, and leaving the others to wait, stepped through. He followed the low-ceilinged passage until he came to an iron door with a small barred window, which he opened with a word. In the center of the cell, a bulky, vaguely human form, wearing only a stained and ragged loin-cloth, lay on a stone table. Shackles, lined on the inside with short metal spikes, loosely held down the thick wrists, ankles and neck. For now, the spikes barely touched the mottled skin. As the lord entered, the creature cringed and turned its grotesque head away, as if even the dim light hurt its eyes.

The lord released the werelight to hang in the air above the table. "I notice your water trough is empty," he remarked. "Blood is so salty; you must be thirsty." He produced a leather bottle from within his purple velvet cloak and shook the liquid inside.

The creature groaned. The Eyascnu reached across its bare chest and placed his thumb firmly on its forehead. "Face up," he commanded. "You are reverting, trying to conceal what you are, and we can't have that."

Slowly, trembling, the creature obeyed.

"Now drink." The creature clamped its mouth shut, but the lord pressed harder on the forehead. The lips opened, and the lord poured the contents of the bottle past the crooked, yellow teeth. He stepped back to wait for the quicker-acting ingredient to take effect first.

A thin scream arose from the creature. With stretching and popping sounds, the chest filled out, the arms and legs lengthened and swelled with muscles. Long grey hairs sprouted on its body, and the eyes bulged like big white mushrooms. He turned them toward the Lord of Shunder.

"Don't look at me," the Eyascnu said in a low, intense voice. "You will never make your face into mine." He stepped closer to the light. "See? My skin is smooth and clean. Yours is full of growths and pustules. Not even your twin would recognize you now."

The creature cried out as its tongue engorged and its

fingers fused into claw-like pincers. With an effort, it uttered half-formed words. "Oo-ooana eiz!"

The Eyascnu barked out a laugh. "You think that matters anymore? Long ago I met that challenge."

"Na eiz!" the creature groaned.

The Eyascnu stood still, as if gazing into some memory. With a shaking hand, he touched the top half of his face, and his voice sank to a whisper. "I was—was only three years old when I discovered that. No one ever told me. How strange. I found out all by myself." He shook off the past. "But I prevailed, my sorcery prevailed. Now I see into the soul. Now my vision reaches to the far future. I have become what my brother once was—a beacon in the night."

The prisoner moaned a reply.

The Eyascnu smashed his fist down on its cheek. "You lie! For that, I could make you eat your own tongue!" Breathing heavily, he clutched the edge of the stone table until he regained control. "My brother is *dead* because of you."

Bones creaked as the prisoner's arms and legs continued to swell under the shackles and press against the spikes. The form on the table writhed and screamed as the points bit down, but the scream ended in a gurgle as the neck also swelled into the metal collar. Blood trickled onto the slab.

The lord waved his hand over the body. "This, vora, is what you truly are. Admit it. This is what drank my brother's blood." He leaned closer. "I understand why you did it. You wanted to be human. You wanted to be more than what you were. A worthy goal. For that reason, I pity you." Straightening, he rattled the chain of binding coiled at his belt. "For that reason I prevent you from expressing the very worst of your bestiality."

The creature lay still, panting in pain.

"So you must see that my justice is, in reality, mercy. I trusted you, and you tried to split me in half. You are a monster, yet I still feed and shelter you. My hope, my firm *commitment* to you. is that you repent. I believe, vora, that even you can be redeemed."

A red flush crept up the creature's face, for now the second potion, fura, was beginning to take effect. The prisoner stiffened and bellowed out its hatred. Veins stood out as it writhed on the slab, attempting to break free. Red drops spurted.

The Eyascnu watched, his face hardening. "The longer you refuse my mercy, the longer you must endure my justice."

A strangled cry burst from the cracked lips.

"No!" The lord pounded the creature's collar with his fist. "I alone am king of this land!"

He turned away and waited until his breathing slowed, then stepped through the door and called for the guards. They appeared with the former proctor. The man's eyes grew huge when he saw the powerful creature pulling on its restraints.

"I did nothing!" he cried. "I *specifically* forbade her to talk to the boy, but the scathi bug disobeyed me."

"I resent," the lord said, "that you force me to act harshly. I resent it deeply." He turned to the guards. "Push him in."

They obeyed, the door clanged shut, and the proctor was left screaming and begging at the window. The lord turned to a thick wooden handle set into the wall to the left of the gate and pulled it down. Mechanisms creaked inside the cell and the shackles binding the creature sprang open. With a rumble deep in its throat, the giant pulled itself off the slab.

The group retraced their steps, and gradually the sounds of shrieks and snarls faded behind them into the pitch black.

Thirsty, his wrist hurting, Teller lay on his bed. A troubled sleep crawled over him. He dreamed of the grate on the floor. It was the black mouth of a tunnel that went down through rock, down endless levels, and into the dark. Far-off screams came out of it, followed by strange, gargling groans, like half-formed words that echoed deep within Oknu Shuld.

Moaning, he turned over. They were hurting him, changing him, forming him into a monster beyond recognition, beyond the reach of any human help. His spirikai simmered like an ember, but he couldn't get it to flare out, and the only thing that burned was himself.

A hand shook him. Teller slapped it away, but a subaltern the hand belonged to pulled him roughly out of bed. "Get dressed," he ordered. "I am here to escort you to your orientation."

Resentment itched in him like a rash. He was tired of people waking him up and dragging him off. He had no idea what orientation was, but he would answer no more questions. No tray had appeared, so it looked like there would be no breakfast. Teller took his time putting on his clothes and then followed the red-cloak, who unlocked gates as he went, down several passages and into a small chamber. The subaltern left him facing a group of children sitting cross-legged on a carpet. They stared at him. All but one were boys, ranging from about eight to eleven years old. The biggest boy, who had russet curly hair that fell over his high forehead, stared at him the hardest. No one spoke as Teller took the only space left on the carpet, in the front.

Except for a desk and chair, the rock-walled chamber was empty of furniture. Three luniku globes hung from the ceiling, and so many worms in one place made his skin crawl.

A blue-robed man strode in and tossed a ledger onto the desk. He had thick hands, a square face, and cold eyes. "I am Master Keel," he announced, "and this is your orientation to life in Oknu Shuld." His eyes traveled over each of them. "The eight of you are here because you are ristas of interest. Your mind-probe has revealed you may possess some smattering of Power that may be worth our time." The way he said "Power" made it clear it was different from ordinary power.

Teller didn't like the teacher's high-and-mighty attitude, but he wanted to learn more about this Power.

"You will begin a course of education," Master Keel went on, "that will quickly reveal whether our interest in you is justified. You will find that this education will last longer than you thought and will be harder than you can imagine. If we find your Power isn't worth our time, you will be eliminated. If you do have Power, we will aid in its growth until it develops enough for us to work with. In the meantime, you will be schooled in our philosophy."

He folded his arms and looked at each student. "Such schooling is necessary because you have been lied to, constantly and consistently, and here we tell the truth. For example. What the people outside call cruelty, you will learn to recognize as strength. What they call ruthlessness, we know to be conviction. Forget what they told you about right and wrong. Here it is right to obey your superiors and wrong not to. It will take courage to learn these things, courage to overthrow years of what ignorant people tried to drum into your heads."

He began pacing. "Some introductory points. Number one: forget your village deities, your green circles, your prophecies, your holy twins, whatever. The Eyascnu Varo is your lord. He is the answer to your prayers. Number two: morue is not used in Oknu Shuld. The purple in all of its forms is for dependents and rustics, not for those the lord appoints to run his kingdom."

Keel stopped and stuck his thumbs into his belt. Looking over their heads, he sighed in a bored way. "We always get the question about fire. 'Where's the fire?' our new arrivals ask. 'Where are the candles, the hearths, the oil-lamps that we used at home?' This is the answer: the Lord of Oknu Shuld is the source of all the light we need. This fact is symbolized by the only flame in this stronghold, which we will view shortly when we visit the Hall of the Eye. Other fires are unnecessary to those with Power. The only true flame is the one inside ourselves, the flame that enables us to compete and to conquer."

Keel took a seat behind the desk and folded his hands. "We have neither the time nor the inclination to coddle the weak or the lazy. You are superior beings and must fulfill your potential. If you don't, you'll die. Any questions?"

There were none, so he opened the ledger, glanced at the page, then looked up at Teller. "You. Seani boy. What's your name?"

If the man knew where he came from, he must know his name. But he answered, "Teller."

Keel leaned back in his chair. "Teller, eh. Teller of what? Tales, lies, what?"

Someone behind him snickered. Heat bloomed in Teller's spirikai, but he didn't take his eyes off Master Keel. "Just Teller. In Widjar, it's T'lir."

Keel included the class in his smile. "So you have two

names?" His smile abruptly disappeared. "Only the Eyascnu Varo has two names here. Perhaps you believe yourself to be better than the rest of us, Teller-of-Lies?"

He disliked this man and didn't care if it showed. "No I don't. And that's not my name. It's *Teller*. T-E-L-L-E-R."

Master Keel's face darkened. He rose from his chair, went to stand over him, and prodded him with his foot. "You do *not*—N-O-T—correct a master of Oknu Shuld."

Teller stared at him. There was nothing this man could do to him that hadn't been done already. "Except when he's wrong."

The room fell into a dead silence.

"Stand up, Teller-of-Lies."

He stayed where he was. "I said that's not my name."

Keel pulled him to his feet. "And *I* said stand up." He slapped him hard across the face.

Teller recoiled. The heat in his spirikai rose up to join the burning in his cheek.

"Tell the class your name."

He had given them many names, over and over. He had answered everything they asked him, and still they made him talk and talk until his throat hurt. Now he was done with that. He pressed his lips together and glared up at the teacher.

Master Keel grabbed his arm. "Tell"—he poked a finger into Teller's chest—"the class"—poke, poke—"your *name*."

"I already did," he said. "Are you deaf?"

The master's eyes widened in shock, then closed to slits. A grim smile stretched his lips. The children nearest Teller scrambled away. Keel's grip on him tightened and he drew back a clenched fist.

A flare, hot and bright, blazed out of Teller's spirikai. It shocked him, blinded him, and a horrible thought hit him as his sight flooded back: this is what I did to Se Gremez!

But Keel only yelped and let go, rubbing his fist. He didn't burst into flames, didn't seem to be hurt much at all. "You little rat," he growled. "You scathi little rat." He made a down-swiping gesture with his clenched fist and, with a loud snap, an invisible lash of pain whipped across Teller's chest. It knocked him to the floor. Again the gesture, the crack, and another blow cut through the front of his shirt. He rolled over, tried to crawl away, but Keel pinned his arm down with one booted foot. The unseen lash struck the back of his neck. He bit his lip to keep from screaming, struggled to twist free, but the foot pressed harder, and the lash cut across his arms, his legs, his back. Master Keel, he suddenly knew, was going to kill him. A part of him roared in protest, but another part whispered, *so what?*

The snapping noise stopped. The foot was withdrawn. Shaking in pain, Teller lifted his head. A figure in a leaf-brown cloak stood at the door, and he recognized Vol Kuat. Master Keel knelt on one knee before him. Everyone in the room was kneeling.

"You have need of Lash already, Master Keel?" the Vol said.

There was no answer from the man's bowed head.

The Vol turned his mud-brown eyes to Teller. Shocked, he saw they had no pupils. "Come with me," the Vol ordered.

Teller struggled to his feet, expecting to see his clothes torn and his arms stained with blood, but they weren't. His skin stung, but wasn't even scratched. He stumbled after the Vol, and at the door looked back.

Keel's glare beamed with hate and an unspoken promise: *I have Lash, and I won't forget.*

Teller met that with a glare of his own: *I have fire, and you won't hit me again.*

The dead-leaf cloak swirled ahead, and Teller did his best to keep up in spite of the pain. Their passing disturbed a dried ivy leaf. Trapped in a corner, it swirled in a tight circle as a gate clanged shut behind him.

Chapter 17

Education

Running away didn't work; he never made it past the back gates, and there was no home to run back to anyway. After two years of rebellion, two years of getting beat up and locked up, Teller finally realized that none of that taught him anything about his Power. So he'd reached an unspoken agreement with the Vols. They would ignore his smart remarks, and he would stop short of open defiance. If he wanted to learn, he had to let the Vols teach him.

Time in Oknu Shuld passed for Teller in a series of oddly disjointed vignettes. Some marked, he supposed, important events. Others just stuck in his mind for a reason he didn't know.

He was staring at a mosaic that covered the small round table. Maybe once brightly colored but now covered with grime, it pictured the faces of three girls, pretty and smiling, with flowing ribbons in their hair. Nice. Except a faint skull showed through each head.

"Pay attention, Teller-of-Lies!"

He jerked his gaze off the table at which he sat with Vol Prome. "That's not my name." He said this automatically, without heat, a game he'd been playing with the Vols for three years now, and hadn't yet lost.

"But it is," the Vol insisted in his rasping voice. "Lies are spoken out of fear and ignorance, to which all lesser beings are subject. Only the lord is free of such weaknesses. Only he is wise enough to grasp the truth and powerful enough to define it."

"So call yourself Teller-of-Lies."

"I fear," Nosce said, "that the mind-damage the Seani inflicted on you will never completely heal. You will never be free of ignorance. Accepting your name is a sign that you understand this. A sign of your ultimate subservience to the lord, and the beginning of wisdom."

"I'm not an ahn, and I won't be re-named." Keya had a beautiful name, but they changed it to that of a bug.

His shrouded teacher pointed to a nearby globe. "Take that off its stand and bring it here."

Teller did so, concentrating on the cool feel of the glass and not on the slowly squirming mass so close to his fingers.

Nosce took the globe with one hand and pulled back his hood with the other. "Look at me."

Teller raised his eyes to the Prome's face. For the first time, he was allowed to see it clearly. He didn't look away, but the sight left a cold spot in his stomach.

The scarred lips moved. "I was once as stubborn and proud as you. I also seethed with resentment. But the lord did not give up on me. He taught me who my master was, and therefore who I was. The pain was excruciating, but it released my Power at last. Now I am his Prome, his first and strongest Volarach, and none dare oppose me." Nosce replaced his hood and the shadow swallowed up his face again. "The more you accept the lord's authority over you, Teller-of-Lies, the closer you will come to your true Power."

"That's not my name."

The hood stared at him. "You've outgrown your clothing again. Go and select others."

He went, but first stopped in his room on the second level. There he scrubbed his face at the basin. His name was Teller. He'd never let them take that away.

The storeroom was deserted. He walked between tables piled with pants, cloaks and vests, looking for a black shirt. He always chose black, although the dim light made it hard to tell one dark color from another. He picked up a shirt that looked black enough.

Most of these garments, he knew, had been sewn by some proud mother who wanted her ahn-child to look his or her best for the Welcoming Ceremony. Now that child wore the dirty-white clothing of a slave.

The shirt smelled moldy, and a feeling of loss seemed woven into it. That feeling lingered everywhere. Walking through the halls, he disturbed it, and wisps of it trailed under his door while he tried to sleep. It came from the ahn, silent and downcast as they did their work all around him. The feeling sometimes grew into a feverish pain, particularly when he was sent anywhere near the narrow stairs that spiraled down to the isav. With an effort, he ignored it and kept his face hard. No one must ever see this weakness. In Oknu Shuld, any weakness was fatal.

"Most of these were gifts to the lord." Vol Ségun chuckled. "Whether given freely or not." He turned his hard, sharp eyes, out of place in such a doughy face, toward a pile of jeweled cups and rummaged through them, the rings on his thick fingers glinting dimly. Unlike Nosce, who always wore a black shroud, this Vol paraded around in robes stiff with embroidery and a cloak of fox fur.

Arms folded, Teller leaned against the wall. The Vols

had decided that thirteen was old enough to foray in the treasure chamber, but he wasn't impressed. The room was filled with tables piled with gem-encrusted swords, boxes of rings, and baskets of medallions. He had no use for any of it.

Beads of sweat formed above his upper lip and, making sure the Vol wasn't looking, he wiped them away on the back of his hand. The chamber, like this whole place lately, felt hot. Even though the corridors were unheated, he had taken to walking them with sleeves rolled up. Night after night, he slept in a smoldering bed. Se Nemez screamed in his dreams, his face melting, his mouth a dripping red hole.

Part of his feverish state, he knew, was a reaction to that background anguish that wafted through every corridor like a poisonous fog. He should be used to it by now, but wasn't. He should've learned a long time ago to ignore it, but couldn't. It seemed to be getting stronger, and so was the simmering in his spirikai. The feeling trembled on his horizon like lightning from a coming storm, and he didn't know what to do about it.

From the table beside him dangled a necklace strung with small black pearls. The sight of it awoke one of his sudden memories. He was holding a pendant on a black braided cord. It was his birth-gift, but his grandmother hid it in a box. There was something engraved on the medallion, but he couldn't quite see it. When he came into the fullness of skora, when he came to the Seani to burn it to the ground, he would find this box, and utterly destroy those who had kept it away from him.

"Take a look at the daggers," Autran said over his shoulder. "It's time you carried one."

"Skora is blade enough."

"Except it's still in its juvenile state."

In grudging recognition of this fact, he pushed away from the wall and sorted through a table piled with knives and daggers. One of these fell to the floor, and he picked it up—a dagger with a hilt of green jade. The blade had been fashioned into a slightly wavy shape. Was it meant to be a flame? He turned it over, and saw V-shaped scorings along a central line. A long leaf? The sight this nudged at a memory, which didn't awaken. Yet he felt it: this dagger was his—something he needed, something he once lost or had to find. He pushed it into his belt.

At that moment, the heat in the room seemed to coalesce into one sharp spear. It stabbed into his spirikai, and the skora inside him flared up so hot and strong it took his breath away.

Nosce's bony finger pressed into the middle of his forehead. "All Powers depend on this Third Eye. That is why all but the greatest of sorcerers can be assailed from behind. Focus your will into this spot. *See* the fire into a bar of light. *See* into existence the sword inside it."

Skora roiled wildly inside him but he couldn't *see* anything. He'd met the Prome in an empty chamber, more of a cave, to practice summoning the fire. That was over a gong ago and Nosce was becoming impatient. "Skora is fire, but you must focus it with ice. If you cannot understand this, then I must enter your mind and demonstrate."

"No." He tried again, but couldn't combine fire with ice. The hood stared at him, and Teller's heart began to race.

"You are remembering what they did to you in the Seani," Nosce said, "how Se Nemes damaged your mind. But I will enter for instruction only. It is the quickest way to release your Power."

Reluctantly, Teller nodded. The black hood leaned closer. Out of its depths, two eye-points glowed. He felt the nudge of Nosce's mind-probe, the cold, wet tip of it, and tensed.

"Do you want to control this Power or not?" Nosce rasped.

Teller took a deep breath and forced his mind open. The probe poured in. It felt like the squid Autran kept preserved in a jar in the laboratorium. He struggled to control his revulsion as it crawled around the place where the skora burned. Then, with whip-like swiftness, its tentacles snatched at the root of his spirikai. Panic seized him; fire flared in front of his eyes, and the probe darted away.

His returning vision revealed the hooded Vol standing stiffly in front of him. "That was not helpful, Teller-of-Lies."

"You were the one who lied! That was no instruction."

"An invasive instruction seems to be the only kind you understand."

Teller clenched sweat in his hands. "I understand just fine. You tried to take it."

A hiss of laughter emerged from the hood. "I merely gauge the fire's strength. Why would I trade a paltry ember for my status here? You have much to learn."

He was practicing in a well-ventilated chamber on level one, with straw-bales as targets. "The more you allow the skora to remain a function of feeling, the less control you will have," the Prome said.

This remark, he'd discovered, was only partly true. Skora leaped up instinctively in the face of a threat, but emotions like anger or fear—if he could keep them under control—fueled that process, and his will guided it. If he wanted to summon fire as a sword or spear, he had to use the Prome's method: form a fiery bar in his spirikai, image it—more like sculpt it—into the weapon he wanted, then project it outside himself and into his hand. If he wanted to sling fire directly from his spirikai, he had to summon the feeling of throwing a rock: the motion in his arm, the urgency in his throat, the forward thrust of his shoulders. None of this was easy, and just because he managed to produce a sword, no matter how fiery, didn't mean he knew how to use it. So he had to practice that part too, with swords of steel brought in by a subaltern who instructed him. Eventually, using a balance of will, imagination, and emotion—mostly anger—he was learning to harness the fire's instinctive nature.

The problem, though, was that skora was basically a defensive Power. He could make it flare up only if he visualized an immediate threat. This meant he had to convince the fire he was in danger and then coolly form it into the weapon he needed. He practiced, aiming for the skill that would eventually allow him to bypass the bar of fire stage and grab a weapon directly from his spirikai.

In all these outward forms the skora was clearly visible; but most of the time it burned inside him unseen, like a fever. He learned how to keep the skora flames low around him as a protective barrier against the ahn-pain, and live numb and unfeeling inside.

"I must warn you," the Vol said. "Do not ever come against me with your fire. My Power is Mirror, which will reflect skora back on yourself."

Sweaty and exhausted, Teller turned away from the blackened pile of what had been straw and wiped his forehead with the back of his arm. "There are no mirrors in Oknu Shuld."

"You lie. Out of ignorance you are a teller of lies. There is a hall here filled with nothing but mirrors." The Prome leaned his shrouded face closer to him. "I am your mirror now, and if you do not heed me, one rota you may find yourself perfectly reflected in it."

The door opened and a middle-aged ahn entered, carrying two buckets. His job was to replace the dead luniku with live ones, and he kept his eyes lowered as he placed the buckets in front of the globe nearest the door. As he picked up the dim sphere, Nosce pointed at him.

"Kill him, Teller-of-Lies."

The ahn stiffened, then raised eyes dark with fear to Teller. But almost immediately the fear gave way to a kind of hopeful wariness, an impossible trust Teller couldn't begin to understand. It was the way all ahn regarded him, with a look he caught with the corner of his eye, a look immediately cast down when he turned to meet it. It was full of that expectancy he seemed to remember from his other life, an expectancy that both haunted and angered him, and it made the skora rise.

"Ahn are mere bugs," Nosce rasped, "and you have already killed. Do it again, Teller-of-Lies."

His stomach knotted, but he remembered what he'd learned. He distanced himself from what he was feeling, set his eyes on the target, and with an effort of will hurled out a white flare. The globe in the ahn's hands cracked. He dropped it as the worms inside burst into flames.

Breathing hard, Teller turned back to Nosce. "That's not my name," he said.

Vol Ségun placed a wide tray in front of him. "So, I've heard you opened the void last rota."

Teller placed a dozen thin strips of copper into the tray and didn't answer. If Autran had heard about that, he already knew his little experiment had been a miserable failure. The scroll he'd been getting his instructions from had been sucked in, as well as most of the other items on the table, and if Vol Kuat hadn't been there to close it, the small rent he'd made would have gotten out of hand.

"I wouldn't talk about it either, if I were you." Autran busied himself at the other end of the table, crushing something in a mortar. "Been down to the isav lately?"

The interconnected chambers on the third level that comprised Autran's laboratorium were isolated, but even here the ahn-pain seeped. Teller kept it at bay by concentrating on the smell of tinctures, the texture of powders, and the dim, twilit colors of poisons. He poured a careful amount of the concoction he had just made over the metal strips and said nothing. But heat crept up the back of his neck.

Autran laughed. "I don't believe it! Nosce, Nosce, how you neglect his education! Surely you're aware, my young apprentice, that the male and female sleeping chambers in the isav are like vast serving dishes." He grinned at Teller. "Surely every fifteen-year-old rista in Oknu Shuld knows succulent bits are available there at any time. Your mind isn't *that* damaged."

When he was sent on errands to the fourth level, Teller had overheard other ristas describe what they did with such access. Much of what they bragged about made him feel sick.

"I suppose then," Autran said, "you know nothing about being with a female."

Up here with the Vols, he was separated from other ristas, but ahn were ever-present. Some of the girls his age were pretty and curvaceous, and at times he felt such swollen arousal it was hard to sleep, or even walk. But he never acted on his desire. He felt too keenly what the ahn suffered to want to add to it like the other ristas did. He continued working while Autran proceeded to instruct him at length on how to be with a girl. Teller pretended indifference, but couldn't help listening.

"There's always those who weep or beg," Autran concluded, "but this only adds to the pleasure. It's even better if one of the little bugs tries to resist, but these are always newcomers, and you have to reserve them ahead of time. Anyway, experiment. Go down to the isav and take your pick, from either the male or female side, and use it in the privacy of your own room. Or you can select several and invite your friends." He looked at Teller dubiously. "But you don't have any friends, do you?"

The question was rhetorical, so he didn't bother answering it. Instead, he thought of Keya, praying under her blanket while ristas stalked among the ahn like morue spiders, picking and taking.

Autran poured a liquid into the tray and set it aside. "After these strips are processed, they'll be brought before the lord for instillation."

Teller looked up. "Instillation?"

"His spell will instill several virtues, obedience and sterility among them."

"What are you talking about?"

The Vol raised his eyebrows. "These will become the collars that control the bugs. How could you not know that?"

But he didn't. These strips would be fitted around the throats of the new arrivals, and the lord's spell would seal the ends shut, forever. It was as if he felt the collar tight around his neck, and it took several tries before he could swallow the loathing that rose behind it.

"Wake up. I've got a task for you." Teller sat up as Autran whisked the cover off the globe next to the door.

Part of what the Vols saw as his "education" was performing tasks, mostly alone, that ahn usually did. These tasks included checking and repairing leaks in the two dams as part of a work crew or digging new furrows up on the cliff. They also included pulling waste-carts out to the garbage heap and climbing up and down the various levels, usually hauling heavy objects—ale casks, boxes of books for the resident scholars, or sides of meat down to the scourery. He didn't care; all the climbing and lifting gave him bigger muscles than many sixteen-year-old ristas in Oknu Shuld seemed to possess; and, sometimes, got him so tired he could sleep for a few hours without the nightmares.

But it hadn't worked this sleep-session. As late as it was, there was an ahn-hunt going on, somewhere on the level below. He'd raised the skora barrier but the terror of the helpless ahn still sifted up from the grate. Relieved at the distraction, he got up and followed Autran to the laboratorium.

On the worktable, next to an open book, stood a mortar full of blue power. The Ségun carefully spooned some of it into a thin-glassed vial. "Hold this in your fist," he directed, "and melt the powder with skora."

Teller didn't ask why; what did it matter? The task, however, turned out to be harder than he thought. He'd have to pull more of the fire away from the protective barrier, and he didn't want to do that during an ahn-hunt.

"By the suckin' voras," Autran snapped after several failed attempts. "I don't have all night."

He knew what would happen, but was still unprepared. He summoned all the fire, the barrier went down, and a surge of anguish hit him so hard he cracked the vial. Giving him a poisonous glance, Autran prepared another while Teller picked bloody shards of glass out of his palm. This time, using his other hand, he managed to fuse both glass and powder into an unusable lump.

"Dammit!" Autran exclaimed. "Don't you know what you're doing yet?"

With the full ahn-pain screwing through him, he struggled to concentrate. After two more tries, he succeeded.

Autran took the vial, which now contained a blue-black viscoid, and inspected it. "Took you long enough." He passed the vial carefully under his nose. "But it's ineerva all right."

Drained of skora and wracked with ahn-pain, Teller propped himself upright against the table.

"This produces in its victim an acute re-living of every wound ever inflicted upon him." Autran chuckled. "Good thing you hadn't made it yet when you cracked the vial." He held the glass up to the light. "The Tierce will find this useful for coating arrows with. You can go back to bed now, Teller-of-Lies."

He pushed off the table and made his way through the door. "That's not my name," he mumbled.

"This page is from a book," Vol Kuat said, "both valuable and dangerous." The slanted brown gaze fastened on Teller, the lack of pupils making it appear blind. He withdrew a single sheet of vellum from his cloak and placed it on the table in front of Teller. "During a battle, pages were scattered and hastily retrieved. They are no longer in order." His voice sounded muffled in the narrow, low-ceilinged room in this deserted section of his domain.

The skora fastened on only one word. "Dangerous?"

"A number of books are dangerous. Over time, you

will receive more pages from this one. Copy them word for word. Do not show them to anyone but me." He indicated the writing materials on the table, then, ducking his head through the low door, left the chamber.

Teller put aside the book he'd been studying, *Faugrit's Treatise on Rista Powers,* and looked at the page he'd been given. It was stained in several places, inscribed with reddish-brown ink, and like most old documents he had encountered, contained no page number.

A creak, loud in the intense silence, caused him to look up at the grit-covered shelves that lined the wall. His eyes ran over pots containing rolled-up scrolls, piles of old books, and—turned sideways—a row of human skulls. Nothing moved. He could hear himself breathing.

The creak must have come from shifting rock, from old wood settling. He returned to the page. The letters were written in a clear hand. Running his fingers over them, he got the distinct impression that a woman had formed them. He picked up the quill and translated to himself as he copied the Widjar words onto another sheet.

"They shall fall out of timelessness and into time, and the niyalahn-ristas will come again…" Niyalahn-ristas. The twin voras who had destroyed the lord's brother. The so-called saviors the ahn secretly prayed for. *"…born in hope as the Toltyr Arulve."* "Toltyr" he didn't know, but the next word made his heart jump. Rulve.

How did that name come to be here, in the depths of Oknu Shuld? The name was in its possessive form, "Arulve," the form of belonging.

Belonging. The word swept in a sudden vision. He was lying in quiet green hands. Tender love washed through him; the gentle wound of compassion pierced his heart. An intense yearning wrung his spirikai, so painful his throat swelled.

Oh god, where did this come from?

He jerked back. It came from mind damage. He belonged to the Lord of Shunder. He belonged here. This was home, the place where he'd found his fire.

He was being hurt, and the skora knew it. It rose up and flamed inside his chest. He let it burn, until the name—the unpronounced name that hovered and haunted—was seared away.

He was holding the quill so tightly his arm shook. He relaxed his grip, took a breath, and returned to the text. *"Blessed are they, alone and chosen, for they shall be called s'eft and t'lir."* He dropped the quill and ink spattered on the table. His brother's Widjar name was S'eft. And his was T'lir. What *was* this book?

The single page told him nothing. The skulls were silent. He found a dirty rag on one of the shelves, rubbed the ink spots from the table, and forced himself to continue.

"But pride crept into the s'eft and corrupted his nika"—his heart, or soul. *"He would live for nothing but his own will. And so the s'eft will grow wroth with the t'lir, and in the battle between them s'rere and sh'kier are lost."* He had no idea what the last two nouns meant. *"Tyranny choked the land. But the people cried out to Rulve, and she will hear them, and in his mercy he will call forth the niyalahn-ristas always yet again."*

The changing tenses were confusing, the whole fragment unsettling. A gritty, scraping sound drew his eyes back to the shelves. A chill fled down his spine. The skulls had turned to face him. "Spukuya!" he cried in Widjar. But why did he command them to be still? A slight earth tremor must have jittered them; or it was a trick of the crawling globe-light. He went back to his work.

"They are opposites, yet called to the same sacrifice and

the same choice. Sayatami, my people!" Listen to me. *"Out of the circle shall come a toltyr, obverse and reverse diverse—"* Here the page ended, apparently in the middle of a poem.

His heart was pounding, but he didn't know why. He sat back and read what he had copied. It resonated—with hope, with mercy, with a sense of urgent destiny.

But all that belonged to a child he no longer was, to a past that had never existed. As to S'eft and T'lir, these names were no doubt known in the Seani and were given to him and his brother out of piety or pretension. The author, whoever she was, apparently wrote of some past or future tragedy, of a cycle of betrayal and refusal; but it had nothing to do with him.

He raised his eyes and met the black gaze of the skulls. A row of empty eye-sockets stared back.

They waited. They had been waiting for a long time, in this silence under the earth.

Suddenly he felt stifled in the confines of the room. He rushed out, taking deep breaths of stale air. Gazes bored into the back of his neck, even after he slammed the door.

"Are you ready?" the Vol asked, turning his sly, slanted eyes toward him.

"Get on with it."

He followed Vol Kuat down a narrow back stair carved into the basalt, through barely lit corridors, and into a remote section of level five. He thought he'd seen most parts of Oknu Shuld in the eleven years he'd been here, but this section was strange to him, and he had no liking for it. They passed a crumbling guardian cairn, still alert enough to require a password, and stopped before double poisonwood doors covered with carvings. The gaunt spiraled eyes, tortured mouths, and prints of outspread hands glistened with amber beads of hardened, lethal sap. With a pointy-toothed grin, the Delver gestured toward them.

They seemed to be designed to keep things in rather than out, so he commanded, "Ephra!"

Slowly, with stops and starts, the doors juddered open. Followed by the Delver, he stepped into a dark-throated corridor. The walls, slick with mold, exuded a rancid breath. Wide enough for four people to walk abreast, the hallway was darker than any he had yet encountered. The globes on their stands were fuzzy with dust, and only a few were partly alive with luniku crawling listlessly over their dead and desiccated companions. The whole place contained a disturbing organic quality, as if it were an alien being that lingered somewhere between putrefaction and evolution. They had entered the Halls of the Goah.

"Few come here," the Kuat said. "Rats or spiders may wander in, but they do not last long."

The hall lay in a stealthy silence, and unrolled itself between dim circles of light as they walked. They passed smaller branching tunnels, a few recessed doors barely visible in the shadows, a drift of what looked like mildewed rags. Teller found himself straining to listen.

A hulking figure appeared out of the gloom. Teller's heart jumped. but it was only one of several cabinets, like upright coffins carved in the likeness of semi-human creatures.

As they walked, the skin on his arms began to prickle, and the fire in his spirikai rose. He heard nothing but their own footsteps on the dusty, marble-tiled floor, yet he glimpsed furtive movements all around him. Inky shadows detached themselves from the darkness between globes and converged behind them. Others oozed out from under doorways. Half-glimpsed forms watched out of corners, and wispy faces coiled in some of the unlit globes. Cautious before as- yet-untested power, they seemed to sense the skora and kept their distance. But Teller could feel their hunger.

"These goah," the Delver said, "are the remains of the once-alive. At times the Eyascnu feeds them with prisoners or ahn. Mostly they prey on what they can get."

He stopped before a black arch looming to their left, blocked by a crusted gate. An almost tangible malice radiated from the passage beyond.

"There dwells Mochlos," Vol Kuat said, "the only goah who has made a name for himself. He has ingested more lives than any of the others and achieved a certain corporeality. Even now, he looks out at us."

The blackness ahead seemed to issue a sly invitation. Of itself, the crusted gate creaked ajar.

"Mochlos beckons," the Delver's voice said. "Will you go?"

Teller's hand crept to the jade hilt of the dagger in his belt, but a blade would be useless in this place, so he let his hand drop. "Why did you bring me here?"

The Delver's brown cloak, patterned like skeletal veins of decomposed leaves, made him almost invisible against the rock wall, and his voice seemed to come from nowhere. "So when you must come again," it said, "you will know the way."

CHAPTER 18

SOUND OF DERISIVE LAUGHTER

"This is all yours," Autran said. He pushed open the door to a room in the rista students' section on level four. "Enjoy it, Teller-of-Lies."

"That's not my name."

Autran chuckled as Teller stepped inside. A quick glance revealed a bed, chest, desk, and two chairs. The chamber was somewhat larger than his previous room and featured a thicker carpet and additional chair, but was otherwise much the same.

"Great location," the Vol said, referring to the rowdy ale-room they had passed on the way. "Remember, your first lecture starts at the next gong. Try to fit in this time." He closed the door.

Teller put away his few belongings, mostly clothes and books. Having been isolated for so long, he found the noise and bustle in this part of the fourth level a source of tension. The Vols had decided that he needed to finish his education and military training with the rest of his class before they all were subjected to what Autran ominously referred to as "The Final Exam." The Vol refused to elaborate on what this exam entailed, but it was a prerequisite to receiving the red cloak of subalternship. Teller wanted that cloak, but didn't want or need encounters with other ristas, and the distant memory of Master Keel didn't make him eager to attend any lectures either.

Something, however, unsettled him far more than that. His awareness of the ahn-pain had been bad enough up on the first three levels, but down here, where many more ahn worked, it was almost intolerable. The spiral stairs that led directly down to the isav and the scourery were centrally located here, and they exuded misery like polluted wells. He couldn't raise the skora barrier high enough to keep out all the anguish, only enough to endure it.

From what he'd heard, a drink called brandwyn might help. Thinking he had enough time to order a cup brought in, he opened the door. The hall teemed with rista students, blue-robed teachers, and foreign visitors who lived on this level, many of whom were coming or going to the ale-room down the curving passage to his right.

"Do you require service, sir?" A kneeling ahn addressed him, leaning out from the niche between his door and the next

She looked about nine years old and reminded him of Keya. Over the years, whenever he had found himself looking for her, for a glimpse of a blue hair ribbon, he had angrily desisted. He needed no ahn for company, nor anyone else. Although he remembered a man he had once cared about: the nearest person to a father he'd ever had.

But Rivere had abandoned him. "There are no healers in Oknu Shuld," Nosce had answered in response to his long-ago inquiry. "No saviors. You should have learned this by now."

The ahn was waiting for his reply. Her eyes were sad, but still held the hint of a sparkle, so the bond with her sister must still be intact. He couldn't send her into a room full of drunken ristas.

"No," he said. "I require nothing." A part of himself was proud of that, but another part wondered if it was true.

"By the suckin' voras," a voice drawled, "look who's here."

Teller turned to see a man with curly, reddish-brown hair, who after a moment seemed vaguely familiar. "You don't remember me, do you? I'm Dahran, from Master Keel's orientation class."

"That was a long time ago." And best forgotten.

"Twelve years." Dahran punched him lightly in the arm. "You've put on some muscle since then."

"So have you." In addition to practicing with sword and skora, and doing the heavy work which the Vols made sure filled the time between his assigned studies, he'd continued running up and down the many stairs and through miles of passageways in his free time. It was all, apparently, paying off.

"Come and join us for a drink." Not waiting for an answer, Dahran made his way through the crowd. Teller hesitated, then followed.

The doorway into the ale-room was lined with a metal frame incised with runes, and as he passed through, a shiver rushed through his spirikai. The skora flared in protest, then sank down. This place, prudently enough he supposed, was one of four areas in Oknu Shuld where all Powers were suppressed. He and Dahran threaded their way through the crowded, noisy room to join another rista at a table in the back. The man, thin with pock-marked cheeks, was idly drawing lines with one finger through a puddle of spilled ale. Like Dahran, he wore a heavy gold chain and several bejeweled rings, but also like Dahran, the dagger at his side was no mere orna-ment.

"This is Noz," Dahran said. "'Needles' Noz. We call him that both for his Power and the charming way he interacts with people." He laughed, but the other man didn't. Before him were two mugs, one empty and one almost.

Noz pushed out a chair with his foot for Teller. Dahran sat down and, without looking around, snapped his fingers. An ahn quickly appeared and placed a foaming mug before each of them.

"So you've finally decided to join the rest of us," Noz said, hunching over his mug and staring at Teller. "And with only—let's see—three months and eleven rotas before the Cloaking Ceremony."

"That wasn't my decision." Far from it.

"So where've you been all these years?" Dahran's smile was pleasant enough, but his eyes held a slight amusement as they ran over Teller's plain clothes and rolled-up sleeves.

"We thought you were dead," Noz remarked. He took a long drink of his ale, and then barked out a laugh. "Made into mushroom compost maybe."

Noz couldn't have known, but his jibe hit home. Teller had turned over that compost for months, working alone in one of Autran's farm-chambers. When it was midday outside, enough muddy light filtered down from cracks in the ceiling to allow the crop to grow. He remembered the graveside smell, the sight of tiny pinheads sprouting as if from a decomposing corpse. "I spent most of my time on the first three levels," he said.

"In the mines?" Dahran's lip curled. "Or in morue packing?"

Teller stiffened. Such menial labor, almost always assigned to ahn, had indeed been part of his "education," but these two didn't need to know anything about that. "As prentice to the Vols."

"Prentice to the Vols, eh?" Dahran exchanged a smile with Noz. "Quite a story, Teller-of-Lies."

"That's not my name."

"Oh. Terribly sorry. I heard it was."

"Apology accepted," Teller said, and got the satisfaction of seeing Dahran's face darken.

"Being isolated all these years," Noz remarked, "that must have been hard. Could have affected your mind." He took a drink, and then turned his head toward Teller. "Did it affect your mind, do you think?" He tapped his temple.

Teller kept his face impassive. The memory flashes had increased lately, stalking him like ghostly straks, appearing without warning to rend and tear. He pointed his chin at the array of mugs sitting in front of Noz. "Not as much as that does."

"This stuff?" Noz gave out a loud belch. "Doesn't affect me at all." He drained his mug, wiped the froth from his lips, and snapped his fingers for another.

"So," Dahran asked Teller, "what's Shacad like? I hear Vol Tierce takes care of his pretty boys. Gets them apprenticeships and so forth."

Teller kept his tone mild. "Never met him. It sounds like you know more about him than I do."

Dahran gave him a hard look, but blew a short, contemptuous laugh through his nose. "I've set up a bug-hunt next gong. There's three of us going, but I'm looking for another man."

"I have a lecture next gong."

"Skew it. We all need a little fun."

"Ol' Dahran here always gets us the pretty ones," Noz added. "Bugs like these." He pulled out his dagger and carved the outline of a nude, voluptuous female figure on the table.

The serving ahn, an older woman, came to collect the empty mugs. She saw the figure as she put the mugs on the tray, and her hands trembled slightly, but the other two didn't seem to notice.

Even suppressed as it was, the fire stirred. "Wouldn't it be more of a challenge," Teller said, "if someone with Power was the target, instead of a collared ahn?"

The woman's eyes flicked at and then away from him, and she withdrew.

Dahran looked at him with a lazy smile. "Are you volunteering?"

"He's asking that," Noz said, "because we heard rumors. We heard something about skora." Biting his thumbnail, he raised his eyebrows at Teller.

Teller took a sip of his ale, his first. It was warm and sour, and tasted like something that belonged in the chamber-pot in the corner of his room.

"So," Noz asked, "do you have skora or don't you?"

Teller put his mug down. "What difference does it make?" Long ago he'd learned there was something about skora he should respect. He didn't want to talk about it much or use it unnecessarily. There was something—sacred—about it.

"Well, you see," Dahran said, leaning forward, "it really does. We have this theory, Noz and I. We think what happened in Master Keel's orientation class never involved skora at all."

Teller leaned back in the chair. "You were there. You saw what was involved."

"I *was* there," Dahran agreed, "but all I saw was Flare. You couldn't keep your mouth shut, and Master Keel made an example of you. He tickled you with Lash, and

I don't recall you doing anything after that except roll on the ground and scream like a girl."

Noz guffawed, and Teller felt his face flush. Coming here was a bad idea. He started to get up but Noz put a restraining hand on his arm.

"No need to get huffy," he said. "It takes a while to appreciate ol' Dahrie's sense of humor."

"Tell you what," Dahran said. "Let's go into the passage, and you can show us what you've got. We'd like to see this skora in action, wouldn't we, Noz?"

"If it exists."

"I don't give demonstrations," Teller said.

The slightly amused look in Dahran's eyes shifted into a darker, more dangerous range. "But you really should." He cocked his head toward the other tables, whose occupants were shooting glances at them. "Because all these people have to know the truth. I've got a certain standing here, and the other ristas look up to me. I can't have them being ignorant. They have to be clear about what you are, Teller-of-Lies, and who I am."

Teller put both hands on the table, palms down. "I said that's not my name."

Dahran scraped back his chair and stood up. "I say it is. I say you have no skora at all, and that you're a scathi liar."

"Scathi bug-lover, too," Noz added.

Teller rose.

Others now were craning their necks, and a few in the back jumped up to see better. Two guards pushed forward. "Both of you," one ordered, a hand on her dagger hilt. "Take it outside."

With a sweeping gesture, Dahran extended his arm toward the door. "After you, skora-boy."

Teller led the way out of the ale-chamber, through a

crowd of ristas grinning and elbowing each other. "Take 'im, Dahrie," someone urged.

The skora leaped up as he passed through the door. Eager to see a fight, onlookers rushed out of the ale-chamber and stood in the crowded passage. Teller glanced around. Ahn knelt in nearby niches that they dared not leave, while others, oblivious, scurried on errands. In a battle of three Powers—Noz was already circling around to attack him from behind—some of them were bound to get hurt. And he'd feel it. He'd feel the needles, the fire, and whatever deadly thing that came out of the rista that faced him. He addressed Dahran. "This corridor is full of people who aren't part of this. I'll meet you anywhere and anytime, but alone."

"The time is now, Teller-of-Lies, and the place is here." Dahran stepped back. His eyes lit up as he clasped his hands, extended the forefingers, and pointed them at Teller's ankles.

Something like an icy stream flowed around them. He glanced down and saw nothing, but his ankles quickly became numb. He recognized the symptoms from the *Treatise on Rista Powers.* Skew it. Dahran was using Entumera.

The rista grinned. "It's interesting what this does." He moved the pointing fingers upward, and the numbness traveled to Teller's shins. "Paralyzes everything, including—when I get up there—the vocal cords." Dahran glanced at the crowd at the door, then back at Teller. "Show us this so-called skora while you still have a chance."

The fire rose hot inside his spirikai, barely control-lable. "This doesn't have to be about Power," he said. "It could be about these." He tapped the hilt of his dagger. The Delver, for whatever dark reasons of his own, had taught him certain moves with it, and Teller was eager to try them out.

"Daggers will come later. When I'm through with you. When my friends and I are having our fun. Right now it's all about Power." He raised the numbness further. "Power that will make you totally helpless. Power that will get you stripped and ripped. But there won't be a skewin' thing you can do about it."

Skora flamed behind Teller's eyes, a fire he didn't want to use. "Get away from me," he said. "You'll get burned."

Dahran's eyes glittered. The pointed fingers rose, and so did the numbness. It hovered at Teller's knees and made it hard to keep standing. "I don't think so, Teller-of-scathi-Lies. If you could do it, you'd have done it already."

Noz was edging to Teller's left, trying to get behind him. He was taking deep breaths to summon a swarm of sharp, four-inch needles that would slam into his back.

Dahran's grin spread. He sent the numbness creeping up Teller's thighs.

The fire seethed, eager to sear the man out of existence, to melt his bones into the rock. He could do it. He could kill Dahran as he stood there. Why not? He lived with one murder and could live with another.

Or could he? How many nights had he dreamed of a screaming man with flesh melting off his face? That's how he lived with one murder. Two would drive him closer to the darkness inside himself, and make it easier to kill again. And the fire, the sacred fire, would never be the same.

"Don't do this," he said. "Stop it now."

With a snarl, the rista jerked his hands upward.

Teller's legs crumpled, and he went down. Focusing as narrowly as he had time for, holding back a good chunk of hate, he hurled a flare at Dahran just as a barrage of needles whizzed over his head. People in the hall screamed and ducked into doorways. Dahran cried out and dropped to his knees, the front of his shirt in flames. All around Teller needles bounced harmlessly off the wall. Not having lodged in flesh, they would soon melt away. He glanced down the corridor—no one else appeared to be hurt—then twisted toward Noz, who was already disappearing into the crowd.

Dahran rolled on the stone floor to smother the flames, then stood, his shirt in sooty tatters and his face bright red. Teller tried to get up, but his legs felt like dead slabs of meat.

"I know what you are," the rista growled down at him, "and soon will everyone else. You don't hunt because you're a skewin' bug-lover, and a bug yourself. You belong with them, down at my feet with a collar around your neck. Believe me, Teller-of-Lies, one rota you'll be kneeling in the niche outside my room as my permanent, personal slave."

The fire lunged inside his spirikai, but he kept it leashed. "You'll have to deal with skora first."

"You think that'll be a problem? Look at who's standing and who's at my feet." With a sneer, Dahran strode past him.

Teller pulled himself up, his legs full of pins and needles of returning sensation. Late for the lecture, he endured the instructor's sustained glare as he took a seat in the back.

The next rota, Dahran appeared in the classroom wearing a confident smile and a new shirt. Gossip circulated: Teller-of-Lies had fallen in submission before Dahran's Power, Teller-of-lies was mind-damaged by years of isolation, Teller-of-Lies had been Shacad's boy toy; Teller-of-Lies was no true rista, only some twisted deformity more like an ahn.

The hunt was rescheduled for the next rota, at the third night-gong.

All that rota, Teller tried to ignore the whispers and the sneers, and concentrate on his studies. But the taunts of mind-damage haunted him, for indeed his mental state seemed to be getting worse. He felt eyes watching him in the crowded halls, in the instruction chambers—the cold eyes of ristas, the anguished eyes of ahn, the yellow eyes of rats that looked out at him from the shadows.

As the scheduled time for the ahn-hunt approached, he retreated to his room. He sat at his desk and took up the Delver's latest copy-work. The rock walls seemed to lean closer, like specters looking over his shoulder. Visions surged, flashing like eye-blinks: a pool caressed by willow branches, people chattering in a fire-lit dining room, a shower of red autumn leaves. A flash, and he was six, lying in warm, jade hands, rubbing the corner of his blanket, half-asleep and permeated by love.

The scene collapsed, and he was sitting at his desk again, his heart hammering. Could these possibly be true memories? Did he really sled down a snow-covered hillside or run with other children on top of a wall? Or were these the remembered dreams of a lonely, mind-damaged child? His thoughts seemed to be spinning farther and farther away from reality, from whatever had been, or *was*, the truth.

The anguish in the room suddenly increased. The hunt had begun. It was taking place somewhere in the winding labyrinth of the deserted Section Forty-two, impossible for him to ignore. The effort to maintain the skora barrier dragged at his strength.

He shuffled through the papers on his desk while breathless terror seeped under his door. It was mingled with the distress of the ahn in the passage outside his room and beyond. Mind-linked as they were, they felt everything just as he felt it: the frustrated longing to help one of their own, the fear for themselves as well as for her. Abruptly, he turned away from the desk, pulled out his dagger, and hurled it against the wooden chest. Again and again he impaled the knotholes, but the *thunk* of the blade couldn't drown out the silent cries. There was nothing he could do for her, for any of them.

Feverish, he pulled off his shirt, poured himself a cup of water from the pitcher, and tossed it down. It didn't help. He knew when the ahn was caught, when the hunting party used their various Powers to toy with her. He knew when one after another they took her, when she suffered beneath them, when she was allowed to crawl away, only to be pulled back.

He knew it when she died.

The rota came when Teller's class, along with several others, began their three months of military training. Everyone was marched down to ground level, taken to the large cavern adjacent to the side gates, and lined up for inspection. The air felt warmer down here; the big gates were often opened for deliveries, the comings and goings of patrols, and the passing of garbage-carts on their way to the massive dumps outside. They were closed now, but daylight streamed through the cracks in long, bright lines. This caused most everyone to squint, even Teller who, thanks to the outdoor work he'd done, was more used to it.

Between the odors of the stables and the garbage heaps, a fresh breeze occasionally wandered in. It smelled like summer. He spotted a pair of bluebirds flitting in and out through the crack above the gates. They'd built a nest in a niche high up in the rock wall. A memory tingled.

He'd seen such birds before, under the eaves of a large house. He couldn't have been more than four or five. A feeling he couldn't name swelled in his throat.

Shacad, Vol Tierce, passed slowly before the rows of ristas. He was a big man with tightly curled grey hair, wrists cuffed with steel, and a muscular chest that strained against the laces of his sleeveless leather vest. His fingers were stained a brownish-red, and a sickly whiff emanated from him. His eyes were lit yet glazed, as if he were still mentally engaged in some recent and compelling activity.

He stopped in front of a rista Teller didn't know. "D'you smell me?" he barked.

The man gulped. "No sir."

Shacad backhanded him across the mouth. "Now do you smell me?"

The rista spoke through bloody lips. "Yes sir."

"'Course you do." The Vol resumed his inspection of them. "That's because I've just spent a few gongs in the strisnu." The torture chamber of Oknu Shuld. "Do well the next few months and maybe you can avoid the place." He grinned. "If not, I'll be happy to entertain you there."

The Vol paused and looked at Teller. His ice-blue eyes narrowed. They raked over Teller's body and lingered on his shoulders. Teller looked steadily past the Vol's ear, even as he felt his cheeks heat up. Someone in the row behind him snickered.

Shacad's eyes jumped away, presumably to the culprit, and a slow half-smile pulled at his mouth. Without turning, he addressed the guard behind him. "Escort that young man to my quarters."

The guard moved. Everyone stood perfectly still as the rista, pale and biting his lip, was taken out. Shacad took up a position in front of them.

"Here is an end to scholarship, to fooling with

potions and texts, to swaggering around like half-fledged roosters. In this chamber all Powers are suppressed, and you can't hide behind Blur, or Needles, or Vermin. Here you will learn other skills"—he showed his big, even teeth—"or bleed."

They were ordered to march out, and Teller glanced up at the bluebirds. They were among the last to lay their eggs; so it must be—he frowned, trying to remember the name of the month, and finally did—Sky-path. About three months ago, then, he'd turned eighteen. He left the chamber, conscious of the birds tending their nest, unnoticed, at the very gates of Oknu Shuld.

In the following months, the ristas acquired expertise with the bow, the sword, and close in-fighting with and without weapons. Everyone was expected to take care of their own injuries; anyone who got themselves badly wounded simply disappeared. Side fights on the ristas' own time were ignored. A couple of these began with ristas eager to take Teller on, and ended when the attackers gained a grudging respect for the green dagger and left him alone. Late one rota, however, Dahran and Noz came upon Teller with weapons drawn, wanting to settle an old score. After a while, Noz found pressing business elsewhere, but Dahran and Teller went on for some time until both, panting and bloody and facing an upcoming session of rigorous calisthenics, decided on a draw.

The weeks passed, and Teller found that the long, sweaty hours, the strained muscles and aching cuts and bruises, and the sleep-sessions cut short by simulated attacks drowned out most of the ahn-pain. The skora, however, added some of its own. Suppressed, yet feeling itself almost constantly attacked, it clawed inside his spirikai for release. Even so, he fell into his cot so exhausted at the end of the rota the worst of his nightmares subsided.

When the training was over, and everyone returned to their quarters on the fourth level, only one week remained before the final exam. Teller found it hard to study. After the brief respite, the ahn-pain surged back even stronger than before. Ahn turned their eyes on him, and it was as if they expected him to unearth something long buried, to remember a lesson learned in an ancient language and from another world.

Inevitably, another hunt was scheduled. This time he was determined to escape his awareness of it. Desperation drove him down levels and passageways where rock walls would serve as buffers, and into the deep silence of the Halls of the Goah. He strode there, the skora as a sword in his hand, and the grotesque shadows fled from him like rats.

One goah did not flee. It turned on him, its eyes filled with hunger. Teller welcomed the attack. It was a force he could meet and destroy. His sword lit up the corridor as he sliced the goah into shreds. These turned into wisps of ash, which coiled for a moment in the air, then collapsed and disappeared into the floor.

He stood purged, the inner tension momentarily released. But as he turned to leave, he knew there would be another ahn-hunt and then another, and he couldn't hide from them all.

Passing the black arch, turning his head away from it, he tried to ignore the sound coming from its depths: the rumble of Mochlos' derisive laughter.

CHAPTER 19

SAW

The cage containing his best trained rat at his feet, Autran stood alone in the Node, a tiny room in his laboratorium that he used when his experiments needed a purer, more finely controlled heat source than the sulfuric steam vents in the lowest levels.

An ahn had pushed the great cauldron aside on its track and departed, leaving it to creak and crack into coolness. Clutching one of the chains that opened and closed the metal shutter, he looked up the shaft that extended two levels to the surface. Through the crystal lens high above, he saw a small circle of twilit sky.

"I alone," he muttered, "have harnessed the heat of the day. I alone have concentrated the beam of the sun. Yet as the Prome wanders around in his hooded little world, I still remain Ségun. Where's the fairness in that?" He kicked viciously at the cage, and the rat squealed in alarm.

He paused a moment as a thought occurred to him. "It's been a while—hasn't it, rat?—since Nosce has mentioned skora. I wonder why."

He looked down at the rat and made contact with the furtive, busy little mind. "*The Prome. He reports to the lord. You hear the word skora.*"

A picture formed in his head. He was hiding under a cabinet. He smelled food and watched bare feet only inches away from his quivering nose. A potato peel fell in front of him.

"No!" Autran shouted. He banged on the cage. "Not the scourery! *Skora*. A report on skora!"

The rat's mind blurred in fear, then produced another picture. From a dark corner on the floor, Autran looked up at Nosce's sparse back. The Prome was kneeling to a figure shrouded in mist.

"And the skora?" the spider silk voice asked.

"I regret to report, lord, that there has been little progress since the last time we discussed this matter."

"He is eighteen years old." The voice was so mild it sent a chill down Autran's arms. "Explain this lack of progress."

The Prome shifted on his bony knees. "The Seani caused more mind-damage than we thought; instilled moral weaknesses more deeply than it first appeared. Teller-of-Lies has difficulty controlling the fire. He could not even defend himself in an alehouse brawl. I speak with candor, lord, not seeking to curry favor with unwarranted optimism."

"A session with Vol Tierce may succeed where you have failed."

Nosce's shoulders twitched at the last word, but he did not—wisely, skew him—dispute its use. "As you wish, lord. Torture may indeed break the stubborn will and release a Power for your service. But there is danger in that course. The Seani-born is at present a somewhat brittle vessel, which may be shattered by physical pressure from without."

"I want no damaged goods. I want a fifth Volarach." He lifted his hand, and one by one extended the long, sensitive fingers. "Prome. Ségun. Tierce. Kuat." He slid out the thumb into a fully extended hand. "And now

Cinc." The obsidian eyes gleamed as he pulled the fingers into a tight fist. "To fully grasp my kingship, I must have a Cinc with fire."

Nosce hesitated, then spoke. "Forgive me, great lord; but Teller-of-Lies may not be the best choice for that honor."

The mist stirred dangerously.

"He will make a useful subaltern," Nosce said, "if he passes the required exam. But being named Volarach…"

"The Seani-born will fulfill my destiny. I have seen it."

"He has certain weaknesses that—"

"All my Vols have weaknesses! Ahn are nothing but weakness, yet still they serve me." The lord's voice suddenly became very soft. "Or do you doubt my vision?"

"On the contrary, lord. I bow to your sight." He proceeded to do so, then straightened. "Please bear with me further. There is another pressing matter, regarding Vol Ségun. He seems—I have to say it, much as it pains me—to be unduly interested in the skora's development. He frequently presses me for information on its progress, to the point where—"

Just then a beetle scuttled across the floor, and the rat darted after it. The report came to an abrupt end.

"Skew you!" Autran shouted. His Power struck out with a buzzing sound and, with a spurt of blood, the rat's head slipped off its body. "Now I have to train yet another of your idiot kind."

That scathi, vora-spawned Nosce! He itched to bring Saw against him, to sever the arms from that scrawny body. But whatever he used against the insidious Vol would be reflected back on him. He gazed at the dead rat within the cage and took several calming breaths.

"This is incredible," he muttered. "Our Prome is

trying to deceive the Lord Eyascnu Varo himself. He points the finger at me, while he waits for the skora to be at the peak of its juiciness. Then he'll bite into it." He rubbed his chin. "It's time for me to taste this skora, and see exactly how ripe it is."

But there were difficulties, and he turned his thought to how they might be overcome.

Teller's first class the next rota was more crowded than usual because the guest lecturer was the famous Lady Shavante. After class, as Teller was leaving the instruction hall, Master Keel called him down from the top tier of seats carved into the rock. The teacher had joined a group of foreigners who had taken the places of honor on the lowest tier.

Teller approached warily. Keel had not forgotten the long-ago orientation class and took every opportunity to make sure no one else did either, at least his version of it. From the gleeful light in Keel's eyes, Teller suspected this was to be another of those opportunities.

"The Lady Shavante has requested an introduction," Keel said grudgingly. Meeting her was, apparently, an honor that he'd rather not see Teller receive.

Probably in her early thirties, the Lady wore a diaphanous garment gathered high under her breasts, and a silver band circled a wealth of tight black ringlets. She carried herself with regal assurance, and her skin was as flawless as a rare and polished wood.

Keel turned to her. "This is Teller-of-Lies."

The lady raised her carefully plucked eyebrows. "So," she said with an arch smile at Teller, "we may not be believing a word you say?"

"What you believe, Lady, is up to you. My name is Teller."

Keel guffawed. "Who lies."

The lady ignored him. "I am hearing the rumor about you," she said, "and am wishing to meet you. Perhaps we learn from each other, no?"

Keel hooked his thumbs in his belt. "I doubt that, Lady. Rumors are rumors, but the fact is your Power is unique here."

"Perhaps," she murmured, looking at Teller from under her lashes, "a small duel might clarify what is being the rumor and what is being the fact?"

Her manner and appearance belied the warrior's mind that was said to lay within, and uneasiness twitched inside Teller. He searched for some excuse, but Shavante looked deeply into his eyes.

Consort to Lord Namakis of Aramjat and a woman of shrewd intelligence, she had come to Oknu Shuld a year ago to work with Vol Tierce to develop her design for a war engine of great destructive power. The Scorpion, as it was called, now stood almost complete in a cavern near the side gate. Its solid arm was able to fling heavy missiles great distances, to smash walls and ramparts, yet its inventor, Teller now saw, was feminine to the core.

By god, he was in the presence of a warrior queen, beautiful and perilous. Why hadn't he recognized that during the lecture? And now, from among all the rista students, she had noticed him. She wasn't hiding the interest in her slightly slanted eyes, and his own interest rose.

But it should not. He wasn't on her level. She was a queen, and he was nothing. He was unworthy even to stand here and gape at her, yet he couldn't tear his eyes away. He wanted—no, he *needed*—to serve her, even give his life for her. He was about to kneel before her, implore that she take him into her retinue, when a corner of her full-lipped mouth lifted in a small, disdainful smile.

The spell broke. She'd almost humiliated him in front of them all, almost ensnared him with the Power of Command. The skora, if it had been a strak, would be growling deep in its throat. Teller kept it leashed, and though it remained invisible to the others, he knew Shavante saw it.

She coolly appraised its strength, but then her gaze sharpened. She began following the fire down to its roots—where she would see his greatest weakness. She would know that he felt the ahn-pain. He raised the skora to block her scrutiny.

"Is there something amiss, Lady?" Keel asked.

Her eyes glowed, as if reflecting the flames. Although dangerous, she was a desirable woman, and on its own volition his body stirred in recognition of that fact. She looked up at him, and her lips curved into a slow, inviting smile. "He burns," she said.

Shavante turned and gestured imperiously towards the door. Everyone filed out, he and the lady last. She put a restraining hand on his arm. "It is not many who are withstanding my Command. That is interesting to me. You will come to my room at fifth night-gong, and we will have our little duel." With a sidelong glance at him, she swept out of the chamber.

He let out a breath he didn't realize he'd been holding. Shavante had barely disappeared down the corridor when an ahn plucked at his sleeve. Volarach Nosce requested his presence.

Teller made his way to the Prome's instruction chamber and joined the Vol at the small mosaic-topped table. The Prome spoke, but Teller was still too shaken to pay much attention. He stared at the tabletop, at the skull-shadows that underlay the three young women's faces. Death lurked under beauty there—very like the

Lady of Aramjat. As Nosce went on, the skulls seemed to emerge, to become more sharply defined, as if they warned him of approaching danger.

"Did you hear what I said?" Nosce demanded.

He started. "What?"

"Look at me."

Teller raised his eyes to the hood.

"Tomorrow you will conduct the Welcoming Ceremony. Tomorrow you will accept your first group of ahn from their parents and lead them into Oknu Shuld."

The rasped words dropped like shards of ice into his stomach.

No. He couldn't do it. He couldn't bring children here, where slave-collars would be fastened around their necks, where they'd be treated like bugs, where their niyalahn bond would be broken and they'd be cut in half. He couldn't bring yet more anguish into Oknu Shuld. With effort, he kept his voice steady. "Get someone else. I have required reading to finish."

Nosce sat back and the hood regarded him. "The lord seeks a fifth Volarach. Did you know that?"

The abrupt change of subject made him wary. "No."

"A Cinc would complete his hand—and make it stronger with skora."

It took a moment for Nosce's implications to sink in. "What do you mean?" he asked sharply.

"I have been speaking to you about the Welcoming. You seem reluctant to conduct it."

In spite of his pounding heart, Teller managed to shrug. "It's as I said. The Cloaking Ceremony is only three rotas from now. All my instructors pile on the work before the final exam."

The black hood radiated intensity. "Consider this a

part of your final exam. Another requirement for the red cloak." The Vol flicked a finger at him. "Now go."

Teller returned through crowded halls to his chamber. There he paced back and forth, barely noticing the comings and goings outside his closed door.

The Welcoming was a monstrous lie. Taking part in it would make him a teller-of-lies. He remembered Keya, proudly telling him she would never do anything to make her collar hurt. He remembered a little boy, his ridged front teeth just beginning to come in, choking at the feet of a glaring rista while the collar tightened around his neck.

The room was getting hot, and he pulled off his shirt. He didn't have the power to change anything here. The collars were necessary to maintain order. He'd even helped make them.

And Nosce had made a point of telling him about the lord's search for a Vol Cinc. A part of him savored the taste of the title. Ristas who despised him, who called him mind-damaged, would have to bow to Vol Cinc. Dahran would be forced to his knees. The Vols, who had rubbed his nose in the bitter truth about his past and called him Teller-of-Lies, would have to make room for him in their ranks. The Seani cowards who had tried to drown him, who pushed him out of their filthy little nest, would go down in flames before him.

The night-gong rang, and for an instant it reminded him of another, deeper sound that had once reverberated in his dreams. It called to something inside him, to something he'd always known was there, to something he must accomplish. He fingered the hilt of green dagger at his belt. Vol Cinc could accomplish much. His fire could sear away the rebels that threatened Shunder, could destroy the vora-infested Riftwood, could even, in many small ways, relieve the suffering of the ahn, along with his own constant awareness of it.

He remembered Keel's long-ago words: *"You are superior beings and must fulfill your potential. Any questions?"* He would be a fool to question that potential, to deny that destiny. Even the ahn recognized it in him.

Someone knocked on his door.

"Ah," the Ségun said when Teller opened it. "You're still up. No doubt going over the rite of Welcoming for tomorrow. Nosce has informed me that you seemed tense." He flashed an oily smile. "I have the perfect remedy." Stepping aside, he revealed a female ahn standing behind him, her head bowed.

She was about his own age. Her thin tunic barely reached her thighs, and it was obvious that she wore nothing underneath. Autran pushed the girl inside and shut the door behind them. He pulled off her hair ribbon, and a cascade of loose. dark curls fell about her shoulders. A deep flush crept up her cheeks.

Like some great wave, Teller's emotional turmoil over the Welcoming receded, only to sweep back as another wave, hot and intense. This ahn was beautiful, brought here expressly for him, and for only one reason. Desire, already stirred up by Shavante, streaked through him, hung heavy on him. Suddenly she looked up, and her eyes widened in horror at something over his right shoulder. He whirled.

Autran loomed over him, but not as he had appeared moments ago. Taller than Teller, an insect form had taken over the Vol's body, which appeared like a misty shadow within it. Glassy red eyes bulged at the top of a long, locust-like face. Antennae waved and chitinous jaws clacked. The creature was armored with bronze scales and equipped with three pairs of angular saw-toothed legs. The top two, viciously barbed, ended in corkscrew claws.

He was facing the Power of Saw.

Teller backed away, pulling out his dagger, trying frantically to shove the skora barrier into the form of a fiery sword; but with a *churring* sound, the creature lunged. Dodging away, Teller banged into a chair, but managed to kick it into the creature's path. Its saw-toothed arms vibrated; splinters flew as the bronze horror reduced the chair to kindling. The middle legs reached for him and Teller raked them back with his dagger. One of its forearms jittered toward his wrist, but the skora barrier flared up to deflect it. Without the fire, he would have lost a hand.

A second pair of arms grabbed him around the shoulders, and the notches dug in. Pain knifed through him and he dropped the dagger, but managed to send out a sputtering skora flare that released him. He bent to sweep up his dagger, but with blurring speed the top two claws shifted, pinned his arms down and dragged him against the insect body. Its scales scraped against his bare chest and the fire inside him guttered like a candle in the wind. One of the middle legs grabbed his thighs, and the jagged edge of the other reached around to position itself against his spine.

The Vol was going to cut him in half.

Clenching his teeth, Teller attempted to reignite the flames with an icy resolve. The two Powers strained against each other. The Vol's blank, globular eyes shifted to look down at him, and the sound of its churring increased. It drilled into his ears, screwed into his brain. He felt the vibration of the deadly leg inch closer to his back.

He concentrated on the fire, on taking the breaths that would build it into another flare, but his head was being battered from the inside, and the top two claws were squeezing the air out of his lungs. The creature's alien face filled his vision. Inches away, a small eye in its forehead glittered like a marble. Teller's sight, like a sheet of paper tossed into the hearth, darkened at the edges. Consciousness began to slip away, and he felt the edge of a cold, saw-toothed leg touch his spine.

Suddenly the eye flicked aside, as if the Ségun had heard something in the hall. The terrible buzzing subsided; the Vol's Power released him. Teller tottered back, grabbed the edge of the desk, and took several deep breaths. He glanced at the ahn, who was huddled in a corner. She seemed terrified, but unhurt.

Appearing normal now and panting a little—a very little—the Vol stared at Teller, and for a moment the locust-face still looked out. Then his whole demeanor changed and he gave a short laugh. "Very good," Autran said. "You do have a few flames after all. Forgive me if my little test almost snuffed them out." He made circles in the air with his hand. "Perfect and strengthen them for the lord's service."

Teller reached back to feel his waist, but his hand came away unbloodied. "Another invasive instruction?" He gasped between breaths. His ears were ringing, and he could hardly hear himself talk. His chest, where it had abraded against the creature's tough scales, felt as if it had been gnawed by rats.

"An apt description, rista. A fine turn of phrase." Smiling, Autran glanced at the ahn, and then at Teller. "Enjoy your evening, Teller-of-Lies. Bring in some good ones at the Welcoming tomorrow. Pretty little bugs, like her." With one last grin at them, he left the room and quietly shut the door.

Shirtless, hot, and still holding onto the desk, Teller shouted after him, "That's not my name."

CHAPTER 20

POWER SURGE

Outside the room, Autran's grin abruptly disappeared.
His eyes searched the passage, but saw no one except ahn
kneeling silently in their niches. Who'd been spying on
him? A volghast? A chill rushed down his back. But no;
what he'd felt had been alive. Another Vol? He stalked
through the halls, putting forth his awareness, barely
noticing the bows and scrapings of those few he passed,
but felt no wisp of that kind of Power.

His fear turned to anger. That scathi, vora-spawned
ahn! If she hadn't given him away, he would have seized
the skora while Teller-of-Lies' back was turned. He
would be walking with it now in his hand, not caring
who'd seen him take it. She would pay for that. His anger
simmered as he thought of the many slow, exquisite ways
he would extract the price, then rose to a boil when he
remembered Nosce's treachery.

It was exactly as he suspected. In his report to the lord,
the Prome had been lying through his teeth. If he had
teeth. Yes, Teller-of-Lies had been struggling, but the
skora was no tenuous flame, easily pulled out. It was a
deeply rooted and powerful fire that licked at the edge of
its apex. Quite soon now, no one would have the strength
to seize it, except maybe the lord himself.

But it was being watched.

He climbed the polished marble steps to the third level. Things were getting complicated, and he was running out of time. Skora glowed in his mind like a treasure surrounded by invisible pits.

When he entered the Node, he was irritated to find the Delver there. In the guise of a green-eyed young man, the Kuat sat at the worktable, idly skimming through the ancient pages of the *Tajemkrew*. Why a shape-shifter was interested in *Regarding Blood*, which listed potions and spells that affected mental and bodily functions, Autran couldn't imagine. The vol-ring seemed to rest lightly on the Delver's finger, and it was rumored that he, alone of all the Vols, could take it off without harm.

"I assume," Autran said immediately, "that you detected the Power surge on the fourth level. It happened a few minutes ago."

"Power surge?" the Kuat said, turning a page.

Autran took his ceramic mug from the cluttered shelf and scooped hot water into it from the cauldron. "The Seani-born you brought here grows arrogant and attacked me when my back was turned. To impress an ahn, I believe." He blew a short laugh through his nose. "He won't do *that* again."

The Kuat looked up. "The nights are getting longer," he said. "That must frighten you."

"What are you talking about? Nothing frightens me."

"The hand of the lord hovers over you. He wants abakal."

Autran drew a tremulous breath. The Eyascnu was indeed becoming impatient. The new siege engine they called the Scorpion was almost finished, and when loaded with the viciously explosive balls, it would make an invincible weapon. The lord had made it plain at the last Volmeet that he expected Autran to produce abakal, since

Teller-of-Lies, according to that rat Nosce, could not. This inability, Autran had just discovered, was a lie. The skora would soon be more than capable of it, but he dared not let on that he knew that.

To hide his unease, Autran selected a jar on the shelf and brought it and the steaming mug to the worktable. If he ever got hold of the skora, the lord would get his abakal all right, enough to blast him right out of his big pretentious throne. He seated himself across from the Delver. "Don't concern yourself, Kuat. The lord will be pleased at my latest developments. I have, for instance, produced a far more potent arrow-tip poison than we have ever seen."

The Delver continued his perusal of the book. "More poison."

"It was ineerva."

The Delver glanced at him, then back at the page.

Autran spooned dried leaves from the jar into his mug. "I still have plenty of hours of sunlight to work with. Especially since a second lens is being brought here from Trey Aughter even as we speak. After it's installed, I'll be able to concentrate the beam even more. This shaft will be like a forge of light, stronger than any sputtering skora that may have been dragged in here. With it, I will produce all the abakal the lord could want." At least he hoped he could.

The Delver folded his arms and sat back in the chair. "I bring bad news, then. Your men returning from Trey Aughter were set upon by falconforms. The crystal was shattered."

The statement hit him like a rock. Autran managed to produce a careless shrug. "Shacad must do something about these falconforms," he remarked. "They hang about the cliff lately, pestering my fieldworkers. As to the crystal, I'll order another. And tomorrow I'll begin different work here." He took a sip from his mug to swallow his growing trepidation. The tea, he suddenly realized, needed honey and the jar here was empty. The bug who neglected that duty would be punished.

The Delver grinned nastily at him, and the sight of a young man sporting a row of pointed teeth was decidedly disconcerting. "I have no doubt you are thinking about 'different work,'" the Kuat said. "Perhaps all the Vols are."

Had it been the Delver lurking outside Teller-of-Lies' room? Autran put his mug down and looked at him squarely. "Except you, of course."

The Delver's appearance rapidly degenerated. The green eyes rolled back and flipped into shiny brown beetle wings; his face and hands crawled with fat insects under the skin. He thumped one teeming arm onto the table and cut a small slit into it with a hard, yellow fingernail. A beetle scuttled out and headed toward Autran's mug. "I have no need for fire," the creature said.

Autran brushed the beetle away. "Oh? With the Power of skora one might move up a notch, eh, Vol *Kuat*?" He emphasized the number with a sneer.

"And thus," the Delver said in his hoarse whisper, "Vol *Ségun* speaks." Two more beetles, antennae waving, rushed out of his arm and onto Autran's mug.

Autran jumped up and swept both mug and beetles to the floor. "I've warned you never to appear before me like this. You're disgusting!"

A gummy mouth, now toothless, opened. Beetles vomited out and swarmed across the table.

Autran jumped back and shouted a command: *"Zura, zabika!"*

Three large rats appeared from nowhere and leaped

up on the table. One snapped up several beetles, and the other two, crouched for an attack, eyed the Delver.

The Kuat sprouted a mottled brown pelt. His jaw lengthened, long fangs appeared, and the chair fell over as a full-grown strak, the fur on its humped back bristling, stood on its hind legs with both front paws on the table. The nails, which were still growing, clicked against the wood. The insects and rats all fled, and the strak gazed at Autran with a menacing grin.

Autran's Power had been weakened with his battle with skora, but he whipped out of his pocket a small vial full of orange liquid, flicked off the cork with his thumb, and waved the glass in front of the strak's eyes. The two glared at each other for several heartbeats. Finally, the strak drew back and folded into the brown-cloaked form of the Delver. It leaned toward him, becoming so transparent Autran could see the back of the chair through it. As a black mist, it fell upon the table and poured onto the floor. Autran hastily stepped aside to let it pass.

"You constantly forget," the mist whispered, "that I am other." It swirled around Autran's shoes and flowed out under the door.

Autran filled his cheeks with air and blew it out. He would have to do something, and right now. Someone powerful must seize the skora for him, someone not being watched, someone he could control. And the deed must be done in a place safe from prying eyes.

He turned his mind to his rat-spies.

They had been busy lately, bringing him several interesting vignettes: a jealous teacher with a years-long grudge, Teller-of-Lies' recent foray into the Halls of the Goah, a proud lady waiting for the Seani-born to come to her room at the fifth night-gong. Well, it was already past the sixth, and engaged as he had been with Saw, Teller-of-Lies had no doubt forgotten *that* little tryst.

Then he thought of Mochlos, and his plan fell into place.

CHAPTER 21

LIASIT

Teller kicked remnants of the ruined chair aside and indicated the one still whole. "Sit down," he said to the ahn. His words, harsh with strain, came out less the invitation he intended and more like a barked order. The ahn obeyed. He sank onto the edge of the bed and breathed until the feeling of almost having been cut to pieces ebbed away.

He glanced at the ahn. Her arms were bare. The thin tunic couldn't hide the curve of her breasts or the dark shadow between her legs. Her body would feel soft under his hand, warm and yielding. She came into this room expecting to be used. Ahn, the Vols insisted, were *for* using. He pushed the thought away; she was trembling as much as he was.

Her hands were clenched in her lap, and for the first time he saw that Autran had bound her wrists with a red cord. Because of the collars, that was totally unnecessary and served only to humiliate. Anger prickling, he rose, pulled the dagger from his belt, and stepped to her side.

She gasped and flinched away.

He stopped, realizing that all she saw was a shirtless man coming at her with a dagger. "I'm only going to free your hands," he said. "Hold them out."

Going down on one knee beside her, he quickly

severed the cord, threw it aside, and sheathed the dagger. She took a shuddering breath.

He stood up. "What did you just see happen in this room?"

She looked aside. "Nothing."

"Don't be ridiculous."

She sucked in her lips, whether in reluctance to speak or, the thought crossed his mind, to retain a burst of hysterical laughter. "I saw Volarach Ségun, under a cloak of Power. A flare of—of fire. And you."

"One flare?"

"Maybe two."

It was as he thought. Most of the time he'd been using the interior skora barrier to protect himself, and not the exterior weapon he needed. He'd have to practice more.

In an awkward silence, he found his shirt, put it on, and groped for something to say. This turned out to be: "What season is it?"

Her cheeks flushed, but she didn't look up. "Autumn. Outside it's the month of Harvest."

Autumn. The word brought no images. He sat on the bed. "What's your name?"

"Gnat."

"No. I mean your real name."

For the first time, she looked directly at him, and her dark eyes were as lovely as the rest of her. They searched his face, gazed directly into his eyes, and slowly filled with that expression of hope, of wonder, that so scraped against his spirikai. Then something like a stuttered whisper flickered in his mind. He blinked.

"You heard me," she whispered.

"No." Something…but no. Even as he denied it, unspoken words flowed into his head.

"You heard me! You're hearing me right now."

The mind-speech. She had spoken to him in the mind-speech. He thought it had been lost, cut out long ago by Se Gremes's probe, but he heard it now distinctly. He found himself trying to answer in kind. "How—how can you...?"

"Most ahn can do this. After our bond with our niyals is broken, it grows back, sort of. But only with each other, here in Oknu Shuld. They say it's a gift from Rulve, to make up for our loneliness. We—we thought we were the only ones here that can speak this way."

The awe in her eyes deepened, and that irritated him. "There's nothing special about mind-speaking," he said. "Several people in the Seani can do it."

She bit her lip and was silent for a moment. "The Seani is your home?"

"No!" His own vehemence startled him. "I was born there, but this is my home."

She dropped her eyes. "The Seani is a good place. The people there are healers and teachers."

"So they'd like you to believe."

There was another pause, during which she studied the floor between them. "My real name is Liasit." She stole a look at him. "We know about what you did for Keya."

He remembered the young ahn, the girl with the blue hair ribbon, who'd dared to speak with him when he first arrived in Oknu Shuld. "What's to know? I was just a boy."

A sudden light leaped into her face. "But you remember it! It was twelve years ago, but you know exactly what I'm talking about. You tried—"

A loud thump against the door caused them both to jump to their feet. They heard the sound of scuffling outside, then laughing.

"He's got a bug in there," a drunken voice said.

"Hey, Teller-of-Liesh," an even more inebriated voice called out, "need shom help?"

There was another thump, followed by a giggle, and then the two stumbled on.

Liasit turned to face him. Her cheeks flared again and she crossed her arms in front of her chest. "I didn't want to come here dressed like this. It shames us both. But the Vol ordered it, and—"

"I know," he said. "You don't have to explain." She was shivering in her thin tunic, so he pulled the blanket off his bed. This time she didn't flinch as he came to her. Instead, her luminous eyes met his.

He stepped behind her and settled the blanket around her shoulders; then, before he could stop himself, freed her hair from under it. She turned and leaned toward him, and although she didn't touch him, he wanted her to. He couldn't remember the last time anyone had laid a gentle hand on him, or when he had done the same to someone else. She stood very still as he brushed her cheek with the back of his fingers, then moved them past the curve of her jaw and down to where a pulse beat in her throat. A little further, and his knuckles grazed against cold metal. Her ahn collar.

He jerked his hand away. It was a collar like many he had made. She would never be free of it, never be free to choose him or reject him.

Her hand also went up to the collar, and her eyes, never moving from his, filled with tears. "Have you come at last, niyalahn-rista? To take these away from us?"

The name hit him like an icy dart. "*What* did you call me?"

Her eyes widened and she drew back. "Niyalahn-rista."

He grabbed her arms. "Are you insane? Or do you want me dead?"

"I'm s-sorry," she stammered. "We never speak openly about you, only in the mind-speech, among ourselves."

"I'm not—" His mind blurred and he could finish only by speaking aloud. "I'm not this traitor. Stop accusing me!"

She threw off his hands. "We don't accuse. It is written."

"Where? Where is it written?" But he knew where. He had seen it, on a piece of vellum in the Room of the Skulls.

"I know what they teach here!" she cried. "That the niyal'arists are nothing but blood-sucking voras. That they killed the lord's brother. That in every generation they rise up to threaten our land. It's all a lie! The niyalahn-ristas are sent by Rulve to buy us back, to redeem the ahn. To bring justice and mercy to Shunder."

Justice and mercy? He barked out a laugh. "And you think I'm this paragon? You think such a one can even *exist* in these tunnels?"

"I saw what you did for me. I know what you tried to do for Keya."

He flicked his fingers against her collar. "*This* is what I've done for you. And thanks to Autran, you know damn well what I'm going to do tomorrow: bring in more ahn to a life of degradation. There are no saviors in Oknu Shuld."

Her face set, she gathered his blanket tightly around her and turned toward the door.

"Keya, don't leave me!" Appalled, he just stood there. The mind-speech had betrayed him, had blurted out years of isolation and loss. To cover his humiliation, he spoke roughly. "I didn't give you permission to go, ahn."

Her back to him, she stopped. "In the mind-speech one cannot lie. Deep down, you are hurting."

Angry denial surged through his chest. "Only ahn hurt here, and I'm no ahn!"

"Then—in this language of the heart, in these words that cannot lie—tell me who you are."

"I'm—" Again he found he couldn't finish, couldn't form the words in his mind for what he wanted to say. So he spat them out verbally. "I'm a servant of the Lord of Shunder. I belong to him, body and soul."

She turned to look full at him, her eyes blazing. "If that's who you are, then do what you want with me. That's why I'm here."

In spite of years of slavery, in spite of a hopeless future, she was still defiant. He pushed past her and opened the door. The tunnel in both directions was empty. "Let's go," he said.

Still wearing his blanket, she went to him, and he guided her to the narrow spiral stairway that led down to the isav. In the midst of the pain that spun up from it, he watched her descend until the top of her head disappeared in the gloom. Only once did she look up at him, but the light was too dim to see her expression.

Back in his room, he flung himself on his bed and stared at the globe-light that writhed across the rocky ceiling. She had dared to confront him, to challenge him with a name. In just the last few gongs, an ahn and a Vol had both thrown names at him: Vol Cinc and niyalahn-rista. Names that resonated, that pulled at something inside him—but which were fundamentally, diametrically, opposed.

"Vol Cinc" would rid him of the empathy he never chose and didn't want. "Vol Cinc" would validate the elusive, dimly perceived destiny that clawed at him as powerfully, as consistently, as the pain he felt from the ahn.

The other name was a whisper, creeping up from his past. Niyalahn-rista. Keya had pronounced it, just before he had prayed for the last time. A wave of bitterness washed through him. The ahn would grasp at any name that shored up their hope—any myth, any shred of humanity, anyone who happened to speak their language.

The night-gong tolled twelve: midnight and the end of the rota. He'd have fifteen hours to wait for the Welcoming. The ceremony, it appeared, was not only a requirement for the red cloak, but also a test of his resolve.

Sleep was impossible, so he practiced moving skora from his spirikai directly into his hand as a sword. Normally he was able to bypass the bright bar stage in eight out of ten tries, but that hadn't worked out so well in the face of Saw. He practiced until he was exhausted, but fell into a restless sleep only after a foray to the deserted laboratorium, where he prepared a packet of the carmine powder called morphous and sniffed three or four pinches of it in his room.

CHAPTER 22

THE WELCOMING

He woke late the next rota, groggy from morphous but with tension still slivering through his veins. He forced himself to take his usual run through the tunnels, then went down to the baths. He left them still feeling dirty inside. He tried to finish reading the lord's autobiography, the *L'garza Wadek*, but instead heard every gong. Time passed at first agonizingly slowly and then too fast. He jumped when someone knocked on his door. The deep gong was ringing five as he opened it.

"We must get this Welcoming done," the subaltern said, "before dinner is served."

He hurried Teller up to the Chamber of Ledgers on the third level, where the records of Oknu Shuld were kept. The room smelled of musty leather and ink. He and the subaltern, the maroon band at the hem of his cloak marking him a Sekrew Bloodknot, passed through the room and into another chamber that contained boxes of rope sandals and piles of grey-worn tunics and pants. This was the first stop for those being Welcomed this rota, where everything would be taken away from them and where they would, for the first time, put on the garb of an ahn.

At the guard-station, the subaltern was given two

hooded cloaks. "How long since you've been outside?" the subaltern asked.

Teller shrugged. "A while."

The Bloodknot handed him a cloak. "Make sure the hood covers your eyes until you get used to the light."

The two were ushered towards an oak door with long brass hinges and an arched top, which one of the guards pulled open. Even though he'd been outside probably more often than most, Teller still squinted against the sudden glare. Someone pushed him forward into a smaller room, and the door thudded shut behind them. Light poured through two narrow openings that flanked a second door opposite the one they had entered. The subaltern unlocked the outer door, and they stepped outside.

Teller jerked the hood over his eyes. For a moment he saw nothing but pin-pricks of light coming through the woven fabric. Then he looked down and noticed his pants. They were a dark forest green. In the worm-light of Oknu Shuld, they had appeared black. A thought came and was pushed aside: *What else have I misperceived in the dark?*

Fresh air wafted against him, carrying the faint tang of autumn leaves mingled with the hint of new-mown hay. He threw back his hood and looked up, blinking, at the over-arching sky.

A few high cloud-wisps glowed a rosy gold from a sun that had already disappeared behind the western uplands, and an arrow of geese was making its squawking way south. He was standing on a high portico, hundreds of feet up, behind a waist-high balustrade. It was a soft fall evening. The dusky shadow of the cliff lay beneath him, dimming the reds and golds of the trees and spreading twilight into the Eeron Valley. A river meandered to where lights clustered at its far bank: the village of Rydle. His gaze lingered there, and he imagined lamp-lit windows and families having dinner together. From somewhere below bubbled up the dusk song of a sleepy robin.

He transferred his gaze to the opposite hillside and searched for more tiny lights. He found them, almost hidden but twinkling faintly among the trees. A breeze fingered his hair and tugged at his cloak as he gazed at them. The Seani.

A memory jumped before his eyes: he was a little boy looking at a map. It hung above a stone fireplace and was drawn in faded blues, greens, and browns on parchment that had turned a dusty ochre with age. Against a background of dark green forest, the map showed the Seani's seven pools, its two creeks, and the Red Lantern Way indicated by a dotted red line. A brown path led to the cow field, where three tiny cows had been drawn. He'd always liked those cows. The pools, too. Some were refreshingly cool on a hot summer's day, and others were so warm that even in winter you could soak in them and watch steam rise from your bare arms.

In one of those pools, they had tried to drown him.

He jerked his gaze away and looked straight down where a stone-paved road, deep in shadow now, wound around the base of Oknu Shuld. To his left, he could see the great entry-porch, with its stairways on opposite sides and its cadre of Vorian Guards, looking foreshortened and tiny from this height.

Suddenly aware of the huge bulk of Oknu Shuld at his back, he turned to look up. It was as if the stronghold did not exist, as if its façade of great stone blocks, many levels and vast halls had disappeared. All he could see was a wall of ivy, moving in waves with the breeze. He bent his head back; the very top of the cliff shone gold in the last of the daylight. Above that, but invisible from here, stretched acre upon acre of morue fields.

The door behind him slammed, and two Sekrew guards, wearing maroon quilted doublets, joined them on the balcony. The subaltern led the group to the right, where a path curved along the edge of the cliff. They passed a narrow stair that was cut into the rock and led up to the plateau, turned to descend a few moss-edged steps, and proceeded through a patio where dead weeds poked through cracks in the flagstones. Guards opened a gate at the far end, and they entered a grassy clearing from which a trail led down to a long series of steps that eventually joined the road to Rydle Bridge.

In the center of the clearing lay the Eye of Welcoming, a flat, slightly concave stone about three strides across. It glittered with minute quartz crystals in white granite, but a pupil of dead black basalt stared out from the center. A few fallen leaves, grey in the twilight, scuttered around the bowl in a brief wind. On the far side stood a small group of adults and children looking up at him, their faces pale in the fading light.

Shifting her weight from one foot to the other and stretching her back against the grinding pain, one of the women squinted at the young man coming down the path. She sniffed. The famous rista wasn't wearing a red cloak; he wasn't even a subaltern. He was comely enough though, tall and with tousled black hair, but what kinda person would call hisself Teller-of-Lies? As he came closer, she noticed he looked sick, or lacked sleep maybe, for there were dark smudges under his eyes and grooves around his mouth.

The pain in her back shot down her right leg. A very bad sign, and she'd run out of morue yesterday. The field

227

man was already frowning at how stiffly she moved, maybe even heard the groans she tried to stifle at the constant bending. He didn't say nothing yet; a portion of her meager store of morue kept him quiet for now.

She hated the purple, hated what it did to her, but it got her to work, didn't it? Without morue to take away the pain, how could she support her children and her sister's?

Just a few minutes more, she told herself. In just a few minutes this Welcoming will be over and she'd have a nice thick package of purple in her hands.

Her ahn-niece, staring at the young man coming down the slope, leaned over and whispered. "He's got broad shoulders, don't he, auntie?"

"Don't you go lookin'. Men're all pricks and yer barely twelve."

"But I ain't blind."

"You just be careful in there, hear? Any man gives you trouble, you report it right away to the matron in charge."

The girl wasn't paying her any mind and still stared. "Ran away from the Seani, they said, when he were just a boy."

"That don't say much for the Se now, does it? Comin' around with promises to help but with no purple in sight."

The man standing next to her craned his neck to see Teller-of-Lies approach. His eyes, feeling as raw and red as his hands, burned from the fumes at work, and all he wanted to do was flop down on the grass and sleep. On the way up here he'd chewed the last of his purple. Taken too much, he did, and that was makin' him feel like a wet rag. He shouldn't have done it, because as soon as this Welcomin' was over, he'd have to look sharp and get back to the tannery. Normally he'd save half a chew for the night, when it would dull the pain in his hands and allow him to get some sleep. But, just for tonight, he could have a full one. Or maybe a little more. After this Welcomin' he didn't have to stint himself, did he? He peered anxiously where the guards were standin' and saw, to his relief, the waitin' packets piled on the ground.

He rubbed his eyes on his sleeve. Maybe if he went to the alehouse and told the owner he'd met this famous rista, he'd get a few hours of employment there after the tannery closed. People who'd be celebratin' the Welcomin' liked to hear about up-and-comers. Maybe he'd get even more hours the day after tomorrow, when half the subalterns and most of the ristas came down after the Cloakin' Ceremony to drink and carouse. Then he might be able to earn enough dinars to pay Undiga for some salve for his hands. He glanced longingly at the morue packets again. Two chews tonight, no more.

He clapped an arm over the shoulder of the ahn-boy standing stiffly at his side. He'd been lucky to get custody of a second niyalahn pair. That way you got both another worker at home and a free purple packet for handin' over the ahn. "Look, lad," he said. "An up-and-comer is presidin' at your Welcomin'. That prolly means you'll be assigned the more important duties. You pay attention now when they teach you your letters."

They'd all been instructed as to what would happen during the ceremony. Bow to the rista in charge and nudge their ahn forward to kneel before him. The official would utter the words of Welcoming to each one, and the subaltern would make the appropriate notations in the ledger. Then the chosen ones would rise and follow the rista up the path.

Parents or guardians were allowed to watch as their ahn marched in procession to their life of service, and if some of the adults shed tears of pride, that was to be expected. They were warned that a few of the younger children sometimes looked back at the turn of the cliff. If that happened, smile and wave. When the children disappeared around the curve, the subaltern would award the morue packets, and everyone would go down the trail and back to work.

They returned to their lives with the blessings of the Lord Eyascnu Varo, and, for a few, with a squirming, steadfastly ignored sense of helplessness and shame.

The Welcoming was agony for Teller. The niyalahn bond was intact in the six chosen children who looked up at him, but they—and he—would soon know the pain its severance would bring. The entire ceremony from beginning to end was a blatant lie. Everything he said, every word of Welcoming, every gesture, denied the hideous truth. He could tell by how they looked at their ahn which of the adults were parents or relatives and which merely collected orphans. He couldn't meet the gaze of an anxious mother who licked her thumb and wiped a smudge from her son's cheek. He couldn't look at the father whose hand lay lightly on his ahn-daughter's shoulder, but squeezed it once just before she stepped forward. A niyal passed a worn rag doll to her sister in parting, and Teller averted his eyes. In only moments, when the gate was shut behind them and their loved ones gone forever, the doll would be tossed into a trunk, and the lid banged down on it.

The last child to kneel before Teller looked to be only five or six years old. He smiled uncertainly, then wiped his runny nose on his sleeve. The sight of him brought a lump into Teller's throat. "He's too young," he said to the father. "A boy this age belongs at home."

The man looked at him in startled dismay. "But—but, sir, he is ready! My wife here made him a new outfit just for this occasion."

"Check the ledger," Teller said to the subaltern.

The officer moved his finger along a line in his book. "There's been no mistake. He's right here: Aron, son of Samir, from Baenfeld. To report at age six." He looked at the couple standing at Aron's side and addressed the man. "Are you Samir? Do you verify our records are correct?"

"Yes, of course," the man said nervously.

The guards, who had been standing about obviously bored, now looked alert and closed in. The subaltern leaned toward Teller and whispered in his ear. "What's wrong with you? You're upsetting them. Even infants in arms are sometimes Welcomed here."

Infants? He had never seen or heard of babies in Oknu Shuld. But once, in the laboratorium, he had glimpsed a special cupboard that contained jars of—his stomach lurched—small preserved hearts and tiny livers. At the time, he had believed they were those of young animals.

The Bloodknot addressed the group of adults. "This young rista is overwhelmed at the honor given to Samir and his family. Not every child of this tender age is deemed worthy. I will say the final oration in his stead." Glancing at Teller with disapproval, the subaltern finished the ceremony.

While the guards were getting the children into line, Aron's mother stepped forward and gave Teller an awkward curtsey. "Sir, our boy has the sniffles," she said. "Nuthin' to prevent him from his work an' that. But will you make sure he gets some thamar tea 'afore bedtime, and—and maybe an extra blanket?" Her eyes, full of trust, implored him.

The Bloodknot subaltern stepped forward. "Don't you worry about him, goodwife. We take good care of the little ones."

Teller turned abruptly away, and looking straight ahead, walked beside the children going up the path. Part way up the slope, a hot little hand was slipped into his. It was Aron's. He carried over his shoulder the pathetic bag of clothing he would never get to wear and was looking back at his parents. Teller snatched his hand away and strode quickly through the gate.

He couldn't eat the supper brought to his room, but paced instead. The memory of that little hand in his wouldn't go away, and it drove him into the hallway where he strode unseeing, until the increasing ahn-pain made him realize he was making his way toward one of the spiral stairs that led to the isav. He hesitated, then went down.

The oily face of the proctor peered at him from the wide archway of the entrance. "May I help you, sir?"

He'd raised the skora barrier so high he could hardly see. "Not two gongs ago I Welcomed a young boy, Aron of Baenfeld. Bring him out to me."

"None of that group is collared yet." The proctor bowed with an obsequious smile. "Tomorrow, sir, he will be ready for your pleasure."

The anguish of the ahn was somehow getting through, clawing inside his abdomen, spreading over his skin in a prickly wave of heat. He grabbed the front of the proctor's shirt. "Now. Forget about the collar."

"There are other young boys here," the proctor said in alarm. "Let me find you one."

Teller shouldered past him and entered the male sleeping chamber. Something hanging from the ceiling brushed over his hair. Leather gloves? But no—the smell. What…? Ah god, they were hands. Lopped off for some infraction and now dried.

He jerked away and stumbled over a man on the ground who recoiled with a startled cry. Row after row of mats stretched as far as he could see in the dark. Pain washed over him in hot, red waves, and he waded through it, searching for one small boy who had the sniffles. "Aron!" he called out blindly. "Aron!"

Startled faces rose up. He thought he recognized them from their niyals in the Seani—one, then another, more faces, all wounded, all doomed. Their eyes pleaded to be saved; mind-words clamored inside his head: *"Oh Rulve, it's him! Niyalahn-rista! Here, here! It's him!"* Their fingers plucked at him, hands grasped him from every side. He turned, struggled to push through them, but was lost among them with no way out.

Guards shoved them aside and dragged him through the archway. "Here's a rista who cannot wait!" one of them said with a chuckle. He returned the green dagger to him, hilt first; Teller had no memory of pulling it on the man. "Go back to the aleroom, sir," someone said. "Or better, to your bed to sleep it off. You have a big rota tomorrow—your last lecture and the final exam."

Laughing, they hustled him back to the comparative silence of his room and left him. He sat for a long time on the edge of his bed, his head in his hands. There were too many of them, too needy. He could do nothing for any of them, nothing except feel how they hurt.

He remembered what the guard had said: the final exam was only gongs ahead. His instructors had refused to talk about it, and for rotas he had dismissed any thought of it. Now it sat like a vulture beside him on the bed.

#

The next rota, Teller, along with Noz, Dahran, and three other students from Teller's original class, were asked to stay after their last lecture. The rest of the students passed out of the tiered chamber, giving them envious looks.

Master Keel addressed them. "Your instruction has now come to an end. You have been chosen as candidates for officer training in one of the lord's three army divisions. The Cloaking Ceremony, your graduation to subaltern-ship, is scheduled for tomorrow." He surveyed them, rocking on his heels. "There remains, however, your final exam."

Everyone grew still.

"The lord wishes proof that you are ready to lead, ready to enter the realm of moral superiority. He wishes to be convinced that your skills have been honed into a sharp, competitive edge. Therefore, in two gongs, all of you will report to Section 22 on the second level."

Section 22 sounded vaguely familiar to Teller—as a boy, Autran had sent him there a few times to collect cave-beetles—but by the looks on everyone's faces, the others had never heard of it.

Noz spoke up. "They say this exam is basically an ahn-hunt."

Keel showed his teeth. "Basically, you are correct. Four ahn will be released into that section with orders to disperse. Each of you must choose one of six tunnels, and if it contains an ahn, find and kill it."

Teller froze. The others breathed out sighs of relief. They already knew all about hunting ahn.

A square-jawed girl with a long braid, however, frowned. "What happens if you fail?" she asked.

Master Keel grinned and rocked from toes to heels. "Good question, missy." He looked around at the others.

"You will be escorted to the strisnu, where you will assist Vol Tierce in his studies. Apparently there are gaps in our knowledge regarding the limits of human endurance to pain and at what point in the dying process a Power no longer functions." His grin grew wider. "A more challenging endeavor than you thought, eh? Further instructions will be given to you in two gongs." With a chuckle, he strode out of the room. The others now looked worried and headed toward the ale-room.

Teller, his stomach roiling, sought the intense silence of the room of skulls. He sat at the ink-stained table and pulled forward another vellum sheet that the Kuat had left for him. His first experience with the ancient pages taught him to avoid translating the words to himself and only do what he'd been told: copy the Widjar letters. He tried to keep his hand from shaking. The point of his quill scratched over his paper, raising letters of black blood. The eyeless gaze of the skulls crept over him. He could move his chair and sit with his back to them, refuse to face them, but what he'd feel across the back of his neck would be even worse.

As he worked, Liasit's face seemed to float over the page, replaced by a look of unspoken accusation in Aron's eyes. Teller blinked them away, focused on what he was doing. Despite his efforts, meaning leaped out of the words that had flowed out of his quill: *"Living the dead surrounding."*

He threw the quill down and stared at the globe next to his right hand, at the writhing worms that constantly sought a way out. He couldn't escape Section 22, couldn't escape the choice that faced him. He must decide whether to pass the final exam or fail it.

He must decide if he or an ahn were better off dead.

Chapter 23

Final Exam

Teller waited with Dahran, Noz, and the three other ristas in front of the iron door to Section 22. The door, flaking with rust, blocked the tunnels of an abandoned, played-out silver mine. Autran once told him that the ahn who used to work here were blinded, all the better to feel the tiny barbs of the silver vein against their fingertips. To the right of the door, a slotted holder held six hand-globes; on a small table below it stood an hour-glass.

Dahran, hands in his pockets, lounged opposite the door with his back against the wall; Noz cleaned his fingernails with the point of his dagger. The other three engaged in a low conversation. The skora jittered inside Teller, and his mouth was dry. The smell of someone's sour sweat hung over them all.

At last the iron door opened and Master Keel and Lady Shavante, holding hand-globes, emerged.

They placed their globes in the holder, then Keel looked from one to the other of them. "Some background information before we begin. None of you know these tunnels, but the ahn inside do. They can find any number of ratholes in which to hide, and their collars have been altered to allow them to ignore any command designed to flush them out." He gestured to Shavante.

"This is being the individual exam," she said. "You

are used to the hunting in groups, but here each rista is acting alone in the tunnel of choice."

"Master Keel told us," one of the ristas said, "that four ahn will be released into six tunnels. What if your tunnel doesn't contain an ahn?"

"We advise," Keel said, "that you figure that out as soon as possible. Then choose another tunnel."

"But another rista will already be in there."

"Exactly."

"That's not fair!"

Keel flashed a grin at them. "It's *not* fair. It's the final exam. What your classmate has so cleverly figured out is that it may become necessary to eliminate a fellow student in order to pass the exam. But I'd be cautious if I were you. If a target ahn was indeed located in your tunnel, and you decided to enter another, you will fail. Any one of you who does not kill an ahn will fail. Those who accomplish their task will receive a red cloak banded with the color of the division to which they will be assigned. Myself and Lady Shavante will monitor the exam. Are there any questions?"

No one spoke.

"Very well then," Lady Shavante said. She turned over the hour-glass. "The bugs are dispersed. You are having one hour."

Looking tense, each rista seized a hand-globe and ducked through the door to Section 22. It opened onto a gritty-floored cave from which several tunnels branched. A few of the students hesitated, glancing at the others. Teller headed for a tunnel but Noz jostled him aside and strode down it. Almost immediately his light and everyone else's disappeared. Teller wiped a sweaty hand on his pants and took the only tunnel remaining, the one on the far left.

The worms inside his hand-globe were fat and bright, allowing him to see several feet ahead. Most of the rock was a nondescript grey, washed in places with tinges of pale yellow or charcoal. A few white spider veins glimmered in the light, traces of ore too thin to be worth the trouble of hacking it out. He walked, shining the globe at the rock walls, the uneven floor, and the low ceiling.

Even though he'd been here before, that had been long ago, and nothing now looked familiar. Any ahn hiding in this tunnel would be terrified, would know that his or her life was unraveling. With this thought came a dim wisp of pain, so faint it could have made its way through the grates from somewhere else.

Perhaps from another tunnel.

He raised the skora barrier so he wouldn't feel anything, wouldn't have to decide if he could use the bond he had with the ahn to hunt one of them down.

He made his way forward, ducking his head when the ceiling lowered or inspecting side passages that soon petered out. He found a storeroom littered with rusted picks and shovels and an empty mining cart with a broken wheel.

As he walked, a door emerged out of the dark at his left and into his circle of light. He pushed against it, but something heavy on the other side prevented it from opening more than a few inches. A desperate old man, hoping to postpone the inevitable? A terrified young girl?

He could pass by without finding out, or he could sink down on this side of the door and wait for the test to be over.

Death was a black lure. It floated in twilit water, promising peace.

But it lied. Death at the hands of Shacad would have nothing to do with peace.

Taking a shaky breath, he shoved the door open and shone the light inside. A chunk of ceiling had fallen against the door, probably in some long-ago earthquake. In the crawling light, he made out a table strewn with broken crockery, a cabinet with its door hanging open, and two sleeping mats covered with debris. An abandoned guard chamber.

He continued down the corridor to where the passageway narrowed, almost touching his shoulders, and then opened again. A few dirty, empty globes unraveled in the circle of light. He crunched over the shards of one that had broken, then stopped. He'd heard something. A sound different from the thudding of his heart.

Ahead in the gloom, the tunnel branched, and the sound seemed to have come from the right-hand passage. He transferred the globe from one hand to the other, wiped the empty hand on his pants, and keeping to the wall, cautiously made his way down the passage to his right. The sound, a slow *pluk-plunk-pluk,* grew louder. The source turned out to be water dripping from the ceiling. It had formed a puddle that filled the center of the tunnel and spread out almost to the walls. On the right, however, just beyond the puddle, he could make out a mark on the floor. Shining the light over it, he saw it was the half-dried print of a bare foot.

Dread squeezed his stomach. He put his hand over the globe to reduce its glare and peered ahead. Nothing but darkness. Conscious of the larvae squirming close to his skin, he moved forward. A sudden influx of pain hit him, so great it pushed past the skora barrier, and he saw a blur of white clothing. The ahn sat cross-legged at the end of the dead-end passage, his head bowed and his hands open on his lap. Over and over he repeated a mind-prayer: "My life is in your hands, oh God. My life is in your hands."

Teller stood over him. The prayer abruptly stopped. With fists clenched, the ahn briefly closed his eyes and took a breath. Then he looked up. Teller saw the earnest, close-set eyes, the high cheekbones, and recognition dawned. The globe almost slipped from his fingers.

Yuin. It was Yuin.

Years fell away. He sat on a bed, next to a little boy who rocked back and forth under a blanket that covered his head. *"I'm dead. Officially dead."* The blanket came down, and the boy's bruised face merged with that of the young man who was now slowly rising to his feet. Years had passed, but the face was unmistakable. He must be Yuin's ahn twin.

"You knew my niyal!" the young man breathed. "You knew my twin brother."

The past rushed over Teller, a chaos of sharp, broken images that still had the power to hurt. The ahn, in contrast, stood with his back straight, gazing at him with that look of expectancy and wonder.

Anger twisted through his spirikai, anger at a peace that would never be his, at demands he could never fulfill. "Why aren't you afraid?" Teller rasped. "Why aren't you afraid to die?"

The ahn merely stared at him, and Teller pushed the globe closer to his face. "Answer me!"

"Rulve has answered. In you, Rulve has answered us."

It was one thing to read the name on an ancient piece of vellum, but to hear it spoken with such level-eyed faith was like a blow to the stomach. "There is no Rulve here! Do you feel him in this dead-end tunnel? See her in the isav? We're trapped here, without hope, and our souls belong to the lord. Nothing is spoken here but lies."

"Rivere doesn't lie. He told us who you are."

Teller stared at him. "Rivere! He's here? Where?"

"Truly, it's better for you not to know."

Teller grabbed the front of his tunic. "Tell me! I *have* to know."

The ahn didn't even try to back away. "He's in the lowest level, in the dungeons near the strisnu."

Still gripping the ahn's tunic, Teller groaned and lowered his head. "Is he in pain?"

"He is there to keep certain prisoners alive, but only for further torment. It scours his soul. But he tries to heal our injuries, tries to keep us from despair. Even in his own anguish, he does this."

Long ago, Teller had begged Rivere to be his father and he had refused; and now he comforted strangers. Now, all alone, he tried to heal the vast and festering wound that was Oknu Shuld. He released the ahn, and for a moment neither spoke.

"How did my brother fare," the young man asked in a low voice, "when you last saw him?"

"It—it was years ago. He struggled with the fact that it was you instead of him who was taken as ahn. Yuin couldn't accept it was just pure chance." His voice turned bitter. "He wanted to believe things happen for a reason."

The ahn, close to tears, looked away. "He searched for meaning in his life."

The words caused the bitterness in Teller's throat to swell. Didn't that also apply to the two of them? He had to swallow before he could speak. "His niyalahn bond was broken. Se—Se Nemez helped him bear the pain."

But they hadn't done anything for the small boy Teller. They were terrified of him, tried to drown him, drown his fire; and when they failed, pushed him into this darkness.

"My name is Gorv," the ahn said.

Gorv? The name turned in his mind. "Keya mentioned you."

From a pocket in his frayed pants, Gorv pulled out a blue hair-ribbon. "I've kept this all these years. I wanted her ribbon with me this rota, when—when I went to Rulve. Keya told us what you tried to do for her, just before she died."

Teller stared at him, and everything drained away. "Died?"

Even here, even knowing what he faced, the young man's face softened in sympathy. "I'm sorry. You didn't know."

How could he know? Who would have told him? The death of one ahn here was nothing. "What—what happened? Oh god," he groaned, "not the luniku."

"No," Gorv said. "We were able to pass her a chunk of inkroot, and she died of it shortly after she entered the chamber."

A cord inside him went taut. He had given up everything to save Keya, and in his darkest hours tried to believe it had been worth it, that his sundering from Rulve had accomplished something, meant something. Instead, it was the death of his last dream, a cruel and crushing betrayal, and a revelation of his own stupid, stupid gullibility. "I thought she was safe," he choked out. "I thought I saved her. For a long time, I looked for her. For her blue ribbon."

Yes, he looked, but never asked. He was too much the superior rista to ask.

"Then you have found it. Keya would want you to have it." Gorv gently opened Teller's clenched hand, put the ribbon into it, and closed it again. "You are here to set us free."

Appalled, he drew back. "What are you *saying*? I'm here to kill you! Oh god, all ahn are better off dead."

"It is peace to me if my death should be at your hands. Every ahn in these tunnels knew you were coming, and we all hoped to be the one you met."

"Please don't," he moaned. "Don't talk like that."

"I will be at peace because I know you are the niyalahn-rista. That you have come at last. You are the savior Rulve has promised, the one who will free us and destroy Oknu Shuld." Gorv smiled, his eyes turning liquid. "You will bring light into this terrible darkness."

Something like hot acid rushed through Teller and he crushed the ribbon in his fist. "I'm not this savior. I'm not anyone, only Seani garbage."

"You long for a brother who is lost. You feel what I feel. You are ahn and niyal and rista, and bear the pain of all."

"No! I belong to the lord, body and soul. Didn't Keya tell you that?"

Gorv gazed steadily at him. "We see someone who gave up his heart's longing to save one of us. We see someone who did not touch Liasit, who protected her and spoke to her in the mind-speech. We see someone who never joined in the ahn-hunts, who went in search of Aron, who alone in Oknu Shuld does no evil deed."

"No evil deed?" he cried. "I made collars for innocent ahn. I made a poison that causes terrible pain. I led *children* into this hell, and one is only six years old. Can't you hear me? I'm riddled with skora, a rista of Oknu Shuld!"

"We see what we see." Gorv inclined his head slightly. "Rivere says we must not bow to you with our bodies, but our hearts bow."

"I'm not the one," he groaned. "My fire burned a man to death."

"We know what really happened. We know what they did to you."

"They didn't do anything to me! I'm no victim, no ahn. They helped me admit the truth."

A clamor arose from down the corridors. "Time is up," Keel's voice shouted. "Come out, Teller-of-Lies."

A sudden memory hit him, and he grasped Gorv's shoulder. "There's a niche on the left, only a few steps farther. It has a hidden cleft in the back. It's narrow, but you can squeeze through and reach another tunnel."

Pain crept into Gorv's face. "I know," he said.

Teller dropped his hand and glanced over his shoulder. Light from hand-globes moved at the far end of the passageway. "Go!"

With a quick movement, Gorv pulled the dagger from Teller's belt. "Y'rulve, niyal'arist." The ahn's face contorted as with both hands he plunged the dagger into his own chest.

The skora barrier leaped, but too late. Teller gasped with Gorv's pain, the hand-globe clattered to the ground, and he caught the young man as he slumped toward him. He lowered him onto the floor and knelt beside him. Blood bubbled around the jade hilt. The light, unbroken, rolled against Gorv's arm.

"It was the only way, emjadi."

"No," Teller whispered. "Gorv, no." He grabbed the ahn's shoulders.

Master Keel shoved him aside as Lady Shavante and two subalterns came crowding up. He shone a globe onto Gorv's body as a stain, black in the dim light, spread over the front of his tunic. Shavante gave Teller a sour glance. "I am detecting your skora from the end of the passage," she said. "You are using it and your dagger both—to dispatch one ahn."

Numb, Teller stood and looked down at the man who had died for him. He pushed the hair-ribbon into his pocket. It joined something else, which he must have put in there without realizing it: the red cord he had cut from Liasit's wrists.

"Vol Prome will have to judge," Keel said harshly, "to see if you broke the rules."

Shavante pulled the dagger from Gorv's body, wiped it on his ragged pants, and handed it to Teller. Her lip curled in disdain. "What he is deciding is no matter to me, but I say you are acting without honor."

Teller took the weapon, its hilt still warm from Gorv's grip, then picked up the fallen hand-globe. They escorted him out of the tunnel.

The group had just turned the corner, leaving the passage in darkness, when two ahn emerged from the niche on the left. One of them carried a dim and battered hand-globe. The other, grey-haired and wiry, knelt beside Gorv and leaned close to his face. "We're here, my son. The other three are with Rulve now."

Gorv's mind-words were barely audible, yet full of luminous awe. "The niyal'arist—he would have—have given his life for me." The last of his breath hissed out of the wound like a sigh, and the light passed out of his eyes.

The grey-haired ahn held the lifeless body close to his chest. "You have saved our savior, Gorv. You have saved him."

The other ahn looked down the empty corridor, where the niyalahn-rista had gone.

CHAPTER 24

AUTRAN'S PLOT

Autran closed the door upon the delectable little bug tied by her wrists and ankles to his bedposts and adjusted his hastily donned trousers. He had ordered that Keel appear before him, but didn't mean *now*. The man had an abysmal sense of timing.

He finished dressing; then made his way to his audience chamber, seated himself on his carved and padded chair—not quite a throne, for that was the lord's prerogative, but near enough—and looked down on the man who knelt before him. Keel had once been square and hard-edged, but now was sliding toward fat. "I asked you here," he said, in a studied mixture of imperiousness and professional concern, "to discuss a pupil of yours and a prentice of mine. It has come to my belated attention that you have filed several complaints against Teller-of-Lies."

"'Belated' indeed!" Keel burst out. "His insolence was obvious even at orientation, but I was prevented from doing anything about it at the time. Now he's grown into a rista who picks fights in the halls, saunters in late for lectures, and consistently maintains an attitude of aloof superiority. He has even made lascivious proposals to our honored guest, the Lady Shavante."

"Ah." Much of this behavior didn't jibe with what his

rats reported, but "lascivious proposals"? Teller-of-Lies must lead a more interesting life than he thought. He pursed his lips to express disapproval. "I can see why you are concerned. It appears this young man must learn respect if he is to do honor to the red cloak."

"That has long been my contention, Vol Ségun. If it had been up to me, he would not be attending the Cloaking Ceremony tomorrow—or ever."

"Oh?"

"This very rota he cheated on the final exam."

Even though his rats had reported the incident, Autran widened his eyes as if shocked. "I would never have thought *any* of our students cheat, especially one who has served as my apprentice."

"I'm sorry, Vol Ségun, but Teller-of-Lies is guileful and very aptly named. I'm not surprised you were fooled."

Fooled? How dare this imbecile throw that word at him! Anger flashed, quickly quelled. He rubbed his chin and put on a thoughtful look. "But didn't you and Lady Shavante agree he passed?"

Keel frowned. "If you've heard about that, then you know we were forced to do so by a technicality in the rules. And, I might add, by subtle pressure from—from those in high places. Not you, Vol, but from certain other Vols who find it advantageous that their protégé rises in the ranks."

"Say no more." *I mean that literally*, he thought. *If Nosce or the Delver heard what you're spouting, that would be the end of you—which wouldn't help my plans at all.* "Unfortunately, student development is, as you know, under Vol Prome's area of supervision, and I understand he has already approved Teller-of-Lies' promotion. Now, if *I* were in charge—" He waved a hand, as if to erase the words. "As things are, I'm afraid our arrogant rista will receive the red cloak with the others." He sighed deeply. "There must be *something* we can do, some way to teach this young man to adopt a more humble attitude toward his superiors. You may stand, by the way," he added.

Keel hauled himself to his feet. He had been looking quite sullen, but now interest dawned in his eyes. "I am at your complete service, Vol Ségun. Have you any suggestions?"

"No, actually," Autran lied. "This is more your area, Master Keel. It would have to involve some challenge that would interest Teller-of-Lies."

The man shrugged. "He seems to have no interests."

Autran spoke with as much patience as he could muster. "I understand he has visited the Halls of the Goah. To practice with skora against the shadows there."

"He might have," Keel said cautiously.

"I seem to recall, Keel, that at one time *you* traversed those Halls."

"Yes, indeed, Vol. In my youth, I killed two of the creatures in a clean-up mission."

"Now there's an idea. Perhaps it's time for another such mission. I've heard that one of the goahs has become overbearing and could use dispatching. Perhaps you can challenge Teller-of-Lies to join you in this endeavor. Then, while he is distracted..." He let his voice trail off.

Keel looked doubtful, and Autran realized he'd have to add an enticement. "Perhaps," he remarked, "the Lady Shavante would like to be part of this plan. It was her honor that was besmirched, after all. And I'm sure she would be interested in seeing your Lash in action."

A small smile flickered on the man's face.

Aha! The scathi idiot wanted to impress her. Using the foreign lady, however, was a bit risky. He didn't want the war-mongering Namakis to hear that his consort had met a lamentable end in Oknu Shuld. But by then he himself would possess skora, and would use it to explain things to the man, if he ever showed up. "It would be of great instructive value," he went on, "for Teller-of -Lies to experience how the Lady's ability can interact with yours. Together they would certainly teach him what real power is."

By the look in his eyes, Autran could almost picture what the man was thinking: Teller-of-Lies helpless under the Lady's Command while Keel plied the Whip. But the dolt still seemed unconvinced.

"Tell me more about this troublesome goah," Keel said.

Autran waved the soul-eating creature aside. "Mochlos is nothing you can't handle."

The man frowned. "Goah now have names?"

"Just my pet name for it, I assure you," Autran said, cursing himself for the slip. "Even though it can bluster with the rest of them, Mochlos is actually quite harmless, which, of course, Teller-of-Lies doesn't know. In any case, Mochlos will be under my binding, and forbidden to touch you. Didn't I mention that?"

"No, Volarach. You did not."

"There will be no such injunction, of course, protecting your former student. How else will the boy learn?"

Looking troubled, Keel chewed on his lip.

Damn the man! "I detect hesitation on your part," Autran said coldly. "Do you actually doubt that your Power *and* the Lady's are greater than your student's?"

"Absolutely not, Vol! The boy's Power is nothing but brag and deception. He needs to be taken down a peg. I was, however, just wondering…" Keel hitched a shoulder, as if to dislodge a troublesome fly.

"Wondering what's in it for you?"

Keel reddened. "I would hardly put—"

"It's a practical consideration, Keel, and I respect practicality. Let me address it." He looked into the distance, as if in thought. "Suppose there were to be a slight shift in the balance of power among us Vols. A shift regarding, shall we say, their numerical designations and resulting responsibilities. The new Vol in charge of student development might be interested in promoting someone intelligent and ambitious, someone who has proved his commitment to the high quality of our students."

Keel's lengthy digestion of this statement produced at last a crafty look. "What about skora?"

Autran raised his eyebrows. "What about it? It's only brag and deception."

He watched as Keel cautiously rose to the bait, hesitated, and then lunged for the hook.

Keel smiled, and the decision to take the skora for himself was plainly written all over his face. "Exactly, Vol Ségun. You can count on me." What he imagined was a secret joke lit up his eyes and his smile turned into a sneer. "I am in truth an ambitious man."

And one ridiculously easy to manipulate, Autran thought, as he gave Keel leave to go.

He returned to his bedchamber and to the naked ahn all spread out for him, but even her moans of pain didn't arouse him anymore. He was too troubled by the dangerous job that faced him. But he wanted his pleasure *now*, and perhaps there was a way he could get it vicariously. He sat back on his haunches and addressed the ahn beneath him. "Describe to me, in every detail, what Teller-of-Lies did to you."

Her lovely eyes widened, then squeezed shut. She turned her face away.

"I'm giving you a direct order."

She still resisted, but the collar began its caustic work. It tightened, and blisters rose up like little opals around her neck. Eventually she choked out that he had cut the cord around her wrists, covered her with a blanket, touched her hair, and talked. Frustrated, Autran slapped her several times, then rolled off the bed. Teller-of-Lies had done nothing to her at all.

He tugged on his breeches, frowning at his apprentice's disappointing behavior. But as he thought about it, an incredible idea occurred to him. In spite of Teller-of-Lies' inexperienced fumbling, could the young rista actually have become emotionally involved? It certainly sounded like it. Perhaps, if all else failed, this wretched ahn could be of use to him after all.

He left her still tied and made his way through the now quiet halls to his laboratorium. Stopping in a shadowy corner in the back, he moved aside a grimy wall-hanging, thrust his hand into the aperture behind it, and pulled a lever. A section of the wall at his right grated open. Taking a hand-globe from the rack beside the door, he stepped down into a small anteroom. It contained a warded, one-piece garment hanging on a peg and a pedestal that held a covered stone jar of unguent. He placed the globe in an empty stand, removed his clothing, and began his preparations to summon Mochlos.

It took a while, for he must be extremely careful, but at last he stood ready, all ten orifices anointed, the garment donned and fastened securely. He stooped to pass through a low door. The next chamber was in reality an old fissure whose throat had been plugged long ago by an earthquake. Its walls and ceiling were covered with powerful runes inscribed into the stone. With a few words, Autran sealed a couple of new cracks that had appeared above the door since last he'd been here, then closed it firmly.

He stood in complete darkness, confident that nothing could get out of the chamber without his permission. Brushing his fingers along the smooth floor, he found the protrusion that marked the exact center of the room and stood there. He began to whisper, and the words of summoning became visible as they wound, faintly glowing, out of his mouth. They expanded, joined and blurred, and formed a tunnel into the dark. Something big appeared at its far end. It rushed down, and with a blast of wind, burst into the chamber.

A scaly neck stretched out and a pair of pale, hooded eyes looked down on him. Fleshy tendrils hung beneath them and two thicker ones, like long mustaches, quivered from the ridge that was no nose. Rodent-like incisors flanked its sharp buck teeth.

Although cold with fear, Autran spoke in a mocking tone. "What a lovely guise you've put on, Mochlos."

The creature's hollow voice echoed in the chamber. "What do you want, Vol?"

"I have something for you."

"Indeed."

"A living form, that you may inhabit and command."

"Failed ristas I have already. They crumble at my touch."

"I offer one different from them."

The neck twisted impatiently. "Ambitious sorcerers bore me. Let me go now, for this place is painful to me."

"The one I will give you is no sorcerer, Mochlos."

"Who then? Speak!"

"Are you aware of the one with skora, who walks alone in your halls?"

The creature stilled. "I am aware."

"He is the one I offer."

Wisps of green suspicion coiled in its eyes. "And what are your requirements, Vol?"

"You may keep the body. Its Power you will hand over to me."

"Why do you need me? Take the Power yourself."

"I am being watched. No one watches you."

"So," Mochlos said, "there are others who want this skora. Perhaps I can make a better bargain with them."

"There is more."

"I thought there might be."

"I offer you your freedom."

The head reared back, and its teeth made a chittering sound that echoed and re-echoed in the dark like a hundred cicadas. Autran hoped that meant it was interested.

Abruptly, the noise stopped. "Only the Lord of Oknu Shuld can give me my freedom."

"Exactly."

"I see. You will use the fire to *become* the Lord of Oknu Shuld." The lids lowered halfway over its eyes: it was either thinking or plotting. "I can take the fire myself, and do likewise."

Autran forced out a laugh. "I'm afraid not, Mochlos. Skora is rooted in the human spirikai, and you don't have a spirikai. No matter how many humans you ingest, you will *never* have a spirikai. For you the fire is useless."

"I can still destroy it."

"Certainly, and the body as well. But what advantage is that to you?"

It shook its fleshy tendrils, apparently thinking. "I will take the body, for it is tall and strong. But I also want the mind and will."

"Fine. After you take all that, bring him, mindless and without will, to the poisonwood doors. I will relieve him of the fire and send you on your way."

Mochlos hissed. "When?"

"Right after the Cloaking Ceremony. Next rota, before the sixth deep gong, he will come to you."

"I will be waiting."

"Another thing."

"Always," the creature growled, "another thing."

"Two others will be with him. They are nothing; ingest them first."

"Who are these nothings?"

"Master Keel and the Lady Shavante of Aramjat."

"I know of them. So be it." The eyes opened wide to glare down at him. "But a word of warning, Autran. Do not seek to change one word of our contract. If you do, I will have my revenge. I will grow huge and silent between the stars, and return in the night for you. Many cruelties I have learned from those I ingested, and you shall endure every one."

The intensity of its words made Autran shake inside. Mochlos could do exactly what he said. But no goah, no matter how great, would be a match for the ruler of Oknu Shuld, especially if he wielded skora plus Powers of his own.

"So be it, Mochlos. Now lower yourself and submit to my binding."

Angry shafts of light darted from its eyes, but Mochlos obeyed. It shrunk until it stood only as tall as Autran, but then it stopped, testing him.

Autran forced himself to put out his left hand, palm down, at the level of his waist. "Under my hand, Mochlos."

The eyes burned, scrutinizing him for any shred of

weakness. Under that gaze the ointment around his eyes begin to dry and the skin on his face shrivel, but he kept his hand utterly motionless.

"In this," Mochlos said, "I choose to obey." It dipped in homage, then rose. "But now I take my turn." A forked tongue flicked out and struck the back of Autran's hand. It felt as if it had been pierced by an icy claw. He drew in a sharp breath, but did not move a muscle.

"Just a reminder," the creature said, "of our bargain."

Autran forced his lips to smile. "Goah, you are dismissed."

Mochlos withdrew in a whoosh of air, and the tunnel closed with a long, low rumble.

Drenched with sweat, Autran stumbled out of the anteroom. His left hand was white and pinched with cold, and he could not warm it, not then or ever.

CHAPTER 25

THE RED CLOAK

It was as if Gorv's death caused a sealed door to burst open inside him, and Teller couldn't shove it closed. His shirt, stained with Gorv's blood, lay wadded up on the floor. He tossed and turned on the bed as ahn-faces whirled around him, as visions tore at him and words echoed: *"Have you come at last, niyal'arist?"... "living the dead surrounding"*...black blood spreading beneath the hilt of his dagger. The wyvern dropped him, tumbling and crying, into the darkness of Oknu Shuld. *"Come out now, Teller-of-Lies. Come out."*

He sat up, burning with fever, the high-gongs ringing in his ears. The Cloaking Ceremony. They told him he'd passed the final exam, and now it was time for the Cloaking Ceremony. His hands shook as he splashed water on his face and threw on a clean shirt. His pants were gritty from the mine tunnels, but it was too late to change them. He rushed through the deserted corridors, down two levels, and burst into the Hall of the Eye.

More heat rolled over him, along with the buzz of an excited crowd that had been invited to this occasion. The great red-veined globes, suspended from the vaulted ceiling and seething with worms specifically selected for brilliance, glowered like bloodshot eyes at the people below. The light cast a shifting, ember glow over well-dressed townsfolk, foreigners with elaborate hair styles, and the line of red-cloaks guarding the perimeter of the hall. Several rows of ahn knelt at the very back, foreheads touching the ground, their faces invisible, their backs lashed with strips of scarlet light.

Three rows of chairs in front, separated by an aisle, were occupied by the honored guests; everyone else stood behind them. The first row included Shavante, the three archons who commanded the three divisions of the lord's army, and the two alterns who governed the villages of Rydle and Baenfeld.

Several quad-commanders joined them, as well as local dignitaries. Blue-robed teachers and foreign guests sat in the second row. The third was full of ristas especially chosen to attend the Ceremony, plus the others who had passed the final exam: the woman with the braid, Dahran, and Noz. Teller didn't want to think about the two who weren't there. He took the only seat left, on the aisle and next to Noz.

Noz took in Teller's disheveled appearance and turned away with a sneer. He was wearing a black shirt with red piping and red fastenings, apparently made to match the color of the red cloak awaiting him, and his boots were so new they creaked when he moved.

Teller shifted slightly so he could see the dais between the heads of those in front of him. Everything seemed etched with fevered sharpness: the lord's unoccupied ebony throne, elaborately carved and wide enough to seat two people; the four drummers, clad in black and silver, who stood behind it; a circle of black earth that lay like an ink-stain in front of it. Until it could dry out from the last krew-let, the circle was left uncovered by its usual ornate carpet. The nauseating odor of blood still exuded from the soil. In the lord's relentless search for s'rere, "the blood that makes the earth dance," each newly arrived rista was required to slash the back of his or her hand and allow drops of blood to fall into the earthen circle. So far, no one's blood had ever stirred it. Teller remembered how, shortly after he was brought to Oknu Shuld, the Delver had performed a private krew-let in his room.

In spite of his efforts to ignore it, a huge and intimidating object on the wall above the throne drew his gaze. It was the Igneous Eye, an oval niche covered with curved red glass bisected by a slit of obsidian. A fire always burned behind the glass, the only fire allowed in Oknu Shuld. Its leaping flames appeared to make the reptilian Eye dart ceaselessly around the hall.

Noz was looking at it too. "That scathi Eye always glares at you," he muttered, "no matter where you sit in here."

Because the lord was not present, neither was the Vorian Guard. The Vols attended in the lord's stead, sitting on polished blackwood chairs on both sides of the throne. The ceremony opened with a drum roll, followed by a brief speech by Shacad, a longer one by Autran, and an interminable one by Nosce. Only the Delver, sitting in his robe like a cobwebbed corpse, said nothing. The fever wrapped Teller in a stifling blanket, the Igneous Eye radiated heat like a furnace, and the anguish of the ahn simmered over his back. His shirt-sleeves clung to his arms, but rolling them up wasn't an option at this formal occasion. With clumsy fingers, he undid the top two buttons of his shirt.

He got to his feet when Nosce called the four of them forward and knelt in a line before the Prome. Four folded red cloaks lay on the top step of the dais. One hem bore the maroon band of the Sekrew Bloodknots, two the cobalt of the Skinners, and one the slate of the most prestigious unit of the lord's army, worn only by archon Rigiati's most elite fighters, the Azanzi Scaths.

Nosce rasped out the words that promoted them to subalterns and, assisted by the archons who commanded the three forces, began bestowing the red cloaks. A sniff of disdain came from Noz when the woman received the maroon and Dahran the cobalt, but he stiffened when the second Skinner cloak was placed over him. Dazed, Teller stared at the remaining cloak. Archon Rigiati passed it to Nosce, who swung it over Teller's shoulders.

He'd been given the slate. He was now an officer among the lord's top two hundred men.

The hood bent and whispered in his ear. "A step, subaltern, on the road to Cinc."

He clutched the front of the cloak, a symbol of hard-won validation, of that destiny to which he had always felt called. From the corner of his eye, he caught a glance of pure hatred from Noz. An urge seized him: to turn to his three colleagues with a smile of contempt, to stand and face the crowd, to pull the grim sword of fire out of its spirikai scabbard and raise it high above them all.

But there would be time enough later for that.

Drums rolled, and the audience applauded, and Teller basked in unaccustomed adulation. But as he went back to his chair, the cloak seemed to get hotter and heavier with each step. By the time he reached his seat, it seemed to weigh as much as if it were soaked with blood. He sat in its stifling embrace, and sweat trickled down his back. Without warning, the visions rushed in. Gorv's face floated in front of him. *"It is peace to me if my death should be at your hands."* Aron's mother placed the child's hand in his. *"Sir, will you make sure he gets some thamar tea 'afore bedtime?"* Liasit's brown eyes regarded him. *"Have you come at last, niyalahn-rista?"*

Noz stood and climbed stiffly past him; the ceremony was over. Teller got to his feet and Shavante stood in front of him. "It is shame," she hissed, "that you are receiving the red cloak. It will always be too big for you, small man."

She disappeared into the crowd. Teller made his way out of the hall, pushing against the throng heading to the reception area. When he reached the quiet of his room, he threw off the red cloak, peeled off his clean shirt, and gulped down water from the pitcher. He sank onto his smoldering bed and covered his eyes with his arm, the far-off sound of revelers echoing in his head.

He longed to jump into a pool of cold water, into a deep green pool, to sink down and let this heat bleed out of him. Memories swirled like a hot wind. *"Se Abiyat,"* a little boy cried, *"the people in there are hurting! They are hurting very much."* A falcon's eyes bored into him, *"I am honored, Emjadi T'lir."* A man rumpled his hair, *"Are you all right, voskat?"* *"No,"* someone cried, *"I'm never going to see the sky again!"* A child's red ball slowly rolled, out of the postern, and into an endless tunnel.

Teller jerked awake, raised his head from the sweat-soaked pillow. A silent figure stood in the doorframe. It beckoned to him.

Lightheaded with fever, he followed it down a crooked maze of oddly deserted passages and into a long and narrow room. Its ceiling was lost in shadows. It contained no globes, nothing but a row of oval mirrors that lined the walls on two sides. They shone with their own silver light, casting their pale, elliptic reflections on the floor like stepping-stones into the dark.

The figure stopped and pointed to the first mirror on the right. Framed in bone, it reflected a face like his: a young man with soot-colored hair and eyes as dark as bog-water. He wore the collar of an ahn.

With a cry, Teller struck the image with his fist. Soundlessly, the mirror shivered and cracked; shards of it fell away.

His companion pulled him to the next mirror. It showed a young man with the same features, but with pale hair and eyes of shining silver. A dark sky loomed over him. In the next mirror the young man lay naked and bleeding on a black circle of earth, his hands and feet tied to stakes.

The figure pointed ahead, to other mirrors.

"I don't want to see any more!" Teller shouted. "Why did you bring me here?"

"Your father called you. You responded."

"That thing wasn't my father! They pushed me out."

"They gave you the courage and the compassion to go beyond the gates."

"They feared me! They feared one of their own children."

"Not as much as you fear yourself, niyalahn-rista."

"No!" That was someone else's title, someone else's tragedy, someone else's refusal. "My name is Teller."

"Teller-of-Lies, then, for you lie to yourself."

"That's not my name."

"Then speak the truth. You are the niyalahn-rista, and the niyalahn-rista calls you, and you must go to him."

Teller awoke with a start. His bed was sweaty, the sheet tossed aside. He was too hot to put on his shirt; had to find air, had to crawl out of this festering tomb. Passing no one in the halls, he made his shaky way up to the third level, to the passage that led to the Garden of Welcoming. The two guards on night-duty were startled to see him, half naked as he was, but they opened the oak door for him. He stumbled out of Oknu Shuld and into a cool, spring night. This time he did not take the path that led down to the Garden; instead he climbed the narrow stair cut into the face of the cliff. It took him past walls of ivy rustling in the wind and onto the plateau. He emerged on a barren shelf of rock facing the east. The breeze blew stronger here, rifling his hair, drying the sweat on his forehead and chest. An old moon hung low over acre upon acre of emerging morue plants. Not far away jutted the outlines of a dimly lit guard station.

He turned to the west, where the cliff angled down in two wide steps into abrupt darkness. His eyes found the cluster of tiny lights on the opposite hillside, shining quietly like far-off stars. Loneliness cut through him. He was a traitor, horribly betrayed. Refused and refusing, he was senselessly lost, mired in lies. The moon cast his long shadow in front of him. It pointed like a black finger to the void below.

Only a few steps. It would take only a few steps. He took one.

Suddenly his shadow was engulfed by another much larger. Downdrafts beat against the back of his head. He whirled. Intense golden eyes looked down at him, outspread wings blocked out the night sky, great claws reached for him.

"No!" Teller screamed. It was happening again, the immensity of fate snatching at him. He dove to the ground as the creature swooped over him, blazing out an emotion, urgent and commanding, that pierced his heart. Arrows zinged past him, booted feet came running.

"A falconform!" a guard shouted. "There! A scathi falconform!"

Shaken, Teller lifted his head. An expanse of feathered back shone in the moonlight as the creature soared over the edge of the cliff. Its cry came back like smoke: "*Leeer. T'leeer.*"

Someone grabbed his arm. "Are you hurt, sir? Did you wound it?"

He climbed to his feet. The cliff seemed to rock under him. He looked down and saw the dagger in his hand. Why hadn't he struck out with skora?

"Skew it!" a voice exclaimed. "It's out of range. Stand down."

"This is Shacad's fault, damn him!" someone muttered. "We need more archers up here."

Teller shoved the dagger back into his belt. A guard hustled him into the station and then down a winding metal stair. "The second time this month!" the woman exclaimed. "First, one of us guards was attacked and now a subaltern." When they reached the bottom, she looked him over. "So you're the new Scath." She flashed him a wicked, green-eyed smile. "Looks like you're off duty right now."

"You address me as 'sir,'" he barked. "I'm a 'sir' and you keep forgetting that." He turned away. "Go back to your post."

Teller made his way through a large square opening, the metal door of which had been rolled into a pocket in the wall. The pounding of his heart slowed, and as he looked around, it was as if he had stepped into the past. This was Section Nineteen, which he had so thoroughly explored when he was first brought into Oknu Shuld.

Or was it? He plunged through the passage, searching for his old room, for the room of green light, but nothing was as he remembered it. The sense of being lost, of being abandoned, swept over him with almost as much force as the falconform just had. Out of the corner of his eye he glimpsed an ahn—Gorv! He whirled, but no one was there.

"Rivere?" he called. "Keya?" But she was dead, long dead, and Rivere had rejected him. His throat tightened as if enclosed with a metal collar, and he clawed at it, trying to swallow. It was mind-damage from the Seani, dogging his footsteps, swirling uncontrolled inside his head. What section was this? What level? Panic jittered in his stomach as deep gongs pounded in his ears.

He blinked to clear his eyes. He found himself sitting on the side of the bed with his head in his hands and staring at his own boots. How did—? Somehow he must have gotten back to his room. Or had never left it.

A knock at the door startled him. Half-expecting more nightmarish visions, he opened it. Autran, Master Keel, and Lady Shavante pushed inside.

"Took you long enough to answer," the Vol said. He looked with distaste at the rumpled bed, the two shirts on the floor, the red cloak tossed onto the chair. "We're here to invite the new Azanzi subaltern on a quest."

It took a moment for Teller to realize that Autran meant him. "Quest?"

"Perhaps mission would be a better word," Autran said. "Keel, explain things to the subaltern here." He rubbed his left hand, as if he were trying to restore circulation to it.

Keel hooked his thumbs in his belt. "A certain demon in the Halls of the Goah has become too big for his britches. The Lady and I go to rid the Halls of it, and we want you to join us. Your skora, my Lash, and the Lady's Command should be more than enough to take care of the problem. What do you say?"

Everything that had been churning in his head—the faces in the mirror, the eyes of the falconform, the panic—was now edged out by wariness. "It's late," he said. "It's been a long rota."

"What matters that?" the Lady said. "I am wishing to observe skora without further delay."

Teller picked the clean shirt up off the floor and put it on. "The Halls of the Goah are in the Kuat's domain," he said. "Let him attend to it."

"Our Kuat," Autran said, taking a seat on the red-cloaked chair, "is off somewhere. I understand you have been down in the goah halls many times. So what are you afraid of, Teller-of-Lies?" For a moment it seemed a pair of globular locust eyes looked out at him from under the Vol's bland gaze.

"That's not my name," Teller said, tucking his shirt into his pants.

Shavante sat on the bed and stared at him. "In Aramjat we are also having demons. I make them to lick my feet."

"The goah you're talking about," Teller said, "is more likely to eat them."

"Skew you," Keel said. "I walked among the goah while you still crawled on all fours. I ordered them about before you could talk. There'll be two of us to protect you, so why not come along?"

Teller saw something that gloated in Keel's eyes, something very like what he saw in Autran's. No way would he be caught up in this. "Some other time," he said.

"Agh," Keel growled. "We've come to the wrong man. We should have approached Dahran."

Shavante arranged her silk garment around her. "In my country, the man is acting; the boy is talking. The coward brags about his great cudgel, but alas"—she raked Teller with a look—"it proves to be as flaccid as a willow branch."

Keel barked out an appreciative laugh. Shavante was getting back at Teller for the tryst he'd never kept by implying something that had never happened. Teller felt heat climb up his face.

"Instead of slaying this Mochlos," Keel said to Teller, "I should bind him and bring him to this room. Only then, apparently, would you do something about him. If you could manage to find a cudgel, that is."

Autran snickered, but Teller kept his anger in check. "Do it, Keel," he said, "if Mochlos lets you." Even though he distrusted this so-called "quest," something inside him needed it. He needed to go against the goah, to illuminate the face of darkness with fire, to wrap it in flames and cast it into the void. But he wouldn't let anyone goad him into it.

Keel turned to Autran. "I *told* you he should never have been awarded that cloak. His wearing it dishonors the Scaths."

For an instant the Vol stiffened at Keel's tone, but then turned serenely to Teller. He spread out his hands. "Let bygones be bygones, subaltern. Forget this pique against a teacher. Use your Power against something worthy of it."

Teller strode to the door and held it open. "Not this rota."

Shavante jumped up. "I will not be dismissed by a dog of Oknu Shuld!" A full beam of Command flashed in her eyes, the essence of authority that must be obeyed. "Down! Down at my feet!"

Even though he was prepared for it this time, the force of her will still shook him. It slammed into the back of his knees to make them kneel, but he refused to bend them.

"Bah!" Shavante said. "When first we meet, I should have made you to cut your own throat."

Autran put out a placating hand. "Now, now. Perhaps

this young subaltern doesn't completely understand the situation. Mochlos has indeed become dangerous. Not to us, of course, who can withstand his lures, but to our servants here. We've come at this late hour because an ahn, by some unaccountable error, has been sent down to the Halls to fill the globes. And naturally"—he shrugged —"we can't allow goah to get a taste for ahn." His eyes hooded, he turned to Teller. "Perhaps you remember the girl. She came here to calm your nerves before the Welcoming."

Everything inside Teller went dead.

"An ahn is making no difference to me," the Lady said. "It is probably dispatched already. The thrill of the hunt—that is the important thing."

Autran watched Teller closely, a half-smile on his lips. "Oh, I think Mochlos may keep the girl alive for awhile. It, too, seeks the challenge of the hunt." He stood up, went to the door, and laid his pudgy, be-ringed hand on Teller's shoulder. "Keel and the Lady will meet you directly, in the Halls of the Goah."

The Lady swept past him. "If he is having the intestines to appear."

Autran leaned close to his ear and spoke in a low voice. "In the Halls of the Goah you will discover your true name. Did you know that, Teller-of-Lies?"

"That's not—"

Autran laughed and departed, followed by the others.

Teller watched them disappear down the empty hall, then turned to the ahn, a grey-haired man this time, kneeling in the niche to his right. "Bring me the ahn Liasit."

The man, thin but sinewy, leaned forward and looked him in the eye. "There is no ahn here by that name, sir."

"You know who I mean!"

The ahn continued to gaze at him, but with a different expression, as if Teller had passed some kind of test. "We do not know where she is. For many gongs, we have not felt her presence." His jaw clenched. "We fear for her." The look in his eyes changed, and for a moment they were Gorv's, full of that hope, that trust, that maddening expectation.

All the ahn kept pulling at him, grabbing at him, tearing the scab off a place where he needed a tough, thick scar. "Why can't you leave me alone?" he shouted. "You come here to die! It's only a matter of time. For anyone here who is wounded. Anyone!"

He slammed back into his room. The luniku globe on his desk writhed with trapped worms. He was imbued with fire, the only such Power in Oknu Shuld, and would allow no one to manipulate it—not Keel, not Autran, not the ahn. His anger was a rising pressure in his chest, rock strata slipping and grating, a terrible, cracking upheaval.

He seized the globe and hurled it against the stone wall. It burst into pieces. Larvae scattered across the floor, along with grey cocoons. One rolled to a stop inches from his boot. It lay there, the cradle of a nightmare. Savagely he ground it underfoot, expecting it to crunch like a dried leaf, but instead it spurted horribly. It left a smear of dissolved life trailing exposed on the floor.

Appalled, he stared down at it, at its naked vulnerability, its voiceless accusation. He hit it with skora, and the thing burned like spilled wax. The floor was littered with cocoons and writhing larvae. With a sheet of flame he engulfed them, but all too soon they were gone, and he was left still blazing. He needed more to burn, much more, more than existed in this small space.

Blind with flames, he broke out of the room. He stumbled down corridors, half ran down twisting stairs and through tunnels, seeing nothing but the fire behind his eyes, and then the glistening poisonwood door. With a word he wrenched it open, and burst into the Halls of the Goah.

CHAPTER 26

MOCHLOS

The Lord of Shunder looked up from his desk as the Prome entered his private study. The glassy black spider-eyes that stared out of his mask were touched with purple glints reflected from the garnet-studded globes hanging from the ceiling.

Nosce knelt on the striped grey and charcoal carpet. "I am at your service, lord."

The Eyascnu's gloved hand finished writing something and then put down his quill. "I am working on my second volume of the *L'garza Wadek*. I am about to record that I have at last added a Cinc to my Volarachs."

The Prome shifted on his knees. "The time, as I've said, lord, is not quite right. The boy still—"

The Eyascnu slammed one hand on the desk and spread the fingers of the other toward Nosce. The Vol's words ended in a gurgle as he grabbed at his neck.

"My vora would find you slim pickings," the lord said. "But it will still tear you apart, piece by piece, and suck the marrow from your bones. I have been patient long enough, my Prome."

The kneeling Vol trembled violently, and with a gesture, the lord released his voice. Sucking in air, Nosce fell forward, catching himself on his hands. "Tomorrow" —he had to clear his throat before he could continue—

"tomorrow without fail you will have your Cinc, great lord."

"I want him to accept his name voluntarily. I want him to put the vol-ring on his own finger."

"Yes, lord."

The Eyascnu picked up the quill, dipped it into a pot of blue-violet ink, and began writing. "Crawl out of here on your hands and knees, Nosce," he said without looking up. "You have leave to crawl out of my sight."

Like a beaten dog, the keys at his belt faintly clinking, Vol Prome obeyed.

Teller seized the fresh hand-globe burning in the triple sconce just inside the Halls of the Goah. The other two slots were empty. Keel and Shavante must have already arrived. But Liasit? The globes on their stands looked as dead as they had the last time he'd been here. If she'd been sent here to replenish them, she hadn't even gotten a chance to begin her work.

If she'd been sent here at all.

He looked down the dim passage. It was a trap. He knew it. His vulnerability to the ahn made something like this inevitable.

But he had to be sure.

Holding the globe high, he moved forward. Flat shadows slid away from him, darted under closed doors, or plastered themselves on the walls between the widely-separated sources of light. He pushed down his fear, forced his anger deep into the coils of his spirikai to fuel the rising skora.

On the floor ahead, an oily-looking mass writhed. He stepped closer. It was a pack of goah, gabbling excitedly as they swarmed over a motionless human body.

Grief tightened the muscles in his throat. He'd come too late. *There are no saviors in Oknu Shuld.*

Moving forward, he managed a strangled command: "Vicofa! Vicofale!" Get away from her! Startled, the filmy-eyed creatures looked up. These were not the hungry shadows that waited in corners, but the rarer kind of goah that had managed to grow patches of ragged flesh on tenuous bones. They all scuttled away, the last goah stumping off on a half-formed leg. The body on the floor was barely visible in the gloom. Steeling himself, he shone the light on it. The eyes and cheeks were gone, but he recognized the face of Keel.

Relief flooded him, to be replaced almost immediately by nausea. One leg had been gnawed away and innards spilled out of the torn abdomen. A broken hand-globe lay beside the body, but there were no worms. They had already been devoured.

He swallowed and moved on. The creatures darted back to the body, and the avid gabbling rose up once more behind him. If the goah had gotten Keel, what chance did a young woman have? At the first branching passage, he raised his light. "Liasit?" he called. "Shavante?"

He listened, but heard no answer. Raising his hand-globe, he made his way to the black arch. The gate stood wide open. He stopped just outside it, knowing he was framed by what little light there was behind him. Ahead in the blackness, he sensed a massive presence, like a beast rising from a primal swamp. A cold eye looked out at him, then sank back into turgid silence.

His heart hammered, slow and hard, shoving fire through his veins. He moved into the tunnel. Something cracked under foot—rat bones, a few wisps of fur still clinging to them. He stepped over them. Ahead and to his left lay a barely discernible bar of light, coming from under a door. He edged his way down the passage until he stood directly outside. Taking a shaky breath, he reached out and pushed the door open. Dim globe-light shone in his face.

The room was exactly like the one he remembered when he had first come to Oknu Shuld. His eyes traveled over a bed, a chest, a chair. A slight movement made them dart back to the bed. Almost invisible in the shadows, huddled against the backboard and clutching his drawn-up knees, a child stared at him with wide brown eyes. The thin body trembled under the white outfit of an ahn and a new collar glinted around his neck. It was Aron.

There was no tray on the chest, no water pitcher, only a globe with a handful of dying larva crawling amidst dead cocoons. The child had been left all alone in the halls of Mochlos.

Anger flared up in Teller, followed by a wave of wrenching sympathy. He stepped into the room, swiftly glancing around as the door swung shut behind him, then inserted the hand-globe into an empty sconce. As he approached, the boy shrank back, trying to hide behind his knees.

"Don't—don't be afraid, Aron," he stammered. He could hardly get the words past the thickness in his throat, hardly see past the pain of remembering that other small boy, so stricken with terror and homesickness that for many rotas he could not speak. He eased down beside the child, but the boy crushed himself still further against the board.

"You know me," Teller said. "From the Welcoming." The boy was pale with fright, but didn't seem to be bruised or cut. "Are you hurt?"

Aron peeked out at him from behind his knees. "N-no," he said in a low whisper. He touched his abdomen. "Just in here. From wanting my m-mother."

She had asked him to care for her child, to make sure he had tea and a warm blanket. Heavy with remorse, with unaccustomed gentleness, Teller took Aron's hand, the small hand he had rejected when the boy needed him the most.

The boy clung to it. "I'm thirsty," he whimpered, "and hungry." He looked up at Teller, and the innocent eyes seemed to ripple. Everything childlike drained out of them, and then everything human. They lit up and squirmed like live coals, black chasing red in fierce avidity. The hold on his hand tightened. Teller jerked back, but the grip held. The child-body swelled, ripping its ahn-clothes, growing into a man-like creature with no skin, only powerful striated muscles and strap-like tendons. Out of the meat-red horror of its face, eyes with no lids glared down at him. A lamprey mouth opened, to reveal a ring of rasping teeth.

With unbelievable strength, the goah flung him onto his back on the bed and rolled its heavy body on top of him. The odor of festering meat made Teller gag. The creature pinned Teller's wrists above his head, clamped its teeth onto the underside of his right forearm, and bit down. Teller gasped and wrenched his left hand free. He grabbed a fistful of the creature's hair, but it pulled out easily. The teeth, like multiple dagger points, bit deeper. Teller pummeled the side of its neck with his fist, but Mochlos continued to drink from him, making a guttural crooning sound as it groped to find and immobilize Teller's free hand. He managed to elude it, but the dim light in the room began turning red. He was losing skora in pain, felt it running out of his arm with his blood.

Struggling under the goah's body, pounding at its shoulder, he screamed a command at it in Widjar: "Eridra, Mochlos! Vicofemi!"

The head whipped up, blood dripping from its mouth, but it did not get off Teller or leave him. Instead it showed its red-tinged teeth in a grin and bent toward his jugular vein.

With his free hand Teller strained to reach his dagger. It was at his left side, crushed under the creature's body. He got one knee up and heaved the goah far enough to pull the dagger out of his belt. The creature's arm came down like an iron bar against his throat just as Teller plunged the dagger into the side of its neck. Mochlos bellowed and let go of his wrist. Teller tore himself away, grabbing a handful of its ripped clothing, and rolled off the bed.

Panting, he staggered back. Blood that looked black in the light ran from his forearm and dripped onto the floor. A shadow darted out from under the door and began scrabbling at the dark spots at his feet. Soon there would be more, coming out of the murk like roaches. With numb fingers, he wound the fabric tightly around the wound in his arm and summoned the fire-sword into his hand. Mochlos stood up beside the bed.

"Where is Liasit?" Teller cried.

"That matters nothing to you. You came in search of *me*, and here I am."

"I came for her!"

Smoke came from its mouth as Mochlos hissed with laughter. "You came for yourself, boy. To destroy and be destroyed. So let me satisfy you. Let me give you death in life."

"That I already have. I want the ahn."

The goah's eyes narrowed. "You make demands, you who do not even know your own name?"

"It's Teller," he grated, "and I want the ahn." The wound throbbed; he had to finish this.

A sly purpose crawled across the goah's skinless face. "If the niyalahn-rista were here," it hissed, "if he were to command me to produce this ahn, perhaps I would obey."

It shocked him that even a goah threw "niyalahn-rista" at him, and for a moment the sword dimmed. "No titles, Mochlos, and no tricks."

Like a giant hand, the goah's power swept Teller's feet out from under him. The sword spun away, and he fell into the shadows waiting on the floor. They swarmed over him. He swatted at them, tried to climb to his feet, but there were too many and they dragged him down.

With no warning, a vision struck. He was falling through cool water, his arms outspread, bubbles streaming past his eyes. He floated, weightless in the green pool, and the longed-for presence poured into him. *Rulve*, a voice breathed. *Rulve*.

He blinked. He lay on a cold rock floor. A brown-clawed hand was reaching down to seize him. "No!" he cried, scrabbling backward on his heels. Skora blazed into a sword, the goah-shadows scattered, and the hand jerked back. He stood, swaying, the fiery weapon bright in his hand. "Liasit," he gasped. "Bring her to me."

The great presence arrowed itself down at him. Teller struck it head-on with the sword. The impact almost wrenched it from his hands, but the goah exploded into hundreds of red-hot cinders. Sizzling, they hit the walls and bounced on the floor. They lay there simmering, then gathered together, and flowed with a gravelly sound down the grate.

The cinders disappeared into silence. His green dagger lay on the floor. Breathing hard, he picked it up and slid it into his belt. He stared at the grate, his whole body tense.

He waited, the sword growing dim and blood seeping out of the bandage on his arm.

From deep in the grate, clicking sounds rose.

No, he thought with a sinking heart.

The clicking grew louder. A segmented leg emerged, striped purple and black, followed by the hairy abdomen of a morue-spider. Scrambling out on needle toes, it became the size of a dinner plate. Another spider followed, and then a third. A shiver of revulsion passed through Teller as the spiders faced him in a half-circle, their eyes glittering, their fangs and mouth-claws working. One crouched, sprung at him. A thrust of the skora-sword dispatched it, but now the other two were three times as big. The one on the left attacked, and the sword reduced it to ashes. The third jumped away, but now it was as tall as he.

"Do me a favor," Mochlos taunted, "and hit me again."

It pounced. Teller darted to the side but not fast enough. A pair of legs knocked him on his back. The spider crouched above him, squatting to inject its digestive juices. With the flat of his sword Teller swept away a pair of legs to his left and rolled free. He leaped to his feet and his eyes met those of the spider, now above him.

"You are tiring," Mochlos said. "You are only a boy and have endured much these past few rotas."

Teller backed away.

"Why do you fear me?" the goah asked. "We are both creatures of the dark. Embrace me. Find rest. How different am I from that lure of black water, from that last step over the edge of the cliff?"

His right arm throbbed, and he *was* tired, to the very death.

"I have lived here," the spider said, "longer than this stronghold has existed. With me, in me, you can wield more power than you can imagine."

It edged closer, and Teller took another step back. "This sounds like that 'death in life' you mentioned earlier," he said. "No thanks." Holding the sword across his body, he glanced behind him. His back was only inches away from the wall. A memory niggled inside his head, and he tried to capture it.

Almost imperceptibly, staring eight-eyed at him, the spider lowered itself into a crouch. "The girl is dead. Fight me no longer and join her inside me."

"You're a liar. I've been called one so long I know the real thing." The memory surged; of a risky experiment he once had tried, a disaster he'd never repeated.

The spider lunged. Holding the sword high, Teller ripped the air between them with fire. "Tekore ephra!" he cried, and dove to the floor.

Just above his head a raging hole tore open. Its edges crackled with thin blue flames, and a strong wind funneled into it. He scrambled to the side, barely getting out of its way before it snatched the sword from his hand and sent it streaking like a comet into the dark. The wind sucked the spider's huge body against the opening as the goah's legs scrabbled for purchase on the edge of the void. Teller crawled toward it and hacked left-handed at the spider-legs with his dagger. They were as strong as wires. The wind whistled around the creature's body as the void tried to pull it in. The sound rose to a shrill crescendo as it began to succeed. Mochlos shouted a word, the spider-body spiraled into the dark, and with a crack of thunder the rent closed.

In the sudden silence, Teller climbed to his feet. The goah was nowhere to be seen. What had it shouted? Was his sword gone forever? But he was still alive, and so must be the fire. Shaking, clutching the back of the nearby chair, he felt for it inside him. There it was, a tiny ember in a banked hearth.

The light in the room shifted, and he looked up. Liasit stood at the foot of the bed, her head turned toward him. She appeared as he had last seen her, dressed in the thin tunic, her long hair falling over her shoulders. Strained and white-faced, she seemed both luminous and shadowed, like the moon reflected in black water.

"Liasit?" he breathed. He moved to stand before her, his back to the door.

"You came here for me?" she asked. "You would risk your life for one ahn?"

Out of the shadows behind her, the voice of Mochlos spoke, lower than before. "Take her. Take her and get out."

He wasn't prepared for that, for any of this. She looked like the young woman who had touched his heart, but Mochlos had already deceived him under the guise of Aron. Keeping his eyes on her, he turned his head slightly toward the voice. "As easy as that?"

The voice seemed to hesitate. "It took me many years to garner what life I possess. She is not worth risking any more of it."

"So you give me permission to escort what might be a powerful goah out of its prison and into the world?"

"She is who she appears to be. If you don't believe me, you will be outsmarting yourself. Take her and leave me be."

"You're a coward and a parasite!" Teller cried. "Hiding under the forms of women and children. Come out and face me as you are." He directed his anger into the skora embers inside him, and they jumped into flames.

"I already have," Mochlos said, "and don't wish to repeat the experience. My kiss on your arm must be hurting. Its poison is creeping toward your heart, but may yet be stopped. Make up your mind. Do you want the girl or not?"

Teller glanced at his forearm. It had swelled up under the makeshift bandage, and a faint purple streak was spreading toward his elbow. He lifted his gaze to Liasit and addressed her in the mind-speech. *"Liasit, tell me who you are!"* He pleaded with her as she once had with him: in the language that could not lie.

"In these halls she cannot hear that speech." The voice of Mochlos sounded fainter. "Take her hand and go."

"I am truly Liasit," she whispered to him. "But a Mochlos-form would say the same. Leave me and get out while you can. You were sent to save all us ahn, not just one."

He looked into her eyes, and they were brimming with sadness. She opened her arms to him. "A last embrace, T'lir; then go."

He stepped toward her, and she to him. But then, as if a curtain had been pulled aside, a different woman looked out at him: Shavante. Her mouth was open as if to scream, but she had no voice. Her eyes were wide with the desperate command of a great sorceress horribly trapped. Using what must be the last of her Power, pulling at his will, she reached out from inside the goah-form in an imperious demand for release, for the gift of death.

The face rippled back into the ahn's, but now he had no doubt. He pulled out the fire-sword and, with both hands on the hilt, raised it. Liasit winked out, and the red, hulking form of Mochlos lunged at him. With all his strength, Teller cut through the muscle-bound creature from top to bottom.

Split in half, the goah shrieked and fell. Shavante's wispy form rushed from between the halves and with a wild cry, disappeared through the ceiling. The goah's body-parts convulsed, quivered on the floor, then lay still.

Teller stared at them, his heartbeat thudding in his ears.

A thin coil of smoke rose from between the goah's sundered body. It thickened, sucked itself rapidly upward into a twisting, ashy column. A voice growled from within it. "You had no right to release her. Shavante was mine."

The chair across the room creaked. It broke into a pile of short, jagged sticks. With a series of loud snaps, the same thing happened to the chest and then the bed. The room trembled. A shower of jagged stones rained down, and the two globes fell and shattered. Teller backed away from the column as its hot wind swept stones, glass, and sticks into a whirlwind that now bristled with sharp edges. From inside the column, a shadowy human form looked down at him, its eyes burning with hatred.

"I see!" Mochlos hissed. "I see exactly what terrifies you. You cannot escape, for accepting it or rejecting it, you are destroyed!" Pale green flickers lit up the face. "I say now your name, and it will fall upon you as my curse." The form bowed, and irony poured out with its words. "All hail, niyalahn-rista! Niyal'arist, all hail!"

Teller erupted in fire, flinging a huge gout of it into the center of the column. Skora roared through it like a chimney.

"Why so angry?" the creature taunted from the midst of the flames. "The fact that you came here proclaims who you think you are. The savior. The emjadi. You came against me to save an ahn. How admirable. And so I say: all hail, niyal'arist, Teller-of-Lies."

"That's not my name!" He poured more fire into the column, and the form itself burst into flames. "Where are they?" Teller cried. "Where are Liasit and Aron?"

Incredibly, he heard laughter. Burning furiously, the creature's arms and hair shot upward like a huge torch. "They are where they were when you first entered here," Mochlos answered. The fire-filled eyes rested on him in manic glee, and in a parody of tears, the face inside the column began to melt. "In your own thoughts."

With a chuckling sound, the entire burning column collapsed. It ran like rivulets of lava across the floor. They flowed toward him, and in utter repudiation he threw out sheet after sheet of skora, engulfing the rivulets, searing the walls, burning away niyalahn-rista, the heavy burden of who they wanted him to be, words that attacked him from the page, visions that clawed at him from the past. Even the darkness burned, for he was blind with fire, deaf with the roar of flames.

Teller backed out of the room and slammed the door shut behind him. He almost fell from exhaustion, but managed to prop himself, shaking in every limb, up against the wall. Slowly his sight and hearing returned.

He didn't know if he had repelled Mochlos or escaped him, but either way he'd failed. He'd fought for people he couldn't save and repudiated names he didn't want, in a battle that won him nothing. His arm hurt, and he stared at it blankly.

Furtive sounds made him look up. Emboldened by his wound, goah were gabbling in the dark all around him. One grabbed at his ankle, and another dropped onto his shoulders from the ceiling. He shook them off, shouted at them in Widjar, sent them scuttling away with flares of fire.

Ahead was the arch of dim light. He pushed off the

wall and staggered toward it. A globe just ahead of him still crawled with worm-light forever trapped. He aimed skora at it and blasted it off its stand.

It was childishly easy and filled him with satisfaction. He entered the main hall and shattered the first globe he saw. A goah hiding beneath it skittered away in terror. Its haste made Teller smile, then chuckle, and he went reeling down the corridor from one globe to the next, laughing and burning.

Sometimes he incinerated the stand first, and let the globe roll part-way down the tunnel before he hit it. He sent fire spinning down a branching hall, and shadows fled out of it in all directions. He engulfed an entire corridor in clean flame and felt the heat tauten the skin of his face, as if it had just been washed. He burst out into fresh laughter, heard his own crazy cackling die back into chuckles, then unravel into an almost soundless keen of grief.

Deep sobs heaved through him. Each one pulled out handfuls of himself—all-encompassing loneliness, a bottomless despair, the bitter knowledge that he had failed the skora and always would. He hadn't found his name in the Halls of the Goah, only the realization that he didn't want to know it. His name awaited him still, in his own inner, demon-infested halls.

But of one thing he was certain: Mochlos was a liar and Autran a lecher. Liasit lived, and he knew where she was.

Numb to everything but the pain chewing at his arm, he lurched out of the Halls of the Goah and headed up to the sumptuous section of level four. It was deserted. The doors of Autran's apartments were locked, but a white-hot flare opened them.

She was barely conscious, but by that look in her eyes

he knew she recognized him. He cut her bonds, wrapped her gently in the blood-smeared sheet, and carried her by back ways down the passages. He stopped to rest in one of the deserted stairwells, and she turned her head against his chest as he cradled her body. He looked away and tried to summon the strength to face the pain of the isav, where she wouldn't be safe anyway, where she and Aron and all the ahn would still be enslaved.

He looked up as three ahn emerged from the shadows. Two were male, and the other was Hanat, the old woman who emptied the chamber-pots in his section. "We will take her, sir," she said. "We will care for her." Carefully, they pried her away from him.

He watched them go, people who had lost everything, except each other. The wound on his arm flared, and he unwound the bloody bandage. The round bite-mark flushed an angry reddish-purple and sent out fainter streaks of the same color past his elbow. He needed ointment—something—or Mochlos would kill him yet.

He stumbled up one more level and into the laboratorium, empty at this late hour. Shaking badly and awkwardly using his left hand, he rummaged through the potions on the worktable. A flask contained a pale liquid, the elixir inside coiling like a diaphanous red worm. Glass clattered against pottery, the flask broke and spilled, and why was he looking for healing medicines in Oknu Shuld? He swiped the containers off the table with his forearm. They went off the edge in a waterfall of jars and vials that smashed on the stone floor.

His eyes came upon a book, the *Tajemkrew. Regarding the Blood*. Autran always kept it locked. Teller slit the hasp with his dagger, and from long usage the book fell open to a certain page. The words blurred, then sharpened.

Memor, he read...*the minikin mushroom...forgetting the true to remember the false.*

A memory speared through him: a bowl of soup with tiny mushrooms floating in it, the prison bars of light and dark, the insidious whisper in his ear; all bringing a relentless flow of heartbreaking memories.

What, exactly, had they made him believe?

With cold rage he burned the page, then the one underneath, until the whole book caught fire. Small flames leaped onto the streak of spilled liquids and ran along the table top.

He turned at a sound at the door. Autran entered. The Vol glanced at Teller's swollen arm, frowned, then studied his face.

"You're not sure who I am, are you?" Teller said. His voice sounded reckless, frayed.

The Vol raised his eyebrows. "Whatever do you mean?"

"You expected Mochlos, not me."

Edging toward the worktable, the Ségun pointed at him. "What's wrong with your arm?" His other hand shot out toward a jar of acid. Before he could touch it, Teller flared his fingers with skora, and Autran jerked his hand back.

Teller laughed. "Confronting Mochlos has taught the skora a thing or two. So, are you going to use your Power against me now? Summon your big grasshopper? Probably not, since my back isn't turned."

Raising his eyebrows, Autran reared his head back. "What are you talking about, Teller-of-Lies? Have you finally gone completely mad?" His eyes flickered, and that was the only warning Teller got. Rats swarmed out of the dimness and assailed him with furious claws and teeth.

Whirling, trying to shield his right arm, he tore them off his shoulders, hit them with fire. Something like a wire whipped around his waist. Teller glanced down at a thin bronze-colored band. He turned. Autran's eyes were lit, his face glowing. "Surprise! Some of us have more than one Power. This is Coil. Didn't know about that, did you?"

Another band burst out of the first and headed for his throat. Teller fended it off with fire, but two of the rats still clawed at him. He reduced them to smoking balls of fur, but by then Coil had whipped twice around his chest, pinning his left arm at his side and squeezing the air out of his lungs. The fire inside his spirikai began to die back. Everything around him grew dim except for Autran's triumphant face, inches away.

"Make this easy on yourself," the Vol hissed. "Stop resisting me."

Teller pounded at the Coils with his right hand, but they only tightened. Black dots danced in front of his eyes; his ribs creaked. Another coil sprung out and shot toward his free hand. With what seemed like his last breath, Teller hit Autran in the mouth with his fist. The Vol seemed to be caught off guard by a physical defense. His head snapped back and the Coils fell away. Snatching a breath, Teller bowled into him with his shoulder as Autran pulled out his dagger.

Grappling, they crashed against a cabinet. It toppled, and drawers popped open, throwing herbs and powders onto the floor. The Ségun's weapon grazed the goah bite on Teller's right arm, and it exploded in pain. With his left hand Teller chopped at the Vol's wrist, and Autran dropped his dagger. With a grunt of effort, the Vol whipped Coils around Teller's legs, pulled him down, and flung himself on top of him. A corkscrew wire began drilling out of the Vol's spirikai and into Teller's.

At such close range, Coil was powerful beyond belief, and Teller gasped in agony. Connected as they were, he couldn't push the Vol's body off him. He struggled to send a flare up the drill that was impaling him. Autran snarled and pushed the Coil deeper.

Out of nowhere, a gauntleted fist dealt the Vol a blow to his temple. Autran cried out, the Coil hissed out of existence, and the Vol was pulled off him. Teller rolled onto his side, drawing in deep gulps of air. Boots of moldy leather wrapped with thongs were planted next to him. Looking up, he saw the edge of a cloak as tattered as a dug-up shroud, then a scraggly fur doublet stretched over a broad chest. A tight woolen hood covered the head, leaving an opening for the face. Grey skin, spotted with mold, stretched over the skull.

A volghast. Its burning eyes were turned, mercifully, not toward him, but toward Autran.

Pressing a hand over his throbbing spirikai, Teller climbed to his feet. But he couldn't hear himself moving. Flames now engulfed the worktable, but he couldn't hear them either. His breath smoked in a room that was freezing cold, filled with the miasma of dead horror that drove out all sound. But not smell. The volghast reeked like an exhumed corpse.

Addressing Autran, the creature moved its bluish lips, its voice resounding through the silence as if from a sepulcher. "The lord requires your presence. He is not pleased." It grasped the unresisting Ségun by the arm and marched him out of the room. The smell, along with the sense of horror, followed them out.

Heat and sound roared back. Flames snapped, the subaltern at the door shouted orders, and guards rushed through with basins of water. Teller looked down at himself to assess the damage. His shirt was torn; but as before, the Vol's Power had left no wound. Although the skin over his spirikai was unbroken, every part of it ached. His arm ached. The skora, intact, jittered in reaction.

A stir at the door made him look up. Nosce entered the room. The black hood made its way steadily through the chaos, striding directly toward him.

Reflexes on a knife-edge, Teller shot a warning flare at him. It rebounded as if it had hit a black wall and caught his right shoulder. Teller staggered backward.

The Vol was untouched and unmoved. "Follow me," he said. "A vol-ring awaits you."

CHAPTER 27

LOWEST LEVEL

Teller gaped at him, and his thoughts flew apart. A vol-ring?

"It is the lord's will," Nosce said, "that you wear it."

Vol Cinc. Nosce had hinted at it, and now he could claim it. Triumphant vindication leaped up in him. A title finally bestowed, power finally recognized.

Another title—far more dangerous, far more threatening—at last nullified.

But why now? Because he had gone against Mochlos and survived? Because he had evaded Autran's traps? Teller glanced at the ring on Nosce's right hand and remembered what it had cost the Vol. There would be a cost for him as well. The skora rose into the simmering, cautious barrier as the Prome left the room. Teller followed, rolling down his sleeve to hide the inroads of the goah-bite.

Dread and anticipation took turns sewing through him as they went down. They reached level seven, where a sign above the entry to a large chamber read: SEKREW BLOODKNOTS, QUAD 3. Soldiers knelt on one knee to the Prome as he passed. On the way back, would they make the same obeisance to him? The thought seemed distant, hazed with improbability.

Ahead and to the left, the light coming from a corridor was acting strangely. It swelled and waned, suddenly causing Teller to remember shadows of swift-moving clouds fleeing across a sunny meadow. But as he got closer, the memory morphed into reality. These were the luniku pits, where clouds of wasps wheeled over the existing light, swarming to lay their eggs, where their buzzing was pierced by the groans and hysterical shrieks of their victims. His skin crawling, hunching his shoulders, he hauled up the skora barrier as far as it would go to block the pain. They turned a corner, and he sagged in relief as they moved beyond earshot, only to find that the next narrow passage felt almost as bad. It could only be the back entrance to the isav.

A narrow flight of stone steps, rounded from use in the center and slick with mold in the corners, descended to level eight. Humid air enveloped him, carrying the faint stink of rotten eggs. Wet, liver-colored bricks led past the steam-filled baths. So much muddy water had collected on the floor they had to walk over a path made of boards that felt unsteady under his feet. Globes set in ill-made arches passed in a blur; the wound in his arm throbbed. Another smell emanated from a corridor to his left—bones and peels boiling in the kitchen stock-pots. It mingled sickeningly with the tang of sulfur from the bubbling pools behind the scourery, so strong it burned his throat

They veered to the right, where the floor gave way to dry rock again, then stopped at a gate guarded by four burly Bloodknots. They all bowed to the Prome. A subaltern, who wore an eye-patch from under which streaked an old scar, swung open the door, motioned for two of the other guards to join them, and all five moved down the corridor.

They passed through a brick arch so narrow they had to proceed one by one. The arch was lined with a band of copper covered with runes and, as Teller ducked through it, the same chill as when he'd gone into the ale-chamber prickled through him. He winced as the skora collapsed. It left him as vulnerable as if he had lost a layer of skin.

They entered a small, circular anteroom. "I must take your dagger," Eye-patch said. Teller hesitated, but the man assured him it would be returned upon their departure, so he handed it over.

Eye-patch knocked at a door made of oxwood, so thick it would render the room beyond quite sound-proof, and pushed it open. He withdrew, leaving the others to descend three stone steps. The door thudded shut behind them, and the two guards took up a position on either side of it. They had reached the lowest level of the lord's stronghold, the sub-basement of Oknu Shuld. A bright light hit him, along with the reek of blood and vomit.

The light emanated from the utilitarian globes suspended from the ceiling; the reek came from every-where—from two rectangular tables in the middle of the room, from the drain in the slightly concave floor between them, from chains and a pulley set into the far wall. Another oxwood door, inset with an iron ring, faced the one they had just entered. Teller looked away from it; the dungeons must lie beyond.

Shacad stood waiting for them, his muscular arms crossed over his open vest. "Welcome to my strisnu, Teller-of-Lies."

"That's not my name."

The Tierce laughed, then turned and surveyed the room, giving Teller time to do the same.

Dark stains permeated the two tabletops. Ropes were threaded through holes at each corner. At the foot of one of the tables stood a high stool, upon which a leather apron had been tossed. Hooks of various sizes decorated the walls. Shelves along two sides of the room held basins, glass containers filled with what smelled like some of the acids he had worked with in Autran's laboratorium, and various metal instruments carefully arranged on velvet pads.

Chills spiraled through Teller's body. This was the chamber in which his destiny—and its price—would be determined.

Shacad's mouth twisted in a half-smile, and his bright blue eyes burned. "You should know, subaltern, that we are here solely for your benefit." The Tierce stepped to the side, to reveal a small table behind him. On its dark surface lay a vol-ring.

It filled Teller's eyes. Thin silver wires, intricately twisted, formed a band that glinted in worm-light and encircled darkness. It drew him, whispered to him, dared him to seize its power. It gleamed with the promise that he was born to wield it. It would slide over his finger, contract to fit perfectly, and snuff out what was left of his soul.

"You have only," Nosce said in his rasping voice, "to tell us your name."

An icy lump congealed in the pit of his stomach, but then anger swept over him in a red tide. Year after year they had picked at this, year after year had manipulated and coerced, year after year had called him a name they themselves should have borne. It was enough. The ring could take his integrity, his identity, his past and future, but never his name.

"Teller," he grated. "My name is Teller."

Silence settled over the room.

Shacad glanced at Nosce, then back at him. "Part of my job here, subaltern, is to give the lord what he wants.

Sometimes a Power deeply buried. Sometimes assent wrung from the obstinate, or eager service from the arrogant. It takes great skill." He turned to survey a shelf full of metal implements. "It demands precision, fine instruments that can probe at nerves, delicate blades that can snip, one by one, the negations, the refusals, the stubborn denials. And if my subject proves unusually intractable, I work on one last, quivering line." He picked up a small pair of tweezers and stared at it. "Upon that I pluck, like the string of a harp, until my—let us call him my partner—surrenders to what he or she truly is." With horribly blank eyes, he smiled at Teller.

Who turned his head in disgust.

"Do not be rude to the Tierce," Nosce said. "He wants what you want."

Shacad put the tweezers aside, moved to one of the stained tables, and thoughtfully placed his hand on it. The black hairs on his finger had grown through the twists in his vol-ring. "As a young man, I was obsessed with my desire to reduce life to its bare essence. But many times I failed and was left with an inert, dead object. I found that extremely frustrating." He rubbed his big hand gently across the stained table. "But now I've learned patience. Now I treat every session as a voyage of discovery."

The black hood turned toward him. "Do you understand what he is saying, Teller-of-Lies?"

"That isn't my name."

Shacad showed his teeth in a grin. "Such an attitude makes our partnership more interesting for me, but a lot harder for you." He raised his eyebrows. "Ever eat oysters, subaltern? No? They're delicious, but you have to crack them open, then dig in with a sharp knife to get at the meat. I probe as deep and as long as I have to, Teller-of-Lies, to get every bit of it."

He spread out his hands. "I'm a big man, but my partners in the dungeons can attest to my sensitivity. They come along with me, you understand, as we explore our limits together." He strode to the door with the iron ring. "See, here's what I mean."

Knowing what was about to happen, Teller braced himself.

The door swung open and red suffering rushed out. It came from victims of what felt like rotas, weeks, of torture. His arm, his abdomen, his spirikai—every vulnerable spot within him flared in resonance and there was no skora barrier to shield him.

A loud clang cut the suffering off. Nosce had pushed the door shut. "We are wasting time. Teller-of-Lies, speak your name!"

He was not like the ahn beyond that terrible door, not weak like them. He would never relinquish his name, not for any promise, not for any lie. He took a steadying breath. "You know it as well as I do," he said. "It's Teller."

Nosce shook his head slightly. "It appears you have learned nothing from me. Must you learn from Shacad how to speak the truth?"

Teller barked out a laugh. "You wouldn't know the truth if it bit you in the leg."

"Seems like you've chosen the hard path," Shacad said, "but the destination is inevitable." He motioned to the Bloodknots at the door. "Take his shirt off."

They grabbed hold of Teller. The sudden wrench on his arm made him gasp; his struggles sent the room spinning. They jerked off his shirt, his swollen arm catching for a moment in the sleeve.

Nosce grasped Teller's wrist and bent his arm to expose the goah bite to Shacad. "He is already wounded," he said to him. "Bear that in mind, for he must be able to wield skora."

"The lord also demands that I be quick about it," Shacad said irritably. "He wants the impossible, Prome."

Nosce released Teller's arm. "This will demand great restraint, Tierce. The moment you break him, stop. Are you able to do that?"

Shacad passed his fingers over his lips, nodded.

"Show me your choice of instrument."

The Tierce led him to a side table. His hand moved down a row of precision tools, hesitated over one, and seized it.

"No," the Prome said, putting it aside. "Do you want to kill us both, as well as Teller-of-Lies?" A wooden box had been pushed up against the wall, and Nosce bent over it. He rummaged through old metal and corroded links until he found what he wanted. He straightened, and placed in Shacad's palm an iron nail about five inches long.

Shacad looked at it with disdain, but Nosce closed the Vol's fingers over it. "This matter is settled. I shall return from time to time to view your progress." With that, he left the strisnu.

Shacad tied on the leather apron, then turned to the basin to wash his hands in short and jerking movements. He dried them quickly and wiped the nail Nosce had given him on the same towel. It left an orange stain. He turned and gestured to the guards.

They dragged Teller to the wall and snapped shackles around his wrists and ankles. The chain rattled, jerked his arms above his head, and he was bound hand and foot with his face against the wall.

"So tell me, boy," the Tierce said, "what's your name?"

Teller swallowed. "Same as it was the last time."

"Sorry, but you're wrong. I'll write it out for you correctly, Teller-of-Lies."

The point of the nail pierced his left shoulder. It dug in, ripped across, and tore down his spine. He clamped his lips tight against the searing pain.

"That was the letter T," Shacad said.

Rivere ran his hand through his hair, and it felt thin and dry, like an old man's. Blue veins bulged under the backs of his hands, which were always cold now. Not for a long time had they been warm with healing power.

But they still possessed enough strength to circle Ronti's scathi neck and strangle him. It would be his final cure. After that he'd never be able to heal again. It didn't matter. His empathy had been staked out for years in the glare of constant suffering. Exposed and helpless, it had shriveled inside him and turned into something hard and dry. Sometimes it felt almost like hatred.

Sitting on his worn mat, he rested his head against the back wall in privacy unique in the isav. The ahn had used ragged blankets and old casks to construct a small, shoulder-high alcove. their gift to him and to those he tried to heal. At the moment, this included Liasit, who lay on a thin mat beside him, asleep from an herbal soporific he had managed to prepare for her.

The medicines in his healer's pouch had been used up only rotas after he was brought to Oknu Shuld, but Hanat helped him develop substitutes that were more or less effective. The ahn matriarch showed him how to scrape off the burvena-mold that grew on the weeping walls and which sometimes prevented infections, how to collect remedial salts that formed on certain walls of the steam-filled caverns beyond the scourery, and instructed him as to which of the hot muds that bubbled down on

VERONICA DALE

level eight could be mixed with crushed roots and used as a poultice for wounds. Ahn who worked in the morue fields surreptitiously looked for the rare root or healing herb that sprouted after earthquakes caused leaks in the dams. These leaks allowed water to seep into the old waterfall bed or into the dry wash on the plateau, and useful plants were occasionally found there. He filled small jars with such things and kept them hidden in his alcove.

He glanced down at Liasit and envied her sleeping state. With standing permission to enter the dungeons only between the first high gong and the second, he knew that time was imminent. In the past, he would have opened his hands and prayed for the strength to perform a duty he dreaded, but for a long time now he had failed to feel Rulve's presence. His need was too demanding, his despair too great.

Drawing up his knees and resting his forehead on them, he remembered how he used to pray for Teller. For the first few years, not a rota passed when he did not ache for the child, beseech Rulve for him, search for ways to reach him. The boy would be burdened by a power he did not understand and with no one to teach him the good use of it. He would be ignorant of the title that was his from birth. But layers of rock had separated him from the bereft orphan who had once asked him to be his father.

A slight scraping sound caused him to lift his head. Two ahn, coming from work to sleep-shift, were creeping past his alcove. But instead of seeking their mats, they were heading to a dark corner where a few other ahn crouched in a forbidden gathering.

These meetings had started after Liasit discovered that Teller could hear her mind-speech, then increased after all

297

the ahn learned that he had been willing to die for Gorv. Hushed excitement rose to a fevered pitch when, only gongs ago, Teller had braved the wrath of the Ségun of Oknu Shuld and rescued Liasit from the Volarach's inner chamber. Long-buried seeds, Rivere saw to his dismay, were erupting into hope all over the isav.

The two ahn, who had been whispering excitedly to each other, slipped into his alcove. Their faces were lit up. "Rivere, we think it'll be any rota now," the young man called Burken said. "Maybe even tomorrow! Have you heard anything?"

"I can almost see it," the other said in a choked voice. "Oh, Rulve! Him striding down here, blazing with power." She pulled at her collar. "Breaking these scathi—"

"I was just telling her we should go to my brother's farm," Burken went on, "me and her and a few others. He'd be glad for the help, if he's still alive. Or we can clear a patch of scrubland and maybe raise—"

"No, I think my uncle's brewery," the woman broke in. "It's in Baenfeld, and he always needs—"

"Lower your voices," Rivere said tiredly. "You're getting too loud."

The woman clapped her hand over her mouth. Burken turned his head to glance over the partition, apparently saw no one, then leaned closer. "We've got to make sure all the wounded and elderly get out safely, Rivere. You and Hanat should start organizing that."

The woman pulled at the young man's arm. "We've got to go. The proctor will be making his rounds." They bent to smooth Liasit's hair and pat her shoulder, then disappeared into the gloom.

Rivere's heart sank. They were so certain. All over the isav, they huddled in small groups, making plans of where they would go and what they would do when the great hour came. They had forgotten the long intervals in which Teller had done nothing. Yes, he had come looking for Aron in the isav, but had still presided at his Welcoming. He gave Liasit a blanket, but never broke the power of her collar. He would have let Gorv escape, but at no real cost to himself: the Vols would never let the one with skora perish. He saved Liasit from the Vol, temporarily, but she was still a slave.

He should have kept Teller's identity a secret from the ahn. In those terrible rotas after they had been separated, when he was first sent down to the isav, he had fully intended to do that. He never breathed the word "niyalahn-rista." It was the ahn who first whispered it to him, a word that, like flint, made a spark in their darkness. Even the smallest child had already been taught how to pronounce the long title that gave them hope.

Young Keya, all those years ago, was the one who had ignited that spark into an open flame. She had rushed down to the isav with her news, as if it were a candle cupped in her hands, her eyes shining with its glow. Teller had befriended her; a rista had befriended an ahn! They urged Rivere to tell them more about the little boy, but still he held his tongue. Then, when the entire isav learned what Teller tried to do for Keya, and at what cost, many of the ahn wept.

The boy's sacrifice wrenched the truth from Rivere, and he found himself telling a few of the elders all he knew. They clutched at every word. But Rivere warned them: to acknowledge the boy before his time would mean death, for them and for him.

Word spread, of course, but the ahn kept Teller as their deepest secret, kept him treasured and hidden in their hearts. With eyes of faith they watched him, hung their hopes on his every action, waiting for the rota when he would acknowledge who he was—the niyal'arist, sent by Rulve as their savior.

But that rota didn't come, and by now Rivere was sure it never would.

Breathing hard, burning lines fused onto his back, Teller climbed yet again to his feet. He clenched his hands, the fingernails digging into his palms, while the goah bite pulsed with what felt like acid. A voice echoed, but he couldn't understand what it said.

The skora inside him, however, did. His encounter with Mochlos had strengthened it, and the fire was greater now than when he had entered Power-suppressed areas before. It raged inside, clawing against the strisnu's restraint, against the shackles that bound him to the wall, wild to flame out against his tormentor. But it was his own body it rent, and he had to quell the anger or it would tear him to pieces. He had to let hatred roll off him and onto the floor; let it flow down that drain behind him.

The voice edged into clarity. "—was E, Teller-of-Lies. The second E. So now, let's hear your name."

He had told him four times already, and four times tensed every muscle in his body while the Tierce cut another letter into his back.

"I'm running out of space," the Vol said. "Guess I'll have to write on top of what's already here." He tapped Teller's left shoulder with the nail. "So we continue, right?"

"Trouble is," Teller said hoarsely, "you keep getting it wrong."

"Fine. Have it your way."

Knowing what was coming, Teller arched his back and took a wavering breath. It rushed out in a stifled cry as with several hard strokes Shacad formed the letter R. It seared into his skin like a brand and ran down, melting.

The Vol leaned closer and spoke in a tight voice. "Your name is Teller-of-Lies, isn't it."

A shudder ran through him, making the chains rattle. "It's not," he shouted.

Shacad made a strange sound, part moan and part gurgle. Another letter ground into him, bright-beaded in his mind. "Is that correct now, Teller-of-Lies? Is it? Answer me, Teller-of-Lies."

A bright hand-globe, visible through the opening in his alcove, was making its way toward him. The proctor. Glancing at Liasit, Rivere got to his knees. Even though asleep, her fingers clutched a trailing corner of one of the blankets that formed his small enclosure. It was the isav's most precious possession. With his own hands, Teller had draped it over Liasit's shoulders. The ahn regarded it as a symbol of Rulve's care for them, a tacit promise they would soon be set free.

The proctor shone his light onto Liasit's face. "Is she dead?" He prodded her with his foot.

She refused to die. The savior was here, she had murmured when they brought her in, even at the gates. "No, sir," Rivere said. "I've given her a drink to make her sleep."

"When will she be ready for her regular duties?"

"Soon," he lied. "Perhaps as early as next rota."

"She'd better be. We don't feed malingerers. Except to the worms." He laughed and moved on.

The place where the ahn had been gathered was now empty. With the approach of the proctor, they had melted into their sleeping mats. The gong he'd been dreading sounded. With a pang of despair, Rivere climbed to his feet. He left the alcove, shuffled past rows of empty mats, and took the tunnel down to the dungeons. Please God, don't let Ronti start moaning again.

He trudged down the narrow steps, pushed open the door, and entered a short corridor that reeked of everything that could come out of a tortured human body. The low ceiling brushed the top of his head, and the whole place was lit by only one globe at the end, where the door to the strisnu was. To his sick dismay, Ronti's moans ground through the air. They irritated him, like fitful torchlight in the face of one trying to sleep.

Four solid locked doors stood on both sides of the passageway, and he knew by name who lay behind each one. Driven not by compassion anymore but by guilt, he dropped to his knees before the first door. A rustle, then a long sigh, answered his whisper. He wedged as much of his hand as he could between the stone floor and the rough bottom edge of the door. It was not far enough for healing, it was never far enough, but fingers quickly covered his.

After a while he moved on. He was too weary to keep rising and then kneeling again, so he crawled from one door to the next, to lie on his side while their fingers touched. If only he could dredge up some feeling for them, some small sympathy, but there was nothing, only the grating irregularity of Ronti's moans. Ronti could stop them if he tried. If he wanted to, he could keep his scathi mouth shut.

He had to force himself to stop at Aron's door. Still disoriented from the severing of the bond with his brother, the little ahn had not yet been touched by Shacad. Their "partnership," the Tierce said, must wait for when he had the time to savor it. As dark-haired as Teller, Aron was only as old as Teller had been when the wyvern carried him here. With all his soul, Rivere dreaded speaking to him, for he knew what awaited the little boy.

The child must be upset by the moans coming from the next cell. Rivere shoved his hand under the door, and immediately Aron grasped the tips of his fingers. His hand was wet, with tears he must have tried to wipe away.

"Rivere," the boy whispered, "is the ni-rista really coming? Will Rulve come too?"

Even here the rumors spread. He pressed his forehead against the floor and swallowed down his anguish. "Yes," he said, keeping his voice steady, telling as much of the truth as he could. "Yes, Aron. Rulve will come for you. You might be"—oh God—"might be hurt for a while, but Rulve will come."

"Today? I mean, this rota? Do you think this rota?"

The boy had been here barely long enough to learn about rotas, yet still had absorbed the faith of the ahn. A sudden blank weariness settled over him. "I don't know," he muttered. "I have to get to the others now." He pulled his hand away and crawled forward.

Useless, unable to do the least, scathi thing, he visited the rest of the prisoners. Finally, he came to the last door, the one closest to the globe and the strisnu entrance. This door was not solid but barred, and he could see Ronti inside. Shacad intended that he should.

Ronti could not see him, or hear him, or move toward him at all. Rivere sat beside the bars and leaned against them. The young man inside was covered with a blood-stained blanket. His head was turned away and all Rivere could see was the matted hair. Ronti was dying. For rotas Rivere waited for him to do it, angry and impatient, as if with an unwanted guest that tarried too long.

Stretching out on the floor, he reached in as far as he

could. His fingers touched only the very edge of the ahn's blanket. It pulled slightly as it rose and fell with every groan. He tried to reach the other with his thought—*squirm this way, lad, where I can reach you. I can make all this end.* But he was no mind-speaker. Without getting his hands on him, he could give Ronti nothing—no warmth, no comfort, and no quick death. He pulled his arm out and just lay there, the ahn's groans grating in his stomach.

The gong rang twice, and a guard appeared at the far door. "Time's up," he said, yawning.

Rivere climbed to his feet. He couldn't go back to the isav just yet, couldn't face whoever would be waiting there, sick or bleeding, hoping for help. Just outside the dungeon, he edged into a tiny, unlit alcove and sat there, his head in his hands. He trembled with bitter self-loathing, his throat swollen with sobs he could not release.

Teller's knees buckled, sending a wrench through his shoulders and forcing his whole weight to hang from the shackles around his wrists. Air squeezed out of his lungs and this time he couldn't get his feet under him. He dangled against the wall and struggled to breathe, twisting under the stinging net of pain that adhered to his back. Someone dragged him upright, and he sucked in air. A cup was pressed to his lips. Water. His mouth was parched and he drank eagerly. But it was a potion that turned to fire in his throat and he choked on it. Behind him, Shacad was talking.

"—awake now? Do I have to keep writing on this messy page? When are you going to tell me your scathi *name?*" He sounded more agitated, more strained.

As if it belonged to someone else, Teller heard his own

voice, dry and cracked, emerging from between his outstretched arms. "You must be deaf," he croaked, "as well as perverted."

A hand grasped his hair and yanked his head back. "Don't you dare judge me! I'm the Tierce of Oknu Shuld, and you're nothing but a bound weakling. You stand here stripped of power like an ahn."

The suppressed skora roiled into reckless anger. "If we"—his throat felt so raw it was hard to talk—"were anyplace else, skora would sear you into the wall."

With his strong fingers still twined in Teller's hair, Shacad pressed the nail-point above his cheek. "We are where we are, and I keep on writing until you tell me what I want to hear. But first, I'll sign my work." Teller tensed, his body rigid, his eyes squeezed shut, as Shacad etched the long letter *S* onto the side of his face. "That will scar, pretty boy," the Vol hissed. "It's my mark on you, and it'll be permanent."

Abruptly the Vol let go of his hair and stepped back, breathing heavily. Teller's forehead banged against the wall, and a hot, thin liquid trickled down his cheek and past his mouth. It dripped onto the floor, big wet spots like the first drops of a storm. It was anger draining away. It had to be, or he was lost. He strained upward, grasped the chain with his left hand, and squeezed it until his rage subsided and all he felt was the sawing, relentless pain.

Behind him, the Tierce was pacing. "Beyond that door," he said, "lies one I've worked with for several rotas. I spent gongs on him, meticulous and disciplined. We came nearer and nearer to the line that vibrates between life and death, Ronti and I, but I never crossed it, never even touched it. But I came close. Very, very close. But I'm a professional, so I hold back, hold back everything, even breath. Yes, it's hard, patience is god*dam* hard."

Teller heard water being poured, splashing into a cup. After a few gulps, the remains were tossed onto the floor. Thirst lined his throat like sand, and he pictured cool water spilling over the stone, rushing in a little rivulet toward the drain, flowing all wasted into blackness.

Shacad's breath touched his ear. "You don't know the deep places where I dwell, Teller-of-Lies. I exist on the bottom of oceans. With my partner in my arms, I sink under the long and rolling swells of heat." He grasped Teller's shoulder, and his voice shook. "Their pain beats through my guts, in my cock, but I'm holding back, holding back"—he squeezed and his breath came in short gasps—"shoving into that wet red place, shoving until—"

Revulsion rose in Teller's chest, and he jerked his shoulder away from Shacad's hand. "You," he rasped, "make me sick, Vol."

Shacad caught a breath. Exhaling a growl, he cut him twice from shoulder to shoulder, then slashed another groove down the left side of his back. "F." He panted. "Four more letters to go. Four more over this scathi bloody page. Read to me, Teller-of-Lies. Read what I've written here."

Nothing could relieve the pain, not even grinding his forehead against stone. "Teller," he etched out. "You're writing Teller."

Shacad turned him so that his forearm, swollen and throbbing now up to the shoulder, was exposed. With the nail he touched the spot where Mochlos had bitten him.

With a hiss of pain, Teller turned his head away.

"Here's where I should've made the O," Shacad murmured as if to himself. "I'll re-write it here, another kiss to add to the goah's."

Teller grabbed the chains in readiness. Shacad's nail cut into his fevered arm, and a cry tore through him as if his will were straw ignited. His knees gave way again, but he hung on with both hands. Red agony blinded him, but when it washed away he was standing, shaking and sick with suppressed fire, his forehead pressed against the wall.

A diffident voice spoke out behind him—one of the Bloodknot guards. "I think the Prome would advise that you leave off for a moment, Vol Tierce."

Shacad uttered a muffled oath and moved away. Metal clinked as he searched through his instruments. "Cell five," he ordered. "Bring me the ahn in cell five."

An instinct in Teller began to keen, an alarm rising into terror, for something was coming that must not come. Painfully, he turned his head to face it. The guards were obeying, were turning towards the terrible door, were grasping the iron ring, were beginning to pull.

It must not open again, not now. It would break him apart. Frantically he twisted around as far as his bonds allowed, tried to call out to Shacad, but his voice emerged as a hoarse croak that blended into the groaning of the door.

Appalling torment roiled out from it as from the mouth of a furnace, the acuity of their pain sweeping into one with his. He tried to shrink into his own huddled center, but he was stretched out and there was no escape. He flicked a glance to the side and saw Aron. His stomach lurched.

The child met his eyes, and immediately fell to his knees, his face furrowed with shock. "Ni—ni-rista!" he cried, "you're bleeding!"

"Be quiet, Aron!" he urged in the mind-speech. "Don't say a word!"

"What's this?" Shacad turned and regarded the boy with narrowed eyes.

The guards hauled Aron to his feet, and he looked up at the Tierce in horror.

"What name did you call him?"

"Say rista! You called me rista."

Aron stood rooted, and the Tierce slapped him. "Rista!" the child wailed. "I called him rista!"

"No. You said another name. What was it?"

Teller groaned inside himself. Niyalahn-rista. Aron would scream it out, the long word so hard for him to pronounce. Shacad would make him repeat it, over and over, and then the little ahn would start to die. All for a lie, all for a title he utterly rejected.

The boy remained silent.

Shacad addressed the two guards. "Tie him to that table."

A jolt went through Teller's heart. Names crowded around him like crows, screeching at him, tearing pieces off him. His dreams were a lie, his memories lied to him, and he had never really known the truth. He was far too corrupted for any niyal'arist destiny, and if he decreed differently, he would be, indeed, a teller of lies.

Aron whimpered as the guards seized him.

Behind him the vol-ring waited, a black maw that would swallow him and save the ahn, for out of its throat would spew the one name that would drown out all others. Teller, t'lir, niyalahn-rista—all would be, now and forever, obliterated by Cinc.

With an effort, he addressed Shacad, his voice sounding hollow between his arms and the stone wall. "Leave the boy alone."

Through simmering red coals of pain, he heard Shacad crunch to his side. "You have something to tell me?"

"What does it matter," he rasped, "what the ahn think they know? What does it matter—if Cinc tells them the truth?"

The Vol's words fell over him like a shower of sparks. "In utter graciousness the lord offers favor to one called Teller-of-Lies. Are you he?"

Bitter tears stung the back of his eyes. Gorv's face swam before him, Keya's warm glance, Liasit's tentative mind-touch—they spun slowly downward with all things lost, and it was a lie to say he knew himself, or ever would.

"Say your name, and be released!"

He wore a cloak of fire, was etched with letters that spelled the truth. He pulled it out of him with a strangled cry. "Teller-of-Lies, Tierce! Teller-of-Lies."

CHAPTER 28

RIVERE'S CHOICE

The chains rattled down. With a long ragged breath, Teller slid to his knees. The two guards removed the shackles from his wrists and ankles, poured more of the fiery liquid down his throat, and pulled him to his feet.

Black in the meager light, a rivulet of blood trickled into the drain on the floor, and when he looked up from that everything had changed. The globes seemed dimmer, as if a film of dust had coated them. A gauzy veil separated him from the pain that floated just above his back and arm and cheek, and he couldn't seem to get objects into proper focus.

They took him to stand before Nosce. How long he'd been present Teller didn't know. The Vol appeared flat, with no depth, like a hooded dream-figure outlined in black. He bowed slightly and held out the vol-ring.

Teller reached across what seemed an interminable distance. He took the ring and pushed it onto the third finger of his right hand. It passed over his knuckle and tightened to fit. The ring felt prickly and cold, like a spider wrapped around the skin.

"The lord will be pleased, Teller-of-Lies," Nosce said. "You have gained wisdom at last, Vol Cinc."

Teller turned his head to look at Aron's white and stricken face. The child seemed to recede down the length of a long tunnel. Only the ring, gripping his finger, felt real.

Nosce addressed the Tierce. "The lord summons you, Vol. In regard to urgent matters above." He indicated two Vorian guards who now stood at the bottom of the steps, along with Eye-patch, another Bloodknot guard, and a second subaltern who held a red cloak folded over his arm. Shacad took off his apron, threw it on one of the tables, and followed the Vorians out the door.

Nosce's hood swiveled toward Teller. "Your Acclamation, Volarach Cinc, will be held two rotas from now." He turned to Eye-patch. "See that the dungeons are cleaned out. When the Cinc of Oknu Shuld is ready to proceed to his new apartments, escort him." Then he departed.

Eye-patch barked an order, and two of the Bloodknots opened the iron-ringed door at the other end of the room. The pain of the prisoners within swept like furnace heat against his spirikai, but the draught seemed to blunt the worst of it. He bit his lip until the door banged shut against the guards' grumbling voices. The remaining guard grasped Aron by the shoulder, and Teller stiffened. After all that had happened, the child was still in danger.

But, he suddenly realized, he could do something about that. He stepped forward on a floor that seemed to tilt and addressed the guard. "Return the boy to the isav. Unharmed." His voice came out in a hoarse rasp.

Uncertain, the man glanced at Eye-patch, but Teller grabbed his chin and thrust his be-ringed fist into his face. The Bloodknot paled, then thumped his chest in acknowledgement. "Yes, Vol." He marched Aron away, the child's head hanging low.

Eye-patch thrust a wad of fabric at him. He looked at

it; it was his shirt. Blood trickled down his cheek, and he wiped it away with the wadded-up garment. He wouldn't go bleeding through the halls. "Find a man named Rivere," he croaked. "Bring him to my room."

"Yes, Vol." With a short bow, Eye-patch returned Teller's dagger and left the strisnu.

It was that easy. At the thought, bitter laughter rose up in him. Easy?

The other subaltern handed him his red cloak. He waited while Teller tried with one numb and shaking hand to get it over his bare shoulders. Finally the man placed it over him. The heavy garment bristled over his wounds.

His escort led him out of the strisnu. As soon as he stepped through the doorway, the skora rushed up. It circled the ring on his right hand like a wary dog sniffing at something unknown and dangerous, then formed the customary barrier around him.

The subaltern picked up two more guards, and all three steered him through passageways and up stairs. There seemed to be too many stairs, weaving skeins of them, but not once did he allow himself to stumble. His cheek burned with the ragged S, and he kept it averted from passers-by. Pain began flickering down his arm and back; the draught seemed to be wearing off.

The guards stopped at a deeply carved double door, and the subaltern pushed it open. Teller stared into a huge room. Several globes—he wasn't sure how many—illuminated padded chairs, carved cabinets, and an ornate desk. They all wavered before him, flat and unreal. He blinked at what he thought was a tall painting, but it was an open door that led to another room. He glimpsed part of a bed, bigger than any he had ever slept in.

He turned to the guards. "Rivere," he rasped.

"As you ordered, Volarach."

The door shut softly behind him, and he was alone. Desperate for water, he entered the bed-chamber, let his stained shirt fall on the carpet, and groped his way toward a ceramic pitcher that stood on a washstand against the wall. Its glaze of gold-leaf spirals passed in front of his eyes as he shakily filled the matching cup, gulped the liquid down, and poured another. The water was half gone when he caught sight of the ring on his finger.

It could get Rivere into his room, but never out of Oknu Shuld. So why had he summoned him? So Rivere would say he understood? Would—somehow—forgive him? But he was Cinc now, the Lord of Shunder's Vol, and could never be forgiven.

He dropped the cup, intending to rush to the door and negate his command, but a shaft of pain cut through him. He stumbled toward the huge bed. A fur coverlet lay upon it, too valuable, too sleek, to stain with blood. He pulled it off and sank face down onto the cool sheets. With his good hand he clutched the pillow as agony leaped upon him like a manic beast.

The sound of scraping and the grumbling of guards brought Rivere out of his alcove. Two Bloodknots were dragging emaciated, blood-streaked bodies out of the dungeon. They were all dead. Ronti was dead. Guards, muttering about having to clean out Shacad's garbage, had done what he could not: ended seven pitiful lives efficiently and quickly. Perhaps Ronti rested now, fully restored, in his Creator's arms. Perhaps they all did.

But where was the little boy? Oh god, was Aron in the strisnu?

A subaltern approached him, coming from that direction. "Volarach Cinc summons you, to assist in preparations for his Acclamation."

Rivere looked at him. There were five Vols now? He followed the man up to the fourth level, his anger building. Seven helpless prisoners had just been slaughtered, and an innocent child was being tormented, yet this Cinc must be immediately served.

They left him in an apartment of dim magnificence, but his mind's eye saw only the bodies of the dead. He entered the bedchamber, his vision still red with their blood, and the sight of the scarlet cloak assaulted his eyes. Hemmed with the slate band of the Azanzi Scaths, it covered the back and one arm of the Vol who lay face down on the great bed, probably sleeping off hours of raucous celebration. An expensive fur coverlet was tossed disdainfully on the floor, next to a wadded-up shirt. A ceramic cup had been thrown onto the thick carpet. Apparently none of these had suited this arrogant subaltern, who had just been so spectacularly promoted.

Silently Rivere approached the bed and looked down at the Cinc of Oknu Shuld. A large dark spot stained his red cloak, no doubt from the ale-chamber. On his right hand, partly covered by the cloak, glittered a vol-ring.

Rivere bent over him. The Vol was surprisingly young, perhaps not even twenty, and he was not sleeping. Rigidity gripped his entire body, and pain creased his face. Rivere jerked off the red cloak. The Vol gasped, for the fabric had adhered to his back. Blood welled up from an array of brutal gashes.

Anger spread out from a tight center and slowly took hold. Rivere was not sickened. Disgust at whatever rites they used was beyond him and he did not care how the lord made them his own. But to expect healing for this, to dirty him with it, expressed such insane malignity that it left him shaking in the grip of murder.

With a cry, he flung himself on the bed and seized the Vol's throat with both hands.

His fingers were not as strong as they once were, but he squeezed them against the windpipe as hard as he could. The Vol flailed weakly under him as he bore down with the relentless pressure of years, with a long and steady outflow of rage, willing his fingers into an iron, choking collar. Let the Vol wear what the ahn wore, he thought fiercely. Let him die as they die.

"No!" Someone grabbed his wrists, pulled them away with a strong and bony grip. "Rivere!"

The Vol fell back onto the bed with a rasping breath. Rivere looked up, into the old, moist eyes of Hanat.

"What are you doing?" she cried. "Can't you see you are hurting him?"

He laughed. "Hurting him! I would destroy him. Now, in his weakness."

She stared at him, her eyes wide. "My God, Rivere! He is Teller. The one Rulve sent to save us."

The flow of things stopped. What was she saying? Teller? Rivere turned again to look at the young man. He saw the left side of his face, the tense plane of his jaw, sweaty strands of hair lying over his flushed cheek and neck.

During his captivity he had imagined Teller's face many times. He remembered an infant in the Seani, crying night after night for his twin, while he knelt beside the crib and reached through the slats to lay comforting hands upon him. He remembered the dark head of a three-year-old nestled against his chest, the curve of a smiling five-year-old's jaw that fit so well into his cupped hands. Oh God, it was Teller who lay there, the niyalahn-rista, the long-waited child of promise.

But he was that child no longer. He had grown into

a traitor who flaunted the red cloak, who laid his niyal'arist power at the throne of evil. A vol-ring shone triumphantly on his hand.

Something inside him crystallized and formed a hard, sharp lump in his chest. "He is the Cinc of Oknu Shuld. His Acclamation is two rotas away. Even now he lies under the marks of his initiation, and they burn him and sicken me. I don't care who he once was. Now he is a monster, who has chosen the vol-ring."

"His choice saved Aron's life! I think many lives."

"What are you talking about?"

"Shacad took Aron into the strisnu. Ronti and the others weren't enough for him. Aron told us Teller was there, chained to the wall and bleeding. But he still mind-spoke to him and saved him from the Tierce. I think—I think Teller tried to help all the ahn, perhaps in the only way he could." Her face crumpled. "I can't understand why this terrible thing happened!"

Rivere seized Teller's right hand and held it up. "This ring, Hanat, is what you don't understand. This *choice* is what you don't understand."

Hanat's mouth set. "We both know who this young man is, and no ring can hide it."

Rivere dropped Teller's hand and looked into the old woman's eyes. He had hurt every ahn, inflicted as much damage upon them as Shacad had to any of his victims. With his healer's words, he had dangled a dream before them, a niyalahn-rista dream that lifted their heads and bred hope out of ashes.

Now all that was gone. "I thought I knew who he was too. But all these years, Hanat, all these years I was lying to you. To all the ahn. I didn't mean to. But—can't you see?—all hope, all salvation here is a lie, and we can't tell each other any more lies!"

She drew back from him. "They were not lies. Our faith is not a lie."

"Teller has chosen evil. Your faith is blind."

"It's not blind! I see a niyal who has mind-spoken to us. I see an ahn who feels what we feel. I see a rista who holds power. Rulve has created him niyalahn-rista and sent him to live among us, and there he is, lying wounded and in need of you. You say Teller made his choice. Now what will your choice be?"

He grabbed her arm. "This moment is a gift, Hanat. Help me destroy him!"

She shook off his grip. "You would choose murder? How is that choice any less evil than his?"

Their eyes locked. Her complete conviction, her utter trust, caused a flicker of doubt.

"We must not allow the ring he wears to destroy our faith," she said, "or lure us into evil. The future will bring salvation, the past will be redeemed, but only if we do Rulve's will *now*."

She shifted her gaze to Teller, and he did the same. Quivering with pain, the young man lay utterly vulnerable with his back in shreds, his arm red and swollen. Rivere remembered—in spite of himself he vividly remembered—a boy whose mind had been raped.

"Rivere," the old ahn implored. "Rulve has put it into you to heal. There is no other way for you." She regarded him silently for a moment, then got to her feet, brought the basin, and put it on the floor before him. "Aron saw tears in his eyes, Rivere. Vols do not weep."

But no longer could he. Teller had been wrenched away from him a second time, and this time forever. He had been torn away even from his own destiny. The terrible loss burned in Rivere's throat and behind his eyes, but found no release in tears.

"Twelve years ago," he said, "when they dragged me away from this boy, I thought Rulve would protect him. I believed that Teller and I must have been brought to Oknu Shuld for a reason, that all this suffering must somehow be Rulve's will, part of her compassionate plan for good. I soon discovered I couldn't help Teller, but I thought it was Rulve's redemption that I could at least help the ahn. But there was too much cruelty, too much death. I could accomplish nothing. Nothing! Rulve forgive me, I could do nothing but hate, and now there is no healing left."

Hanat crouched before him and stroked his hands, as if trying to bring the power back into them. Gently, she turned his head to look at Teller.

Rivere's habit of deep seeing was dragging him inevitably toward compassion. He couldn't help it. He could feel the terrible pain of Teller's choice. For the ahn, for himself, for this young Vol, the consequences were just beginning.

"Tell me," Hanat said, "what I should do."

She knew what to do, better than he. She was the true healer here, and perhaps not only for Teller. "Go and fetch our jars," he answered wearily.

She soon returned, but even her gentle ministrations hurt Teller; every touch of water or salve on his back caused him to gasp. She gave him some of their precious lethean, and with a shudder, he let go and slumped into unconsciousness. This made everything easier as she cleaned his wounds and covered them with a thin layer of burvena.

Rivere, meanwhile, worked on Teller's forearm. An angry bite-mark—from what creature he would not speculate—glared on the underside of it and the skin was tight with swelling. Already a faint line of reddish-purple had reached past the elbow on its silent and purposeful journey to the heart. Rivere made several quick incisions to bleed out the poison, then placed Teller's arm in a basin full of brine to draw out what remained.

Hanat noticed blood on the pillow, and when they turned Teller's head, found another wound on his cheek. They cleaned and coated it, but Hanat feared there would always be a scar there to shame him. As if, Rivere thought distantly, the ring would not do that enough.

When they were finished, Hanat packed the medicines away, touched Rivere on the shoulder, and left the room. He pulled up a chair beside the bed, on Teller's right, and sat down with a sigh. The cuts on the young man's back and cheek no longer bled, most of the pain-creases had left his face, and his breathing was shallow but regular.

Rivere remembered a small boy sitting on his lap, who turned to him with bright, hopeful eyes and begged him to be his father. But at that time the memory of his own son, killed in Oknu Shuld, cut too deeply in his heart. Without knowing any better, he had proudly brought his own little rista up to the Garden of Welcoming. Taking his son by the hand, he had condemned him. What if he had condemned Teller also, on that day so long ago, when he turned away from a child who needed him for one who no longer did?

He cried out in his heart to Rulve. *Why did you create him if you knew he would be corrupted?*

There was no reply. There was no divine plan, no salvation for Shunder, no hope for the ahn. Teller was lost.

The young man lying on his stomach stirred. "Rivere?" he whispered.

Rivere leaned closer, need swelling painfully in his chest. "Teller! Whose are you?"

He turned his head toward him, winced, then opened his eyes. They were liquid with returning pain. "Teller-of-*Lies*," he rasped. "Can't you read it?"

"What do you mean? Read it where?"

With a bark of derisive laughter, followed by a long and jagged in-breath of pain, Teller waved his left hand toward his back.

The wounds were just visible under the burvena poultice: long, angular cuts, except for a few that were curved or even round. They trembled on the edge of meaning. They were, he suddenly realized, letters.

The cut on Teller's face now jumped out at him. It was an S, the signature he had seen before on Shacad's victims. He saw that Hanat had treated Teller's wrists, which were raw and scraped. But he had not thought to find any of these marks on a Cinc of Oknu Shuld and didn't at first recognize them. Neither had he recognized the bitterness and defeat engraved on Teller's face.

Perhaps his first estimate of the wounds had been wrong. Perhaps they were no chosen rites, but a savage imposition of the Eyascnu's will. A ghost of hope flickered in him, but he remembered the ring on Teller's hand, hidden now under the pillow.

"The vol-ring. How could they force you to wear it?"

The lines around Teller's eyes and mouth deepened. He withdrew his right fist from under the pillow. It was clenched tight against the sheet, the knuckles white. He opened it, fully exposing the ring. "Rivere"—he swallowed—"I put it on myself."

The twisted wires winked slyly up at him, chosen evil, secure in its ascendancy and ultimately victorious.

Teller's averted eyes filled with tears. Trembling, he turned his hand palm up and slowly extended it toward

Rivere. Begging to be taken, to be held, to be understood, it was a wordless plea.

But it came too late. He could not reach out, could not take Teller's hand. The ring had forever desecrated it. "You chose what you chose, Vol Cinc."

A vein pulsed in Teller's throat. He squeezed his eyes shut and slid his hand back under the pillow.

Chapter 29

Acclamation

The old ahn salved his back, gave him lethean to drink, and brought meals he could not eat. A subaltern set out new boots for his Acclamation. The Prome went over the ceremony, including his three brief responses. A nervous tailor from the village brought bolts of cloth and measured him for new clothes, assuring him that he and his assistants would get them finished in time. Teller chose fabrics of unrelieved black. Some of his former attire, the tailor pointed out, had actually been dark blue or green; but for years, in the dim light of Oknu Shuld, Teller had believed it was black. Now it would be.

His Acclamation proceeded in a lethean blur. He was escorted to the main aisle at the rear of the hall, where the light from the red-veined globes crawled over a great smear of shabby white on either side: the backs of obeisant ahn, crushed down on the marble tiles like trodden-on cocoons. Even through the pain-draught, he felt them.

The sensation joined the distant simmering on his back and the pulling sensation of the S on his cheek. The Igneous Eye tinged the faces of dignitaries, foreigners, and village elites with red; the purple plumes of the Vorian Guards clashed sickeningly with doublets of slate, cobalt and maroon; and the massed crimson of subalterns' cloaks blazed against his eyes.

At a signal from the master of ceremonies, he walked up the center aisle while the section of rista students bowed low. A select group of Azanzis, Bloodknots, and Skinners clashed swords against shields, and all five archons thumped their chests. He took his seat in the front row, the last in the line of Vols.

With a roll of drums, the door at the back of the dais was thrown open, and the whole assembly, including the Vols, fell to their knees. The Lord of Shunder entered. It was the first time Teller had laid eyes on the Eyascnu Varo, to whom he had pledged his body and soul.

He appeared to be a middle-aged man, strong and confident, who took his place on a throne big enough for two. Smiling, and wearing a simple silver crown made of twisted wires set with amethysts, with a ring to match, he raised his arms to the applause of the crowd. He gave the impression of putting aside the trappings of power, wearing no cloak, only a silk loose-sleeved shirt striped with purple and black, and black trousers that tapered into his soft leather boots.

As Teller knelt there and the ceremony went on, a deep uneasiness filtered through him. The lord's mouth and aquiline nose were clearly visible, but the eyes were blurry smudges. Teller blinked several times to clear his sight, but the effect remained. Even worse, a disturbing aura crept out from the throne. It seeped into his draught-dimmed brain like ink. To take his mind away from it, he focused on the round carpet in front of the throne. Its weave depicted purple morue flowers, prickly leaves intertwining, and—from the corner of his eye he saw them, but when he looked directly at them they merged into twigs or stems—morue-spiders poised for the hunt.

Contrary to what Teller had expected, Autran was present. The Vol, after all, had tried to seize a Power that belonged to the lord. Apparently he had paid at least something for that: Autran looked thinner than he had only rotas ago, and his glassy eyes bulged out of a face that seemed longer and more gaunt. At a gesture from the lord, Nosce came forward to address the assembly. Under a cloak of increasing pain, Teller shifted his weight on his knees. The Vol's voice buzzed in his ears while waves of power emanated from the throne. The lord's smeared eyes stared at nothing, but the great Eye, burning behind its red glass on the wall above, watched him constantly.

The Vols came forward—Autran walking with an odd, spindly gait—to put their clasped hands between the long and elegant hands of the lord. Then it was Teller's turn. He climbed to his feet and went to kneel on the carpet before the throne. It gave slightly, covering soil made friable by years of blood spills. He extended his folded hands, and the lord's icy grip surrounded them. The lord bent over him, and for a split second, the white face filled Teller's vision. A wave of horror washed over him.

The lord had no eyes. There was nothing above the nose but a smooth expanse of skin.

Still gripping his hands, the lord leaned back slightly. Teller's vision shifted, and he saw he'd been mistaken. The Eyascnu Varo appeared as before. It must have been the lethean, or a trick of the light. His hands were released, and it was time for the three questions required by the rite.

Teller had, in essence, answered them as a child, but now he was doing it as an adult. Now he understood what he was giving, what it had cost, and what he would get in return.

The red lips, gleaming and moist, parted. "Do you pledge your body to me?"

Teller, his palms sweating but his gaze steady, repeated the practiced answer. "Yes, lord,"

"Do you pledge your mind to me?"

"Yes, lord."

"Do you pledge your soul to me?"

"Yes and forever, true lord."

With a gracious nod, the Eyascnu Varo made an upwelling gesture with his hands. Numb, his throat dry, Teller got to his feet and turned to accept the crowd's applause.

It was over. He stood there, the lord's Vol. Scarred and drugged, he was the Cinc of Oknu Shuld.

Half healed, only a rota after his Acclamation, Teller came down to the isav. An honor guard of Scaths accompanied him, to the flusterment of the proctors. Teller raised the skora barrier so high against the ahn-pain that it inflamed the letters on his back. Better to feel that than the anguish he was about to inflict.

He stepped onto a proctor's small dais. A sea of faces, pale in the cavern-light, floated in front of him: that of the boy Aron, Liasit, Hanat who steadied her, and others whose names he didn't know. The ghostly presence of Keya and Gorv moved among them like shadows. All were silent, but their eyes shone with adulation. All had been fitted with new collars for the occasion. Row upon row, with a rustle of worn and ragged clothing, they knelt for him. Not with foreheads touching the ground, as they did for the other Vols, but with heads up and that look of expectant trust in their eyes. So many.

He forced himself to raise his clenched fist and display the ring, forced himself to move it from right to left. "Do you see this?" he asked. "It proclaims me Volarach Cinc."

His eyes stayed level upon them. "My name is Teller-of-Lies. Most of what you believe about me is a lie."

They looked from him to the guards and back. They did not understand, and he had to make sure they did. Late last rota, he had folded in half Keya's blue hair ribbon and the red cord he had cut from Liasit's wrists, twisted them into one strand, and made several knots along the length. He'd stuffed it deep into the pocket of his pants, a constant reminder of all the things he could not do. Now, his hand out of sight, he clutched it.

"I belong"—there was no hesitancy, no lump in his throat, no crack in the firmness of his voice—"body, mind, and soul, to the Lord of Oknu Shuld."

No one moved or even seemed to breathe. The light in Liasit's eyes turned to puzzlement.

He lowered his arm and spoke loudly, harshly. "I come here with a direct order. No longer will you speak the word 'niyalahn-rista.' No longer will you spread that lie. That name, that belief, is forbidden."

Their faces cracked with different emotions: devastation, anguished betrayal, and in some, a dawning anger. They did not see what he kept hidden in his pocket, nor could they see the scars on his back, forever marking him a teller of lies. He raised his fist again, and the vol-ring they did see, and that was what destroyed their hope and kept them all alive.

"For as long as you live, that name is not to be mentioned. Should you forget, your new collars will quickly remind you. There are no saviors in Oknu Shuld."

The pain of the ahn had increased so much that the skora couldn't block it anymore. He turned away, stepped from the dais, and left the ahn abandoned and bereft. He had succeeded in destroying their only hope.

#

His wounds healed. They didn't burn so much when the water down in the baths touched them. They gradually turned to scars that caught against the finely-woven fabric of his shirts. When he washed his face, he could feel the roughness of the S on it. At first he had turned his head aside when others approached him, but now he wore the scar as openly as he wore the vol-ring.

The ring clung tightly to his finger, so tight that he could not twist it, could not insert even the tip of his dagger between it and his skin. At times it itched, as if the wires were growing into his hand and putting down roots. It also deadened things. The day and night gongs seemed muffled in the long and shadowed halls. No longer did he hear tormented cries rise from the grate, and only the wind moaned in the ventilation shafts. The only feeling that remained was the pain of the isav, for it was too ingrained in Oknu Shuld for him to escape it.

He dreamed vividly, the exact opposite of how he lived, but upon awakening only snatches remained, to sting and wink out. He wondered, briefly, if the other Vols dreamed.

He never summoned Rivere again. But he arranged that the healer receive anonymous packets of ointments and herbs from apothecaries in Rydle. The proctor was informed that Rivere was under the personal protection of the Cinc; that Aron, Liasit, and Hanat belonged to him and were not to be mistreated in any way. From time to time, he quietly sent down to the isav extra blankets and rations of food, only to learn they disappeared among the proctors and guards. Citing wasteful destruction of the lord's property, he ended the ahn-hunts, but the ristas complained to Shacad, who reinstated them. He declared to the Procurement Committee that children nine years and under were of little use in Oknu Shuld and would no longer be Welcomed; but Procurement was under the rule of Nosce, and Teller's declaration was overruled.

Along with the Azanzi quad-commanders, Teller spent much of the fall and winter outdoors, in training with archon Rigiati. This involved learning horsemanship, a talent for which he had a surprising and seemingly natural ability. He became acclimated to rain and snow, learned how to melt into the folds of the valley while observing the movements of the Bellstone rebels, and became adept at drying a rain-soaked cloak with carefully controlled waves of skora. All this prepared him for his main duty, which was to scout a northern route across the valley and into the Riftwood that would avoid rebel ambushes. He set out alone, and his mission took him seven days.

He had just returned when a minor earthquake damaged one of the log cribs that formed the East Dam, causing more water than usual to leak into the back walls. The lord sent orders for Teller to fix that, so he gathered a repair crew and went out. The job, cold and muddy to begin with, turned dangerous when a part of the wooden crib, filled with rock and earth and positioned between two of the four massive oak buttresses that supported the dam, began to slip away.

They shored it up, but not before a tumbling boulder crushed the foot of one of his men. When the work was done, and as he was making his tired way through the frozen morue fields and back to the guardhouse, he was acutely aware of the ahn who were replenishing the mulch that protected the plants from the last of the winter winds.

Shivering in their ragged cloaks, they knelt to him but did not look up at him. Mindful of the knotted cord in his pocket, he stopped in front of a little girl. His shadow fell over her bowed head. He groped for mind-words, but there were none. He had said them all already. She turned her face to the side, but not before he saw a tear trickling down a cheek ruddy from the cold. She was in despair, but alive; he was a Vol and chose to feel nothing. He, too, turned away.

After going down to the baths to clean up, he received a message from the lord to meet Vol Ségun in the Node. Autran's lips had gotten so thin as to be almost non-existent, and the outline of his arms and legs under his clothing appeared angular and stick-like.

"Allow me to congratulate you, Vol Cinc. I wuzz"—he cleared his throat—"was called away immediately after your Acclamation and could not speak to you at the time." He turned his large, cold eyes on him. "Since the lord has seen fit to make you a colleague of ours, I have decided to hold no ill will regarr-ding"—the word came out like a gargle—"our last meeting."

His attitude rankled, but rumor had it that the lord had severely punished him, so Teller only asked, "What do you want?"

Autran pointed to a box on the floor. He did so awkwardly, having to straighten his downturned wrist to do so. The box was full of earthen balls about six inches in diameter that appeared to consist of mud and chopped, dried herbs. "I made those a while ago. Now they must be fired." Stiffly, he turned his whole body to look at him, apparently expecting questions.

But Teller had none, for he knew what these harm-less looking objects were. Only skora could change them into the explosive weapons called abakal.

Autran said, "The lord has long wanted theezz." At the buzzing sound, both arms jittered uneasily. "To defend his army." He made vague circles with his hand.

"Tranz—*change* them as you did with ineerva, but I think you will need a greater fire."

He did indeed need a greater fire, but when he was finished, the dull clumps of mud had become twelve glittering balls of what looked like rough-edged black glass. It had taken him almost a gong, and the repeated efforts to summon skora in the absence of any threat left him drained. With a disturbing half-crouch, Autran stalked away. Teller helped himself to a packet of morphous and retreated into his quarters.

The sleeping powder lasted only a few hours. Unable to fall back to sleep, he ordered a dram-jug of brandwyn brought to his room, put on his cloak, and took the jug up to the plateau.

It was cold and very late, with dawn about two gongs off. He left the light of the guardhouse behind him and walked away from the cliff edge and toward the dry wash. On the hillside across from it burned several camp-fires that belonged to the 'brak troop that guarded the plateau from the east. The fires seemed unreal, as if he were a ghost looking at them through the barrier that separated the dead from the living.

He reached the East Dam and settled down with his back against one of the now-dry buttresses. A dim light shone from the top of the Node-shaft to his right, and here and there much fainter lights glowed from some of the ventilation shafts. There was no wind. He saw his own breath, heard the creaking of the buttresses, and felt the weight of the dark waters of Insheer Lake looming up behind him. He took a swallow from the jug.

At this late hour in winter, the stars of the Great Triangle were rising. When he was a boy, they used to shine with delicate, ethereal colors, especially in that magic moment when they were caught in the star-frames of the Quela. Rayuel, a faint green, lingered closest to the earth, then golden S'gan, and reddish Marhaut at the apex. Now they hung dull and colorless in a flat sky.

The guard on duty, one of the Scaths who had attended his Acclamation, sauntered over and bowed. "Do you mind some company, sir?"

Teller shrugged.

The man studied the Triangle in the east. "They say that the Seani curs howl up at that during some kind of ceremony. They call it the Spera, but Vol Shacad calls it the Spear. And its point is aimed straight at the Seani's heart." He snorted, then glanced down at Teller sitting in silence. "If you don't mind my saying it, Vol Cinc, most of us think you'll soon become the tip of that spear."

Teller said nothing, only took another swig from the jug, and the man moved on. He sat, drinking the brandwyn, until the waning moon rose to his left and cast long shadows into the night.

Chapter 30

The Final Command

Some rotas later, two gongs after dinner, the lord called a Volmeet. It was Teller's first, and he knelt stiffly in the lord's private audience chamber with the row of Vols to his left. Skora-stripped as he was—all Powers had been repressed outside the door—everything in the room exuded danger. Purple light from the morue-shaped lamps writhed over the floor like goah; the heavy drapery behind the lord's throne swayed eerily from time to time, as if the vast recesses behind it breathed; and the faceted gazes of the insect sculptures lurking in the shadows behind him all seemed focused on the back of his neck. Fog wafted over the dais where the Lord of Shunder sat, blurring his face. Now that a hall full of people provided no distractions, the sheer weight of his power seemed to have doubled.

Occasionally the fog thinned, to reveal part of a crown the lord wore low over his forehead. It glittered with two rows of black stones. They stared directly at Teller, like the spider-eyes he had confronted in his battle with Mochlos. His breath caught, and he remembered the disturbing vision of the lord's face during his Acclamation. Except at that time he thought he saw no eyes, and now there were eight.

"We welcome our new Cinc," the lord said. His voice

had a clipped quality to it, like the clicking nail-toes of a morue spider. "My hand is now complete. Teller-of-Lies has followed my orders in an exemplary manner and is to be commended." A few of the Vols stirred, as if such praise were unusual and resented. "Finally, my great vision for Shunder is about to become reality." He gestured toward Shacad.

The Tierce thumped his chest and addressed the Vols on either side of him. "The rebels of Bellstone Forest have long strangled our efforts to expand. They hold the Gap. We always thought this passage between the forest and the western reach of the Riftwood was the only way we—"

The Lord of Shunder waved his hand impatiently. He wore a tight-fitting pair of gloves, something, Teller was sure, he had not seen at the Acclamation.

"To be brief," Shacad said quickly, "ancient maps have recently come to light. They show a string of guard-towers that comprise an arc—a series of stepping-stones, if you will—that runs along the western edge of the Rift-wood and then curves east. The towers were abandoned long ago, but the lord saw immediately that they could become a route that would bypass the Gap altogether. We could enter the Riftwood north of the Gap, fortify the towers that curve south, then strike in a pincer move-ment from both directions. To sum it up, before the rebels know we are even there, Bellstone Forest would become nothing but a piece of meat between our jaws." He leaned back with a satisfied look. His lower cheek bulged with an exploratory tongue, as if it tried to dislodge the said piece of meat from dinner caught in a molar.

Next to Teller, Vol Kuat leaned out from the line of Vols to look at the Tierce. "Ah, but the King of the Rift-wood will object to these forays, might he not?"

Shacad pressed his lips together, swallowed whatever

he had found, then grinned. "Of course he will. But a force led by skora"—he extended an arm toward Teller—"will overcome his objections."

A Vorian guard approached the throne with a tray upon which rested a deeply incised crystal glass filled with amber liquid. A gloved hand reached out of the fog and took it. "In his recent scouting expedition," the lord said, "Vol Cinc has found a northern route across the valley. Therefore"—by the sound of his voice, Teller knew the lord had turned toward him—"you will lead a small force along that route and into the Riftwood. You will find the exact location of these towers and repair them. You will first remove whatever wards are upon them and cast others for my purposes. We will form garrisons around them, and skora will burn a path between them. Thus we will build a fortified road that will lead to our conquest of the south." The lord paused, the fog wisped, and the row of eyes assayed him.

Teller steeled himself not to look away. There was, and would always be, only one answer. He had given it months ago when he slid the vol-ring onto his finger. "Yes, lord."

The other Vols gave their various reports as the shadowy form sipped from the amber glass, but the heavy unease in the chamber made it difficult for Teller to concentrate. At last the lord's voice said, "You are all dismissed."

No one dared to sigh in relief, but everyone quickly climbed to his feet.

"Except you, Teller-of-Lies."

Wary, Teller waited in silence as the last of the Vols filed out and the heavy doors bumped shut.

The lord, barely visible within a swirl of fog, stood. "I am bestowing upon you a very great honor, volarach, because you remind me somewhat of my brother. He too had the skora"—his voice turned vicious—"until the niyal'arist vora sucked out his life. Rise and follow me."

Teller obeyed as the Eyascnu descended from his throne and walked among his sculptures to take up a position behind a bloodwood stand. It was illuminated by a globe directly above it and held something covered with a cloth. The crown of eyes now dangled from the lord's hand and a deep hood, like the Prome's, covered the top half of his face. Even so, the force of the invisible gaze within crawled over Teller's face like a swarm of ants.

"I wish to show you," the Eyascnu said, "my latest work." He pulled the cover off, to reveal an angular metal sculpture about three feet high. The lord ran the tips of his gloved fingers over a spiral spine, following it to a copper triangle impaled on the top. This face was depicted without features and only showed a deep crease between two tormented, downward-sloping eye-slits. The arms looked human, spreading up and out as if begging, but the wrists ended in inarticulate pincers. Eight angled spider-legs, straining upward, supported the spine.

"This is *Arachniman,*" the lord murmured, looking down at his creation. "The subject, as you see, is becoming a spider. He tries to scream, but has no mouth. He reaches out—for help, perhaps—but his appendages are such that he could never grasp it. He yearns to escape what is happening to him, but cannot. He is fully conscious of his hideous state, yet is prevented from articulating his desperate desire to die. His only hope is that he will be ground into the dirt by something larger than the obscenity he is."

There was a long pause. "Have I not expressed this perfectly?" the lord asked.

Repelled, Teller couldn't answer. The hooded figure stared at him. Then, with a suddenness that startled him, the lord cast back his hood and smiled. Under the globe light, his face jumped into plain view.

Teller froze. The skin exhibited the slightly rough texture of thick, white paper, and the crimson mouth seemed ready to drip red paint. But the worst was what appeared on the empty expanse of skin above the nose: two crudely drawn spirals. They could have been the work of an evil child, its eyes alight with glee, its hand pressing so hard on the stick of charcoal that flecks of it broke off. Yet somehow the spiral eyes saw him. They bored into his soul like an auger and then, with a sensation that made him dizzy, reversed direction and began to pull him in.

Teller jerked his head to the side, the repressed fire inside him clawing for release. Something like the mind-speech wisped into his head: the hint of an emotion he couldn't identify and didn't want to.

"You are dismissed," the lord said. His face again hooded, he turned away.

Teller made his way out. Alone in his well-appointed room, he wondered what had happened, if he had somehow displeased the Lord of Oknu Shuld. Probably not, because he had walked out of the room alive. Several sniffs of the carmine powder helped dispel the pitiful, unsettling vision of *Arachniman*, and allowed him to fall into a twitchy sleep.

Three rotas later, at the second deep gong, he joined his small scouting party at the side gates. He'd chosen its members from the Scaths: a subaltern and six armsmen from its 'brak division, the Hewers. His horse was Kon, a dun gelding with strong legs and feet. Descended from the wild horses of the northern plains, Kon could forage for himself, tended to blend into the background, and was not easily frightened.

The Kuat had warned him about the Riftwood's many dangers. "Speak to nothing with twiggy hair," the Delver had said, "and trust nothing unduly fair." Teller barely listened. Nothing worse could live in the Riftwood than what dwelt in Oknu Shuld.

It was a cold and cloudy afternoon toward the end of Herb-Bearer, the tail of winter, and Teller wore a new cloak. Tweaked by a memory he couldn't quite revive, he'd ordered a mottled brown and grey-green garment made of a similar dead-leaf pattern as the Delver's cloak. Hooded, lightweight but warm, and so thickly woven it shed the rain, it would hide his passage from watching eyes.

A few snowflakes materialized out of the grey sky as they set out. He and Alrum, the Azanzi subaltern, were mounted, but the 'braks were not. Although they could ride if necessary, they prided themselves on being able to travel through wooded terrain as well as any horse, and with equally great burdens on their muscular backs. He and Alrum had packed carefully, and the 'braks carried the various tools they'd need for repairs and enough dried food to sustain them until they could hunt for their own.

Following the route Teller had mapped out, they traveled without incident until dark, then made camp in a hollow that afforded some protection from the wind. They made no fire, lest it be seen by Bellstone patrols. Rising before daybreak, they moved on until the Riftwood rose up stark before them. Teller ordered his band to stay hidden until he found the first tower and returned for them, and rode forward alone.

Kon's breath made steamy whorls in the cold air. Clouds lowered above the Riftwood and shrouded the

337

tops of the bare and silent trees. He climbed a slight slope covered with dead grasses and bleached, fallen tree limbs. Today was the first of Seed. A dismal month, Teller thought, muddy and grey, encapsulated in a hard shell.

He dismounted and led his horse through the thicket at the outskirts of the forest. His cloak snagged on thorny twigs, branches slapped at his face, and roots tried to trip him. The Riftwood seemed to exude a hostile force, not easy to penetrate, but at last he emerged into a clearing under the first of the great trees. Bending his head far back, he looked up the gnarled trunks and past branches full of tight ocher buds until they disappeared into the cloud-mist. Not even the sound of a bird broke the silence. He reached into his pocket and fingered the red and blue cord, tightly twisted and knotted, that he kept always with him.

It took him only a day to find the first watch-tower, for most of the old maps had agreed on its general location. He circled the round wall, observing the tight-fitting stone blocks, the black openings that faced different directions on each level, until he came upon the entrance. In a crevice by the half-open door a woody vine had gained a foothold. At the sight of it, a memory flashed—he was a boy, climbing a thick vine—then it was gone, leaving only an echo: *"Hurry up, Teller!"*

The memory resonated with what he'd been feeling since he entered the wood. A sense of urgency, as if something, as yet far off but which had to be dealt with, was approaching.

While Kon foraged nearby, Teller dispelled the faded vestige of a ward that remained around the tower and replaced it with a stronger one. He led his horse into the tower for the night, ate some bread and cheese from his saddlebag, and stretched out to sleep. He dozed fitfully, and at one point dreamed.

He was surrounded by a thicket of thorns. A tall, pale woman stood in front of him, and when she lifted up her eyes, they shone with an eerie silver light. Holding a basket of seeds in one hand, she offered him a silently burning torch with the other. "*Set fire to this thicket, emjadi, and burn it all away. Make the soil clean, so these seeds may be planted.*" He took the torch and brushed it against the thorn bushes. Flames immediately sprung up all around him, and he too caught fire. Her silver eyes watched him as he burned, as he stood like a lightning-hit tree while the thorns settled into char and he stood in the center of a fertile black circle. The woman walked around it, throwing handfuls of seeds from the basket. They drifted down like snow and melted into the ground at his feet. With a moan, he awoke. It was dawn.

He rode back to camp, and by midday his band arrived at the tower and began setting it to rights. Teller worked alongside the rest of them, but could not forget the dream. The silver eyes, like those he'd seen in the hall of mirrors, seemed to underlie everything he looked at.

Over the next few days, the band cleared the area around the watch-tower, pulled out the debris inside, and, using planks planed from the trees they had chopped down, repaired the floors of both levels. The horses were stabled in the ground floor, which now had a door, while Teller and Alrum slept on the first level. The umbraks bedded down on the second, whose ruined roof was still partly open to the sky.

The nights were clear and frosty, but also, in spite of the ward, uneasy. The Hewers were assigned night-duty two at a time, and they sat on the half-finished observation deck on the top of the tower, back to hunched back, their deep-set eyes warily sweeping the forest below.

About mid-afternoon on the third day of Seed, a strange incident occurred. Teller was alone on the ladder, inspecting the opening to the now-finished deck, when a sudden pain shot down his back. He took a sharp breath and clutched the ladder for support. The pain ran from his left shoulder, stabbed like a broken rib into his right side, and ended at his waist. What *was* this? He reached under his shirt but felt only the rough scars, and no blood came away on his hand. As the day wore on, the pain became somehow distant, and by nightfall, it seemed almost to belong to someone else.

They worked all the next day, but at night Teller lay restless on his mat while the off-duty 'braks snored above him. Sometime before dawn, a 'brak cried out and everyone rushed up to the deck. Ogwush, a veteran of last summer's attack against the falconforms and the leader of the Hewer band, had shot an arrow into the trees, claiming something was out there. Alrum passed around a jar of ineerva, and the 'braks, their small eyes glinting, dipped their arrows into the thick blue poison and laid them out to dry.

Dawn of the next day was more like twilight, for a heavy fog obscured the trees. They searched for what had disturbed Ogwush, but found no tracks. Teller wasn't able to leave on his mission to find the second tower until the fog lifted, so it was almost noon when he gave orders to the subaltern, saddled his horse, and rode off.

He headed south, but soon found the going hard. The terrain always seemed easier to the right, which would edge him deeper into the wood, so he was constantly forcing his way through brambles, over rocky ravines, or around huge fallen trees. Coming upon a vernal pond, he stopped so his horse could drink, and the many reflections of the misty sun, half-hidden by trees, looked out of the water like silver eyes.

The memory of that gaze followed him, and the feeling that something was approaching dogged him. His back itched with the memory of someone else's pain. At dusk a thunderstorm grumbled over the Riftwood. Lightning momentarily brightened Teller's way around the massive tree trunks, but the thickness of the forest muffled the thunder. Rain whispered high above him, and a few great drops fell on his hands, but very little seemed to reach the ground. The storm passed.

On edge, he made camp under a wide-limbed oak that, like most of the ancient trees around him, seemed quite dead. He tied his horse to it, rubbed him down, and cast a temporary ward around them both. He ate a meager meal that he had no stomach for, wrapped himself in his cloak, and lay on his woolen blanket on the ground under the tree that sheltered him.

As the night deepened, the tree began to glow, as if the very sap were visible, until every branch, every twig shone softly. Even the roots gleamed with faint phosphorescence that wound ever more dimly into the earth. It must be one of those trees that glimmered like this only in the dark of the moon, which this night was. He fell asleep watching the trunk slowly course with light brought up from the loam.

The murky passage at his back, the Delver stood before an iron door, locked against the vast caverns beyond. A monstrous form on the other side, breathing raggedly, clutched the bars. With a convulsive effort, it succeeded at last in spitting out a word. "Ia–Iahsons?"

"There is no doubt now. The sons of Riah are the niyalahn-ristas."

"Esss," the creature hissed, "Esss!" It licked its lips with a lizard-like tongue and moved its grotesque head within inches of the Kuat's.

"Wask has found the blood that makes the earth dance," Vol Kuat said."

The tumescent eyes lit up, then clouded with a question.

"The one who possesses it is T'lir's brother. He has already left Ullar-Sent and entered the Riftwood."

The creature's claws around the iron bars tightened. "En? *En?*"

Vol Kuat's double voice, though low, set off whispered echoes. "Compared to the years you have already waited, not long. Even now T'lir traverses the same wood as his brother. I will make sure their paths converge."

"Owes? K-K'nu owes?"

"Not yet. Only when I bring Teller and his brother before his throne will the Eyascnu discover they are the ones he seeks."

The other threw its head back, shook the bars, and roared in frustration.

"Control yourself," the Delver said. He turned away, his pupils mere slits. "Soon the niyalahn-ristas will walk into Oknu Shuld."

Teller started awake from a haunting dream of torches, of horror and loss, that fled almost immediately into the dark. The tree still glowed, but more faintly. Dawn must not be far off. He sat up. It was, he suddenly realized, the sixth of Seed. He was one year older: nineteen. One year of many that stretched endlessly ahead in a dead, grey line.

His forehead and spirikai ached—old throbbings that

stirred a dim memory. He had felt this pain as a boy, as a twin missing his brother, and Rivere's healing hands had made it go away. Now, once aware of the pain, he couldn't ignore it, and as he packed away his belongings and saddled his horse, it grew worse.

He was about to mount when a rustle made him turn toward the oak tree. Its glow had disappeared in the grey light, and a shadowy figure sat with its back against the trunk. Its cloak caused it to blend into the background, and only the bark-like face and pupil-less brown eyes were clearly visible.

"Someone wanders," Vol Kuat said, "not far away." He looked into the distance, then back at Teller. "You are ordered to meet him at the second tower, and bring him directly to me in Oknu Shuld."

The pain in his head and beneath his ribs throbbed with portent, ached with longing. "Who is this wanderer?"

"Your brother. He is needed in Oknu Shuld, and you must take him there."

Teller stiffened. Questions churned, and for an instant blanked his vision. "What? Why should—?" He was staring at nothing but a pile of dry, dead leaves. The Delver had vanished.

As if he heard a call, he turned his head. A brother he had not seen in nineteen years was somewhere in this wood.

End of Book Two

QUESTIONS FOR DISCUSSION

1. In Book One, *Blood Seed,* the falconform Yarahe told Sheft, "A community must provide support and safety for its members, so they may find the true identity within." How did this work out for Teller, Sheft's twin?

2. Several recurring symbols are found in *Dark Twin.* Two of them are the globe lights and the red and blue cord that Teller makes. What meanings do they have for Teller or for you?

3. Tolkien, a linguist and a Christian, coined the term "eucatastrophe," a terrible event, a catastrophe, that is redeemed. We might think of his definition as "the dark tunnel that leads to light." In Book One, Sheft found a glimmer of light. Does Teller find it in this book?

4. Teller must choose between three different names: Teller-of-Lies, niyalahn rista, and Vol Cinc. What do you think of the choice he makes toward the end of this book? How does his choice differ from the one Sheft made at the end of *Blood Seed?*

5. Why is it so hard for both brothers to accept who they are? Did you or someone close to you ever struggle with self-acceptance?

6. Let's face it, none of the Vols in *Dark Twin* are particularly likeable. But just for fun, which one most intrigues you and which one most repulses you? Why?

7. One of the themes that appears in both books is that of fatherhood. What is Teller's reaction to the idea of "father," and how does it change? What about Sheft's reaction?

8. How is Teller different from his twin? How is he similar? Who do you think had the harder time growing up?

9. For most of Book One, neither Sheft nor the reader know who Sheft is. In *Dark Twin*, the reader knows almost from the beginning that Teller is niyalahn-rista, but Teller does not. What difference did this knowledge, or lack of it, make to you as you were reading the books? What difference do you think it made to the brothers?

10. Psychologist Carl Jung wrote about the shadow, the dark part of ourselves that we fear, are challenged by, or are ashamed of. But Jung maintained that, if rightly acknowledged, the shadow could reveal an inner light. What or who is Teller's shadow, and is Teller successful in dealing with it?

Thank you for taking the time to read *Dark Twin*. If you enjoyed it, please let your friends know that and consider posting a short review on Amazon and/or Goodreads. Word-of-mouth referrals are an author's best friend and much appreciated!

I invite you to sign up for my private email list for giveaways, sneak peeks, and notices about the next Coin of Rulve books. I won't spam you or share your address with anyone, and you can unsubscribe at any time.
http://eepurl.com/bGCRQf

ABOUT THE AUTHOR

Veronica "Vernie" Dale writes genre-bridging fiction that includes dark fantasy, romance, psychological intrigue, and the inner journey. She is the author of a short story anthology and two novels, and her work has received commendations from Writer's Digest and Writers of the Future. Vernie holds two master's degrees and is a graduate of the Viable Paradise Science Fiction and Fantasy workshop. With twenty-six years of experience as a pastoral minister, she is also a member of Detroit Working Writers and Phi Beta Kappa, as well as an Ethical Author of the Alliance of Independent Authors. "I love dark chocolate," she says, "and am a real fan of what you might call the Holmes-Data-Spock archetype." Visit her at www.veronicadale.com.

LOOK FOR

TIME CANDLE

BOOK THREE OF

THE POWERFUL NEW

FANTASY SERIES

COIN OF RULVE

*Promised saviors—dying in poisoned pain
Desperate freedom-fighters—struggle to find a cure*

After a life-long separation, twin brothers Sheft and Teller finally meet in the deadly Riftwood. Teller, however, has been ordered to bring his brother into the Spider-king's underground stronghold. He must decide if he will betray Sheft or help him reach the Seani, the small resistance community secretly working to free their country from the king's reign of terror. Teller's decision results in disaster. What follows is a tale of risk, heartbreak, and courage, plus a race to find the antidote for a mysterious poison that has left Sheft and Teller with only thirteen hours to live. Mariat, meanwhile, strives to outwit the fierce boar-men who have captured her and then must face the most wrenching decision of her life.

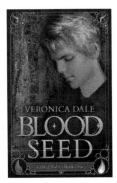

THE MUST-READ
NOVEL THAT
LAUNCHES THE SERIES:
BLOOD SEED: COIN
OF RULVE BOOK ONE

Sheft—maligned, hunted, chosen.
Mariat—the woman determined to save him

Growing up as a despised foreigner in the backward village of At-Wysher, eighteen-year-old Sheft hides a dark secret. He is being stalked by Wask, a deadly entity that haunts the nearby Riftwood. He keeps himself apart; yet beyond what he had ever dared to dream, he and Mariat fall in love. Sheft can't bring himself to tell her the truth about his deepest fear, nor can he share with her the devastating realization of who he is discovering himself to be. But when he must take part in a secret annual rite designed to protect the village from Wask, he confronts the true magnitude of the evil arrayed against him. It threatens to strip away his life, but will first break his heart.

"intense, powerful, and compelling" … "an impeccable read with a troubled hero and highly imagined mysterious entities that are sure to engage readers on many levels. Highly recommended" …"To readers who enjoy dark fantasy settings, but who still prize romantic fiction above all else: you won't be disappointed!"

ABOUT THE
COIN OF RULVE
SERIES

Coin of Rulve consists of four novels that comprise one story arc. It is about twin brothers Sheft and Teller, born in a small resistance community called the Seani. They are the promised redeemers, called to save their homeland from the reign of terror imposed by a brutal lord. In order to protect them from the lord who hunts them, the brothers are not told who they are and grow up in separate lands. Surrounded by cruelty and suspicion, Sheft and Teller each feel a call they cannot understand and struggle to believe in their own power for good. They desperately need the help of the Seani, as well as the strength of two extraordinary women, to confront the shattering realization of what the Creator Rulve has called them to do.

A tale of lost innocence and tender love, told against the plots of the powerful and the providence of the Creator, *Coin* describes the spiritual quest as a dark journey toward a distant light.

"A new approach to this genre"… "the story keeps getting better and better"… "a page-turner" … "wonderfully sympathetic characters and gifted prose"…"Wowza!"

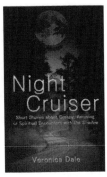

ALSO BY VERONICA DALE
NIGHT CRUISER: SHORT
STORIES ABOUT CREEPY,
AMUSING OR
SPIRITUAL ENCOUNTERS
WITH THE SHADOW

Whether it's a whispered invitation from the basement, a lost but dangerous wizard, or a spirit that has haunted a family for generations, ten different people must deal with the dark side. These insightful, award-winning tales flip from fantasy to faith, and from horror to humor to hope. We all have a shadow, a part of ourselves we'd rather not see, but only by dealing with it can we find the inner light.

"If you're intrigued by clever writing, crave fascinating stories that pack a lot in a short space, and appreciate an author who never lets religion get in the way of her highly spiritual and deeply psychological message, take a wild ride on the Night Cruiser."

"The stories are fun, spooky, and strange."

See more about the *Coin of Rulve* series and *Night Cruiser* at www.veronicadale.com